Silver Totem
of **SHAME**

The Meg Harris Mysteries

Death's Golden Whisper
Red Ice for a Shroud
The River Runs Orange
Arctic Blue Death
A Green Place for Dying

Silver
Totem
of SHAME

A Meg Harris Mystery

R. J. HARLICK

DUNDURN
TORONTO

Editor: Allison Hirst
Design: Courtney Horner
Printer: Webcom

Library and Archives Canada Cataloguing in Publication

Harlick, R. J., 1946-, author
    Silver totem of shame / R.J. Harlick.

(A Meg Harris mystery)
Issued in print and electronic formats.
ISBN 978-1-4597-2169-2

    I. Title. II. Series: Harlick, R. J., 1946- . Meg Harris mystery.

PS8603.A74S54 2014   C813.6   C2013-906072-3
                                            C2013-906073-1

1 2 3 4 5   18 17 16 15 14

Conseil des Arts   Canada Council   Canadä   ONTARIO ARTS COUNCIL
du Canada   for the Arts   CONSEIL DES ARTS DE L'ONTARIO

We acknowledge the support of the Canada Council for the Arts and the Ontario Arts Council for our publishing program. We also acknowledge the financial support of the Government of Canada through the Canada Book Fund and Livres Canada Books, and the Government of Ontario through the Ontario Book Publishing Tax Credit and the Ontario Media Development Corporation.

Care has been taken to trace the ownership of copyright material used in this book. The author and the publisher welcome any information enabling them to rectify any references or credits in subsequent editions.

                                                          J. Kirk Howard, President

The publisher is not responsible for websites or their content unless they are owned by the publisher.

Printed and bound in Canada.

Visit us at
Dundurn.com | @dundurnpress
Facebook.com/dundurnpress | Pinterest.com/dundurnpress

Dundurn   Gazelle Book Services Limited   Dundurn
3 Church Street, Suite 500   White Cross Mills   2250 Military Road
Toronto, Ontario, Canada   High Town, Lancaster, England   Tonawanda, NY
M5E 1M2   LA1 4XS   U.S.A. 14150

To Jim

ONE

He liked the staccato beat of rain drumming on the roof of the carving shed. It felt good knowing his ancestors would've heard this sound on Haida Gwaii while working on their own totem poles, and not the incessant thrumming of traffic crossing the bridge less than thirty metres above his head. The sound drove him crazy, until his hands started moving over the wood. Then the noise faded away with the steady rhythm of his carving.

But with no shed of his own or hope of having one until he was out into the "real world," he had to rely on the charity of the only Haida carver he knew, Ernest Paul. Ern made a lot of money from carving totems and liked to brag that he had one standing in pretty near every major capital of the world.

Last month, Ern was in Tokyo for the raising of his latest, a huge fifteen-metre pole of red cedar that some Japanese billionaire had commissioned for his garden. At $6,500 a metre, only rich guys could afford them. The guy even had the nerve to insist that four watchmen sit on top instead of the usual two. They were supposed to represent his four kids, which wasn't exactly in the Haida tradition.

But as Ern said, when a client paid the big bucks, he got what he wanted, which wasn't all that different from when the chiefs in the old days commissioned their poles.

He carefully laid his long-handled tools out on the table. Some were Ern's castoffs; others he'd made himself. Though they might not have the sharpest edges, they were his, about all he had to show that he was a carver. That and the two-inch scar from the time a chisel had slipped and sliced his hand almost to the bone. Fuck, it had hurt. A lot of blood had spurted out, much of it on the killer whale he'd been carving on one of Ern's smaller commissions. That was the first time he'd faced Haida anger in its full fury.

In time Ern had calmed down, although the master carver hadn't let him near another commission until now. And this wasn't especially important. It was a pro bono for the new healing lodge being set up in Vancouver's Eastside. If he cut himself this time, Ern wouldn't care. Besides, the blood would add to the legend of the pole.

He ran his hand over the smooth cedar and traced his fingers along the stenciled outline of the eagle he would start working on tonight. He remembered the first time he had cut into cedar. It'd felt like coming home. With that single cut he'd known this was where he belonged. This was who he was, a carver, not the lawyer his mother wanted him to be. He could almost feel the hand of an ancestor guiding his adze as it sliced into the soft, almost buttery, aromatic wood.

He breathed in the rich scent of the cedar. He imagined this is what it smelled like on Haida Gwaii, a place he'd never visited, despite it being the home of his people.

Only in his dreams did he walk amongst the giant cedar and Sitka spruce trees that covered every inch of the mountainous islands. Someday, when he had the money, he would go. But he wouldn't tell his mother. She wouldn't like it. Just as she'd be upset if she found out he was in Ern's studio carving tonight instead of studying at the university.

He jerked his head up at a sudden sound that came from the back of the large, open workroom. He walked to where various lengths of logs lay stacked against the back wall. Although the brightness of the overhead lights didn't reach this far, he could see well enough with the light from the bridge filtering through the shed's transparent roof. Nothing looked disturbed. Likely the noise had been made by one of the stray cats that called the shed home.

He glanced out a back window. The tide was up. A big yacht was churning through the channel into False Creek. The lights of downtown Vancouver hovered beyond.

He returned to his carving and was soon lost in the flow of the movement. His chisel bit into the outline of the eagle's beak. He would make it a strong, commanding beak, worthy of the king of birds. He felt a special affinity to the eagle. As a child, when his family vacationed on Galiano Island, he loved to watch them soar with the clouds and wished he could join them. He wondered if he belonged to the Eagle clan, but since he knew nothing about his birth mother, he'd never know. He couldn't ask his adoptive mother. She wouldn't know. She wouldn't think it important.

He didn't hear the rustling nor see the shadow moving from behind the stacked logs. He only became aware of a presence when the cold steel of a blade suddenly bit into his throat. By then it was too late. His one thought as he watched his blood gush over his almost perfect eagle was that this was going to make one hell of a story.

The man stared at the lifeless body. He waited. When he was sure he was alone, he picked up the boy's adze. Too bad about the kid; he would've made a great carver. But the matriarchs would've never let him be simply a carver.

The man continued where the boy had left off, etching the outline of the eagle's beak ever deeper as the blood flowed into the crease. He would make changes to this eagle. After all, he had a story to tell.

TWO

"This is the famous Bill Reid sculpture *The Raven and First Men*."

Our young female guide pointed to a massive wood-carving squatting on a slab of granite. The morning sun slanting through the dome skylight washed it in an unearthly glow, while at the same time it created shadows that gave the work a menacing, almost predatory aspect.

A rather well-endowed first man, I thought, chuckling as I ran my eyes over the buttocks and dangling parts of one of the men trapped inside the giant clamshell. A huge raven with a beak that could peck out more than eyes prevented their escape by sitting squarely on top of the shell.

I turned as I heard another chuckle and saw Eric grinning at me. He knew what I was thinking. He should. Since we'd finally tied the knot, we'd probably spent more time in bed than out of it, and much to the embarrassment of our young guide he now wrapped his arms around me and gave me a resoundingly loud smack on the lips.

Realizing this wasn't exactly the kind of reverence we were supposed to be giving such a magnificent piece of art, I extricated myself from his embrace.

"Bill Reid was Haida, wasn't he?" I asked.

"Yup, probably the most famous Haida artist," replied the young woman, who looked to be in her late teens. Her smile had a nervous hesitancy to it. From the outset she'd acted distracted, as if she'd rather be somewhere else.

On the recommendation of a colleague of Eric's, we were taking a tour of the Museum of Anthropology at the University of British Columbia. It was reputed to have one of the best collections of Northwest Coast native artifacts in the world. We had arrived in Vancouver a couple of days earlier, mainly because Eric was attending the annual general assembly of the Grand Council of First Nations, but also so we could get to know the west coast of Canada better.

"The Haida, I know, are full of stories. No doubt this carving has its own tale to tell." Eric raised a questioning brow at the young woman whose rippling ebony tresses and dark eyes suggested she was also native.

At my insistence, Eric had worn his beaded deerskin jacket instead of the scruffy windbreaker he preferred. I'd felt that it was only fitting that he showed his respect by wearing this beautifully crafted example of Algonquin artistry made by his grandmother for his grandfather.

"You're right," she replied. "The raven is such a trickster, always playing tricks on the world and its creatures. This sculpture depicts the ancient Haida story of creation. According to our legend, the raven found a clamshell on a beach in Haida Gwaii. That's the Queen Charlotte Islands, in case you don't know the traditional Haida name."

"It means 'Place of the Haida,' doesn't it?" Eric asked.

"Not quite. It means 'Islands of the People.' *Gwaii* means 'island' and *Haida* 'people.'"

Eric ran his fingers lightly over the bald head of one of the human beings. "What craftsmanship. It feels as smooth as polished stone."

"Sorry, you're not supposed to touch it." She smiled apologetically then glanced in the direction of voices echoing from outside the rotunda. Nervously biting her lower lip, she stared at the sound for a moment before returning her attention to us.

"According to our legend, a number of human beings protruded from the clamshell. They didn't want to leave. The raven toyed with them before finally persuading them to climb out onto the beach. They were the first Haida."

"Interesting," Eric said. "It's quite different from the Algonquin creation story, which says man—"

"It's the one about Turtle Island, isn't it?" the guide interrupted. "I've been studying the creation myths of various First Nations in one of my anthropology classes."

"So you're a student at the university."

"I'm in third year anthropology. I wanted to learn more about my own people and the other first peoples of North America. I just volunteer at the museum part-time."

"Are your people from the West Coast?"

"Yup, I'm Haida."

"I envy you Bill Reid and other Haida carvers. They've done so much to help your people gain a sense of pride in being Haida."

"Yeah, I guess they have. Art's always been a key part of our culture. I'll show you some more awesome examples of Haida art in the Great Hall."

She led us down a ramp and into a cavernous room filled with light, the sun's rays slanting through staggered glass walls. Monumental totem poles filled the room. They stretched up to the ceiling, their wood silvered, their carvings eroded by weather and time. A group of young men and women, some native, some not, were scattered amongst them. A number sat cross-legged on the hard stone floor, while others perched on small folding stools. All were drawing in sketchbooks. They stopped talking as we approached.

Our guide greeted them, running her eyes from one student to the next as if searching for someone. "Where's Allistair?" she asked.

A pudgy young man with a brush cut and nose ring shrugged, while a young woman in glued-on jeans with turquoise and bone choker clasped around her neck said, "We waited for him, but he never showed."

"I guess he got caught up in class," our guide replied. I sensed both disappointment and relief behind her words.

"Are these fellow anthropology students?" Eric asked.

"No, they're studying at the Emily Carr University of Art. They come here to learn about the ancient art of carving and the stories depicted on these old poles."

"That's on Granville Island, isn't it?" I asked.

Nodding absently, she pulled out her phone and started to dial. But she changed her mind and returned it to her pocket.

"We passed the school yesterday. It's down the road from where we're staying," I said, feeling the need to fill up the strained silence.

Continuing to ignore us, she pulled out her phone again and stared at it for a few seconds before returning it once more to her pocket.

"Please go ahead and make your call," I said. "We'll take a look at those poles over there to give you a bit of privacy."

"Sorry. It's nothing. I'll call later." She smiled wistfully. "He probably won't answer anyway."

"Oh dear, man problems?"

"Yah, what else. But hey, I'll cook him his favourite meal and we'll be golden, eh? Isn't that what love's about?"

"You know the old saying: The way to a man's heart is through his stomach."

"Or, as in our case, the woman's heart." Eric wrapped his arm around my waist and held me close. How true. No matter how grumpy or annoyed I was, he could always cheer me up with a sumptuous meal. I kissed his cheek with a renewed surge of love and then stepped back, not wanting to upset our guide further. Although she was laughing with us, I still sensed her underlying pain.

"What can you tell us about these poles?" Eric asked, pointing to a nearby line of towering giants. "A friend told me to make sure I saw them. Apparently one of her Haida ancestors carved one of them."

"Do you know her ancestral village?"

"She didn't give an actual name, but said it was near the southern tip of Haida Gwaii."

"That's where my ancestral village of SGang Gwaay is located. What was the woman's name? Chances are she's a relative, eh?"

"Louise O'Brien."

The young woman laughed. "She's my auntie. Not exactly a relative, but a close family friend. Her village isn't far from mine. Let me show you the pole she was talking about."

She led us to a corner of the vast room, where two of the shorter poles stood side-by-side, one braced against the glass wall and the other against a cement pillar. She pointed to the smaller of the two, although *smaller* hardly described its massive breadth. "This is the one from Louise's village. It's a very good example of a frontal pole." Her face beamed with pride.

"Such a magnificent heritage," Eric said wistfully. He craned his neck to study the chiseled features of what looked to be a man-sized bird with two huge eyes peering over a hole in its face. The figure squatted on top of a curious four-legged creature perched on its haunches.

"What do you mean by frontal pole?" I asked.

"There are actually three types of totem poles. The frontal poles are the ones with the most carvings. They were placed at the entrance to a longhouse, usually one belonging to a chief. They proclaimed the highborn status of the chief and told a story about him. That's what the carved figures, or crests, as we call them, are about." She pointed to the top bird-like figure. "This is an eagle. Notice how large the eyes are. We Haida have a thing for making our eagle eyes very bold, unlike other Northwest Coast nations." She laughed again, and now seemed more relaxed.

She pointed to the hole. "We like to make the beaks bold too. There was probably once a large pointed one protruding from this hole. The eagle means that this pole likely belonged to a chief of the Eagle clan, which makes sense, since Louise's village was an Eagle clan village. The other—"

A tune I recognized as an Arcade Fire song cut her off and had her scrambling for her phone. But the eager anticipation reflected on her face vanished when she read the caller's name. She slipped it back into her pocket without answering.

I mouthed to Eric, "Not the boyfriend."

Squeezing my hand, he whispered in my ear, "Love's never easy, is it?"

"It sure ain't," I replied, remembering our own tumultuous times.

Eric turned back to the young woman. "Do you know how old this pole is? It looks to have weathered many a storm."

"No one knows for certain, but since Louise's village was abandoned in the late 1800s, it's at least that old, likely older. The same goes for most of the other poles in this exhibit."

"I guess if they had remained in the villages, they would have disintegrated long ago," I said.

"Yup, back to Mother Earth where they really belong. But the archeologists wanted to preserve them, so they took them, mostly in the first half of the 1900s. Because the poles were so large, many were cut into sections for easier removal. This one was probably triple if not quadruple this height."

"Were they taken with the approval of the Haida?" Eric asked.

She shrugged, although I thought I detected a flash of anger in her eyes. "You probably know from your own tribe's experience that we rarely had an option. Sure, some Haida were just as keen on preserving them as the archeologists. But I think most were just taken. Since people no longer lived in the villages, no one was around to stop them."

She started walking toward a doorway. "Come, I want to show you some mortuary boxes." She led us into a smaller room filled with an assortment of wooden masks and boxes. She stopped beside a box about the size of a wine carton. Made from a reddish wood, which I took to be red cedar, its sides were elaborately decorated with a variety of carved creatures. Though the painted features had faded with age, I imagined at one time the brightness of the reds, greens, and blacks would have made them seem almost alive.

"A chief from my ancestral village was once buried in this mortuary box. I think one of my ancestors made it."

"You must be proud to see it displayed in this museum," I said.

"Yes and no. It's an awesome example of a bentwood box, but I don't like how it got here."

"Are you saying it was stolen?" Eric asked.

"It had to be. These mortuary boxes are sacred. There's no way anyone in the clan would have agreed to it being removed from the village."

"Because it contained human remains," Eric said, more as a statement than a question.

"Exactly."

"Do you know what happened to the remains, if they were treated with respect?"

"Respect? You've got to be kidding. There are supposed to be hundreds of human remains stored away somewhere in the bowels of the museum, just like any other artifact."

"But if people were buried inside these boxes, why would anyone want to take them?" I asked.

"Because the thieves thought they might contain treasure. Our chiefs liked to be buried with some of their valuables."

"Like gold and silver?"

"I suppose the archeologists thought so, but they would've got one whopping surprise when they opened the boxes. The most valuable thing would've been bits of abalone shell. Gold wasn't exactly on the radar back then."

At that point a young woman with blond braids and a gauzy floor-length skirt poked her head into the room. She appeared to be crying.

"Becky," she called out hoarsely. "Can you come here a sec?"

"What's up?" our guide asked as she joined her. The blonde placed her arm around Becky's shoulders and began whispering into her ear.

"No!" the young Haida woman shouted. She burst into tears and the other woman slowly led her away.

Within minutes the blonde returned, brushing tears from her eyes. "Becky's really sorry, but she can't finish your tour. She's asked me to take over."

"What happened?" I asked.

"Her boyfriend was found dead this morning."

THREE

I woke up to a gently rocking bed and the sound of a boat passing outside the window. I stretched and turned to snuggle into Eric, but felt only cold, empty sheets. I was about to call out to him when I remembered his early breakfast meeting. Although it was after ten, with the rain splattering against the window there seemed little point in leaping out of bed.

We were staying on a houseboat belonging to Matt Miller, one of Eric's former hockey buddies, now coach of the Vancouver Canucks. The houseboat was in between renters, so Matt had offered it to Eric for free. With visions of a basic cabin floating on a barge with only the bare necessities, I was very pleasantly surprised to discover we would be staying in an ultra-modern two-storey building complete with a roof garden that would rival any land-based home. It even had a humongous flat screen TV and wireless connectivity for Eric's iPad, along with a fully equipped kitchen that had brought a huge grin to his face.

The building had more windows than solid walls, many of them overlooking the broad channel of False Creek, across to the skyscrapers of downtown Vancouver and on to the snow-capped mountains beyond. Last evening, despite the chilly early May air, Eric and I had climbed up to the roof garden to enjoy one of his scrumptious dinners while enjoying the magical view.

Despite the houseboat's land-based amenities, I was frequently reminded that we were floating on water. It rocked slightly whenever a large boat passed. The line of sight rose and fell with the tides, along with the floating walkways that took us out of the small community of ten houseboats and onto the dry land of Granville Island. The invigorating sea air was also a constant reminder, as was the water surrounding the building; though on one side it was masked by a boardwalk that served as the street. Fortunately, Matt's houseboat was at the end of this "street" of four houseboats, two on either side. This premium location provided an unobstructed view of beautiful Vancouver. Two of his neighbours had sizeable sailboats moored beside their houses. Not a bad life, eh?

I couldn't fathom why Matt didn't live in this fabulous house, until I learned from Eric that he lived in one of those quintessential multi-storied West Coast cedar homes built into the side of a mountain overlooking Horseshoe Bay. Little wonder that Vancouver real estate prices were the highest in the country.

I crawled out of bed and slipped on the ivory silk kimono my mother had given me as a bride's gift along with a slinky silk nightgown that invariably slid to the floor before the night was over. Sadly, Mother's weak heart had prevented her from coming to the wedding, but my sister Jean and her family had driven the seven long hours from Toronto to attend the simple ceremony in the Migiskan

Reserve's tiny wood-frame church. They even bunked in with Eric and me at Three Deer Point in the rambling Victorian cottage I'd inherited from Great-aunt Aggie.

I would say this about Jean: although she had a heightened view of her place in society and didn't hesitate to remind everyone that she was a judge and the daughter of one of Toronto's Establishment families, she was as gracious and as friendly with our friends as she was with her own. She readily accepted Eric's bear hug, even going so far as to kiss him longer than I would've liked. A couple of months later, during our stay at their ski chalet in Collingwood, she took me aside and told me that marrying Eric had been one of the best decisions in my life. I heartily agreed.

I tripped down the stairs to the stainless steel kitchen wondering how to spend my day. Eric didn't think he'd be free until late afternoon. Until then, I had the day to myself.

Last fall, after Eric resigned as band chief of the Migiskan Anishinabeg, he was hired as a special advisor to the Grand Council of First Nations, the nationally-based organization that served as a focal point for bringing the interests of the many different First Nations in Canada under one umbrella. Many viewed this as a stepping-stone for Eric's eventual election to Grand Chief. Dan Blackbird, the current incumbent, wouldn't be running again when his term was up next year. He was putting his support behind Eric.

The plan this year was for Eric to get to know the issues facing First Nations across the country and for them to get to know him. Before coming to Vancouver, we'd been in Yellowknife and several remote communities in the Northwest Territories meeting with Dené chiefs and elders. I loved this chance to explore Canada and meet the people inhabiting its many diverse wildernesses.

Sadly, one of the reasons I was able to join Eric was the death of our much-loved Sergei. His last days had been painful not only for him but also for us. It was with mixed feelings that we made the heartbreaking decision to have him put down. We were all devastated, especially our dog's best buddy, Jid, the boy he had saved several winters before. Although both Eric and I wanted to get another dog, I was reluctant. I needed to properly mourn Sergei before I could accept another bundle of squirming fur into my heart.

I smiled when I saw that Eric had primed the coffee maker before heading off. All I had to do was press a button. After one too many of my decidedly inconsistent pots of coffee and similar food-preparation disasters, he had taken over the cooking duties, which was fine by me. It meant that I did dishes detail, which wasn't exactly my love either. But at least I did a better job of keeping the dirty dishes at bay than my husband did.

Husband. I loved saying that word. Although I rather liked the sound of "Meg Odjik," Eric had suggested I keep my maiden name, Harris. Traditionally, Algonquin women didn't change their names when they married.

This morning he also left me a bowl brimming with chunks of melon, papaya, and mango, along with a container of plain low-fat yogurt and some homemade granola picked up at the Granville Market. Eric was trying to change my eating habits. I tended to favour calorific foods like cream-filled doughnuts, poutine, cheeseburgers, and the like. And my body showed it. So he was bringing healthy foods into my life: leafy greens, fruits, vegetables, fish, and game. To tell the truth, although I'd initially feigned resistance, I didn't mind at all. In fact, I was gaining a real appreciation for their natural, unprocessed flavours, while my body was gaining a familiarity with thinness. So far, I'd lost ten kilos and was able to get into clothes I could only dream about before, like the slinky black dress Eric bought me for the Assembly's Closing Feast.

A glance outside told me the rain had stopped. Worried it wouldn't last long in this city of changeable weather, I gulped down my breakfast, threw the dirty dishes into the dishwasher, and got dressed. Though the clouds were breaking apart by the time I stepped onto the walkway, I still wore my rain jacket. Several times yesterday, Eric and I were surprised by a sudden shower despite the skies being more blue than grey.

With the tide out, it was a steep climb up the ramp to terra firma. I followed a path bordering the shore toward a group of buildings. A rainbow-coloured water taxi bobbed past, and then another. Looking more like rubber duckies than boats, they darted back and forth, ferrying passengers to various points along False Creek. It looked like a fun ride.

I decided to check out the Emily Carr University of Art to see if it was worthy of the name of this famous Canadian artist. Carr's name alone conjured up images of swirling green and cathedral forests. But at the sight of the boring monolithic buildings with their corrugated metal and concrete walls, I felt she would be shuddering in her grave at the lack of artistic imagination.

On the other hand, I knew she would let out a belly laugh at the cement trucks parked in the grounds of a nearby factory. Giant spears of green asparagus covered the drum of one of the trucks, while enormous red apples covered another.

I was about to turn back to the school to see if its interior was more promising, when a crowd of onlookers caught my attention. They were standing in front of a building cordoned off by yellow police tape. Next to them were parked several police cars and a forensics van. Curious, I joined them.

FOUR

The police tape blocked off a single-storey building that resembled the Haida longhouses we'd visited at the museum yesterday. Massive timbers supported a low-pitched roof, which appeared to be open to the elements, since I could see the metal struts of a bridge through it. But the debris that seemed to be floating on air suggested it was made of glass or acrylic. Three of the walls were open, with only wire mesh to keep out intruders, while the back wall was solid wood except for two narrow windows. The mast of a sailboat drifted past one of them.

Several cedar logs of varying length and thickness were stacked near the back wall. Along one side of the vast open interior stretched a workbench with an assortment of tools, large sheets of drawing paper, and pieces of wood scattered over its surface. Nearby stood a short, partially carved totem pole, while another much longer length of timber extended horizontally over a couple of wood supports. Black outlines of various exotic creatures were sketched along its smooth surface. Several appeared similar to those we had seen yesterday carved into the ancient poles.

My attention, however, was riveted to the middle of the room, where a set of empty wood supports stood as if waiting to be put to use. I felt a chill at the sight of a pool of blood on the ground next to them. The blood flowed out from the upper torso of a yellow chalk outline of a person with arms flung out. Several numbered plastic tent markers radiated from the outline. A man clad from head to toe in a white forensic outfit stood next to it snapping pictures, while a woman, similarly clad, dusted the surface of a nearby table and the tools spread over it. Another forensic investigator was consulting with a man dressed in street clothes, who acted as if he were in charge.

"I guess someone was killed," I said to the boy standing next to me.

Sporting a bulging knapsack, he was the only person in the group of mostly teenagers and early twenty-types not plugged into an iPod. "Yah, yesterday," he replied.

With a sense of foreboding, I asked, "Was it a man?"

"Yah, I think he was a student at my school."

"Do you know if his name was Allistair?"

"Yah, you know him?"

"No, but I was with his girlfriend yesterday when she received the news."

The poor girl.

At that moment a young woman wearing the *de rigueur* student uniform of skin-tight jeans with plenty of bare midriff forced her way through the crowd to a small park next to the building. Her curly hair was the same flaming red colour that had prompted my friends to call me "Carrot Top" at her age. Clutching a bouquet of wilting flowers, she knelt in front of a

27

squat newish-looking totem pole (judging by its reddish colour). Bunches of flowers lay at its base. She bowed her head for a few minutes as if in prayer then placed her carnations next to a drawing of a stylized bird propped against the pole. The creature reminded me of the eagles painted on the mortuary boxes.

"That's his memorial," the young man said.

"Did you know him?"

"Not really. He wasn't in any of my classes, but I'd sometimes see him here carving, usually at night when I was on my way home. I figured he was in the native arts program."

"Do you know how he died?"

"Some kid said his throat was cut. Awful way to go, eh?" The student winced. "That blood's probably his. And the outline's got to be where they found his body. Fuck, this is just like *CSI*." His voice quivered with excitement.

I cringed at his insensitivity. But he was barely out of his teens, and seeing something that reminded him of a TV show was likely more exciting than respecting the memory of the murdered boy.

A short, barrel-chested man who'd been standing in the park staring intently at the shrine walked up to the mesh wall of the building and called out. With his slicked-back salt-and-pepper hair and his broad face seamed from life's trials, he looked to be a good thirty or more years older than most of the other onlookers. The pained expression on his face suggested that he wasn't exactly indifferent to Allistair's death.

The plainclothes cop approached. The two men conversed for several minutes, until the first man broke away, saying angrily, "I have a customer waiting for that pole."

He stomped back through the park and took up station next to the totem pole with the makeshift shrine. He crossed his arms with annoyance and glared at the world at large.

"Do you know who that man is?" I asked my informant.

"Ernest Paul. He's the owner of the carving shed. He's a famous Haida carver. I guess he's ticked off 'cause he can't use his studio."

"Surely he's more concerned about the boy who died."

My informant merely shrugged. Then, muttering "Got a class," he turned his back on death and made his way through the crowd.

Ernest Paul paced back and forth between the make-shift shrine and another older pole, silvered with age. Each time he reached the older pole, he would slam his hand against one of its eroded animal carvings, whirl around, and stomp back to the newer one, its carvings almost jumping off the wood. He would stare at the growing pile of flowers for a few seconds, then whisk back around and return to the other pole.

After several minutes of this restless pacing, he shouted. "Hey, what are you doing about my log?"

"What log?" the detective yelled back.

"The one the kid was working on? That red cedar cost me a fortune and now it's gone."

Questioning glances passed between the forensic cops, as the detective motioned Ernest to come inside. "Why didn't you mention this earlier?" he asked, pulling out his notebook.

Before the carver had a chance to explain, a silver BMW squealed to a stop behind us. A well-dressed mid-dle-aged woman with her blond hair more out than in a ponytail jumped out of the car and shoved us aside. She burst through the police tape and ran straight to Ernest. Pummeling his chest, she cried out, "How could you?"

The carver winced but made no attempt to stop her. Instead he planted his feet as she continued hitting him.

"You killed him!" she shouted.

The detective approached. "Please, Mrs. Zakharov, you shouldn't be here."

At that point a grey-haired man dressed in boardroom attire came up behind her and pulled her away.

"Oh, Dmitri, our son is dead." She collapsed wailing into his arms.

The man led her back to the BMW, where he coaxed her into the passenger seat. He then walked to the Mercedes parked behind it and spoke to the chauffeur before returning to the driver side of the BMW. In tandem, the two cars drove away.

Only then did I notice the slim figure of Becky, our guide from yesterday and the girlfriend of the woman's dead son, standing forlornly at the side of the road where the cars had been parked. I couldn't remember seeing any interchange between the two women or any acknowledgement by the grieving mother or the father that this young woman who had loved their son was also grieving.

Biting her lip as the tears trickled down her cheeks, Becky's eyes followed the cars until they disappeared behind a building. Her gaze then turned to the studio. She took a few hesitant steps in the direction of his shrine but stopped and glanced helplessly around as if uncertain. I was about to come to her aid when the young blond woman who'd brought her the dreadful news ran up and draped an arm around her friend. Watching Becky collapse in front of the flowers, I ached for this young woman who no doubt thought her life had come to an end too.

The carver, his arms hanging limply by his side, his face a mask of stone, remained rooted where the woman had accused him of killing her son.

FIVE

The Right Log

He parked the logging truck behind a warehouse but within sight of the dock and clambered up onto the back to make sure the pole was secure. The log's fresh smell brought back good memories of other red cedar poles he'd carved. The wood tingled as he ran his fingers over the smooth surface. The grain was good, straight, with no visible knots. And the milling was perfect. It was ready for carving. His hand trembled at the thought of slicing into its buttery wood.

The totem pole was already calling to him. He could feel the figures wanting to come out and how they would flow one into the other. But it was too soon. He didn't know the full story. Although he knew the ending and the beginning, there were parts in the middle he had to work out.

He was sorry he had to move the kid's body from his first totem pole. It would've made a fitting deathbed. After all, it was the boy's heritage, as it was his own. They both came from a long line of master carvers or *Gya k'id ll Gaay Ga*, as he liked to call himself. If only he knew how to pronounce it properly. It wasn't easy twisting his tongue around these strange Haida words, words he should've spoken since birth.

He traced his finger over the dark area of the stain. It was still moist where the boy's blood had flowed into the groove. Over time, the stain would blend and become one with the wood. It, too, was part of the story. As was the silver trinket he'd seen fall. He'd almost forgotten it. But when he spied it glimmering on the ground next to the body, he remembered. He tucked it away in his pocket for when it would be needed.

He'd barely had the energy to remove the heavy log from the shed. Thanks to Salaana, the right equipment had been close at hand. Now he had to get the log to Haida Gwaii so he could complete the story.

SIX

The lumbering dark clouds that had been threatening to release their drenching load throughout most of the day finally let loose just as I was preparing to join Eric for dinner. He'd called an hour ago to suggest that we join a group of his colleagues at a restaurant in Gastown. Although I wasn't keen — I felt like a fifth wheel at such gatherings — I knew he wanted to, so I agreed.

The torrent blotted out the opposite shore. It pummeled the roof of the houseboat, sending water gushing from the gutters. The building hummed with the noise. I hoped that by the time I had to leave the rain would've been reduced to a sprinkle.

I really wanted to wear my new rust-coloured wool slacks, two sizes smaller I might add than I used to wear, and the brown leather loafers bought to go with them. But let's face it, it was a stupid idea. They'd get soaked. My other options were jeans or an old pair of baggy wool slacks dating from when my figure was fuller, options I wasn't keen on. Besides, I wanted to look svelte for Eric.

Before we married I paid little attention to my clothes, since the bulk of my time was spent tramping through the woods. And Eric never indicated that my clothes mattered to him. But after watching his soft grey eyes light up when I first wore these new slacks and the matching forest green silk blouse, I knew he cared. He'd even bought me a silk scarf of greens and browns with a hint of turquoise to compliment the outfit. To hell with the rain, I'd wear them. But I'd keep the shoes and matching purse dry inside a plastic bag until I reached the restaurant.

I zipped up my rain jacket, careful to place the hood so that it didn't destroy my hair. But with frizzy hair, there wasn't much damage that could be done anyway. My first husband had insisted I have it straightened, but I'd never felt that it was me. After we went our separate ways, I let my hair return to its natural curly ways. Nowadays I kept it reasonably short. My only attempt at a beauty aid was touching up the fading red and hiding the emerging grey with Flame by Clairol. But even this might stop, for Eric preferred the natural look. And to tell the truth, so did I.

The dispatcher said the cab would take fifteen minutes. Even though I couldn't keep an eye out for its arrival from the houseboat, I decided to wait inside until close to the estimated time and then race to the pickup spot. But after ten minutes I started to worry I would miss it, so I grabbed a large golf umbrella from the closet and headed out into the deluge.

Instead of abating, the rain's intensity had increased. I splashed up the ramp, but the taxi hadn't yet arrived. Not willing to wait, I headed down the lane to the main road hoping to meet it. No such luck. And without a cellphone, I couldn't call. This was one of the rare occasions when I wished I had one. But with no reception at Three Deer Point, it had never made any sense to have one.

I gave up on the taxi and headed to the nearby Granville Island Hotel, hoping to find one parked out front. The cabstand was empty, but a five-dollar tip had the doorman calling one for me. I waited by the entrance under the protection of the glass portico. My trail shoes were decidedly wet, so was the bottom of my slacks. But the rest of me was dry.

A cab drove up and emptied itself of two passengers. I started to walk toward it when a man brushed past me and jumped inside, shouting for the driver to get him to the airport fast. The doorman merely shrugged and indicated the next one was mine. So much for my five-dollar tip. I moved to the front of the portico, careful to keep out of reach of the slanting rain.

By now I was a good ten minutes late. I debated running inside and using a payphone to let Eric know, but feared I would miss the next cab. The hotel doors slid open behind me and two men emerged. They were arguing, judging by their raised voices. Though I couldn't make out the words above the rain pounding on the portico roof, I thought one of the voices sounded familiar. Before I had a chance to turn around to check, another cab arrived. I was already climbing inside by the time the last passenger was stepping out.

As the cab sped away, I peered through the rear window and recognized the slicked-back hair and paunch of the master carver, Ernest Paul, the man who just this morning was accused of murder. Since he was walking free, I could only assume the police hadn't reached the same conclusion as the dead boy's mother. As for his companion, I noticed, before the hotel retreated from view, that in sharp contrast to the carver's casual, slightly sloppy appearance, the man with the short-cropped black hair and stocky build was dressed in perfectly pressed grey slacks and a blazer.

As we zipped past, I saw that the police tape no longer blocked access to the carver's studio. If Ernest Paul was so keen on getting on with his carving, as he'd loudly insisted this morning, why wasn't he there? Or had he used it as a ploy to hassle the police? Maybe Allistair's mother was right. Maybe he was involved.

After a nail-biting snail-crawl through downtown rush hour to the rain-swept streets of Gastown, I arrived at the Salish Feasthouse a good thirty minutes late. I splashed through puddles and into the restaurant where I hastily switched into my dry loafers and stowed my wet gear in the cloakroom. After carefully draping the silk scarf around my neck and smoothing down my hair, I followed the maître d' into the dining area. Fully expecting to find Eric casting anxious looks in my direction, I sighed with relief when I found the table empty. I sat down to catch my breath.

I found myself enjoying the warmth and coziness of a longhouse. Rich cedar paneling covered the walls and the peaked ceiling, while massive cedar beams extended from one end of the room to the other. The walls were alive with eagles, killer whales, and other West Coast native renderings in the form of woodcarvings and colourful prints. Most of the long wooden tables were overflowing with diners and food, which, given the enticing aromas, promised to be delicious.

I had just ordered a pot of hemlock tea, one of the house specialties, when I heard the sound of stamping feet and clattering umbrellas amid boisterous laughter at the front door. My heart jumped when I recognized Eric's grey-streaked mane of black hair among the group of men and women.

He waved and started toward me with the confident stride I knew so well, of a man wholly content with his life. Of medium height with a husky build, his easy self-assurance invariably made him stand out in a crowd. I watched eyes turn in his direction as he strode, beaming, dimples erupting, toward me. My heart fluttered as it usually did, making me feel like a lovesick teenager, which was ridiculous. After all, we'd been married a good eight months and were supposed to be set in our old married ways.

We embraced as if we'd been away from each other for considerably longer than half a day. His colleagues' laughter and joking banter soon had us breaking apart. As everyone spread around the wooden benches on either side of the table, Eric introduced me. Although I had previously met a couple of the men, including Dan Blackbird, the Grand Chief, the rest I was meeting for the first time. I have a terrible habit of forgetting names, so the only name that registered was Louise O'Brien, only because it had been mentioned yesterday.

While Eric remained standing talking to Dan, the elderly woman carefully inched her way along the bench to sit beside me. "These old bones sure can't take a hard seat like they used to." Her dark eyes twinkled with life. "It's wonderful to finally meet you. I've heard so many good things about you from your husband."

I squirmed with embarrassment and changed the topic. "We enjoyed meeting your niece Becky at the museum yesterday."

"A lovely girl, isn't she? We're all very proud of her." Her red and black appliqué jacket barely stretched across her ample bosom and stomach.

"I'm afraid we were with her when she got the bad news about her boyfriend. How is she doing?"

"The poor child. Such an awful thing to happen." The twinkle vanished. "I only found out a short while ago."

"I saw her again today. She seemed in a bad way. I hope she'll be okay."

"The poor dear is very upset and rightly so. She loved him very much. I suggested she join us tonight. It's not good being alone at a time like this. I'm the closest to family she has in Vancouver. Although I'm not exactly family, just an auntie who has known her since she was in diapers."

With her sympathetic manner and short curly white hair freshly primped at the hairdresser, she reminded me of everyone's favourite grandmother. But if the steely glint lurking behind the twinkle were anything to go by, I'd say she was a grandmother with a firm hand who'd be less inclined to spoil her grandchildren than offer them heartfelt advice.

SEVEN

Eric climbed over the bench to grab the spot on the other side of me. "I hope your day wasn't too boring without me." He chuckled.

I yawned. "Funny, it only just started to become boring." Then I punched him gently in the ribs. "Seriously, I did have an adventure. Remember our museum guide?" I began telling him about the crime scene. Partway through, the woman sitting on his other side interrupted me by asking him a question. Smiling apologetically he turned to answer and became caught up in a heated discussion on some issue pertaining to the Grand Council.

With everyone around me engrossed in conversation, I found myself studying my mug of hemlock tea until I felt a nudge.

"Don't mind us, dear," Louise said. "It's been a busy day and we haven't quite left it. Eric says you have a lovely place in Quebec. Please tell me about it."

I began describing Three Deer Point to her and the features that made the century-old Victorian cottage such a comfortable place to call home, like the wraparound porch where I liked to sit and ponder the ever-changing view of Echo Lake or the massive stone fireplace that pours soothing heat into the front room on a cold winter's night. But after several minutes, I realized her thoughts were elsewhere, so I stopped talking just as the waitress was placing large wooden platters piled with a cornucopia of native delights on the table.

"Potlatch platters" the menu called them. The one in front of us overflowed with plump fried oysters of the giant variety and bright pink spot prawns, both unique to the cold seas off the West Coast. A large side of barbecued salmon filled another platter. Farther down the table, a third contained a haunch of venison smothered in a juniper berry sauce, while another was piled high with contributions from eastern Canada, wild rice and fiddleheads. It was going to be quite the feast.

Eric's eyes sparkled with delight as he reached for an oyster. Cutting it in half, he placed one half in my mouth and ate the other. Muttering "delicious" in unison, we both reached for another.

"I hope you're taking notes," I said. "I expect to see some of these dishes on our table back home."

He grinned and poured himself a hefty glass of white wine, while I stuck with the hemlock tea. I was enjoying its faintly licorice taste. I no longer drank alcohol. After one drunken episode too many last year, I decided that alcohol and I didn't get along and never would, so I gave it up. Amazingly, I hadn't found it difficult, even with Eric having his nightly glass of single malt. At first he'd stopped drinking altogether, but when I realized that he missed his scotch and occasional glass of wine, I insisted that he go back to his old habits. I found I was no longer tempted to sneak a drink, nor did I find myself eyeing his glass longingly. On the plus side, I felt healthier, more energetic, and more ready to take on life's challenges, which these days didn't seem quite so insurmountable.

We continued to share tantalizing morsels until Eric was again drawn into a conversation, this one with two men across the table. Although he tried to include me, I had no idea what they were discussing, nor was I particularly interested, so I concentrated on eating.

After a few minutes I noticed Louise was also keeping to herself. Thinking she might be worried about her niece, I asked about her.

"A lovely girl." She sighed. "Such a shame. Two sweet, innocent kids who weren't hurting anybody."

"Do the police know who killed him?"

"I doubt it. And they won't try very hard to find out either."

"Of course they will."

"Hrmphh! For an Indian? Don't kid yourself. But then you wouldn't know."

I felt my back stiffen and was searching for a diplomatic response when she said, "Forgive me, child. That wasn't fair. Please excuse the grumblings of an old lady."

"There's no need to apologize. I've had my own experience with police wearing blinkers." I paused to help myself to another oyster. "But I hadn't realized Allistair was native."

She sighed. "He was a good Haida boy and a natural carver from what Becky says. So he must've come from a long line of carvers, although he didn't know. He was adopted and had no idea who his birth parents were, not even his clan."

"Your people have two main clans, don't you?" Eric asked, leaning across me to reach the platter of barbecued salmon.

Loud guffaws spilled over from the other end of the table. After exchanging a few jibes accompanied by a couple of wry comments from Louise, Eric turned his attention back to the salmon. He passed Louise and me a slice of the tender flesh before placing one on his own plate.

Louise smiled. "Nothing beats salmon, our people's lifeblood. If I'm not mistaken, this spring salmon, or *taagun*, could be from Haida Gwaii, where the run has started."

"I envy your people's bounty," Eric replied. "I'm afraid my Algonquin ancestors had to search far and wide for their food."

"We were fortunate. But we always made sure we paid our respects to *Salaana*, the spirit who lives above." She paused to enjoy another bite of the delicious fish. "To answer your question, every Haida is either an eagle or a raven. I'm eagle, whereas Becky is raven. I had worried that her boyfriend might've been a raven, especially if they'd decided to marry. Traditionally, we can't marry within our clan."

"So Allistair would've needed to be an eagle?" I asked after savouring another tender morsel of salmon.

"That's right. Mind you, the young today don't pay much attention to such things. Many don't even marry within the Haida Nation. But who am I to talk." Her eyes creased in merriment. "I married an Irishman from Belfast. Met him when he was working at the military base in Masset at the north end of Haida Gwaii. He was a sergeant with the British Army, on a special assignment with the Canadian Forces. We spent several years moving around to various British bases, then he left the army and we came back to Masset, where he got a job as a civilian."

"Do you have children?" I asked.

"Two sons. Both married white girls and moved away. One's living in Edmonton and the other's in Seattle."

"I imagine you don't see them often."

She chortled. "One of the reasons I like to work on GCFN committees, I get to travel. I'm heading down to Seattle tomorrow to spend a few days with the grandkids and then back to Haida Gwaii for a very special occasion — I'm witnessing a pole raising."

"A totem pole? Like the ones I saw in the museum yesterday?"

"Yes, but more colourful, for it will be freshly painted."

"How exciting."

"Yes, a very exciting time for us. A member of my clan will be raising it to take the name of a chief. It has been many years since we've had a potlatched chief."

"A potlatch is about giving away goods, isn't it?" Eric asked.

"You've been doing some reading." She smiled. "The chief holds a potlatch ceremony to reward witnesses to the pole raising by giving them gifts. It includes a big feast and lots of dancing. In the old days these potlatches would go on for days. If you and Meg don't have any immediate plans, you should think of coming. It would give you a chance to get to know us Haida better and for us to get to know the next Grand Chief of the Grand Council of First Nations."

Eric laughed, while my ears perked up. This could be fun.

"Please, I'm not the only one in the running for Grand Chief. There are some good contenders. When did you say this would take place?"

"On Saturday, which is, let me see …" She pulled out an iPhone and checked the calendar.

"Five days from now," I offered. "Let's go, Eric. It sounds like a lot of fun and I'd love to visit Haida Gwaii."

"We'd have to change Friday's flight and I have an interview with CBC early Monday, so we'd have to be back in Ottawa by Sunday night. I don't know. It would be cutting it pretty tight."

"I'll check the flights. I'm sure we can get an early one on Sunday."

"Let me know," Louise said. "I'm sure the new chief would be very interested in meeting you."

At that moment her face broke into a welcoming smile. Our guide from yesterday was making her way toward us.

"Becky, how are you doing, dear? I'm so glad you decided to come."

EIGHT

Trying to keep her tears in check and not succeeding, Becky walked around the table greeting those she knew and introducing herself to those she didn't. All expressed their sympathy with either a bear hug or a consoling pat. She clung to Louise for several long minutes before turning to Eric and me. At first she didn't remember us, and when she did, she broke down, muttering, "I'm so sorry I ran out on you."

"Please, you have nothing to apologize for," Eric said, taking her small hands in his large ones. "You have our deepest sympathy."

We shuffled along the bench until there was enough space to squeeze her slimness between Louise and me. Finding ourselves in a shoulder lock, Eric slipped his arm around me, nuzzled my ear, and continued eating with just his right hand. If he needed to cut something I could hold it down with my fork while he sawed away with his knife. We'd call it communal eating.

"Oh Auntie, it's all my fault," Becky wailed.

"Hush, child, and eat something. It'll make you feel better." Louise filled her bread plate with oysters and prawns and passed it to the distraught girl.

"But Auntie, you don't understand. I got him killed. If I hadn't kicked him out, Allie would be alive."

"Now, child, you can't go blaming yourself. His death had nothing to do with you."

"But it did. We were supposed to be studying together, but we got into a terrible fight. I was so mad at him I kicked him out of my apartment. He must've gone straight to Ern's."

"Child, these things happen. It's unfortunate, but you mustn't blame yourself."

"It was such a stupid argument. He wanted to give me his bracelet. But I didn't want it. So we started shouting at each other and before I knew it he was slamming the door in my face."

Door slamming could certainly lead to trouble, as I well knew. I snuck a glance at Eric and wondered if he remembered the time he slammed the door on me. It had almost ended our relationship.

"So you didn't kick him out, did you, dear?"

"No … but I should've accepted the bracelet. It was a really nice silver one. It looked old. It belonged to his real mother, so I felt I couldn't take it. Now I wish I had. Then I'd have something to remember him by."

"You can ask his stepmother. I'm sure she'd be happy to give it to you."

"You kidding? That old witch wouldn't give me anything. She didn't think I was good enough for her precious son."

I felt like an interloper listening in, but with Eric caught up in another Grand Council discussion, it was difficult not to hear. Besides, having been with her when she first received the news and then seeing where her boyfriend had died, I felt involved.

"Don't pay any attention to that nonsense," Louise replied. "You're much better than her. You have the blood of one of the great Haida chiefs, Nang Sdins, flowing in your veins."

The girl's long black hair rippled as she nodded. She dabbed her eyes with a Kleenex before taking a tiny bite from one of the prawns.

"It serves her right that he was carving when he died," Becky continued. "She hated him carving. She wanted him to be a hotshot lawyer. She wouldn't even allow him to go to Ern's shed. But Allie didn't care. He wanted to be a carver more than anything in the world." She paused as she helped herself to another succulent prawn. "You know, Auntie, when he carved he became a completely different person, more whole, more complete, more Haida."

"I'm sure he had the blood of master carvers flowing in his veins. I know you said he didn't know his real parents, but did he ever try to find out? It would be nice to close the circle and let his Haida relatives know of his death."

"He tried, but the hospital where he was born had no record of his mother, who died giving birth to him. And his birth certificate has the Zakharovs as his parents. He knows nothing about his real father. Mrs. Zakharov probably knows more, but she won't tell him."

"Poor child, to be brought up knowing nothing of his heritage. At least he was trying to reclaim it through carving. Come, child, eat up. Try some of this delicious *taagun.*" She cut a generous slice from the fresh side of salmon that had just replaced the one we'd devoured and placed it on Becky's plate.

I could still taste the delicate flavour that came from being barbequed on a cedar plank. According to Eric, it was a traditional way of cooking salmon for the peoples of the North West Pacific coast.

After finishing off the oysters, prawns, and making good inroads into the salmon, Becky turned to me. "I really am sorry about yesterday."

"As my husband said, you have nothing to apologize for. It must've been a terrible shock. I'm so sorry."

"It was. When he didn't come to the museum I thought he was still mad at me. He was so sweet, so kind, so wonderful. Why would anyone want to kill him?"

"What did the police say?"

"I've no idea. They won't tell me anything. I'm just his girlfriend. But they sure grilled me. Maybe they think I did it?"

"Did they treat you badly?" Louise interjected. "Perhaps we should get you a lawyer."

"No, Auntie, I don't need one. I didn't kill him. How could I? I loved him too much." She burst out in a fresh flood of tears.

"There, there, child," Louise said, wrapping her arms around the young woman.

"Is it possible it was an accident? That someone else was the real target?" I hazarded.

"I don't know," Becky said, straightening up. "I know he wasn't into drugs or gangs, the things that usually get guys killed. But the totem pole he was working on is gone. Surely he wasn't killed for a stupid cedar log."

"There were plenty of other logs to take," I said. "Besides, I think it'd be pretty difficult stealing a log without proper equipment. Do you know how big it was?"

"About eight metres. And it would weigh a ton. Not exactly something you'd stick into your back pocket."

"So the only way it could've been removed was by a logging truck with a crane," Eric said. "I doubt there are many logging trucks wandering the streets of Granville Island. There's got to be witnesses who saw it."

Becky's face lit up. "Ern has a truck. He uses it to transport the logs and the poles when they're finished. But why would he steal his own log? And more importantly, why would he kill Allie? He's always been so nice to him, teaching him the techniques, giving him his old tools, and letting him work on commissions. Mind you, he wasn't paying him anything. But Allie didn't care. He saw it as a chance to learn."

On the other hand, his mother hadn't thought the man was so nice. And she hadn't hesitated to accuse him of murder.

Becky's phone rang, with the same ringtone as yesterday. She spoke a few hurried words, then snapped it shut. Popping another prawn into her mouth, she scrambled out of her seat.

"Sorry, Auntie. I've got to go. Thanks for the food. And thanks for being there."

"You take care of yourself, child. I'm going to Seattle tomorrow, but I'll be back in a few days and then I'm going to Skidegate. Why don't you come home with me? I think some time with your family would do you good."

Becky leaned over to give her auntie a kiss on the cheek. "I'll let you know."

With a hasty goodbye, she left.

The three of us watched her push through the crowd of people milling at the entrance. Noticing her lively step, I couldn't help but envy the healing powers of youth.

NINE

The Journey Begins

His lungs filled with the tangy sea air as the cold wind whipped his thick hair into a frenzy. It felt good to be back on a boat. It'd been a long time since he had stood in a prow. Thank god he hadn't lost his sea legs. He braced himself for the coming deluge as the bow plunged into a wave and came rising back up, water splashing over him. He laughed. It felt like a goddamn orgasm. Mind you, it'd been a while since he'd had one of those too. This time he let out a war whoop.

He licked the salt from his lips. He didn't mind the water's numbing cold. The sun rising over the snow-capped peaks of the mainland would soon dry him. This must be how the ancestors felt when their giant canoes crashed through the open seas.

It was a good ten years since he'd spent this much time on a boat; not since he was running his own. But the big companies had moved in and the fishery had collapsed in seas that had fed his people for generations. With too many boats and not enough fish, he'd been forced to sell *Water Sprite*. She'd been one hell of a boat.

He more or less grew up on her. He was just a little

fry when his dad first took him onto her slippery decks and anointed him with oolichan oil, the smelly fish oil that had made him cry and stink so much that no one wanted to come near him for a week. It was supposed to make him a good fisherman, and he supposed it had. After Dad died and he took over *Water Sprite*, it was like Salaana was speaking directly to him. Even as the fish were disappearing, he managed to find where they were hiding and would bring in a decent haul, enough to keep him in logs and carving tools.

Carving, that was his real love. From his earliest memories, he knew in his bones that he was *Gya k'id ll Gaay Ga*. But that was not to be. His father had always been a fisherman, so too his grandfather. Besides, when he was young, there was no money to be made in carving.

Though he was pretty upset when he had to sell *Water Sprite*, he thought it would give him the chance to spend more time carving. But it hadn't worked out that way. He had gotten sidetracked, took a wrong step. Carving eventually brought him back. And now he had another pole to carve — likely his last.

It'd been tricky spiriting the boy's pole away from Ern's shed. Thank god for the truck. Even if the cops eventually found it, it didn't matter. He and the pole were long gone from Vancouver. Besides, he left the truck in a place that was sure to throw them off the scent. They'd never suspect in a million years that the pole was hiding behind boxes of ATVs, stoves, and fridges on a supply barge heading north through Georgia Strait.

Once again Salaana was looking out for him. It was pure luck that his old fishing mate was starting his run back up north. When he drove the log down to the loading docks on the Fraser, he was hoping to convince one of the operators to load it onto a barge to wait for the next tug going north. So when he saw his boyhood buddy tying up his tug, he almost whooped for joy. It didn't take long for Joe to get the pole loaded onto the barge and hidden from view.

Here he was, many hours later, heading north to Haida Gwaii on his buddy's tug with the kid's log trailing behind a good kilometer or more. In a few days he'd be stepping onto the beach of the ancestors. No one would ever think to look for him or the pole there.

TEN

"Let's go for a walk," I suggested after the cab dropped us off. The rain had stopped, leaving the night air feeling clean and refreshing, although the temperature had dropped. "We both could do with some exercise after that wonderful feast."

Eric grimaced.

"*Unh unh*, I won't take no for an answer." I prodded his stomach, which felt pudgier than normal. "You especially need it. Too much wining and dining lately."

"You're right, my *Miskowàbigonens*," he said, using the Algonquin spirit name he had given me. It meant Little Red Flower. He wrapped his arm around my waist and kissed my forehead. "But I tell you, I'm dead tired. It's been a long day and not an easy one."

I grabbed his hand and propelled him toward the ramp. "You can tell me about it on our walk. But first, let's get out of these clothes and into something more comfortable."

With the tide at its highest, the ramp was almost horizontal to the dock. The houseboats, now close to the same level as the shore, appeared to be standing on *terra firma*. However, the undulating movement of the walkway didn't let us forget that we were over water.

"You looked terrific tonight," Eric said when we reached the front door. "I got several comments on how attractive my wife was." He embraced me.

I pulled his arms away and said rather testily, "Why didn't they tell me?"

This sharing of confidentialities between men made me feel more like a chattel than a wife. Still, I couldn't deny that I wasn't flattered.

"Probably because they didn't know you. It was their way of saying they approved of my choice."

I bristled even more. "Approval? I wasn't aware that you needed their approval. Did they slap you on the back and give you a nudge, nudge, wink, wink and ask how good I was in bed?"

"Look, Meg, you're taking it the wrong way. Besides, two of the compliments came from the women. One in particular used to have me in her sights until I made it known that we could only be friends."

"Oh, who was that?" I attempted to sound unconcerned.

I tried to hone in on which of the women my onetime rival could be and realized all four — I wasn't counting Louise — were possible. Their ages were right: mid-thirties to late forties. None was bad looking, although the one with the shimmering black hair and crinkling green eyes was particularly attractive. Then I remembered her mentioning three children and a husband waiting for her on a reserve near Whitehorse.

There was one woman though, the youngest of the four, who seemed to give me a thorough once over, such that I felt as if I were under the microscope. She was the least attractive, with her acne-scarred complexion and scraggly brown hair. But she did have the kind of smile that made you forget about her shortcomings, a smile she bestowed upon me once I passed inspection.

"My *Miskowàbigonens*, you have nothing to worry about," Eric said, sensing where my thoughts were dwelling. He knew me too well. "You are my one and only." We shared a long, lingering kiss.

"Maybe we should forget the walk," I said, rather huskily.

Eric grinned wickedly. "Perhaps we should. But you're right. I need the walk. I need to clear my head, so let's change. The faster we're back from the walk, the sooner we can ..." He didn't bother to finish the sentence, but instead leaned over for another temperature-raising kiss.

Within minutes we were walking along the path, skirting the shore of the island. As much as I liked my new outfit, I felt considerably more comfortable in my usual garb — jeans, long-sleeved T-shirt, and a fleece jacket (with my rain jacket tied around my waist in case the rain returned). I could tell Eric was more relaxed, too, in his jeans and windbreaker. Although we'd both grown up in the city, me in Toronto and Eric in Calgary, we were confirmed country types and much preferred the casualness of rural living and the clothes that went with it.

Despite being in the middle of one of Canada's most thriving cities, walking along the shore of Granville Island felt more like walking in the country. Perhaps it was the proximity of the sea. This afternoon I'd watched a Great Blue Heron searching for tasty tidbits amongst the rocks at low tide and two gulls quarrelling over a crab, while a black spec soaring high above the water might have been a bald eagle. The island's low buildings gave it a small-town feel, while the mountains looming above the city reminded you that the wilderness was only a few short miles away.

But the night regalia of the towering skyscrapers twinkling at us from across False Creek and the drone of traffic crossing a nearby bridge reminded us that we were surrounded by bustling humanity. This was reinforced by a yacht festooned in party lights and reverberating with loud music that was churning up the channel.

"If we had to live in a city, I would want it to be Vancouver. What about you?" I asked.

"As long as it's in one of those townhouses," he said.

We had rounded the end of the island, which was really a man-made peninsula, and were overlooking a bay that separated Granville Island from the southern shore of False Creek. Eric was pointing to a number of two- and three-storey buildings stretching along the opposite shoreline.

"Only if we win the lottery. Given their prime location and that spectacular view, those places have got to cost a million or more."

"I guess we'd better start buying tickets, eh?" The two dimples I loved erupted on either cheek.

I kissed them. "Then we'd better be ready for the big win. Let's walk over and choose one. We can cross at the end of this inlet." I tucked my arm through his. "Tell me about your day."

Starting with the breakfast meeting, his day had been an endless cycle of back-to-back meetings. Some boring and going nowhere other than putting attendees to sleep, while others were filled with argumentation and dissention with little chance of agreement.

We crossed over to the south shore and walked along the brick pathway edging the shoreline, careful to avoid the puddles scattered over its uneven surface. Undulating mounds of rhododendron pregnant with fat buds and other flourishing shrubs separated us from the rows of townhouses. Up close I could see that the buildings had been artfully designed to capture individuality. Choosing one would be difficult.

Eric scanned the staggered collection of windows and balconies. "Not bad, eh? I could see myself spending the day sitting in any one of those windows contemplating the changing Vancouver scene."

"When you're ninety, maybe. You can't sit still long enough to contemplate anything right now." I gave him a playful jab in the ribs.

As we ambled along, Eric filled me in on a particularly contentious meeting of the Culture Committee he chaired.

"It took every trick I knew in the art of diplomacy, which isn't much, to get the two groups to stop arguing," he said.

"I'm sure you had them purring like pussycats in no time. What were they arguing about?"

"The ownership of ancient cultural items that have remained within a community, and who gets the money when they're sold."

"I thought the money was shared by community members."

"Usually, but that's mainly because the concept of ownership isn't traditionally a part of most First Nations cultures and these items are often so old that no one knows who they belonged to." He stopped talking and pointed to a three-storey unit with an expansive second-floor bay window jutting out over the garden. "What do you think of that one?"

"Not bad, but I like that one with the top-floor sun-room better. In this rainy climate I think the more light we can bring inside the better."

An interior light shone on a woman watering orchids, while in the neighbouring unit a man was sitting next to the window reading in the soft glow of a table lamp.

"We're getting distracted. Let me finish what I was talking about and then we'll get back to deciding on our future home."

But that was not to be. A fluffy grey and white Shih Tzu broke free from its owner and raced toward us. Our heads almost collided as we bent down to pet it. Overjoyed, the dog squirmed around our legs as the woman, all apologies, hastened to retrieve it. We glanced at each other mournfully as the unhappy animal was dragged away.

Eric squeezed my hand. "I say we get a puppy when we get back home."

"Maybe...." I said, although I knew I wasn't ready. The thought of replacing Sergei was still too painful. I steered the conversation back to the meeting. "So, someone on the committee doesn't want the money from one of these sales to be shared. Were they talking about a specific case?"

"He didn't say, but I had my suspicions. Let's face it, most of our communities have few items that date from early times. Either they were traded for next to nothing or they didn't survive because of their fragility."

"Isn't it really up to the individual community to decide how they want to handle this?"

"I agree. But Louise was quite adamant that we—" He stopped dead in his tracks. "Christ, it can't be...." His eyes were fixed on a woman who'd just entered the brightly lit ground floor of a townhouse set slightly back from the others.

"How did you know it was her?" I asked, immediately recognizing the woman. "You weren't with me when I saw her this morning."

"It may be many years since I've seen her," he growled, "but I'd know my goddamn sister anywhere."

"Your sister? But that's Allistair's mother."

ELEVEN

"Allistair? Who's he?" Eric snapped back.

"Remember? The boy who was killed yesterday, the boyfriend of Louise's niece."

"Right. Sorry. I forgot."

"Are you saying that woman is your sister?"

The woman approached the window. Worried she would see us staring in; I ducked and tried to pull Eric with me. But her red-rimmed eyes and distracted manner suggested her focus was on her murdered son and not on us. She flung the curtains closed.

"Stepsister." He ran his hand through his hair. "This boy was Haida, right?"

"Yes, he was adopted. That's what Louise said."

"Christ, she did the same thing. Like mother like daughter."

The minute the words were spoken, I knew he was talking about his own adoption.

"Let's keep walking." I had to calm him down.

During the ups and downs of our relationship we'd both kept secrets from each other, until a near tragedy forced us to admit that if we wanted to continue together, we had to be completely open with each other. After my painful confession to him about my brother, he had told me about his own childhood and his adoption by a white family in Calgary.

"I learned from my Algonquin grandmother when I finally located her that my real mother was killed in a car accident when I was about two," he recounted before we were married. "My dad had taken off shortly before I was born, so my grandparents were the only family left to take care of me. But the local priest and the Indian agents didn't think they could look after me properly or provide the so-called 'necessary education' to make me a contributing member of Canadian society. Yeah, right. As if that mattered to my grandparents.

"So I was taken from the rez and sent thousands of miles away to Calgary for adoption. I guess the authorities wanted to make damn sure there was sufficient distance between me and my heritage. My grandparents later told me that my leaving was like losing an arm or a leg. You see, I was their last remaining family. My mother was the only one of their four children to survive into adulthood."

Needless to say, Eric had no memory of any of this. His earliest memories were of being a young boy growing up in a family with two older siblings. It wasn't so much that his adoptive parents were bad parents; it was that they denied him his culture. When he started asking why he was darker than his fair-haired siblings and his parents, they finally had to admit that he was adopted. But they suggested that his parents might have been Italian. So he grew up not knowing that he was native, let alone a member of the Algonquin Anishinabeg.

"They wanted to stamp the Indian out of me," he said, not bothering to hide his bitterness, "though I didn't find that out until years later, when I finally put two and two together. They were much harder on me than the other two, kept insisting I needed more discipline for reasons they never bothered to explain. I assumed it was because I was adopted. They made sure I received a good education. Spared no expense and sent me off to one of the best private schools in Alberta. It was there I found hockey, my lifesaver."

Eric proved to be a natural and before long was playing in AAA. At an away game in Winnipeg he was approached by a woman who wanted to know if he was from the Buffalo Point Reserve because he looked like the grandson of a friend of hers. He vehemently denied it, insisting he was Italian. Later, when he was mistaken once again for native, he started to wonder.

"It terrified me," he said. "It'd been drummed into me since I was a boy that Indians were nothing but lazy drunkards. I didn't dare ask my parents. To convince myself that I wasn't one, I set out to become the best hockey player in the league and the best student in the school. It almost killed me. Between the hours I was spending working out in the gym, in hockey practice, and studying, there weren't many left for sleeping. I was a walking zombie, barely able to function. Then I met Uncle Joe. He was a Dené elder from the Northwest Territories and the wisest man I've ever known. Simply put, he told me to stop running."

Eric went on to describe how this wise old man, who'd spent more time in the bush than with a roof over his head, convinced the confused young player to accept and be proud of his aboriginal heritage. Uncle Joe

opened the door to the traditional ways, to the Creator
and Mother Earth, to smudging ceremonies and the like.
He invited Eric to participate in a healing circle and sweat
lodge. But it was only when he attended his first powwow
that he felt he'd finally returned to his roots.

"I was very nervous," Eric confided. "This was the first
time I was going to be in a large group of my own kind and I
felt like a fish out of water. I was terrified of doing and saying
the wrong thing. I felt I had nothing in common with any
of these people. But I shouldn't have been worried; within
minutes of arriving with Uncle Joe, someone stuck a mallet
in my hand and invited me into the drum circle. Soon I was
drumming with the best of them. I swore I could feel my
ancestors talking to me through the rhythmic beating of the
drums. It was the first time I truly felt like an Indian."

By this time Eric was playing Junior 'A' hockey in
Medicine Hat, so it was easy to keep his adoptive parents
ignorant of this side of his new life. But when the season
was over and he returned home wearing a bone choker
around his neck and a hawk feather in his Stetson, he
confronted them. At first they denied it, insisting he was
Italian, but when he threatened to leave and never come
back, they admitted that he was native. Needless to say,
they were all apologies about hiding it from him, but they
truly believed it had been for his own good. Unfortunately,
they knew nothing about his mother or her reserve. They
only knew he had been born in Quebec.

"With the help of Uncle Joe, it took me eight years
to find out I was Algonquin and another two to find the
reserve where my mother had lived. In the meantime, I
continued with hockey, advancing from the juniors to the

NHL. The day I hung up my skates for the last time, I learned that my mother's parents were still alive. I hopped on the next plane east and headed to the Migiskan Reserve, where I walked into the waiting arms of my grandmother." His eyes had glistened as he remembered. "The two of them so wizened and small, their backs stooped from their hard lives. Kokomis was blind. Nokomis had lost several fingers from frostbite while tending his trap lines. But they opened their arms and invited me into their lives.

"Sadly, my time with them was short. Kokomis died a year after we were reunited and Nokomis a couple of years later. I never returned to Calgary. The Migiskan Reserve was having its difficulties. I decided that I would use the skills and the education I had acquired through my adoption to help our people. I moved in with my grandparents. I was still living in their bungalow when you found me." He grinned.

At the time he said little about his step-parents or his step-siblings, and I hadn't asked. I supposed I had the impression that despite their misguided views they had been basically good parents and that he and the two other children had gotten along the way most siblings get along in such relationships. But given his reaction to the sight of his stepsister, this clearly wasn't the case. It was time he told me.

We continued walking along the shore in silence. Although the lights of downtown Vancouver still shone brilliantly from across False Creek, the din of the city had died down and the traffic over the bridges had diminished to a trickle. The city was going to sleep.

I noticed a bench standing a little off the path, facing the water.

"Eric, let's sit down and you can tell me about your sister."

TWELVE

"You told me that your stepsister was a few years older, but I don't think you mentioned her name," I said, settling onto the bench beside Eric.

Although I could feel the dampness of the wood seeping through my jeans, I ignored it. I squeezed his hand and received a warm answering squeeze, which I took as a good sign. He hadn't shut me out.

Eric placed his arm around me. "I'm sorry. I've acted like an idiot, but seeing her so unexpectedly was a real shock. What did you ask me again?"

I repeated the question, adding, "If you really don't want to talk about her, it's okay. I understand."

"I should've told you sooner. I'm sorry." He kissed me on the cheek. "Safe to say it's a part of my life I'd rather forget about." He paused. "At one time Cloë was the person I was closest to in my adoptive family." He brushed a wayward strand of hair from my face. "You're right, she is older, by four years. She married Dmitri Zakarhov, a Russian bobsledder who defected from the Soviet Union after the Calgary Olympics. Our family name was Teresko. I changed mine back to Odjik. I can't remember if I told you that."

"You said you changed it after you reunited with your grandparents."

He chuckled. Another good sign. "Yeah, my stepfather wasn't too happy. He saw it as a slap in the face for the years and money he'd put into raising me. I think I gave him the finger along with some equally complimentary words. I didn't see him again for twelve years, until my stepmother's funeral fifteen years ago. I haven't seen him since. I don't even know if he's alive or dead."

He lapsed into silence. I could hear water dripping from the trees behind us, and the sound of waves lapping against the rocks below. Clouds were beginning to hide the top floor lights of the skyscrapers downtown. Was rain on the way?

"My mother meant well. She was a good person in her misguided way. She understood and accepted the name change the same way she accepted my desire to reclaim my heritage. But the old bugger wouldn't let her have anything to do with me. After years of jumping to his commands, she wasn't about to do otherwise. I never saw her again. But thanks to a neighbour, we were able to keep in touch.

"Mike, my stepbrother, followed his father's lead and was very glad to see the end of me. He'd always resented me and didn't hesitate to call me a 'fuckin' injun.' I guess he wanted to make sure I was good and gone so he wouldn't have to share his father's money with me."

"I'm so sorry. It must've been hard. I'm sure you loved them at one point."

"My mom, yes, my dad, never, although I had a healthy respect for his heavy-handedness. As for Mike, it was mutual dislike from my first memories. He was seven years older and treated me like his personal punching bag.

But, hey, he taught me one thing — how to stand up for myself. When I finally bulked up from playing hockey and could give as good as I got, we retreated to our own separate corners and had very little to do with each other."

He grew silent and stared out over the water.

The tide was retreating. The seaweed covering the rocks glistened in the glow from the streetlight behind us.

"Don't get me wrong, Meg, it wasn't an unhappy childhood. I had many good moments. In fact, if my real mother hadn't died, I'm not sure my life would've been any better growing up on the rez. At that time, life on the Migiskan wasn't too prosperous and Kokomis said that my mother had a drinking problem, so it would've been difficult. But enough about me…." He held an open palm to the sky. "I feel a few drops. We'd better get back."

I remained seated. "But you haven't told me about Cloë. Besides, my bottom's already quite wet. A few more drops won't hurt me."

But he stood up and pulled me to my feet. "It's late, and I have another early meeting. I'll tell you on the way back."

"Oh no, I was hoping you'd get a chance to sleep in."

"Unfortunately, not tomorrow. But it's the last day of the Assembly, so the next day I'm all yours. And don't forget the big event tomorrow night, the Closing Feast. You'll want to look your best, so I think a good night's sleep would only add to your … ah … lustrous beauty." His grey eyes twinkled as he ruffled my hair.

"Lustrous beauty, eh? I like that." I tried to regain control of my hair. "But it won't work. Flattery will get you nowhere. But I could be bought off by …" I smiled wantonly, not bothering to finish the sentence.

The glint in his eye was enough answer for me.

"Let's get going. But I still want to hear about your sister."

He nodded, striding beside me. "There isn't really much to tell. As I said, when we were growing up Cloë and I were close. She liked having a baby brother and treated me as such. She even came to my defence when Dad came on a little too hard. She was his little princess and could penetrate his tough veneer in a way none of the rest of us could."

"So why did you get so upset when you saw her just now?"

Although I couldn't see the rain, I could hear it approaching across the water. Within seconds it was upon us. I flipped up my hood and zipped up my rain jacket. Eric didn't bother, but at least he'd put on the jacket.

I repeated my question.

"I heard you," Eric replied abruptly.

We walked on, albeit a bit faster. The rain pounded us, and the ground around us. I wasn't going to push him. He would tell me in his own time. The townhouse where we'd seen his sister came into view. While I glanced at the now darkened windows, Eric kept his gaze fixed on the path in front of us.

As we crossed back onto Granville Island, he finally spoke up. "Sorry, Meg. I'm not trying to avoid the question. I'm just trying to come up with an answer that makes sense." He paused. "The last time I spoke to her was at Mom's funeral, and we didn't exactly part on friendly terms."

Rather than taking the scenic shore route, we took the more direct route to the houseboat. The rain persisted. The bottoms of my jeans were drenched as were my trail shoes. Though Eric had finally zipped up his rain jacket, he still got pretty soaked.

"After I moved to Migiskan, we exchanged a few let-ters and some phone calls, but for the most part I ignored her," Eric continued. "She was trying to get me to see their side and I didn't want to. I was too angry."

"This doesn't sound like you. I've never known you to be mad for longer than a few minutes."

"You didn't know me back then. I was a man on a mission, intent on eradicating my white upbringing. At the funeral she wanted me to say a few words about Mom and I refused."

"If you disliked your adoptive family so much, why did you go to the funeral?"

"Simple. I loved my stepmother. She had treated me kindly and with love. I wanted to pay my respects. I wanted to say goodbye to her. But Cloë and I started shouting at each other and I ended up leaving before the service even started."

"And you've had no contact with her since?"

"No, not a single phone call or letter. I didn't even know she was living in Vancouver. No, that's not quite true. I found out she was living here just before we left home. She sent me a note suggesting that we meet while I was in Vancouver. She'd read in the newspaper that I would be attending the Assembly."

"And you're just telling me this now?"

"Yeah, I guess." He grinned sheepishly. "I knew if I mentioned it, you'd insist I see her … and I have no inten-tion of doing so."

"But Eric, you said the two of you were once very close. Surely you must still have some feelings for her."

"I didn't tell you everything. I imagine, like most siblings, as we grew older we became more caught up in our own lives. I was away at boarding school most of the year, and only came home for holidays and the summer months. She was caught up with her friends and had little time for me; in fact, she became a bit of a bully. She and her friends used to gang up on me. But I was okay with that. I would play tricks on her to get even."

"What kind of tricks?"

"The kind of tricks younger brothers play on their sisters. A frog in her bed, Saran wrap on the toilet seat." He chuckled. "Of course, that only made her madder at me."

"I can't say that my sister and I were any different."

"What hurt me the most, though, was her coolness after she learned I was native. She didn't call me names or treat me badly like Mike, but she would go out of her way to be busy whenever I suggested we do something together. And she no longer came to my hockey games. Before, she used to make an effort to see every Calgary game. Basically, she ignored me."

"Did you ever bring this up with her?"

"No, I didn't. I suppose I was afraid of the answer. Our mother's death finally told me how much she had come to hate me. The argument we had at the funeral was only part of it. Mother was fairly well off in her own right, so when she died she left the three of us an equal amount of money. Cloë joined forces with Mike to try to prevent me from getting my share."

"Oh Eric, how awful."

"It was a terrible time, but the will held and I did get my money, although I didn't want it anymore. I gave it all to the band council."

"I don't blame you for not wanting to see her. Still, she

71

has opened the door. Maybe you should see her, or at least talk to her. Did she give a reason?"

"Something about putting our past quarrels behind us. But if I know her, she won't let them rest and we'd just end up fighting again. Nope, I'm not going to go through that door. I'm very content with my life now." He squeezed my hand. "I don't want to ruin it by dredging up all those old feelings."

"I know it's hard. Remember the agony I went through when I finally faced up to my guilt over my brother's death? But it was worth it. For the first time, I felt at peace with myself. This is probably something that's been eating away at you for years without you knowing. You once had a close relationship with your sister. Maybe you can have one again."

"I doubt it."

"Don't forget, she's just lost her son. She was really distraught when I saw her this afternoon. Maybe a brotherly shoulder to cry on is what she needs to help her through this."

"She's got a husband."

We were standing under the overhang to the front door of the houseboat, facing each other. I could see more hurt than anger in his face.

"Why don't I visit her and see if there's anything I can do to help?"

"No, I don't want you seeing her."

"But Eric, it's times like this that family is needed most. Can't you put your differences aside, just this once?"

"We'll see." He slipped the key into the lock and opened the door. Without another word he stepped inside.

I followed, knowing from the firm set of his jaw that he had no intention of changing his mind.

THIRTEEN

Coming Home

The rain slanted across the bow, catching him full in the face. *Typical homecoming*, he thought as he pulled the rim of his ball cap down over his forehead. Although clouds hid the mountain tops, they weren't low enough to blot out the distant island completely. He could make out the faint white line of waves crashing against the shore.

"Haida Gwaii," he whispered to himself as he felt the rush of adrenaline he always felt when sighting the land of his people. And as he always did, he paid silent homage to Salaana, the god of this ancient land.

He peered through the greyness for the lights of Scav's boat. According to Joe's GPS they should be within a few miles of where Scav was supposed to meet them. If he wasn't, he was up shit creek. He'd sweated buckets yesterday worrying over how to get the kid's log to Llnagaay without prying eyes broadcasting it up and down the islands, but he'd finally come up with the perfect solution: Scav and his Red Rocket.

He'd called him every hour on the ship-to-shore. But the bugger wasn't answering. The first few times he figured Scav was out doing what he did best, scavenging the seas for whatever flotsam crossed his path. By late afternoon, he'd begun to worry that the bugger'd gone off to the Bahamas or Seychelles or whatever warm-sea island he'd decided to visit this year.

Without Scav he was screwed. He'd have to bring the log through Masset at the north end of the islands where the tug was headed. Where there were too many spies. By the time the log was loaded onto a truck, the whole island would know.

He'd finally reached Scav about ten o'clock last night. The bugger had been shopping. He'd gone to Queen Charlotte to stock up on supplies. He would've been back sooner, he said, but he'd been persuaded to have a beer or three with a couple of draft dodger buddies. Just what he needed to put him in the right frame of mind for the five-hour trip back to Turkey Point.

He'd never understood why Scav called his place Turkey Point. There wasn't a single turkey within a thousand kilometres of these islands, and Scav's place sure wasn't on a point.

"So, Scav, you'd better be here," he muttered under his breath.

If his eyes weren't playing tricks on him, he swore he could see more land than he could five minutes ago. The clouds must be lifting. But he still couldn't see Scav's big red Zodiac.

It had been pure brilliance when he thought of using Scav. Only Scav could get the log to Llnagaay without alerting the whole island. No way did he want people to know he was back and that he would be carving the kid's story.

Well, not exactly the kid's story, but the clan's story. Not a good one that. He'd always known the beginning, and he had a rough idea about the middle, but until he recognized the bracelet on the boy's wrist he didn't know the end. But maybe it wasn't quite the end. Maybe the silver trinket in his pocket would stir up a new ending.

He no longer felt the vibration of the tug's engines under his feet. For the past hour the captain had been lowering the speed to reduce the forward momentum of the barge. It's not as if the tug could stop and expect the barge to stop too. One of the crew had already gone back to the barge in the runabout to man the crane. Jumping onto Scav's boat would have to be quick. He hoped he could do it. Then they'd have to race back to the barge so they would know exactly where the crane dropped the log into the water.

Thank Salaana it was calm. If the waves were like the ones they'd slammed into yesterday when they reached open water at the north end of Vancouver Island, it would make grappling the log and towing it outright danger-ous. Still, it didn't take much wind to get these seas going. He was already feeling an increase in the sting of the rain against his face.

He spied Scav's Red Rocket at the same time as the tug's horn let out a thunderous blast. The fun was about to begin.

FOURTEEN

Come morning the situation seemed no better. Though Eric refused to talk about his sister, I knew he was grappling over what to do. He had spent most of the night shifting from one position to another. When he wasn't trying to sleep, he was standing motionless staring out the window. When I tried to get him to talk, I was told to go back to sleep. I hadn't had a good sleep either, so neither of us was in a fit mood for breakfast conversation.

However, before he left, he did leave the door open.

Determined not to let the situation fester unresolved, I offered again to speak to his sister. This time, instead of turning me down outright, he growled, "Do whatever you want." I took that as a sign to go ahead.

After picking up a latte in the Granville Island Market, I walked over to the south shore and along the pathway we'd taken the night before until I reached her townhouse. The drapes were still drawn across the ground-floor windows. As I was debating whether or not to disturb her, the curtains were suddenly whisked open. My natural reflex was to duck. By the time I realized I should be waving to catch her attention, she'd disappeared into the darkness of the room.

Unfortunately this was the back of the townhouse. I would have to climb over mounds of budding rhododendrons to reach the door partially concealed by a climbing rose. I didn't think she would appreciate that. The unit was in the middle of a long row of townhouses with no visible street access at either end. I did notice a path alongside the right side of the row. Figuring this would lead me to the street on which her place fronted, I took it.

By the time I reached the street, I was having second thoughts. How would this woman, whose son had just been brutally murdered, react to my turning up without warning saying I was her sister-in-law? Would she believe that I was her estranged brother's wife, or would she think I was a journalist trying to get inside her house ... or worse, her son's killer? While I hesitated, the decision was taken from me. A familiar silver BMW drove past with Eric's sister in the driver's seat.

On my way back to the houseboat I decided I would call her, introduce myself, and go from there. There were two Zakharovs listed in the phonebook. I called the one with a downtown Vancouver address. She hadn't yet returned, so I left a message identifying myself as Eric's wife and saying that if she didn't mind I would like to drop by later this afternoon. I didn't leave a contact number. Not knowing what the houseboat's number was, I was reluctant to leave Eric's cell number. When unexpectedly confronted with his sister's voice, he might say something he would later regret.

Several hours later I arrived at her townhouse. Before I had a chance to lift my hand to the doorknocker, she was opening the front door.

"Are you Meg?" she asked. "Eric's wife? I'm so glad you called."

This visit wasn't such a bad idea after all.

"Please, tell me how he's doing. I've thought of him often over the years."

She appeared calmer today, less distraught, although there was an aura of sadness about her. She was quite a beautiful woman, with her light blond hair, every strand in place, and cornflower blue eyes that showed signs of her grief. It was little wonder Eric had felt he wasn't part of the family. She was dressed to perfection in cream suede pants and a teal blue cashmere sweater. I tried to forget I was wearing faded blue jeans and my ten-year-old fleece jacket, but decided, why bother? This was who I was. She'd have to accept it.

"It's wonderful to meet you," she said, ushering me into a living room reminiscent of my sister's Toronto waterfront condo; vibrant Persian carpets scattered over dark cherry wood floors, delicate antique mahogany tables offset by cushion-bedecked sofas and chairs made of pale cream leather, and walls of the same pale cream colour covered with art, several by well-known Canadian painters. My nostrils twitched at the rich lemony aroma of furniture polish, another reminder of my sister's place.

"I knew Eric was in town for the Grand Council of First Nations Assembly," she said, settling into one of the chairs and motioning me to do likewise.

I hesitated before remembering that my jeans had been washed the day before our trip. I sank into the buttery-soft leather without worry until I recalled my wet bottom of last night. Oh well. If they'd gotten dirty, there was nothing I could do about it.

She continued. "I've seen his name in the paper. I gather he's in the running for Grand Chief. Mom would be so proud of him."

So she cared enough to keep track of him. Maybe there was hope for reconciliation. All I needed to do was convince Eric.

"I'm dying to hear all about you and Eric," she continued. "But first, let me offer you a glass of wine, some single malt, or whatever you'd like."

"Just a cup of tea, if you don't mind."

She frowned. For a second I thought she was going to insist I have something alcoholic until she smiled and said, "Of course, no problem."

While I waited, I wandered around the room admiring the paintings. A David Milne landscape was particularly striking. It reminded me of the forests around Three Deer Point. Although we'd been gone less than a week, I was already starting to miss it.

Cloë returned carrying a silver tray with a perfectly polished tea service and a delicate bone china teacup. I felt like I was back at my mother's partaking in her traditional afternoon tea. The only difference was this tea was a tangy cloudberry herbal tea from Nunavut and not my mother's usual smoky Queen Victoria tea from Murchie's. I mustn't forget one other difference: Cloë's crystal tumbler of whiskey. The door to the liquor cabinet was always kept firmly shut at Mother's teas.

She started to bring the glass to her lips, but stopped as it was in mid-air. "Is he coming?"

I struggled to come up with a reply that wouldn't hurt her feelings.

She didn't wait. Instead she gulped down a large measure of scotch and said, "So tell me how the two of you met and how long you've been married."

I told her about myself, and about Eric and our relationship while wondering if I should bring up the estrangement between the two siblings. At last I ran out of things to say. Actually, it was more like I suspected that Cloë was no longer listening. I stopped talking and poured myself another cup of tea. With the air between us tense with things left unsaid, we continued to drink in silence. A wind chime tinkled outside.

Finally, just as I was summoning up the nerve to speak, the doorbell rang. Clearly startled by its suddenness, Eric's sister remained ramrod still, clutching her glass with such force that her fingers were turning white.

The doorbell rang out again.

She didn't move.

"Would you like me to answer it?" I asked.

Rousing herself with a shake of her head, she set her glass down carefully on a coaster. "No, I'll get it. It's probably the police…." She left without further explanation.

She didn't need to. I suspected she'd already had many visits from the police and would have many more until her son's killer was found. Perhaps it was time to leave.

I thought I heard a gasp before a low murmur of voices drifted from the direction of the front door. I waited for her return. The voices continued. Uncertain about staying longer, I got up and started toward the front hall. Passing close to a mahogany cabinet with lead glass doors, I noticed, resting on one its shelves, a wood carving of a fish, possibly a killer whale, in the style of

Northwest Coast native art. Next to it stood a couple of intricately carved miniature totem poles also made from cedar. Several modern glass sculptures were crammed onto the shelf below, almost as if they had been hastily placed there. On the shelf above the carvings stood a photograph in a silver frame with what looked to be white down scattered around it.

The dark eyes of a young native man stared back at me. Although the camera caught him just as his lips were twisting into a smile, there was little hint of this smile in his dark amber eyes. Instead there was startled annoyance, almost as if he'd been surprised by the photographer and wasn't exactly pleased. One eye, the right one, drooped slightly as if the skin was pulling it down. Regardless, he was one very handsome young man with the kind of boyish charm that would have women falling over them-selves to be his girlfriend. A young man who'd had his entire life ahead of him.

At that moment Cloë stepped back into the room. Behind her walked Eric.

FIFTEEN

I could tell by the faint crack of a smile on Eric's lips that he wasn't exactly thrilled to see me. I was about to protest that he had given me permission, well … sort of, when he said, "I'm glad the two of you have had a chance to meet. I hope I didn't interrupt anything."

Cloë answered, "Meg and I have been having a wonderful time getting to know each other, haven't we?"

I nodded appropriately. Using one's best manners seemed to be the norm at the moment.

"I'm so glad the both of you found me," she continued. Please make yourselves at home, while I get you something to drink. Eric, a beer? I'm afraid my only hard liquor is single malt and I'm not sure …"

"I can appreciate it? Is that what you were going to say, Sis?"

I cringed and waited for the blast, but it didn't come. Instead Eric said, "I would love a splash of Lagavulin if you have it."

"I have Glenfiddich."

Eric pursed his lips. "I guess a Speyside will have to do. You should try an Islay whisky sometime. You'd like its peaty flavour."

She glared back at him, but kept her retort to herself.

I relaxed. One sibling fight avoided.

He sat down on the sofa beside me, placed his arm around my back and pinched my bum. Fine. Take it out on me.

"I'd love some more of that delicious cloudberry tea. But we have dropped in rather unexpectedly, so if you have something you need to do, let us know and we can arrange to meet at another time," I said, thinking the sooner we ended this reunion maybe the better.

"No, no … I'm happy for the company." Her eyes rested on her son's photo before turning back to us. "Besides, we have a lot of catching up to do." She slipped out of the room with my empty teapot and her empty glass.

"Eric, I'm so sorry," I whispered. "I shouldn't have pushed it, but I guess—"

"Sh-sh. I'm glad you're here. I will admit I was a bit ticked off when Cloë told me. But now that I've had a chance to think about it, it's better. Forces us to act like human beings." He grinned.

"I thought you had a full afternoon."

"I did, but when I looked at the schedule I realized I could play hooky." He paused and glanced out the window at a cyclist on the path where we'd stood last night peering into this very window. He turned back to me with his eyes twinkling. "As much as I hate to admit it, your nagging worked. You're right. It's high time I forgot the sins of the past. I don't have a lot of family. Apart from you, Cloë's about all I've got."

83

"And you are about all I've got too," his sister said, gliding back into the room.

She set the steaming teapot back down and handed Eric a crystal tumbler with a respectable amount of scotch. Then she resumed her seat and gulped down another healthy amount from her own refilled tumbler before continuing. "To bring you up to date on my life, Dmitri and I are divorced. We have been for several years. It's the usual story, another woman. And Dad's in a home with Alzheimer's. He doesn't have a clue who I am anymore."

"I'm sorry. It hasn't been easy for you, has it?"

She sighed and took another sip of scotch. "You probably don't know that your dear brother is in jail."

"Jail? What for?"

"Embezzlement. He stole 20 million dollars from his clients."

"I'm not surprised. It couldn't have happened to a nicer guy. But 20 million bucks is a lot. How did he manage that?"

"It was one of those Ponzi schemes that came crashing back to earth when clients starting asking for their money. I was one, but fortunately he only took me for a few hundred thousand. I should've known better. As you well know, Mike liked to skate close to the law. Since I testified against him, he's wanted nothing to do with me, which suits me fine. Though he finally married, I never liked his wife. Too money-hungry for my liking. After his arrest, she divorced him. They never had kids." She fixed her eyes on her son's picture. "So you see, you're all I have." Her eyes brimmed with tears.

84

Eric watched his sister thoughtfully before getting up and walking over to the photo in the cabinet. "I'm sorry to hear about your son. He was a fine-looking young man."

"You know," she whispered, clenching her hands against her breast. The tears spilled onto her cheeks.

"It's the reason for my visit. This is a time for families." He pulled her to her feet and hugged her.

She wept silently into his chest. Finally she pulled herself away. "Do you know how he died?"

Eric nodded. "Have the police found the person who did it yet?"

"I don't know. They aren't saying much. But who would want to kill my sweet innocent boy who never harmed anyone?"

"Tell me about him." Eric resumed his seat beside me.

She hesitated. "You know he's native?"

Eric nodded.

"I hope you don't mind. I know it wasn't easy for you, particularly when our parents pretended you weren't native, so I wanted to make it up with Allistair. From the moment we got him as a tiny two-month-old, Dmitri and I did all we could to ensure he knew he was Haida."

"Do you know what happened to his mother?"

"It's a sad story. I was doing volunteer work in the ER at Vancouver General when the paramedics came in with a young native woman who'd been stabbed. She was eight months pregnant. The doctors were able to save the baby, but couldn't save the mother. He was a fighter this little guy. I fell in love with his fighting spirit. So when social services decided to put him up for adoption, I persuaded Dmitri that we could provide a good home for him."

"Why didn't the authorities give the baby to the grandparents?" Eric asked.

"The woman had no ID and the police weren't able to establish her identity. They only knew she was Haida."

"But surely they could've made the effort to find the girl's relatives on Haida Gwaii. There can't be more than a couple of thousand living there," Eric said a little too strongly.

Cloë's paleness became a bright pink as she searched for a response.

I patted Eric on the knee, muttering, "Now's not the time."

"The authorities tried … I think," Cloë said, biting her lip. "But you know how it was and still is at these agencies, not enough resources for the workload. I don't think anyone had the time to go to Haida Gwaii. Besides, the baby needed a lifesaving operation. We were the best equipped to help him. You see, he was born with a defective heart."

"I'm sure it was the right decision," I interjected. "Besides, I gather you did what you could to ensure he learned about his Haida heritage."

She raised an eyebrow at me, as if questioning how I would know.

"Sorry, I was told he was a wood carver. Are those some of his carvings in the cabinet with his picture?"

"Yes." She walked over to retrieve the two miniature totem poles and the carved fish. "Look at the fine detail in these poles. He carved them when he was only twelve. The orca he carved a couple of years ago. He based it on a sculpture by the famous Haida artist Bill Reid."

Keeping the killer whale for herself, she passed each of us a tiny pole, both about ten centimetres in height. I breathed in the faint cedar smell. The exaggerated features of the miniscule birds and animals seemed to leap out from the wood. I felt as if the cedar had become their prison and once freed from its entrapment, they would spring forth into life.

Eric ran his fingertips lightly over the undulating contours of the carving. "He was very talented." He didn't voice what was doubtless uppermost in all our minds, a talent that would never be realized.

"Meg said he was carving a totem pole at the time of his death."

She glanced at him helplessly. "He wasn't supposed to be in the carving shed. He was supposed to be at the university library studying for a major exam he had the next day. He was in second year political science. I so wanted him to do well. I was hoping he would eventually help his people by becoming a lawyer. But that man — that so-called master carver — was trying to twist his mind into thinking carving was his heritage. As if Allistair could help his people by gouging out bits of wood."

"Totem poles play a significant role in Haida culture," Eric answered.

"I know they do," she said between clenched teeth. "But as a lawyer he could've done so much more for the Haida."

"Perhaps he could've become both," I interjected, wanting to ease the tension. "You must have many happy memories of Allistair."

"I do." She caressed the orca carving, running her fingers idly over its arched back. "Many…. He was a very sweet boy."

"And you loved him dearly."

"And now I have to bury him." She lapsed into silence, while Eric and I fidgeted, trying to come up with a fitting response.

Eric took a final sip of his scotch and broke the silence. "I'm sorry, Sis. I overreacted. I know you did the best you could for the boy."

Raising a tear-stained face to her brother, she said, "No, you're right. He was very proud of being Haida and I didn't pay enough attention to it. He always wanted to go to his people's homeland and I never took him." She paused. "I was afraid. It's a simple as that. I feared someone would recognize him as their grandchild or nephew and would take him away from me. But now I want to set it right."

She banged the orca down onto the coffee table and closed her eyes for a few seconds. "Although I plan to bury his ashes here in Vancouver, I want to sprinkle some of them on Haida Gwaii. I also want to see if I can find out if he has any living relatives. They've probably been wondering what happened to his mother all these years." She paused before turning her porcelain features toward her brother's distinctly bronzed face. "Eric, can you help me?"

"I'm not sure what I can do."

"I guess … I was thinking that because … you're … ah …"

"I know, you think because I'm native that I have an in, that I know every native in Canada—"

"Eric," I hastily interjected, "I'm sure that's not what your sister means. She's probably thinking that the Haida community might more readily answer your questions

88

than hers. You yourself know how native communities will close their doors to whites."

He took a deep breath. "Okay. I'll make some inquiries. Tell me what you know about the mother."

She glanced at me and muttered thanks before continuing, "Mary is the only name I have for her. The police were never able to come up with a last name. We buried her. I didn't want her ending up in a Jane Doe grave. I want to bury Allistair beside her."

"Are you sure she was Haida?"

"A woman she hung around with said she was. It was terrible the kind of life she led. She was living in an abandoned house with little more than thin blankets and newspapers to keep her warm."

"I don't suppose they found her killer?" Eric asked.

She shook her head. "The police thought it was either her pimp or a john, but were never able to come up with any suspects."

"A pimp or a john?" I exclaimed in disbelief. "She was eight months pregnant. Surely she wasn't turning tricks."

"It's awful, isn't it?" Cloë replied.

"It happens, especially if she was feeding a habit." Eric sighed. "I doubt the cops put much effort into finding her killer. Was there any mention of her clan? As you know, the Haida have—"

"I'm perfectly aware of the two clans," she cut in. "I doubt the police knew or cared, but I suspect she was of the eagle clan."

"Why do you say that?"

"I'll show you." She rose from her chair and headed into the hallway.

Hearing her climb the stairs to the next floor, I said, "Eric, I know this is difficult for you and I can see she does have her faults. But she's going through a really rough time too. Can't you try to be a little more understanding, please?"

He squeezed my hand. "Yes, my *Miskowàbigonens*, you're right. It just is—"

Eric stopped talking at the sound of his sister's footsteps echoing on the hardwood floor outside the living room. She came in holding a circular band of gleaming silver in the palm of her hand.

"This bracelet was found in the woman's belongings. You'll see that the predominant figure is an eagle."

She passed it to me. An intricate design of Northwest Coast native art was etched into the finely polished silver. I recognized the eagle in the centre of the design by its oversized beak and bold eyes. There were a couple of smaller eagles intertwined with what looked to be a fish and another fanciful creature with bulging eyes. In several places the design was almost worn smooth.

"This looks quite old and very valuable," I said. "If she was as poor as you say, I'm surprised she didn't sell it."

"I found it hidden inside a pouch that was with her other belongings. The police found it in a garbage bag near where she was stabbed."

"Could she have been killed for this bracelet?"

"I doubt it. He would've taken it."

"You're right." I wondered if this was the bracelet Allistair had wanted to give to his girlfriend.

"My son treasured it," she said.

Holding the bracelet under the brighter light of a table lamp, Eric peered intently at the inside of the band.

"There looks to be some marks here, but I can't make them out. Maybe they identify the artist, and if so that might help to identify her."

She walked over.

"I see what you mean. She did have one other item on her at the time — a flat piece of a green translucent stone that she was wearing around her neck. I think it's jade, but I've never had it verified. It's a rather curious piece with a strange design carved on one side. I could never make out exactly what the design was."

"Do you have it handy?" Eric asked. "It could also be useful."

"It should be upstairs. No, wait a minute. Allistair would've been wearing it. I'll have to follow up with the police to ensure I get it back." She paused. "I'd better call now, otherwise I'll forget."

She slipped out of the room and within minutes was returning, her face twisted with annoyance.

"Damn those police. You can't trust them. They say they don't have it. But I know Allistair was wearing it when he left the house that morning. He was never without it. It's probably mixed up with their other evidence."

"Or maybe it was taken by the man who killed your son," I hazarded.

SIXTEEN

Where It Began

Despite the build-up of surf, Scav's salvaging equipment easily towed the kid's log the five kilometres to Llnagaay. And with the beach on a dead calm lagoon, the landing was a cinch. The tide also behaved itself by reducing the beach to a narrow strip. Hell, maybe Salaana was on his side.

But hauling that sucker up the steep incline of loose stone to solid ground gave him and Scav one hell of a workout, even if they had help. They used the time-honoured Haida method of pulling the massive dead weight over smaller logs using Scav's power winch. But the ancestors would've used woven cedar bark instead of nylon rope. And instead of electric power, they would've used slaves to do the pulling.

After he and Scav got the log onto the flat land beyond the beach, they hauled it farther into the trees to hide it from prying eyes. Not that there'd be any prying eyes. Nobody ever came this far south. Too far and too isolated.

He liked the idea of using Llnagaay. It seemed fitting to carve the log where the clan used to live. After all, the story was about the clan and its shame.

They winched the log onto several trestles Scav made from driftwood. It lay next to the moss-lined pit of a once mighty longhouse. He could see the outline of one of the cross beams covered in the same thick, spongy moss that had moved in when his people moved out. Unlike the rest of the house, this beam hadn't been completely reclaimed by Mother Earth. Because of the size of the pit, he figured this had probably been a chief's house, which seemed like what the Iron Men called poetic justice, for it had been a member of a chief's family who pretty near ruined the clan.

So you traitor, if your spirit's caught up somewhere in the trees, pay attention. Most likely though, your spirit's hanging out in some museum, where your burial box is stacked away in storage along with all the other stolen burial boxes. I'm gonna tell the story of what you did to bring shame to our clan.

SEVENTEEN

I snuggled deeper into Eric's sleeping warmth, pulling the duvet tightly around us. To think I'd been stupid enough to believe I could live without him. Stupid and too pigheaded to admit I was wrong.

A faint murmur whistled through his lips. Although he didn't snore, he did snuffle intermittently throughout the night, sounds I'd come to love. It told me that he was very much alive, something that had been in doubt last fall. Physically, he'd fully recovered from the ordeal, although the scars around his ankles would always be a reminder. But mentally, he still bore the wounds.

Occasionally, I sensed a tenseness underlying his usually calm demeanor, particularly when entering a dark room. And he hated to be alone. After returning home with me to Three Deer Point, he would follow me from room to room, unable to bear being by himself. Eventually he was able to abide being alone as long as Sergei was with him and the door left open. After Sergei died, I would leave him absorbed in his reading, only to have him join me several minutes later. I didn't mind. I wanted to be with him. But there were times when I needed my own space. Perhaps a puppy wasn't such a bad idea.

The sun filtered through the curtains billowing in the breeze of the open window. The air felt cool on my face and smelt of the city and the sea. I snuggled deeper into the warmth. It looked as if this morning was going to be a contest to see who could wait out the other before one of us gave up and leapt out into the cold to close the window. Mind you, after last night's late hour, more like early morning hour, since it was close to three when we finally shut the door on our guests, I could stay here for the rest of the day. From the sound of Eric's steady breathing he could too.

Last evening's Closing Feast lived up to its billing. The servers brought in platter after platter piled high with grilled salmon and halibut, boiled spot prawns and fried oysters and roast bear, moose, and venison. Of course the wine flowed along with the beer and scotch.

I couldn't deny that I was tempted, sorely tempted more than once to have a sip, just a tiny sip of wine. But when the urge hit, I followed Eric's advice of turning my thoughts to something equally desirable, like making love on a carpet of moss with the summer sun filtering through the trees. In the early days, after I'd gone completely cold turkey, the urge was difficult to ignore, but after many months of no alcohol, I'd learned to shove it aside whenever it raised its ugly head, which it rarely did these days.

My first Closing Feast, I wasn't sure what to expect. After hearing the patronizing comments made by some of Eric's friends, I worried that I'd be given a few pats on the head and left to twiddle my thumbs like a good wife should. But Eric made sure I was included, and although I knew little of GCFN affairs, I was able to fling my fair share of quips into the boisterous conversation.

The ceremonial opening by the elders of the Musqueam Nation, whose traditional territory encompassed Vancouver, was gripping. Wearing hand-woven blankets and a variety of headgear from cone-shaped cedar bark hats to headbands with dangling strips of fur, the elders entered the banquet hall to the solemn beat of a drum and behind a gyrating procession of dancers wearing costumes that tinkled and chimed. After welcoming us to their territory and offering thanks to their gods for the bounty of the land, we diners pounced on this bounty.

The evening closed with the return of the dancers. Several, sporting grotesquely painted carved masks, twisted and turned with the movements of the animal whose mask they wore. I recognized the gull by the dancer's outstretched arms and white mask with a gold beak and a train of white feathers. But I had to be told that the stomping dancer wearing the black animal mask with a toothy grin and menacing eyes was a bear.

Many diners joined the dancers, stomping and twisting with the best of them. Despite Eric's entreaties, I chickened out, in part because I didn't want to draw attention to myself with my flaming red hair. Although no one suggested that I didn't belong, I nonetheless felt like an interloper. Hopefully in time the feeling would disappear.

I felt more relaxed when several of Eric's colleagues joined us along with their guitars back at the houseboat to finish the night with some country tunes, particularly after I learned that two of the men and one of the women were married to whites. It made me feel more acceptable.

I was sorry Louise had already left for Seattle to visit her son. I'd enjoyed her company. I couldn't convince Eric to go to Haida Gwaii for the pole raising, despite finding a Sunday morning flight from Haida Gwaii that would get us to Vancouver in time to connect with an Ottawa flight that would arrive late Sunday with plenty of time for Eric's early Monday morning interview. But Eric, having been the victim one too many times of the vagaries of weather and equipment screw-ups, wasn't willing to chance it. Before she left, Louise invited us to visit her next time we were back in British Columbia. I'd do what I could to make this happen.

I chuckled remembering Eric's boisterous singing last night. I hadn't known he could carry a note, let alone sing like a warbler. Well, not quite, but he had a clear tenor voice and could do a good rendition of a country twang. I added my own slightly off-key alto and became completely caught up in the music, despite not knowing many of the words. I just hummed, stomped, and clapped with the rest of them. It had been a fitting end to the evening.

But way too late. Long gone were the days when I could do an all-nighter and go about my business next day with barely a yawn. Judging by the soundness of Eric's sleep, I'd say he was feeling it too. And given the amount of scotch and wine he consumed last night, he was going to have one doozy of a headache.

I stretched out, then curled back up against him. His hand found my naked bottom and gave it a comforting pat, then he sighed and turned over. Thinking he was awake, I whispered quietly, but got no response other than a snuffling whistle as he sank deeper into sleep. I closed my eyes and felt the bed rock with the passing of a boat. I had no idea how late it was and didn't want to know. We could stay in bed the whole day for all I cared.

But it was not to be. A little while later, I awoke to the sound of the bell and someone pounding on the front door. I struggled out of bed and searched for my silk kimono, while Eric sputtered and groaned beside me.

"What time is it?" he growled. He reached for his watch and knocked it onto the floor. "Damn!" He leaned partially out of the bed and rummaged around to retrieve it. "Christ, it's two o'clock."

The doorbell rang again and the hammering resumed.

"Christ, who in the hell is making that goddamn noise? It's killing my head." Eric fought with the duvet, before finally winning and gaining the floor. But he clung to the bed to steady himself.

"Oh dear, did we have a wee bit too much to drink last night?" I said with no little amount of smugness.

He growled.

"Better cover yourself up." I tossed him his sweat pants.

Making sure that the kimono covered all the bare bits, I cinched it in tightly. In the interests of propriety and warmth, I added my pashmina, wrapping it securely around me. It had been a bride's gift from my sister, who'd been intent on sprucing up my very meagre and countrified wardrobe. I ran down the stairs, shouting "I'm coming."

I chuckled when I heard the slam of the bedroom window closing, soon followed by the sound of my husband stumbling down the stairs behind me.

I figured it must be one of our guests from last night, who had forgotten something. No one else knew we were staying in Matt's houseboat. Until I saw Cloë's red-rimmed eyes peering at me through the door.

EIGHTEEN

"I'm *sho* glad you're here," Eric's sister gasped as she stumbled through the door. I flung out an arm to keep her from falling. "I was worried you'd already left."

"What's wrong? Has something happened?" I asked, alarmed by her unexpected and disheveled appearance. Her normally perfect hairdo looked as if a cyclone had blown through it while her silk blouse with its fuchsia and orange flowers clashed with her Harris Tweed jacket. And she was wearing jeans, plain ordinary discount store jeans, clothing I didn't think she would ever condescend to wear.

"I can't bear to be alone."

I turned my head away from the expulsion of alcohol fumes. It was enough to make me drunk.

"I guess we'd better get you some coffee," Eric said rather too brusquely as he came up behind me. He gripped her by the underarm and steered her toward the kitchen.

"Eric, I'm *sho* glad you're back," she slurred. "You always know what to do."

Eric's only reply was to firm his lips in disapproval.

When we reached the sterile brightness of the ultra modern kitchen, not yet recovered from last night's impromptu party, he let go of her arm. But she wobbled and would've fallen if he hadn't taken hold of her again. He steered her to one of the moulded leather kitchen chairs and sat her down without any hint of his usual gentle touch. I was surprised to see his annoyance with her drunkenness. He'd been the poster boy of understanding and patience in handling my drunken episodes.

"This has to be a very difficult time for you, Cloë," I said. "Losing a child is never easy, and particularly in such a terrible way."

Her eyes brimmed with tears. "*Sho* awful. Why me? Why always me?" She tried to support her head in her hands with her elbows resting on the kitchen table. But she missed and her head slid down her arms to the glass, where she left it. She giggled. "*Shee*, everything happens to me."

She was much drunker than I thought. I glanced at Eric for help, but his face remained closed as he set about making coffee.

She raised her head. "Everyone leaves me. Daddy, Mummy, Dmitri ... and now Allistair. They all leave me. Even you, Eric. But you're back." She giggled and cast her eyes around the kitchen. "*Nishe ki'shen.*" Her eyes stopped when she spied a line of empty beer bottles on the black marble counter. "Got any more? I could do with *shome.*"

"You've had enough." Eric slid a not quite empty bottle of scotch behind the Cuisinart. "How did you find me?"

"Meg said you were *shtaying* in Matt Miller's house-boat. Everyone knows Matt. He throws great parties."

Eric shot a glance of irritation in my direction.

"Please, don' get mad. I don't wanna be alone."

"You must have a friend who can keep you company."

"But family is better, isn't it?" I interjected, not liking Eric's attitude. She was hurting. Surely he could see that.

"Do you want something to eat? We're about to make breakfast," I asked.

I headed for the fridge intent on getting some eggs, but Eric stopped me. "I'll make it. You might want to put something else on."

Only then did I notice the flimsiness of the silk clinging to my bare flesh. I blushed, wrapped my pashmina tighter around me, and headed upstairs.

When I returned more suitably attired in jeans and a sweater, Eric was hovering over the stove intent on making perfect scrambled eggs. His sister sat with her head still resting on the table, while steam rose from the coffee mug beside her. Silence reigned but for the swish of the spatula.

I pulled up a kitchen chair beside her. "I'm glad you came. We want to help you as much as we can."

No response as her head remained immobile on the table, her breathing steady. "Eric, I think she's gone to sleep."

"Christ. Like mother, like daughter." He divided the eggs evenly between two of the three plates and added slices of smoked salmon. "Might as well eat up and then we'll get her home."

He placed one of the plates in front of me. It smelled delicious, but I pushed it away. "She looks so uncomfortable. Let's move her to one of the chesterfields in the living room."

I expected her to wake up when I tried to sit her up. Instead she slumped back onto the table without waking.

"Let me do it." Eric scooped her up into his arms and kicked her chair out of the way with more force than I thought necessary.

I followed him into the living room, where I was convinced, given his present mood, he would dump her in a heap onto one of the leather chesterfields. But he surprised me. He lowered her gently onto the dark red cushions, careful to straighten out her arms and legs, while I placed one of the numerous kilim-covered cushions under her head. I retrieved a blanket from upstairs and tucked it around her. Her eyes remained closed, her breathing steady. Other than a slight adjustment to her position, she gave no sign that she knew she'd been moved.

"Such a shame," Eric said, watching her. "I thought she would avoid the family curse. But I can see she's become a drunk like her mother."

"You don't know that. It could be an overreaction to the death of her son."

"Possibly, but I suspect she has problems with alcohol. I saw signs of it at our mother's funeral."

"You cured me. Maybe you can help her."

"I doubt it. You were ready. If she's anything like her mother, she likes to wallow in self-pity."

Since Cloë had begun to snore slightly, I felt there was little danger in her overhearing us.

"I'm sorry to hear that your stepmother had problems with alcohol."

"Sadly. In some ways I was lucky, since I spent most of my boyhood away at boarding school. I didn't have to contend with her drunkenness, not like Cloë, who bore the brunt of it. Dad chose to pretend his wife wasn't a drunk and my brother took off with his friends. That left my sister to deal with it. She emptied the liquor bottles Mom used to hide around the house. Whenever Mom was in danger of passing out, she helped her up to the bedroom. When I was home from school I helped, but often I found some excuse not to."

"I'm surprised you didn't run as far away from me as you could the first time I passed out on you."

"By then I'd had a lot more experience with my drunken friends. Besides, I loved you." He kissed me softly on the forehead.

We were standing side-by-side, arms around each other, looking out the window toward the heights of Vancouver. Beyond, the snow-capped mountains sparkled against the blue sky with only a few clouds to remind us of the rain of the last two days. An aqua-cab bobbed toward us as if saying hello before scooting past. Behind us, Cloë groaned. I turned in time to see her resettling into a new position before sinking deeper into sleep.

"Your sister had a rough childhood and now she's going through another terrible time."

"Don't get me wrong. Mom wasn't always drunk. She would go through periods of heavy drinking and then for whatever reason she'd stop and go for months without taking a drop. At the time I wasn't sure what triggered the episodes. Only later did I learn that Dad liked his bit of flesh on the side."

"That can make any woman drink."

"As I said, the man was a bastard. But Mom was a terrific mother when she wasn't drinking. So you can't really say Cloë had a terrible childhood. She was Dad's little princess and could do no wrong. I think she became rather spoiled because of it. But she did vow to never drink like her mother, so I'm surprised by this."

"You're not entirely an angel yourself. How's your head treating you this morning?"

He rolled his eyes and grinned. "I'm trying to ignore it."

"Maybe the unravelling of your sister's marriage got her started … like the demise of mine got me drinking."

"I know I'm being harsh with her. But hell, Meg, I can't forget how she tried keeping me from my share of Mom's money. Her talk of family is nonsense. She didn't think me family back then."

"Family relationships are never easy." I hugged him close and kissed him gently. "Your sister needs you. If you could try to put your anger aside this once and help her, I think it would go a long way in your own healing."

He held me tightly for several long minutes, before breaking away.

"I'll try," he said.

NINETEEN

We left Eric's sister asleep on the couch. Although Eric felt we should take her home after we finished eating, I persuaded him otherwise. Knowing she was afraid to be alone, I worried that she would continue her binge in the emptiness of her townhouse.

Yesterday we'd discussed exploring Stanley Park and having dinner after at the Asian fusion restaurant Matt had recommended. Instead, Eric went to the market to buy supplies for dinner, while I enjoyed a surprisingly warm sun on the roof terrace. We didn't dare leave his sister alone, worried that she might do something unpredictable on waking up in a strange place.

She awoke while we were sitting at the dining room table enjoying the cioppino Eric had painstakingly prepared. We'd turned off the lights and were letting candlelight and the lights of Vancouver filtering through the wall of windows set the mood for the evening. To add to the romance, a fire crackled in the fireplace separating the living room from the dining room.

And very romantic it was until a pale face appeared out of the gloom. I let out a faint gasp before realizing it was Eric's sister. Apologetic for causing us so much trouble, she joined us for dinner. But she ate little and spoke little. Before the end of the dinner, her eyes were closing. So I guided her upstairs to one of the empty bedrooms where I helped her out of her clothes and tucked her in for the night. Eric and I continued to enjoy the rest of our meal, particularly the salmon berry torte he'd found in a tiny out-of-the-way bakery, until we too gave in to sleep and headed upstairs.

I was deep into a dream about being chased by a monster salmon when I awoke with a start. Not sure what had wakened me, I lay in bed listening. Eric continued to sleep. I could hear waves lapping against the houseboat and the distant drone of cars passing over the bridge. Laughter drifted in from nearby. But none of these sounds would've wakened me. Then I heard the tinkle, a very quiet, gentle tinkle, but a tinkle nonetheless, coming from downstairs.

I slipped on my moccasins, wrapped my kimono around me tightly, and threw on the pashmina. I padded along the hall toward the stairs, glancing into Cloë's room as I passed. It was empty. I found her in the living room sitting in the dark with a blanket wrapped around her in a winged-back chair she'd pulled up to the window. Her hand held a glass filled with Eric's scotch and a single ice cube that chimed when she brought it to her lips.

I shoved the chair's twin beside her and wished I had a blanket too. It was chilly. Only dying embers remained in the fireplace. I debated throwing on another log, but figuring I'd soon be back in bed, I sat with my legs tucked under me and my pashmina spread over like a blanket for warmth.

"I always knew Matt had a better view than I did," she said, continuing to stare at the reflection of the city lights rippling across the water. "I like being this close to the water. Maybe I'll get a houseboat. But then I'd miss my garden." She sipped the scotch slowly. "An Islay scotch isn't bad. But I much prefer a Speyside."

So why are you drinking it? I wanted to ask, but instead I said "How are you feeling?"

She raised the glass and jiggled it with another clink. "The perfect remedy for a hangover."

"I know. I've been there. I used to add a splash of cognac to my coffee. Eventually it became a splash of coffee in my cognac."

She chortled.

"I stopped, and so can you."

"But I don't want to." Her glass jingled again as she raised it to her lips. "Besides, I'm not an alcoholic. I can stop anytime."

"That's what I kept telling myself."

Clouds had descended since we'd gone to bed. The skyscrapers were disappearing. I thought I heard the distant sound of a foghorn in the bay beyond the bridge. The city lights grew dimmer. The night closed around us until the opaqueness swallowed our view. Still, we continued to stare out the window.

"The ... the police are going to release Allistair ... tomorrow. I was supposed to go to the funeral home this afternoon to make arrangements. But ... well, you know what happened...."

"Is that what starting you drinking?"

She murmured, "I suppose." The glass tinkled as she took another sip. "I'll have to make another appointment." I felt her eyes turn toward me. "Can … can you come with me? I … I can't do it alone."

"We'll both come with you."

She reached for my hand and squeezed it. "Thank you."

"What about your ex, Allistair's father? He should be helping you with this."

She sighed. "He had to go to Hong Kong. Some big important meeting … But he said he'd be back for the funeral."

"Is that the story of your marriage?"

"Yeah, I guess. But I didn't leave him." She paused. "He left me." She laughed bitterly. "The usual boring story — another woman."

"If it's any comfort, that's what ended my first marriage."

We giggled together.

"I hope you cleaned him out," I said.

"How do you think I can afford my townhouse, my BMW, and my clothes?" She laughed so loudly I worried she'd wake up Eric.

"He's got more money than he'll ever need. The least he can do is give some of it to me and his son." But as she said these last words, she suddenly realized that Allistair no longer needed it. Her laughter changed to sobs.

I placed my hand on hers while she cried, expecting Eric to emerge at any moment. But he didn't, which was par for the course. I was the one who woke up at the merest sound and agonized over whether I should crawl out of bed and check it out, while Eric slept on like Rip Van Winkle.

After her weeping subsided, I invited her to join me for a mug of hot chocolate. I expected her to refuse, but she followed me into the kitchen, leaving the empty tumbler behind. I hoped it meant she'd stopped drinking, at least for the moment. But when I passed her the steaming mug of hot chocolate, she poured in the last of Eric's Lagavulin.

"This'll keep me warm." She placed her hands around the hot mug and gently blew on the scalding milk before gingerly taking a sip.

With the blanket clutched around her and my shawl around me, we returned to the living room and resumed our vigil of the murky darkness.

The hot chocolate felt soothingly warm. "Tell me about Allistair. He sounds like he was a good kid."

"He was all a mother could ask for."

For the next hour, she told me about her son as only a loving mother could, from his first baby teeth to his high school graduation, when he was voted by his class to be its valedictorian. Although he didn't have the stamina because of his weak heart to play hockey or other team sports, he loved sailing and was a member of the Kitsilano Yacht Club, where he raced his lightning and often won. Apparently, he had a bedroom wall of ribbons and trophies to show for it. If she'd had any problems or difficulties with Allistair, she didn't mention them, nor would she. This was a time to remember only the good. I found it curious that she made little mention of his aboriginal roots or his plan to reclaim them, though she brought up her disappointment again in his desire to be a carver instead of a lawyer. He'd even been considering dropping out of university, but she said she'd stopped that.

She finished by saying, "So much promise ... and now ... now he's dead."

I clasped her hand, waiting for the tears. Instead she said, "I've made a sorry mess of my life." She paused. "Allistair was the one bright spot in it. If there is one thing I'm going to do, it's to make damn sure the bastard who killed him pays for it." She slammed her empty mug down on the windowsill.

"I'm with you on that. Do you know if the police have any leads, any suspects?"

"Just the guy who stole his totem pole. Apparently they found Ernest's truck abandoned in a field in the Richmond area, minus the pole of course."

"Do they have any idea who he is or where he went?"

"I don't know. They aren't telling me anything."

"I was at the carving shed the other day when you accused Ernest Paul. Why do you think he did it?"

"My son's dead because he was in that damn shed. If that bastard hadn't lured Allistair with his promises of becoming a world-renowned carver, my son would be alive today."

"So you don't really think he did it?"

"I have no idea. But I wouldn't put it past him."

"Can you think of anyone else who might've wanted your son dead?"

"He didn't have any enemies. How could he? Everyone liked him. No, it has to be something to do with Ernest Paul." She spat out the name. "I bet someone wanted to kill him and killed Allistair by mistake. He's not the upstanding genuine Haida carver he pretends to be."

"Are you saying he's not Haida?"

"His mother was, although I believe his father was white. But all this bumpf about his carvings being the voice of the Haida is nonsense. He grew up in Vancouver. A friend of mine went to high school with him and didn't know he was Indian until she read it in the paper. He had nothing to do with Haida culture until he was an adult."

"No reason why he couldn't have learned about it then. Look at Eric."

I felt her eyes focus on me, although I kept looking out at the fog. I was sorry I'd brought up Eric's name. I wasn't ready to get into a discussion about him.

"Yes, you're right. He could've. But people say the only reason he took up carving was to make money. And believe me, he makes a lot of money. He has a big house in West Van to prove it. He charges anywhere from $1,000 to $2,500 a foot for a totem pole and gets people like Allistair to do the actual carving for next to nothing."

"Isn't that fraud?"

"He probably follows the same techniques the old master painters used, creating the design and adding his finishing touches. This way he can churn out a lot of poles."

"So he's rich. Is that a reason for someone to want to kill him? Unless he's made enemies along the way?"

"I gather Ernest isn't exactly liked by his fellow carvers. According to a friend of mine, a collector of Northwest Coast Indian art, some carvers view him as too mercenary and others complain that he takes away all the business from them."

"But isn't that just the normal course of doing business?"

"I suppose. But if Ernest wasn't the target, that means Allistair was, and I can't accept that. There isn't any motive."

"There is a missing totem pole."

"Do you really believe someone would kill my son for a piece of wood?"

With no obvious answer, I remained silent as did she. Together we continued to stare out the window. From the kitchen came the sound of the refrigerator clicking on, and from upstairs, Eric's gentle snoring.

"Remember Allistair's jade medallion I told you about," she said. "The officer I spoke to yesterday called this morning to say they've searched the shed thoroughly and didn't find it. They assume the killer took it. They want me to come in to give them a description. I have a photo of Allistair wearing it. I guess that would work."

"Do you want me to come with you?"

"Thanks, but I'll be fine. I just need someone to come with me to the funeral home."

"Do the police think the pendant might have had something to do with Allistair's death?"

"How could it? It's just an ordinary piece of jade, and not a particularly valuable piece at that. Hardly a motive for murder."

I turned at the sound of footsteps on the stairs and saw Eric, rubbing his eyes. "Ladies, what in the world are you doing up at this hour of the morning?"

We squirmed like a couple of teenagers caught doing something wrong.

TWENTY

The Village

It had been one hell of a wet night and damn cold too. His old bones were feeling it this morning. The pain didn't help either. Long gone were the days when he'd take off for a week's fishing and sleep on whatever beach happened to be on hand when night arrived.

Thank god, Scav had a spare tent. Yesterday with the rain coming down hard, still was for that matter, there was no way he was going to build a lean-to out of cedar boughs like he used to or the ancestors did when they were off on one of their voyages. Their spirits were probably jeering at him huddled under the flimsy tent fabric that glowed like an orange pumpkin. Given the holes in it, Scav had likely found it on a beach, thrown away by kayakers. He was managing to keep Scav's sleeping bag dry by placing it off to one side away from the worst of the drips.

He sure as hell could do with a nice soft mattress. He could barely move. But he was going to have to soon, if he wanted to start on that log today. Without electricity he'd have to rely on natural light. While the days were getting longer, it still wouldn't give him enough daylight hours.

And with the log lying under the thickest part of the cedar canopy it would get dark sooner. He'd try Scav's headlamp tonight to see if that provided enough light.

Yesterday, he'd gone exploring. It'd been some years since he'd walked where the ancestors had lived and died. They'd done a good job of picking this site. With such a narrow entrance to the lagoon, it could easily be defended against rival clan attacks by sea, while the steep, almost cliff-like mountain slopes prevented attacks from land. Little wonder the ancestors had occupied this site for thousands of years.

Years ago he'd followed a faint trail that took him up through a narrow pass and into a high meadow overflowing with salal and salmon berry bushes. The trail would've been the clan's escape route when an enemy attack got a little too hot. But his people had been mighty warriors; the greatest in Haida Gwaii, if his *nanaay*'s stories were anything to go by. There was no way they would've been run over by another clan. More likely it would've been them running over the other clan's village.

He wondered if this was the trail the traitor betrayed on that disastrous night almost a century and a half ago, when the bastard helped the cowards sneak into the village like thieves and not like the warriors they were supposed to be. Haida warriors didn't hide and skulk. They advanced on their enemies howling and banging their canoes. He imagined the trail would've normally been guarded. But on that fateful night it wasn't. *Nanaay* said that the first the clan knew anything was wrong was when they heard the keening. He figured that if the path had been properly guarded he'd be carving a different story today.

114

Since a tiny fry he'd called his grandmother by the Haida word *nanaay*. It had never seemed right using the English word. She'd been a major force in his life. Too bad she was no longer around. But then again, she would've done all she could to keep him from carving the story. She believed the clan's shame should be kept hidden. But most everyone knew something terrible had happened, they just didn't know what.

He wished he'd been around when Llnagaay was at its height. According to Nanaay, over twenty-five longhouses had filled the meadow bordering the beach. Lines of sky-high frontal and memorial poles, some two and three deep, had announced the village's wealth to anyone who dared approach. But the place would've stunk with the rotting remains in the mortuary poles and the mounds of decaying fish entrails and shells. Today nothing was left but a meadow overgrown with towering cedar and Sitka spruce. A few pole-length mounds of moss and moss-lined longhouse pits were the only reminder that a once mighty Haida village had been the masters of this shore.

He wondered if the small pox germs that had killed off the ancestors and forced them to abandon the village were still around. But he figured it happened so long ago, their potency would've worn off by now. Besides, he wasn't worried He'd been vaccinated as a kid. Plus he'd inherited over a hundred years of immunity to the Iron Men's diseases, something the ancestors didn't have when the Iron Men first came to these shores.

A curious name, Llnagaay. Unlike other ancient villages with names like Hik'yah Llnagaay, meaning

"Windy Bay Village," or SGang Gwaay Llnagaay, meaning "Red Cod Village," it was simply called Llnagaay, meaning "The Village." People once called it by the clan name, but no one called it that now, not since the shame.

TWENTY-ONE

"Are you sure you don't want me to drive, Sis?" Eric asked. He was sitting in the passenger seat of the BMW next to his sister.

Cloë had just missed running a stop sign. If Eric hadn't called out a warning, she would've creamed a bike crossing the intersection. He'd already offered to drive us to the funeral home, but she had insisted that she could handle it.

"I'm fine."

"Arranging your son's burial is probably one of the most difficult things you've ever done. I know you have the strength to handle it. But please, no one will think any the less of you if you let others share the load."

"I'm okay. I can do it." She stopped at a red light with a sudden jerk, throwing all of us forward.

After yesterday's drunken episode, she'd seemed more in control, until now. She hadn't complained of a hangover. She was even handling the prospect of meeting the undertakers better than yesterday.

"If I drive, it'll give you a chance to prepare yourself," Eric persisted.

Her hands gripped the steering wheel until they were almost white. A car suddenly backed out of a driveway. She swerved to avoid it, barely missing the bumper, and then jerked the car to a stop in the middle of the road. Thank god there was no following traffic. She released her shaking hands from the steering wheel.

"You're right. It's too much." She jumped out of the car and ran around to the passenger side. Eric gave her a brotherly hug before getting into the driver's seat. I expected tears. But she seemed to be trying her best to remain steady. We continued driving in a silence broken only by her occasional direction to Eric on our route.

I was lost in my own thoughts, when she suddenly spoke up, "Eric, you have to help me find Allistair's Haida relatives."

"I've already said I would."

"When are you going to do it? I can't bury Allistair until I know."

"I was going to send pictures of the bracelet to a Haida friend of mine. It could take her a couple of weeks to track down the girl's relations, if there are any. And that's only if the bracelet can be used to help identify them."

"I can't wait that long. I want to bury him now."

"I'm sorry, but I don't see how it can happen any sooner."

"Eric, don't forget Louise invited us to Haida Gwaii for this coming Saturday's pole raising," I interjected. "We could take the bracelet with us. There's bound to be a ton of people at this event. Surely someone will recognize it."

"It's a thought, but don't forget that interview Monday morning. I can't miss it."

"I know, but remember I found a flight that will get us back to Ottawa by late Sunday night."

"What if the flight's late?"

"I doubt it would be ten hours late."

"What if it gets cancelled?"

"You're making excuses. Remember how overjoyed your grandparents were to finally have you back in their lives. This could give another family a chance to finally learn what happened to a long lost daughter."

"Oh Eric, could you go, please," added his sister. "It would mean so much to me."

"How do you know we can still get seats on this flight?"

"Give me your cell and I'll find out."

"You're right. Let's do it."

By the time we arrived at the funeral home, we were booked on a Friday flight to Haida Gwaii and on flights back to Ottawa on Sunday.

Handing him back his phone, I kissed him on the cheek, while his sister smiled and said, "Thank you. I really appreciate it."

But her smile vanished with the approach of a man in a dark suit, suitably sombre as only undertakers can be.

TWENTY-TWO

I watched the jagged northern coast of Vancouver Island slide under the plane as we headed over the deep blue of open water. To the east the snow-drenched coastal mountains of the B.C. mainland stretched up toward the Alaskan Panhandle. We'd left Vancouver a little over an hour ago on the flight to Sandspit, the main airport on Haida Gwaii. We almost missed it.

My heart was still racing from our frantic dash to the boarding gate only to find that it had closed. Eric, thank goodness, managed to convince the airline staff to allow us through. It hadn't hurt that there were three other passengers who'd also arrived late. Given that the plane was at the opposite end of the scale of a Boeing 747, six missing passengers would've put a sizable dent in their passenger load. I say six, because we were three. I supposed four if you counted the urn, except we didn't mention it at the check-in counter.

Twenty minutes before Eric and I were to leave for the airport, his sister called to tell us that she was coming with us to Haida Gwaii. She was at the crematorium, where she was picking up her son's ashes, and would be at our place in thirty minutes to take us to the airport. She hung up before Eric had a chance to convince her otherwise.

Needless to say she was late. By the time Cloë found a parking spot at the airport and we walked the distance to the departure level, we knew we were in trouble. When the attendant at the check-in counter said there was no time to check baggage, we ran. Fortunately the plane had a valet service so we were able to get our luggage onto the aircraft.

Now here we were. I was pretending everything was okay by looking out the window at the passing scene far below, while Eric fumed beside me. Cloë, with her son safely stowed in the luggage bin, sat three rows behind us. In the rush to catch the plane, we hadn't had a chance to learn the reason for her joining us. Last night we'd left her townhouse with the understanding that she would fly to Haida Gwaii at a later date to sprinkle some of her son's ashes on his homeland. With no whiff of alcohol on her breath, I couldn't blame this sudden change on a fit of drunkenness.

I watched a couple of boats, more like black specks against the deep blue, churning through the water, one after the other, with barges trailing some distance behind them. The barges seemed so disconnected from the tow-boats that I wondered how they prevented boats from running into the towing cables.

The plane began its descent. In the window across the aisle, jagged pinnacles rising above wisps of cloud came into view, while out my window lines of whitecaps drew closer. A spit of sand suddenly spread beneath us and we landed. We taxied past a group of men waiting to board one of two large transport helicopters parked on the tarmac, which I later learned would ferry them to one of the many fishing camps on the west side of the islands.

The airport was of a size one would expect of an airport servicing an island community of only a few thousand people. The main hall was packed. Many people were waiting to board the return flight to Vancouver. A dozen or so fisherman, recognized by the latest in fishing paraphernalia, were lined up at another gate. The rest of the hall was filled with family and friends craning their necks in search of arriving loved ones or acquaintances.

Amongst the throng I recognized Ernest Paul with a welcoming smile planted on his broad face. While Cloë studiously ignored him, I watched him greet a silver-haired gentleman of the distinguished variety and his platinum blond companion, at least half his age with boobs that extended well beyond the normal and a 1960s beehive hairdo. I'd noticed them on the plane, sitting a few seats in front of us. They appeared to be the kind of passengers who were more at ease in the wide luxury of executive class than the narrow confines of economy, the only class available on this flight. Given Ernest's somewhat obsequious manner with this man, I took him to be a client. Perhaps he was journeying to Haida Gwaii to see where the carver got his inspiration.

While pointing out Ernest to Eric, I noticed him glance in our direction. He started to raise his hand as if to greet Cloë before abruptly turning away. I suspected the memory of her accusation changed his mind. His gray-haired client was not so easily put off. He smiled broadly and waved, "Cloë? Cloë Zakarhov? Is that you, *cherie*?" before walking purposively toward us.

"Damn," Eric's sister muttered, before fixing a greeting smile on her face. "François, imagine seeing you here."

She held out her hand, which he grasped warmly in both of his before pulling her close and pecking her on either cheek in the typical Gallic manner. His companion teetered behind him on spiked heels that more properly belonged on the marble floors of a luxury hotel than on the dusty floors of a backwater airport. Her toothy smile had slipped a degree.

"It is wonderful to see you, *cherie*. It has been such a long time." He continued to hold her close. "But I find it curious to see you in such a wild place. This is not like you."

As Cloë struggled for a response, he continued, "*Mais oui*, your son, he was Haida, wasn't he? Such a delightful young man. I was so sorry to learn of your tragedy." He gave her another warm hug, before stepping back, almost colliding with Ernest, who had come up behind him. "Please, I am forgetting my manners. Let me introduce you to the best totem pole carver in the world."

With her face stonily impassive, the slim, immaculately dressed woman stared at the overweight carver who seemed to squirm as if waiting for another accusation. Finally after what seemed an embarrassingly long time, Cloë broke the silence. "We've already met." She ignored Ernest's offered hand, which became occupied with the key chain dangling from his belt.

Turning to the Frenchman, the carver said, "Mr. Champagne, it looks like your luggage has arrived. If you could show me your bags, I'll put them in my car."

Clasping Cloë's hand once again in both of his, François said, "We should plan to have dinner. Give me a

call. I'm staying at The Eagle's Nest in Queen Charlotte."
Continuing to ignore Eric and me, he turned and followed
Ernest, with his teetering companion struggling to keep up.

As they vanished into the crowd, Cloë turned to us.
"I'm so sorry. I forgot to introduce you. But it's probably
just as well. You wouldn't want to know that man."

"Who is he?" Eric asked. "He seems familiar."

"He was a business associate of Dmitri's until they had
a falling out. Dmitri suspected he was making some under
the table business deals, but was never able to prove it.
François is now CEO of a rival forestry company."

"Now I remember. His company was at the centre of
one of the big logging protests on Vancouver Island a few
years back. As I recall, he faced the protesters at the barri-
cades and convinced them to let his company do selective
logging of the old growth. But he went back on his word
and cleared the whole damn side of the mountain before
anyone could stop him."

"That's François for you, all charm and no honour.
He'll do anything to make a buck."

"Charm indeed. He did rather come onto you, didn't
he, Sis?"

"Is this brotherly concern taking over?" She smiled.
"Don't worry. I stay well out of reach of his roving hands.
He acts that way with every woman. Besides, I'm too old.
He likes them barely out of the cradle and, as you can see,
with boobs out to here." She extended her arms as far as
they could go. "His first wife got fed up with all his affairs
and left him. She took him to the cleaners." She chortled
and glanced at me knowingly. "If that woman with him is
his wife, she must be number four or five. I've lost count.

I have no intention of having dinner with him. So let's stay well clear of him. By the way, where are you staying?"

Eric smiled wryly. "At the Eagle's Nest. And you?"

"Oh dear. I was going to ask if you thought they might have a room for me at your hotel. I'm afraid I made the decision so quickly that I forgot to book a room."

Eric groaned. "And if they don't have a room, what are you going to do?"

"I'll find one at another hotel."

"It might not be close by. Do you plan on renting a car?"

"Forget I asked," she snapped back. "I'll make my own arrangements." She flung an angry glance at her brother before stomping across the hall to the only car rental booth in the airport.

I gave Eric my own evil eye and was about to call his sister back, when his brotherly concern finally kicked in. "Cloë, come back. I'll check our hotel for a room. If they have one, you won't need to rent a car."

She walked back as he tried his cell. "No signal. I'll try outside."

Cloë and I watched him thread his way through the thinning crowd toward the exit. Through the glass doors I could see François and his companion climbing into a dark blue Range Rover being driven by Ernest.

I turned back to my sister-in-law. "I'm sorry, Cloë. I think Eric's still getting used to having his sister again. He doesn't mean to be so abrupt."

She shrugged. "He wasn't the easiest of brothers."

"I thought the two of you were very close when you were growing up."

"We were ... but you know how it is ... you grow up and other things become more important in your life." She paused. "Like hockey. It kind of went to his head. But that's a long time ago and now we're back together again." Although a smile spread across her face, it didn't quite reach her eyes.

Her comment left me confused. It sounded as if she was blaming Eric for their falling out. I was tempted to bring up the fight over their mother's inheritance but decided against it. Now wasn't the time.

"We were surprised that you decided to come with us. We assumed you'd wait until Eric had a chance to locate some of Allistair's relatives."

"That was my plan, but after Dmitri told me he was too busy to come, I changed my mind. I didn't want to do it by myself."

I squeezed her hand and said words I didn't completely believe, but knew would make her feel better. "I'm glad you came."

I found Eric's sister a bit of an enigma and wasn't entirely certain if I liked her. There was just something about her that left me cold. I was hoping these couple of days together would give me a chance to change my mind and come to like her.

Eric walked back through the airport entrance. With a thumbs-up he signalled success, then nodded his head in the direction of the car rental booth.

A man with close-cropped light brown hair and dragging a wheeled suitcase approached Cloë. Despite his casual clothes, he had an air of officialdom about him. "Mrs. Zakarhov, I see against my advice you decided to come."

"This trip has nothing to do with you, Sergeant Antonucci. I came with my brother and sister-in-law to scatter my son's ashes on his ancestral lands."

"Once again, ma'am, I'm sorry for your loss. I would like to remind you that we are doing all we can to find your son's killer. But it's a small community here on the island, where everyone knows everyone's business, so I would appreciate if you stayed away from the investigation."

"I think, Sergeant, that the only thing that matters is that my son's killer is caught. How it's done is immaterial."

"A word of caution, ma'am. It could be dangerous. So please leave police business to us." After a perfunctory good-bye, he continued out the exit to a waiting RCMP SUV.

"What was that all about?" Eric asked, arriving just as the detective left.

"He's the sergeant in charge of the case," Cloë replied. "One of his underlings told me they've learned that the man who stole Allistair's pole, and their prime suspect, is here. Antonucci got quite angry when he found out that his man had told me."

"Is this the real reason you came?" I asked.

Her eyes flashed with anger. "I want to spit on the bastard when they clamp on the cuffs."

TWENTY-THREE

The Eagle's Nest was a fitting name. When I stepped onto the deck outside our room, I found myself locking eyes with a bald eagle. Although we were at the same level, I realized he was roosting on the top of a tree. We stared at each other for a few seconds before he turned his head away as if he had other things on his mind.

To further emphasize the steepness of the terrain, the roofs of neighbouring houses seemed to cascade down the slope to the main street of Queen Charlotte far below. Beyond lay the broad channel we'd crossed by ferry and the mist-wrapped mountains of Morseby Island where we'd landed. We were told that this channel, Skidegate Inlet, severed the archipelago into two distinct halves with the southern half comprising the mostly uninhabited Moresby Island and numerous smaller islands. The northern part was primarily a single island, Graham Island, where the majority of the people lived. It included two Haida communities; Skidegate in the south and Old Masset in the north. The pole raising was taking place in Skidegate, a short drive from where we were staying.

Although we'd shared the ferry crossing with the Vancouver cop, there'd been no further interaction with Eric's sister, other than his pointing her out to his RCMP counterpart. The master carver and his client were also on the ferry. But with a number of vehicles separating us, we didn't have to worry about protecting Cloë from François's advances. By the time we inched our way off the ferry, they were gone.

Our hotel turned out to be a bed and breakfast with rooms in the main house and in several cottages. The house, with an A-frame sloped roof and balconies stretching across the front, looked as if it should be standing beside a ski hill, while the cottages were the typical box-like structures found lining the shores of crowded Canadian lakes. Cloë had a room in the main house, while our room was in the farthest cottage. Ours had a front window view onto what I would come to know and love as the essence of Haida Gwaii: rain forest–carpeted mountains tumbling into shifting seas.

If Cloë hoped to avoid her amorous Frenchman, she would have to stay away from our cottage. When we arrived, Ernest Paul was carrying several leather suitcases into the room next to ours. Both Ernest and François raised their eyebrows in surprise when Eric introduced himself as Cloë's brother. Ernest mumbled something about it explaining everything. Not bothering with niceties, Eric got straight to the point and asked if Ernest had any idea who'd killed his nephew.

"I wish I knew," the man replied. "He was a nice kid and had the makings of a master carver."

"The boy was murdered in your shed. You must have some idea who killed him. The fact his killer stole the log he was working on says he's going to do something with it other than split it into firewood. And, if the police are right, he's gone to a lot of trouble to bring it all the way up here. What's so special about that log?"

"The bastard stole my damn truck, that's what. And the log I paid good money for," Ernest fired back, then stopped abruptly. "What did you say again? That last part."

"I said he's brought the log here."

"You kiddin' me?"

"That's what the police told my sister. Any idea why he would do that?"

"Bloody hell," he muttered.

"This guy's a carver, isn't he?"

Ernest remained silent.

"And you know him, don't you? You have to. I bet every carver in your community keeps tabs on one another."

"Ah, *messieurs*," François said, sauntering up. "I think this is a conversation best discussed over a glass of Beaujolais, *non*? Would you care to join me?" He walked into the kitchen and placed a wine bottle on the counter and proceeded to open it with a corkscrew he took from his pocket.

"François, I'd love like hell to join you, but I have a bunch of errands I gotta do before dinner," Ernest replied, glancing at his watch. "Look, I'll pick you and Sherry up in an hour and a half, okay?" He was slamming the front door behind him before the Frenchman could reply.

François turned to Eric. "That leaves us. And I won't accept no for an answer. I am most interested in getting to know the brother of the lovely Cloë — and his charming wife."

I could see my husband hesitating. François had the distinctive aura of the ruling class, which Eric innately distrusted. Nonetheless, I said, "Eric, you go ahead. I'll unpack. We don't meet your sister for dinner for another hour."

Since this man was the head of a major forestry company, I thought it wouldn't hurt for Eric to get to know him, even if he wasn't an especially upstanding CEO. Clashes between native communities and logging companies were becoming all too frequent. If Eric did become head of the GCFN, such a contact could be useful.

I left the two of them in the living room settling into rattan chairs. Each held a wine glass swirling with the dark red liquid and wore nice-to-get-to-know-you smiles. Though it was difficult to tell what lay behind François's smile, I knew from the steely glint in Eric's grey eyes that this wouldn't be a friendly conversation.

Partway along the hall, I passed François's companion, still teetering on her too-high heels. We exchanged polite insipid smiles and first names and continued on our respective ways, she to join the men and me to our room. I hesitated for a moment wondering if Eric needed my protection, but then decided that I was being too "wifey." Still, if Eric didn't come to the room within a respectable time, I would go in search of a cup of tea.

But he surprised me. He joined me in less time than it took to drink a glass of wine.

"What did you do? Toss the wine down in one gulp?" I jammed the last of my clothes into the top drawer of the chest.

He chuckled. "A fine vintage, but I couldn't leave my wife, an even finer vintage, all alone, especially in a room with such a magnificent bed."

It was indeed magnificent: a four-poster mahogany bed with a lace canopy that seemed more fitting in a Victorian manor house than in a vinyl-sided bungalow. But I wasn't going to give in that easily. "Vintage! You're calling me vintage?"

He grinned devilishly. "A vintage that has mellowed and ripened into a sumptuous taste with a hint of chocolate on the nose, long curvaceous legs, and a full fantastic body." He grabbed me and together we tumbled onto the bed, narrowly missing the empty suitcase, which was quickly pushed to the floor.

"You know, Eric, we seem to spend more time in bed than out of it."

"That bothers you?"

I answered with a titillating kiss.

Cloë was snapping back the pages of a fashion magazine when we arrived rather shamefacedly a good twenty minutes late in the cluttered front room of the main house. Like our cottage, it was a jumble of fake antiques and discount store furniture overlade with cutesy knickknacks and walls dripping with crocheted hangings and framed calendar artwork. A fire crackled in a stone fireplace. On the end table beside her stood a mug of tea with a layer of congealed milk floating on its surface.

She didn't scold us, but instead said rather tersely, "I've found a restaurant. According to our innkeeper, Jimmy's Gastropub is the best in this godforsaken town. Can you imagine, there are only two decent restaurants, plus a pub with no doubt the standard godawful pub fare? How in the world do people survive?"

"Not everyone can afford the luxury of fine dining," Eric quipped. "Besides, you have a Master Chef here." He flung out his arms in ta-dah fashion. "With the bounty of the sea at our feet, we can eat royally tomorrow night. After that you're on your own."

"You're really leaving Sunday?"

"Yup."

"But what if we don't find Allistair's birth family tomorrow?"

"I figure half the Haida Nation is going to be at this pole raising. I think the chances are high that someone will know who the bracelet belongs to."

"But what if no one does?"

"Then you'll just have to continue on your own."

"But how can I? They won't own up to me. Remember, I adopted him. I'm the enemy. If there was one thing I learned from you, it was that." She started to weep.

I wondered if it made sense for me to stay behind to help her, but before I could make the suggestion, Eric said. "I don't think it will take long to locate his birth family if any are still around. I've done some Internet research and have discovered that, like totem poles, the designs engraved in these bracelets tend to be family crests. I'm hoping that the crest will be quickly recognized."

"And if not?"

"Then either the design on the bracelet is not a family crest or Allistair's relatives no longer live on Haida Gwaii. But enough talk. I'm starved. Let's go find this fancy restaurant of yours."

TWENTY-FOUR

It looked as if "Jimmy's" better defined the restaurant than "Gastropub." The cavernous room with fake mahogany panelling, scuffed vinyl flooring, metal chairs, and Arborite-topped tables could only augur mediocre food. The giant photos of hockey players covering the walls didn't suggest gourmet fare either, nor did the large flat screen TV over the bar currently airing, what else, a hockey game.

"Not exactly my idea of a gastropub," Cloë muttered as she turned to leave. I was about to join her when Eric stopped us.

"Smells pretty good to me," he said. "And look at all the people. They wouldn't be here if the food wasn't any good."

It did smell good, but there didn't seem to be any free tables.

The reed-thin man who'd been drying glasses behind the bar walked over to us, flipping the towel over his shoulder as he slicked back the few remaining grey hairs on his head. I could tell he was about to tell us there was no room, when his gaunt face lit up. "Is that Lightning Odjik who used to play for the Flames?"

Confused, I turned to Eric, who was beaming. "It's been a long time since I played for Calgary. I'm surprised you recognize me."

"I never forget a face, and certainly not the face that scored the winning goal in the final game of the 1989 Stanley Cup playoffs. Man, you made me five hundred bucks that day. I thought for sure I was gonna lose and then you came through in the final second of the game and scored with that perfect shot. A bit late, but I'd sure like to shake the hand that kept me in beer that week."

Clenching Eric's hand in a vice-like grip, he pumped it up and down.

Extracting his hand, Eric pretended to wince as he shook his fingers. "Man, that's some grip. You must've played hockey yourself."

The guy laughed. "Yer kiddin' me, eh? With a puny body like this, no way. I drove a skidder in a logging camp before I took up the restaurant business. The strong hands come from pushing all those levers." He laughed again. "I tell you, Lightning, I cried, really cried the day you left the Flames for the Leafs. I thought you were a traitor going east like that. But I guess you had no say, eh?"

"I didn't want to leave either, but there wasn't much I could do. The Flames' owners made a lot of money off me with that trade."

"Within a year you were out 'cause of that recurring groin injury. Must 'a hurt like hell leaving hockey like that."

"It wasn't one of my happier moments, but hey, life goes on, and I'm doing what I love best with the woman I love best." He wrapped his arm around my waist and pulled me close.

Here we go again with this chattel business, I thought, starting to resist. But realizing this was to be expected in the man's world of hockey, I relaxed into his side and put on my best dutiful wife smile.

We both turned around at the sound of chairs scraping along the floor. A couple was leaving.

"Jimmy," Eric said, taking an educated guess. "I see you have an empty table coming up. Do you mind if we take it? Your food has come highly recommended."

"Sure, go ahead. It'll give me real pleasure to serve the great Lightning Odjik." He hastily removed the dirty dishes from the table and scrunched up the paper placemats.

"Lightning?" I asked as the owner scurried away.

Eric's dimples erupted. "As in 'greased lightning.' In my day I was one of the fastest guys on ice."

"I guess you never saw Eric skate, did you, Meg?" Cloë said. "He was a ballerina on ice. I used to watch every game."

Eric turned to his sister in surprise. "Why, Sis, I never knew that. Thanks for the loyalty."

Unsmiling, she stared at him before continuing. "There are a lot of things you don't know about me."

She scowled at the mishmash of patrons crowding the room. With the predominant apparel being jeans, T-shirts, running shoes, and the occasional ball cap, casual was in. Unlike Eric and me, who were still wearing our jeans, Cloë had dressed for dinner in her urban best: a pair of dark brown wool slacks and a camel blazer over a pale blue cashmere sweater. A burgundy pashmina was draped around her shoulders. To tell the truth, I wished I'd worn my pashmina too. The walk down the hill to the restaurant had been chilly, with a cold wind rising off the water.

"Are you sure you want to eat here?" she asked.

"You're just going to have to get used to country casual," Eric replied. "So unless you want to go without dinner, I suggest you sit and try to enjoy yourself."

She shoved a strand of hair behind her ear before pulling the chair out with a resounding screech.

If she acted this way during our entire stay, it was going to get downright boring and unpleasant. Judging by the less than pleased expression on Eric's face, he was having similar thoughts. But his expression perked up as he glanced over the menu.

"It looks like we've hit seafood nirvana."

"I can't stand fish," his sister replied. "At least they have filet mignon. I'll order that."

Eric's fan arrived with clean cutlery and new placemats with maps on them advertising the delights of Queen Charlotte.

"We have a couple of specials on tonight," he said. "Fresh-caught Coho from the north, and halibut. But Lightning, for you and your missus, I have something even more special — a couple of Dolly Vardens caught by my buddy early this morning."

"What do you think, Meg?" Eric asked, barely able to contain his enthusiasm.

"What in the world is a Dolly Varden?" I asked with some suspicion.

"A variety of trout," Jimmy replied. "Tastes a lot like char. But don't ask me how it got such a crazy name. Someone said it's from a character in a Dickens book."

After the owner left with our orders, Eric turned to his sister. "My friend Louise said you are very welcome to come to the pole raising tomorrow. She's picking us up around ten o'clock. I'm not sure how long it will take, but there's a potlatch after that I imagine will go on for hours. So, plan for a long day."

"I'm not interested. What about Allistair? When are you going to look for his relatives?"

"As I said, my plan is to ask around at tomorrow's events. I think you should come."

While he was speaking, I watched a new group of diners arrive, namely Ernest Paul, François, and Sherry. Many sets of eyes watched the group as they walked over to a recently vacated table. The restaurant had suddenly become very quiet. The carver nodded at several people and shook hands with others. But I didn't get the sense that the attention was directed at him. Rather the focus seemed to be squarely on the Frenchman, who appeared to be totally unaware of their interest. He smiled in our direction before doing his gentlemanly duty and pulling out the chair for Sherry.

The silence gradually gave way to conversation with a tense edge to it. Occasionally eyes flitted back to the new diners as they chatted amongst themselves and perused the menu.

Heads turned when a bottle slammed onto the counter at the far end of the room. The heftier of two men drinking at the bar shouted, "I'm not gonna drink with that traitor!" He lumbered over to Ernest's table, raised his middle finger at François, and shouted, "You bastard. How dare you show your face on these islands?"

He stomped to the exit.

"You coming, Siggy?" he shouted, holding the door open.

His companion, who had long, straggly grey hair and a curious rat's tail of a beard, slid off his bar chair. I caught the gleam of a gold earring as he turned. Shorter and slimmer than his buddy, he sauntered up to François, hissed "asshole," and spat on him. Without missing a step, he strode over to join his grinning friend.

The sound of the door slamming left the room in stunned silence.

Wiping the spit from his jacket with a handkerchief, François tossed the insult off with a shrug. Though, I did catch the French word for "idiot" before he turned to Ernest to ask for his advice on the menu.

TWENTY-FIVE

Conversation in the room didn't return to its former energetic level. I noticed many diners were leaving, some with half-eaten meals on their plates. By the time a steaming bowl of spot prawns landed on our table, the restaurant was empty apart from our table, François's, and a couple of other obviously tourist-occupied tables.

"What was that all about?" Eric asked his hockey buddy.

"Goddamn logging," Jimmy spat out. "It's always caused a shitload of trouble, what with the constant fighting between the tree huggers and the loggers. But that guy over there did what no one else ever done. He got them fighting on the same side."

"Not an easy achievement. What in the world did he do?"

"His company clear-cut one of the few remaining stands of mature cedar and Sitka spruce after the moratorium was put in place."

"What moratorium?" I asked.

"The Haida had a big protest a few years back over logging on sacred land and won. Everyone paid attention to the moratorium until that bastard arrived. He brought in an off-island crew, and before anyone realized what was going on, they clear-cut half the island. He not only got all the tree huggers mad at him, he also got all the local loggers spitting mad. The two groups even set up common protests." He chuckled. "I can't imagine what he's doing here."

"Probably buying a totem pole from Ernest," I said.

"Those two got a lot in common. Ern's got his own share of enemies. Some of the traditional carvers don't like the way he's commercialized totem pole carving." His grin revealed a large gap where a bottom tooth was missing. "More like they're jealous of all the money he's making."

"I saw his studio in Vancouver. Did you know that a young man was killed there recently?"

"Yeah, I heard something about it. Kid was supposed to be an up and comin' carver, eh?"

"He was my sister's adopted son." Eric motioned toward Cloë, who seemed to be paying more attention to the cutlery in front of her than the conversation.

"My condolences, ma'am. Not easy losing a son."

"No, it isn't," she replied. "He never had a chance to visit his ancestral lands while he was alive. So I've brought him to pay homage to his ancestors."

Sensing his confusion, I hastily added, "She's brought his ashes to sprinkle on the land."

"That sounds like a fine idea. Does he still have family here?"

"I don't know. He was a baby when I adopted him. Nothing was known of his parentage other than that his mother was Haida. I'm hoping to trace his birth family. Do you know anyone who we could ask?"

"I don't rightly know. Once we were all one big community here in the Charlottes, Haida and whites living together, eh? But ever since the government said they couldn't get their Indian benefits unless they lived in Skidegate or Old Masset, they pretty much stick to themselves now. With so many of us out of work with the collapse of the fishery and logging industry, the Haida are now the rich ones with all their government money. So there's a lot of resentment. Too bad. I had a couple of real good Haida friends. I don't see them much anymore. But I suppose you could start with the band council office. If you don't know which community his mother came from, best try both. One's in Skidegate and the other's in Old Masset."

"Thanks."

"What's the mother's name? When I was working in the logging camps, I used to know a lot of Haida. Chances are I might know her family."

"I'm afraid I don't have a last name. Mary was her first name."

"It's gonna be tricky. Mary's pretty common. How far back you talking?"

"About nineteen years."

"As I say, it's gonna be tough. A lot of girls leave these islands."

"I have a bracelet that belonged to her. I'm hoping someone will recognize it."

"One of them fancy gold ones all the Haida women wear? I hear tell that the more bracelets a woman's got, the more she's supposed to be loved and the more shit her man probably got into. It's blackmail if you ask me." He chuckled. "Something you gotta realize with Haida women, they wear the pants. The poor men don't stand a chance. I had me a Haida girlfriend once, and I tell you

I never met such a bossy woman. One day I finally had enough. I told her I was going out for some cigarettes and never went back. She hounded me for months after, so much so that I hid out in the camps for a good year." He chuckled. "But boy, she sure was a looker."

"The bracelet is silver with an intricate Haida design carved into it," Cloë persisted. "It looks old."

"Like I said, try the band offices."

"Thanks, you've been a big help."

"You folks here for the pole raising?"

"Yeah, we're looking forward to it," Eric answered.

"Should be a good one. Time was there weren't no pole raisings. The authorities outlawed it. Was the missionaries' doing. Said it was unchristian. When it was finally okay, no one had the money to become chief. 'Cause, you see, not only do they have to pay for the pole and its carving but they also gotta hold this big potlatch after. The new chief has to feed and give out gifts to everyone who watched the pole raising. I hear tell there can be hundreds of people and it can cost the poor bugger up to a hundred grand to put on a half-decent one. I can think of better things I'd rather do with my money. They say the more money you spend, the bigger the chief you are. So tomorrow's gonna be expensive 'cause this is for the chief of one of the most important clans in the islands. You guys should get yourself a nice gift."

TWENTY-SIX

Preparing the Log

He spent most of yesterday planing the log, smoothing out the nicks and gouges from the trip north. It sure was a beauty. He'd never worked on one so near perfect. Usually the logs he carved were full of knots, mostly because they were second-growth. This had to have been one big grandmother of a red cedar, a thousand years old or more, the kind of tree that demanded respect. And the kind of tree you're hard-pressed to find these days with all the logging that's been done on the islands. He wondered where Ern had found such a monster. And why he'd wasted it on the boy instead of keeping it for himself.

Thank Salaana, Ern had already sheared off the back and hollowed it out the Haida way. He didn't have the strength or the tools to do it. And it needed doing with such a big log. It made for easier handling and allowed it to dry more evenly, keeping the grain from splitting. This prep was done a ways back, for the wood was good and dry. In fact, a little too dry, so the damp of Llnagaay should keep it moist, making it better for carving.

He sanded away the black outline of crests the boy had drawn over the log. That was the boy's story, not his. But it hadn't really been a story, just a series of animal crests in Haida formline flowing one into another without any real meaning. They were likely figures Ern had told him to draw. How could the boy carve a story when he'd known nothing about his Haida roots, let alone his clan's stories?

From the way the drawings flowed one into another, he could tell the kid'd had talent. There was good harmony and balance. He would've made a good Haida carver, maybe even a great one. Too bad it would never come to be.

When he started to erase the eagle at the bottom of the pole and plane away the carving where the boy's blood had flowed, the log stirred and tingled. It wanted him to stop, so he did. He would keep the boy's initial cut, still dark where the blood had sunk into the wood. But he would add motifs to the eagle that would identify the boy, for his killing was part of the story. Though probably not the end of the story, for stories never end.

By the time he finished preparing the log, his hand was throbbing real bad, so he called it a day. He crawled back inside his orange pumpkin with the bottle of rye Scav had sold him. He'd pretty near finished it off, which was bad. He'd sworn off booze. But hell, what did it matter now?

In the morning, his hand still throbbed along with his head, so he took his time getting going. After a bracing cup of steaming tea, along with the last of the rye, he made his way to the log. He ran his hands up and down the wood, waiting for figures to emerge. He stared at it, breathed on it, talked to it, willing it to speak.

He wandered over the remnants of the old village, walking where the ancestors had walked, waiting for them to speak. He tried to decipher the crests on the only totem pole not completely buried in moss. Time and weather had pretty well blunted its silvery features. The only thing he could make out was the angled beak of an eagle, which was to be expected since this village belonged to his clan, the Greenstone eagles, or *Hlgaa K' inhlgahl Xaaydaga*, as Nanaay had taught him. One of the few Haida words he knew how to pronounce.

He stopped by the pit where Nanaay had said Old Chief's longhouse had stood and sat on the spongy mound of a once enormous crossbeam. The hole was little more than a deep mossy indentation in the ground with two thick spruce trunks rising from the far end. At one time it would've been a swimming pool–size hole with two levels of platforms surrounding it, large enough to house an extended family of forty or so, including slaves. Old Chief would've made sure it was the largest in the village, overpowering the other longhouses, so no one would dare ignore his highborn status and his power as chief of the Greenstone clan.

As the afternoon wore on and the rain found its way through the dense cedar canopy, images swirled through his mind: eagles, hummingbirds, ravens, beavers, even a killer whale, and of course the picket fence. He'd better not forget the picket fence, for it was that hare-brained visit to the gold miners' camp at the mouth of the Fraser River that led to the shame.

What a mighty paddle that trip must've been, over a thousand kilometres of open water in the only canoes that could make such a journey, the giant canoes the ancestors hollowed out of a single monumental cedar. That was why the Haida were so unbeatable and so safe in the island homeland. No mainland tribe dared travel the hundred-and-fifty-kilometre distance in their small dugout canoes. But the ancestors hadn't bargained on the Iron Men and their sailing boats, which could travel even farther. And when they finally came to Haida Gwaii, the Haida were invincible no more.

TWENTY-SEVEN

Although I couldn't see the start of the procession, I could hear the drummers above the heavy breathing and shuffling of the men inching along the road in front of us. They were transporting the massive totem pole the traditional way, with manpower. A good sixty or so men, split between the two sides, had hefted the pole at the carving shed and were now carrying it along the road to the place where it would stand for the next hundred years or more.

Louise O'Brien had picked Eric and me up at the Haida Heritage Centre about an hour ago. Although we'd invited Eric's sister to join us for breakfast, she never appeared. Last night Eric had offered her the use of our rental car in case she wanted to follow up on Jimmy's suggestions for tracking down Allistair's relatives, but she turned him down. So I wasn't sure what she intended to do today. Maybe she just wanted some time to herself as she tried to adjust to life without her son.

We'd driven along the coastal road to where a crowd was gathered at the Skidegate carving shed. A blustery morning, waves were crashing onto the beach. The wind whipped the clothing of the waiting throng of several hundred people. Low scudding clouds hinted at rain.

We arrived just as the men were carrying the eighteen-metre totem pole onto the road. Gaily painted carvings of assorted Haida creatures seemed to leap out of the top two-thirds of the pole while the bottom third had been left untouched. According to Louise, this section would be buried in a deep hole that'd been dug in a less traditional way: with a backhoe and an excavator.

The unwieldy pole was being carried on lengths of sturdy four-by-four fence posting placed every metre along its length. Four men, two to each side, hefted each four-by-four to waist height. Judging by the laboured breathing and the odd red face, the task was onerous, even with this amount of manpower.

Though it took a good forty-five minutes to get there, the pole's final resting place was little more than a few hundred metres along the road at a large suburban brick house. Struggling to walk in sync, the men maintained a pace that was more a crawl. Whenever one of them looked as if he was about to collapse, another was ready to take his place. Although most of the men were young and sturdy, there was the odd grey-haired gent, no doubt intent on proving he still had it in him. I could even sense Eric flexing his muscles beside me, wanting to test himself. Thankfully we reached the destination before he had a chance.

The men carried the pole along the side of the house to the oceanfront. A fitting place for a totem pole, I thought, to stand guard on a grey stone beach overlooking the sea's endless cycle of tides. The men collapsed with relief as they dropped the carved end a little too heavily onto a crib of planks, knocking several to the ground and causing the pole to wobble dangerously. Before it could fall, several men grabbed the dislodged planks and shoved them firmly underneath, while others angled the un-carved end toward the yawning hole. Once firmly in place, the men laughed and gave one another congratulatory slaps amidst cheers from the crowd. The air vibrated with excitement.

Louise cheered and clapped with the rest of them, as did Eric and I.

"Sorry you came?" I tugged at Eric's buckskin sleeve. We were both appropriately dressed in deerskin jackets with plenty of rippling fringe and colourful beading. Eric's jacket, made by his grandmother, was smooth and supple, almost silk-like with age, while mine, his wedding gift to me, was still a bit on the stiff side and rustled when I moved.

His reply was a broad dimpled grin as he raised his arm in triumph and let out a war whoop.

I smiled to myself. Just like a man. Show him a macho activity with lots of sweat and muscle and he's as happy as a pig in … well, you know what I mean.

Louise was wearing a black ankle-length blanket with a wide bright red border. Flowing creatures in red appliqué cavorted across the back. I recognized the bold eyes and sharp beak of an eagle and the long pointed beak of a hummingbird. The border and designs were edged with shimmering white buttons, hence the term "button blanket." Her broad face beamed from under a high, flat-topped cedar hat with a similar design painted in red and black on the woven bark.

She turned to embrace a young man who greeted her. From the moment of our arrival at the carving shed she had been and still was being accosted by people from the community. Judging by her broad smile and the crushing hugs, she was enjoying the attention. Clearly, she was well respected in the community.

"This is a very big moment for us," she said. "My clan, the *Hlgaa K'inhlgahl Xaaydaga*, or Greenstone Eagles, hasn't had a clan chief pole raising in more than a hundred and forty years, not since we left our ancestral village, Llnagaay."

"How exciting for you," I said.

"We've had other pole raisings in Skidegate, but they were for public buildings."

"I gather becoming chief can be pretty expensive. Someone mentioned it could cost up to a hundred thousand dollars."

"It has to be costing Harry at least that if not more. But I suppose it's not too different from the old days, when only the highborn had enough wealth to raise a pole and hold a potlatch. It usually took them many years to amass the necessary number of gifts for the potlatch."

A woman with a young girl in tow came up to say hello. They chatted for a few minutes before Louise turned back to us. "Where was I? Ah, yes, the cost. Harry MacMillan, the man who's becoming chief today, has made a lot of money in the computer business in Vancouver. Although he hasn't lived on Haida Gwaii for a good number of years, he's returning home to reclaim his heritage."

I ran my eyes over the crowd, looking for a likely candidate. Instead, I noticed another man, tall and lanky with a grey-streaked ponytail, clambering over the railing of the deck behind the house. Unlike others wearing their traditional garb, he was dressed in threadbare jeans and a scruffy windbreaker. He strode across the deck to where a group of men and women stood, appearing very regal in their Haida button blankets, vests, and headdresses. He stopped directly in front of a much shorter man with close-cropped hair who looked vaguely familiar. Jabbing a finger into the man's chest, he started yelling at him. He finished his rant by spitting in the man's startled face.

Everyone gasped.

While we watched in stunned silence, the bully calmly jumped off the deck, shoved his way through the shocked crowd, and disappeared around the side of the house without a backward glance.

As if a signal had been exchanged, an eagle that had been watching from a nearby spruce lifted his wings and with an angry squawk flew off after the man.

"Oh my goodness," Louise said.

"Is the man who was just insulted the new chief?" Eric asked, just as I realized that he was the man I'd seen at the Granville Hotel with Ernest Paul.

"Yes, yes he is." Louise shook her head. "This is terrible."

She paused as people swarmed around the new chief. Some offered him sympathy while others held back as if unsure of what to do. A youngish, light-haired woman, maybe his wife, passed him a corner of her button blanket to wipe the spit from his face.

"Oh, Johnnie, what have you done?" Louise muttered.

"I take it you know the guy who did it," Eric said, offering his arm for support. She appeared quite shaken.

"Unfortunately I do. He's my nephew, Johnnie, the son of my younger sister. He has a greater hereditary right to be Greenstone chief than Harry. You see, my late sister and I are the only direct descendants of the sister of Old Chief, the last potlatched Chief Greenstone. In Haida culture heredity runs through the maternal line."

"So why isn't Johnnie becoming chief?" Eric asked.

"Money. He doesn't have any. Although he earned a fair bit in the logging camps, he spent it all on liquor and hare-brained get-rich schemes, like growing greenhouse cucumbers. I'm afraid Johnnie isn't worthy of becoming chief, nor is his brother Colin. Although Harry isn't an ideal choice, he is a better choice than either of my nephews."

"You mentioned that you had two sons," I said. "Couldn't one of them have taken it on?"

"Yes, but neither of them wants it. They both moved off island years ago and have no desire to claim their heritage. Besides, neither makes enough money. Harry is the son of a cousin, a very distant one. We share great-grandmothers. Although Rose is also descended from Old Chief, it is not in the direct maternal line. That's her with Harry. She will become senior Matriarch when her son becomes chief."

She pointed to a large woman with hair that seemed a little too jet-black. She was wearing a red and black button blanket, more elaborate and more bedecked with buttons than Louise's and easily twice the size, which it needed to be in order to cover her expansive girth. She wore it with a haughty confidence that she no doubt felt her due as the mother of the soon-to-be chief. At the moment she was bending over her son, who was much shorter than her, and appeared to be berating him rather than offering sympathy. The woman who'd offered Harry a corner of her blanket stood outside this mother-son circle as if cast aside.

"This must be difficult for you, Louise," Eric said. "I assume this means that you will no longer be Matriarch."

She shrugged. "It is our tradition. I inherited my Matriarch position from my mother. While my brother was looked upon as chief by our clan, he never formally took on the name through a pole raising and potlatch. He was killed in a boating accident twelve years ago. Usually the chief's sister is the Matriarch, but because Harry is an only child, his mother is taking it on."

She paused as she glanced back at her distant cousin, who continued to loom over her son and jab her finger into his chest. Although the anger expressed in his face suggested he wasn't the least happy about the shocking insult or her badgering, he seemed to be silently accepting both.

"Please, don't get me wrong, this is a great moment for the Greenstones. After more than a hundred and twenty-five years we will finally have a potlatched chief. I'm glad. I'll still be a matriarch of the clan, just not the senior one."

"Auntie," called a voice from behind us. Allistair's girl-friend was squeezing her way through the crowd. "Wasn't that just awful?" Becky exclaimed when she finally reached us. "Have you ever seen such a thing?"

"No, I haven't, child."

"Does this mean Harry can't become chief?"

Many of the people around us turned in our direction. It would seem they, too, wanted to know the answer.

"Johnnie did a very shameful thing, child. It reflects badly on all of us. But it's up to Harry now."

TWENTY-EIGHT

It looked as if Harry was about to take up Louise's challenge. Brushing his mother aside, he tucked his wife's arm under his and together they strode to the deck railing. The wind tugged at his black and red blanket and ruffled the fur fringe of a band of woven fabric tied around his head. Although his wife had regained some composure, I doubted she ever gave off the bold confidence I sensed in many of the other Haida woman. No doubt her mother-in-law did her best to trample it down.

"Folks," the soon-to-be chief called out. "We won't let that little episode stop us, will we? What do you say? Is it time to raise the pole?"

At first there was only an exchange of raised eyebrows and shrugs, with many questioning glances in Louise's direction. But after what seemed an embarrassingly long silence, the cheers rose from the waiting crowd until they reached a resounding crescendo. The witnesses were willing to forget the insult and celebrate in the naming of a new chief.

When the shouting subsided, Harry directed his gaze to Louise. Acknowledging her rank as the clan's Matriarch, he asked, "Well, Auntie? Is it a go?"

Silence reigned but for the sound of waves grinding the gravel on the beach behind us and Louise's heavy breathing. Everyone held their breath. She fiddled with a silver bracelet on her wrist. The crowd waited. Even Harry's mother had lost some of her bluster as she stared anxiously at her distant cousin.

Finally, Louise straightened her shoulders. "It was a shameful and cowardly act, but I will not let it ruin this momentous occasion. Please begin."

I felt more than heard the collective sigh of relief, immediately followed by loud clapping. Eric relaxed his grip on my arm.

"Dodged that one, didn't they?" he whispered in my ear.

A sudden burst of drumming brought our attention back to the pole. The throng of several hundred crowded around. Because of Louise's honoured status, we, along with Becky, were pushed to the front, where we saw several people standing in ceremony next to the pole, still resting on the crib. An elderly white-haired woman, regally bedecked in her red and black button blanket, started chanting in Haida. While everyone dropped their gaze to the ground, Becky leaned over to Eric and me and whispered, "She is blessing the pole."

The elder threw bits of white fluff over the pole. It scattered and soared with the wind. One clump attached itself to Eric's sleeve. So delicate, I couldn't feel it when I picked it up. I tickled his nose with it, prompting him to sneeze. We laughed.

"Eagle down," Becky whispered. "We scatter it as an offering of peace and friendship."

When a heavy-set man and two others similarly attired in blankets began dancing beside the pole, Becky said, "That is the carver and his apprentices. They are breathing life into the pole. The carver always comes from the opposite clan to the chief. So Denny is a Raven. He's a cousin of Harry's wife."

When the carvers finished dancing, Harry, his mother, and his wife filed down the stairs from the deck and approached the pole where it angled into the hole. Each in turn threw what looked to be blue beads into the yawning depths. Louise was invited to join them.

When she returned, she whispered, "In the old days we put a slave in the hole."

I glanced up in shock only to chuckle when I noticed the mischievous glint in her eyes and the laughter in Eric's voice as he whispered, "My little red flower, she's tugging your chain."

The carver approached Harry. Ignoring the strands of wind-whipped hair gyrating around his face, he shouted a few words in Haida, then asked, "Can I raise the pole?"

The soon-to-be chief gave his solemn permission, though the glint in his eyes betrayed his restrained excitement. He shouted, "Move back everyone."

As we started to move back a man approached us. He glanced first at Louise as if seeking her approval before turning to Eric. "Sir, we'd be honoured if you would assist us in raising the pole."

He pointed to where men were lining up beside four separate lengths of heavy rope radiating out from the front of the pole. The ends were tied around a thick wadding of material placed around the pole a metre or more from the top.

Before replying, Eric sought my consent with raised eyebrows. Although I worried the strain might be a bit much, I knew I couldn't say no, so I reluctantly smiled my support.

"I would be honoured," Eric said. "Although I'm not exactly at the top of my game, I can still bench press two hundred with the best of them."

To emphasize this, he jokingly raised his arms in a strongman stance and, with a sprightly spring to his step, followed the man to one of the lines. The man placed him in the centre of the line of about a dozen men, beside a couple of others of middle age. I hoped this meant the middle would be the least strenuous.

Although Eric was in good shape for a man in his early fifties, his abs weren't quite as hard as they once were. With his busy schedule and extensive travelling I found he was more inclined to relax in his favourite chair than go out for a jog as he used to when he was band chief. Lately I'd been pestering him about getting more exercise.

Louise, Becky, and I pushed and shuffled our way back with the rest of the crowd, away from the pole and onto the loose pebbles of the beach. With the rising tide, we were forced to spread out along its edge. Hopefully we were well out of range of the pole should it fall.

The four lines of men, their hands gripping the ropes, began spanning out. Eric's line was on the far left. I waved, but with his head down, his back braced, he was too busy pulling to notice.

A number of people continued to linger near the pole. I thought I spied the bleached blond beehive of François's companion, but wasn't sure.

"Move back everyone!" a man called out.

A few moved farther back as the pole rose into the grey sky. I felt a few drops of rain on my face and worried that it might make the rope too slippery.

I noticed with considerable surprise Cloë's blond head amongst the group still lingering near the base of the pole. Amazingly, she was standing next to François, a man she'd said she wanted nothing to do with. He was leaning back taking photos of the rising pole. I wondered what charm he'd laid on to entice her to come not only to the pole raising but also with him.

As the pole rose higher into the air, the carvings became more visible. "Louise, some of those carved figures look like the ones you have on your blanket."

"You're right. The eagle, hummingbird, and dogfish. Quite well done, aren't they? Those are our clan crests. You'll soon see a beaver with its big teeth. The two figures at the top with the tall hats are the traditional watchmen. They face the sea to watch out for our enemies. Harry will have other carvings to tell his own story. Maybe he'll have a beaver typing away on a computer." She chuckled.

"The dogfish is an interesting crest. It means that the dogfish woman was one of our clan's ancestor's. Our stories tell us that she was carried away by a dogfish, which is a small shark, and became one herself. But she was able to transform herself back into a human."

"Get back farther!" the man shouted again.

The pole rose steadily, then stopped as the men pulling on the ropes stopped. The three watchmen hovered as if undecided about moving higher. Then they slowly slipped backward.

"Don't stop! Keep pulling!"

The ropes strained and groaned as the men strained and groaned. The watchman began to inch back up. They sat on top of the head of a huge eagle with two very bold eyes and a fish tail sticking out of its large hooked beak.

"Keep at it guys! It's moving again."

The hummingbird with its straight, almost horizontal beak shifted ever more vertical.

"Hey you! Get out of the way!"

At that precise moment, a rope snapped, then another. They whipped toward us. Without thinking, I pulled Louise to the ground.

A shriek rent the air and the ground shuddered as the pole landed with a booming thud.

Silence.

Then, "Oh my God!"

TWENTY-NINE

A high, piercing shriek spiralled above the sound of the wind and the waves.

"Eric!" I screamed.

While the people around me remained motionless, trying to absorb what had happened, I scrambled to my feet.

Completely forgetting about Louise, I raced around and over people to where I'd last seen my husband. The line of men lay clumped on the ground like collapsed dominos. I found him sitting on a clump of grass rubbing his hands.

"Are you okay?"

"Christ, what happened?"

"A rope broke, maybe two. Are you hurt?"

"My bum's sore and my hands hurt like hell. But otherwise I'm okay." He held his hands out to reveal angry red rope burns on both palms.

I winced at the sight of the torn skin. "We better get some ointment on those."

He pulled his hands away and hid them in his pockets. "It can wait."

"Poor baby, afraid it'll sting." I ruffled his hair and kissed him on the forehead. "I'm very glad you're okay."

We both turned at the groans coming from a man lying on the ground near us. As far as I could tell, he lay where he'd fallen. His eyes were tightly closed; he grimaced in pain.

I leaned over him. "What hurts?"

He gasped. "I think I did something to my back."

Before I could tell him that I'd get help, a teenager ran up calling out "Dad!" Close behind him was a stocky woman about the same age as the injured man. Tears streamed down her cheeks. An older, silver-haired man, his brow creased with worry, limped up behind them. In the distance I could hear sirens. After suggesting they don't move him until medical help arrived, I turned back to Eric.

"I tell you, Meg, there was nothing we could do. When I felt the sudden dead weight of the pole, I tried to hold on, but the rope slipped through my hands like it was greased and down I went crashing into the other guys. I sure hope no one has been seriously hurt."

The shrieks that continued to rise above the other sounds told another story.

Most of the men slowly struggled to their feet. Family and friends crowded around. Two broken lengths of rope lay forgotten on the ground. Apart from the man with the injured back, two others remained seated. Both had been at the front of their lines when the ropes snapped. One had a deep gash across his face; the other cradled his arm.

"Christ, Meg, I think someone's trapped." Eric pointed to a group of men struggling to lift the pole where it angled over the ground. It had landed against the sloped back of the hole. Something was sticking out from under it. *A leg?* A camera lay abandoned on the ground nearby.

The sirens grew louder.

"I'd better go help."

Before I could tell Eric there were more than enough men, he was racing to the hole. I followed.

The shrieking continued. It sounded as if someone was yelling "Bo-Bo!" over and over again. I saw Eric's sister trying to pull a woman away. Shit! It was Sherry. Her face was twisted in anguish.

Unable to raise the log, the men scattered with the arrival of a backhoe. I recognized the grim face of Harry at the wheel. He angled the shovel under the pole and slowly lifted it up. Several people carefully pulled the body out, then Harry lowered the pole back down.

I didn't dare look. I already knew it was François, and given the tremendous weight of the pole, he would bear little resemblance to the elegant man I'd met yesterday. There was no way he could've survived.

I ran over to where the two women stood. Sherry twisted out of Cloë's grip and crumpled to the ground beside … Her husband? Her lover? I didn't know which. She was slapping his face and kissing it, yelling at him to wake up. But his expression remained serene in death. His white hair was still neatly coifed, but his electric blue eyes were open, staring up as if he had registered what was about to happen. Apart from those transfixed eyes, though, there was no hint on his face of the horrible death that had befallen him.

His body was another matter. Someone had quickly covered him with a Haida blanket. I could see the blood seeping into the beak of the raven and along its wing. Where François' chest and abdomen should be rising from the ground, there was only an unnerving flatness. Blood started to trickle from his mouth and nose.

People moved aside as the paramedics rushed in with their stretcher. At the sight of the body, their pace slowed. They allowed Sherry a few minutes before Cloë gently pulled her away. Eric was at her side. She collapsed weeping into his arms.

Cloë stood forlornly beside him.

"Are you okay?" I asked her.

"I'll be fine." But she was shivering, whether from the cold or from shock, I didn't know. I wrapped my arm around her shoulder.

"It was awful, Meg. It took us a few seconds to realize what was happening after the ropes snapped. By then the pole was falling and François didn't know. Someone shouted for him to get out of the way, but it was too late." Tears were seeping down her cheeks. "I'm not exactly a fan of François's, but to die this way…. I wouldn't wish it on my worst enemy."

"What in the world was he doing under the pole?"

"Pictures. The fool was taking photos of the pole going up. It was Ernest's idea. He said it would be nice to have a good set to record the momentous occasion. Since François had his expensive Nikon, he offered to do it. And now he's dead."

"Speaking of Ernest, where is he?"

"He dropped us off and left. Said he'd be back in time to take us home."

"Why wouldn't he want to stay for such an important occasion?"

"Probably another deal. The only thing on that man's mind is money."

The paramedics placed François's body on the stretcher and headed toward the ambulance.

"Meg," Eric said. "Since Ernest isn't here, I think we'd better go to the hospital with Sherry. She'll need someone with her."

"Of course, but how are we going to get there? You left your car at the Heritage Centre."

"I'll drive," said Louise. Like the rest of us, her face was stark with shock. Fortunately she appeared none the worse from her tumble to the ground. "A terrible tragedy. Someone from my clan needs to be with this poor woman." She glanced at Harry, who seemed more interested in talking to his mother than involving himself with the dead man.

He stopped talking as the stretcher passed by though. For a moment I thought he was going to approach Sherry, but his mother said something and he turned his attention back to her. Louise muttered, a low *harrumph*, but she didn't stop to speak to them.

The police had arrived. Their SUV, lights flashing, was parked next to the ambulance. They were arguing with the paramedics over the removal of the body without their say-so. But since the damage was already done, they relented and let them load the dead man into the ambulance. As it pulled out, we followed with Sherry in Louise's car.

THIRTY

Old Chief

He caught a rare sight this morning, the dorsal fin of a killer whale slicing through the water just outside the lagoon. Given the height of the fin, he figured it was a good-sized bull. From the way the fin flopped over it'd been through a few battles too. He'd read somewhere that the bulls were momma's boys. As long as their momma was around they thrived. It didn't sound all that different from the Haida. Though the men strutted around like bulls, there was always some damn woman behind them pulling the reins.

The elders say people who die at sea come back as killer whales. Whenever he saw a big bull like this one, he liked to think it was his dad. Poor bugger drowned more than twenty years ago when his foot got caught in a net. A hell of a way to go.

Some believe seeing an orca brings good luck. He sure hoped so. He needed all the luck he could get if he was going to get this damn story finished in time. He sure hoped Scav didn't get ornery drunk while he was in Charlotte and blab about him and the log to a drinking buddy. You never knew who might get angry and try to stop him, or worse, call the cops.

He wasn't worried about somebody turning up out of the blue. There was no reason for anyone to come to Llnagaay. There was nothing to see. Nothing to steal. Anything of value left when his people left, or more likely when the museum guys stole them. No one had been here in years, apart from himself. And he never told anyone he came, except Scav. Many of his people were afraid to step on these shores, afraid the ghosts of shame still lingered. But he didn't care.

Sure there were ghosts. He felt them last night. Heard their whispers in the trees. Felt them brushing the sides of his tent. But given all the people who died after the small-pox came, there had to be a lot of spirits hanging around.

Nanaay said that before the Iron Men came, over five hundred people lived in Llnagaay. When his people were forced to leave, only about sixty remained, many of them children. They couldn't survive on their own, so they went north, to where the survivors from the other villages in the southern islands went, to Skidegate, another clan's village where the Methodists had set up shop.

But his people didn't go there straight away. They didn't want to live with the Iron Men. And they didn't want to live in another clan's village. They were a proud clan. They didn't want to admit defeat. So they set up a new village down the inlet from Skidegate, but it didn't work out. People still died. After a few years they went to the missionaries, to their medicine and food.

Old Chief never saw his clan's defeat. He died a few years before people starting dying. He was the last great chief of the clan. Chief Greenstone was his official name, but everyone called him Old Chief because he was the chief for such a long time. He took it over as a young man barely out of boyhood, when his uncle, the chief at the time, was killed in a raid on a rival clan's village.

The carver picked up his marker and began drawing what he would later carve using the forms that were central to Haida art. He started at the top of the pole where the story began, and the story began with Old Chief. He'd make him a proud and powerful eagle worthy of his clan's chiefdom and not the figure of shame the Blue Shell Ravens had made him out to be.

From what Nanaay said, he'd been a good chief until that shameful moment. Though she didn't really know, since she'd been born in Skidegate long after Old Chief died. It was her nanaay who told her he brought great prosperity to Llnagaay, making it the most important village in the southern islands. But this wealth wasn't all good. It made other clans jealous.

He boldly outlined the shape of the eagle's head, at an angle to command respect. The eyes he made sharp and intelligent using the circle within the S-form that defined Haida eyes. He added another interior circle to show wisdom. The beak was blunt and curved like an eagle's, but he drew it larger than the eagle's head to emphasize Old Chief's power. When carved it would protrude at a commanding angle from the eagle's body. The wings stretched down on either side of the eagle's body. And since you can't have empty space in Haida art, he filled them with ovoids and split U-forms to represent feathers.

Nanaay had told him that the clan's wealth came from the great sea voyages Old Chief undertook with other clansmen to distant lands. So he drew the long, pointed bow of a dugout canoe sticking out from under one of the wings. She thought they might've gone as far as Hawaii, because the old stories spoke of mountains of fire and wondrously coloured birds.

He was going to draw a fiery mountain inside the other wing, but decided not to in case it wasn't true. But there were stories that Old Chief's ceremonial blanket was made from thousands of tiny red and yellow feathers taken from birds that sure didn't fly around these islands. So he thought, what the hell, if he drew a fiery mountain inside the wing it would become part of the Old Chief's legend whether it was true or not, so he drew it. He liked the idea of the ancestors paddling thousands of kilometres to Hawaii and back. He stuck a feather in the beak of the eagle. After it was carved he would paint this bright yellow, a colour rarely used on Haida totem poles. But he wanted this feather to stand out so people would know how great Old Chief was.

At the time of his death, Old Chief's potlatch pole was supposed to have eight rings on it, meaning he had accumulated enough wealth to hold eight different pot-latches. But Nanaay never mentioned if the clan had erected a memorial pole or mortuary pole after Old Chief died, as was his right as Chief Greenstone. He expected it had to do with the shame.

He figured if there had been a mortuary pole it would've disappeared pretty soon after the village was abandoned. All those museum guys looking for treasure. And if a feather blanket had existed, it vanished along with everything else. No one knows if anyone got the real treasure, because no one knows where it was hidden. He only knew no one had seen this treasure, let alone talked about it, in over a hundred and fifty years.

To make sure no one ever forgot Old Chief's important status, he drew a potlatch pole with eight rings rising from a top hat sitting squarely on the head of the eagle. At the eagle's feet he placed a large ovoid filled with ever smaller ovoids. Later, when he finished carving, that is if he were lucky, he would paint it another non-traditional colour, a bright shiny green, the colour of the eelgrass that swirls in the water of the estuary across the channel from Llnagaay.

This would be the greenstone, whatever it was. He had no idea what the greenstone was or what it looked like. He'd never seen a green stone or rock anywhere on Haida Gwaii, let alone at Llnagaay. When he'd asked Nanaay why the clan was called the Greenstone Eagles, she would only say that it had always been the name. But she did tell him that when she'd asked her own nanaay the same question, she'd been hushed and told never to ask that question again.

THIRTY-ONE

The hospital visit was short. It turned out Sherry was only the girlfriend and had no official connection to François. His current wife, whatever number she might be, was on a cruise in the Mediterranean and the only person authorized to handle arrangements. After tearfully giving the cops the contact information for the dead Frenchman's office, Sherry climbed back into Louise's car and drove with us to the Eagle's Nest.

She may have only been his mistress, but she clearly loved the man. Her tears hadn't let up since the accident. Her mascara ran in blackened streaks down her cheeks, while her hair had collapsed. She'd shredded more tissues than she'd used. But she still teetered undeterred on her spiked heels and clattered up the front stairs of our shared cottage without the need to lean on Eric. Rather than retreating to her suite, she remained with us in the front room.

She downed a healthy measure of Eric's single malt scotch, as did Eric, Cloë, and Louise. With his hands encased in thick bandages, applied at the hospital, Eric couldn't hold on to the bottle properly, so I poured. He could barely manage the glass either, but stubbornly refused my help.

I was very tempted to join them, but I gritted my teeth and put the kettle on for a cup of tea instead. I wasn't going to let the unnerving death of François get me drinking again.

After the scotch, Sherry kicked off her heels. "I guess I don't have to wear these anymore. Bo-Bo liked me wearing these things. Said they made me look statuesque." She raised her hands above her head as she stretched out this last word. She rubbed first her left foot, then her right, before tucking her feet under her as she sank back into the floral cushions of the rattan chair.

"Five years we've been together, Bo-Bo and me. Jeez, I still can't believe it. I don't know what I'm gonna do without him."

She told us how she'd first met François at a bar in Whistler where she'd been working. It was love at first sight and he hadn't looked at another woman since, except, of course, for his wife. But she didn't count. She was just some stuck-up bitch — her words not mine — he could parade in front of his company's board and at cocktail parties. Besides, he didn't sleep — my word not hers — with her anymore.

Sherry had accepted that François would never marry her. Divorcing his current wife had been a nonstarter. She had too much money. Besides, there were the three kids. Spoiled brats, she called them. If she and François had married they would've been a part of her life. This way the wife got to deal with them, while she enjoyed François all to herself.

She punctuated this last remark with giggles, which soon turned to tears as she remembered this would no longer be the case. I wondered if she realized that in death they would be even further separated, for the wife would take up her place as François's chief mourner and pretend that Sherry had never existed.

While Sherry was recounting her story, I watched Cloë carefully, worried about the effect this tale would have on her, a tale that so closely paralleled her own — except in her case she was the scorned wife. I could see Eric was equally worried. When his sister asked for more scotch, he insisted I dilute it with a generous amount of water. But apart from taking frequent sips, she showed no outward reaction. Instead she seemed to be genuinely commiserating with Sherry's distress. Maybe Cloë felt a certain affinity to Sherry, since both their loved ones had died violently.

The bereaved mistress was regaining control of her emotions when Harry MacMillan and his mother arrived at our front door. "I've come to pay my respects to Mrs. Champagne and to say how sorry I am about the accident," Harry said.

"We are so sorry, dear," his mother chimed in. "Such a terrible tragedy."

Sherry, not bothering to correct Harry's mistake, invited the two of them to join us with all the dignity of a grieving widow.

For a moment Harry seemed a bit taken aback to see Louise sitting in one of the rattan chairs, but he quickly recovered. "Glad I found you, Auntie. We need to talk."

She nodded. "It can wait till later."

"I think you could do with some of this." Eric pointed at the scotch with his bandaged hand. "Please, help yourself."

Harry shook his head. "Thanks, but I haven't had a drop in ten years. As upsetting as this is, I'm not going to start now."

I gave him the thumbs up, one reformed alcoholic to another. "How about a cup of tea?"

"I'll have some scotch." Rose poured herself a more than generous amount and dropped into a rattan settee designed to seat two, but which barely contained her ample frame.

Resplendent in a muumuu-style dress, she no longer wore her button blanket or other Haida regalia, nor did Harry. This morning's death had obviously affected him, for he looked somewhat ragged around the edges. His khaki pants had lost their crease and his checked sport shirt was smeared with dirt.

Harry grabbed a kitchen chair and pulled it up beside the settee where Eric and I were sitting. "You're Eric Odjik, aren't you? The new Grand Chief of the GCFN."

"Hoping to be is more like it. The election isn't until next year," Eric replied. "And this is my wife, Meg. I'm sorry we're not meeting under better circumstances."

"Yes, an unfortunate and terrible accident."

"Have the police determined what caused the ropes to break? They looked relatively new to me. Thank God." He held up his bandaged hands. "Old ropes would've made mincemeat of my hands."

"Damn, I never thought. I guess the other guys will have rope burns too. Look, Eric, I feel really badly about this. Is there anything I can do?"

"Don't worry about me. My hands'll be back in shape in no time. I just find it strange that two of the four ropes would break like that."

"I can't for the life of me figure out why either. They were mooring ropes, supposed to be only a few years old. Denny, the carver, got them off a friend's boat. They should've been able to handle the weight of the pole."

"Don't you find it curious that both broke at the same time? I could see one going, but two?"

Sherry straightened up. "What are you saying? That someone killed my Bo-Bo on purpose?"

"No, not at all," Harry jumped in. "It was an accident, nothing more."

"Maybe those guys at the restaurant killed Frank," Sherry continued as if she hadn't heard. "They sure hated his guts. You guys saw how they treated him last night. That skinny bastard even spat on him."

"I know feelings can run deep around here, but not enough to kill. This was just a horrible accident. I believe your husband was unfortunate enough to be standing in the wrong place at the wrong time," Harry said.

"All for a stupid picture. Look, guys, I'm feeling kinda shaky. I'm going to go to my room, pop the pills the nurse gave me, and lie down, okay?" Picking up her shoes, she unfolded her legs and stood up.

"Why don't I keep you company?" Cloë suggested. "I'll pour us both some more scotch."

"Thanks. But I just want to be by myself, okay?" Ignoring the proffered refilled glass, the grieving mistress padded down the hall in her bare feet and disappeared into her room.

Momentarily silenced by the rejection, Eric's sister continued to stare at the empty hallway before pouring the departed woman's scotch into her own freshly filled glass. "I'm feeling rather shaky myself. I think I'll go to my room."

I watched her progress through the window. With her head bowed, her shoulders hunched, she seemed so forlorn I almost ran out to keep her company.

Eric, sensing my unease, said, "We've all had a rough few hours. That scotch'll put her to sleep, and when she wakes up she'll be fine."

Figuring he knew his sister best, I poured myself another cup of tea, placed some chocolate chip cookies on a plate, and passed them around.

"What do you plan to do now, Harry?" Eric asked.

"I'm not sure."

Without bothering to wait until she finished chewing her cookie, Rose said, "We gotta get the pole up. You can't be chief without it. Ain't that right, Louise?"

"But Awaay, the pole killed a man. It's cursed," her son said.

"Harrumph, it'll be part of the pole's story. Long after you're dead, people'll be talkin' about the great Chief Greenstone and his famous pole."

Louise glanced at her cousin with disgust before saying, "Harry, do you have enough money to have another one carved? It would be better to have one that doesn't have this shameful story."

"It cost me eighty grand. No way I can come up with more. As it is, I had to remortgage my condo. Plus I've got a bundle invested in potlatch gifts." He winced. "I suppose I can return most of them, but hell, I'm going to be the laughingstock of the Haida. The chief-that-never-was. No, I've got to go through with it. I've no choice."

She nodded grimly.

He stood up, his face set in determination. "We've got to go, Awaay. I need to find out when the police will be finished at my place and find a logging winch. It's the only way to get that damn pole raised now. I sure as hell wished I'd gone that route in the first place."

"You'll need witnesses," Louise said. "I assume most people have gone home."

"I don't see us having a problem getting them back. Everyone'll be dying to see if the pole will fall again." His mother punctuated this comment with a loud laugh.

A phone rang. Harry reached into his jacket pocket.

"Harry MacMillan here."

As we listened to the one-sided conversation, we watched Harry's face grow steadily grimmer. I thought I heard the door to Sherry's room click open.

"Yup…. Yup…. Damn, you sure…? So what happens now…? Right. I'll drop by the station on my way back to Skidegate."

He ended the call. "That was the RCMP. They say the two ropes were intentionally cut. It's now a murder investigation. Damn! Just what I need."

Sherry's voice shouted from the hallway, "See! Didn't I tell you?" The door slammed shut loudly as she retreated back into her room.

Rose turned to Louise and snarled, "It's all your god-damn fault. You don't want Harry to be chief. I bet your damn nephew cut the ropes to bring shame on Harry. And *you* probably put him up to it." She struggled out of the chair. "Come on, Harry. Let's get outta here."

Without waiting for a response she charged her way to the front door, but before she reached it she turned around and pointed at her rival. "Harry's gonna be chief. You hear? Whether you like it or not!"

As she flung the door open, it banged hard against the wall. She stomped out.

Her son slowly rose from his chair. "Auntie, I'm sorry about this. But you know my mother can get a bit carried away. I know Johnnie had nothing to do with this. The police will find that a logger did this. Those guys don't like us Haida any better than they did this poor man. I could see them using the pole raising to make a statement."

Halfway to the door, he stopped. "Auntie, once I've talked to the police, I'll let you know what's happening. I still want to get the pole raised today and have the pot-latch tonight. We can't let all that good food go to waste, can we?" He smiled apologetically. With a nod in our direction and a quick goodbye he was gone.

The door closed with a click, leaving behind a ringing silence. Neither Eric nor I dared break it. I felt at a loss, unsure of what to do or say. Louise just sat there, seemingly lost in her own painful thoughts.

For Louise's sake, I hoped her nephew had nothing to do with this. It would be better if the ropes had been cut by a disgruntled logger, as Harry suggested. Still, if François was the target, how would the culprit have known he would be the one standing under the pole when the ropes broke?

Then I remembered Cloë mentioning that Ernest had suggested François stand there to get some photos of the pole going up. But what would the carver's motive be in wanting his client dead? From what people were saying, he'd be more interested in getting money from the man than settling old scores. And let's face it, there were much easier ways to get rid of someone.

Eric finally broke the nervous silence in his usual thoughtful way. "It's been a tough day for you, Louise. How about Meg and I drive you back to your place and we'll pick up our rental on the way?"

She continued sitting, lost in thought as she played idly with her bracelet. The rain that had threatened earlier had begun to beat a staccato against the windows. I watched rivulets form on the roof of the neighbouring cottage.

"It's starting to rain," I said. "We'd better go before it gets worse."

"The shame, the shame," Louise whispered, her lips barely moving, her gaze fixed on the streaking rain. "It's all my fault. And I don't know how to make it better." She paused. "If only one of my sons had wanted to be chief, if only ..." Her voice trickled away into silence.

I moved to help her up from the chair, but Eric stopped me. "Let her do it in her own time," he whispered. So we waited and watched as the rain fell with more determined force.

At last Louise straightened her back and cast her dark brown eyes fully on us. "Life is full of 'if onlys,' isn't it? But we can't go back. We can only keep going forward." She stood up. "Eric, I think I'll take you up on your offer to drive me home."

I grabbed my jacket and Eric's red one as we headed outside into the rain. On our way to Louise's car, Becky and her mother arrived in a silver pickup complete with shiny chrome and roof lights. They'd been searching for the Matriarch and had just learned from Harry that she was with us. It was decided that Becky would drive her auntie home, while her mother would take Eric to get our car.

Before climbing into her car, Louise turned to Eric. "I know this has been upsetting, but I would really appreciate it if you could come to the pole raising. Your presence will help bring respect to the ceremony. Meg, you too."

With the image of François's bloodied and flattened body still fresh in my mind, I shook my head. "Sorry, but I don't think I can."

Louise nodded in understanding.

"I'll be there," Eric said. Though he'd managed to put his rain jacket on without difficulty, he couldn't grasp the zipper pull with his bandaged hands. I reached to zip it up, but he brushed me aside with a grin. "I'm okay. A little rain won't hurt me."

"At least put up your hood."

"Yes, Mummy." Grinning, he flipped the hood over his head. But at this point I wasn't sure what good it would do. His hair was already plastered against his skull.

"When do you want me, Louise?" Eric asked.

Becky answered from inside the car, "Harry said it would be around 4:30. He figures the police should be finished by then."

"Eric, I'd also like you and Meg to come to the potlatch after," Louise continued. "It will be important that we give the new Chief Greenstone all the respect we can."

"We'd be honoured to come, wouldn't we, Meg?"

"Yes," I said with some reluctance. I felt uneasy about attending a big celebration after such a tragic death.

As if reading my mind, Eric said, "Louise, I understand your need to restore harmony to your clan. But at the same time, the dead must be respected."

"I feel the same way. I will make sure Harry pays homage to the memory of the poor man. Please bring his girlfriend, if she's up to it, and your sister."

Louise climbed into her car and off she and Becky sped down the steep road, now more a river than asphalt.

I glanced at Eric's bandaged hands. "You can't drive. I'd better come with you."

"I'll be fine. See." He gripped the door handle of the truck and wrenched the door open, but not without a few winces of pain. "Besides, I want to see a few people before the pole raising. You'll only get bored. I also think it might not be a bad idea for you to stick around to make sure Sherry and my sister are okay."

THIRTY-TWO

I was about to go into the cottage to check on Sherry, when I noticed Cloë leaving the main lodge. Suitably fortified against the rain in a bright blue Gore-Tex jacket, she was walking with determination. I called out, but either she didn't hear me or she was ignoring me, for she continued without a backward glance down the steep incline that led to the main road.

I ran after her.

"Cloë, wait up!"

No response. Finally, when I was almost behind her, she jumped at the sound of my voice.

"Oh, it's you."

"Sorry, I didn't mean to startle you. I saw you walking and thought I would join you."

She shrugged. "If you want. I'm going to the police station to see if they know anything about Allistair's Haida family. I don't imagine Eric had a chance to ask around this morning."

"We'll try at the potlatch tonight."

"Are they actually going through with it?"

"I believe there's too much at stake to cancel. But

Louise said they would have a ceremony to pay homage to François. She invited you to join us."

"Not on your life. I couldn't celebrate, not with the image of that pole falling on him. It was terrible. And Sherry's screaming ..." She winced. "By the way, how's she doing?"

"I was about to check on her when I saw you. I have a feeling she'll be fine. She strikes me as someone who doesn't remain down for long. Do you know François's wife?"

"I knew his first wife, and she was a wonderful person. I think he was on wife number three when he and my ex went their separate ways. She was one stuck-up bitch."

"Sherry's exact words. Must be the same wife."

"If it is, I don't blame François for fooling around. But then he fooled around on every woman he hooked up with, including his mistresses."

A car turned onto the road and started the climb up the hill toward us. With barely enough room, we were forced to walk in the stream coursing down the side of the road. Thankfully, my feet were snug in my Gore-Tex-lined trail shoes. Cloë's Gucci loafers, however, were soaked, but she seemed too focused on our destination to worry about wet feet.

"Sherry sure acted as if she loved the guy. Do you think it's possible he could've been fooling around on her?" I asked.

"If he had been and she found out, I pity poor François." Cloë picked up her pace. "I've got to get to the station before the officer leaves."

The single-storey detachment was in the middle of the town — if Queen Charlotte could be considered to have a middle of town. From what I'd seen so far, it seemed to sprawl raggedly along the shore with commercial and government buildings scattered along the main road and most of the residences sprinkled in the heights above.

After being told that the staff sergeant was busy, we sat down on metal chairs facing a wall of Canada's Most Wanted posters. Scanning the collection of unsavoury faces, I wondered about the chances of any of these criminals turning up here, on the edge of the world. Mind you, the remoteness of the archipelago's many islands would offer plenty of good hideouts.

A door opened and out of the office stepped the Vancouver policeman who was working on Allistair's case. He raised his eyebrows in surprise at the sight of my sister-in-law.

"Mrs. Zakharov," he said, "I trust you're enjoying your stay in the Queen Charlottes."

"You had better say you've found my son's killer," she retorted.

"You know I can't discuss the case with you. Suffice it to say we are working on it."

"Have you found the man?"

"Please, Mrs. Zakharov, I will inform you when it's appropriate." He turned to a man in an RCMP uniform who had followed him out of the room. "Thanks, Jean-Louis, for the info. I'll let you know what transpires."

With a curt nod in Cloë's direction, he headed out the front door before she had a chance to say another word.

The Mountie held out his hand. "Staff Sergeant Galarneau. What can I do for you, Madame Zakharov?"

Staff Sergeant Jean-Louis Galarneau wasn't exactly your ramrod straight, muscular, six-foot Mountie in red serge; rather, he was quite squat and verging on flabbiness. His navy Kevlar vest seemed to be acting more like a corset than protective garb. But he did have a head of thick dirty-blond hair cut short in Mountie style and a stern "I'm in charge" demeanour.

"What was Sergeant Antonucci saying? Has he found my son's killer?"

"Please, madame, I know this is a terrible time for you, but you must understand it is not possible for me to discuss it with you."

"Can you at least tell me if you know who you're looking for?"

"I can only tell you that Sergeant Antonucci has identified a suspect he believes has come to these islands."

"I know. The man who stole Allistair's totem pole, I want to know if you have a name."

"Please, madame, I cannot help you. If you don't mind, I must be going. I am very busy."

I hastily intervened. "Sergeant Galarneau, if you have a few moments, the reason my sister-in-law has come to see you today is to see if you can help locate her dead son's birth family. You know that he was Haida?"

He started to turn away, but for whatever reason changed his mind. Perhaps buried under his aura of officialdom lurked a human heart. "I can give you five minutes."

He ushered us into a cold, sterile office, bare of furniture but for the *de rigueur* faux wooden desk, wooden chairs, and metal shelving. Apart from a photo of a young blond woman with a towheaded boy, the only other items that could be considered personal were two posters hanging on a drab green wall, one announcing the Musical

Ride in Calgary a few years earlier and the other enticing people to visit the Gaspé Peninsula. Through the narrow window I could see that the rain had stopped.

I waited for Cloë to speak, but when she didn't, I provided my version of her son's story and that of his birth mother. From time to time Cloë would nod in agreement. For whatever reason, she seemed content for me to carry on. Perhaps it was too painful for her. At the end of the short but sad story, I said, "My sister-in-law is hoping that you might be able to locate the parents or family of this young Haida woman."

"But, mesdames, this happened almost twenty years ago."

"Couldn't you look through your files to see if there are any missing women from that period?"

"There won't be a missing persons report."

"How can you be so sure?"

"I know. Even though I have only been at this detachment for two years, I have learned from my experience at other detachments where there is a high native population that missing persons reports are rarely filed. Many kids leave the reserves looking for a better life in the cities. Some keep in touch with their families, but many don't. For the ones who don't, I have rarely seen a parent bother to report them missing. They assume their child has a good reason for staying out of touch or that the child will eventually turn up, probably broke and looking for someone to take care of their kids."

"Couldn't you at least have someone check, just to make sure?"

He sighed. "Okay. What was the year again and the name of the woman?"

When he finished jotting down the information Cloë gave him, he said, "You should also check with the Vancouver police. Perhaps the parents contacted them directly."

"They didn't," Cloë said. "At the time of my son's birth, the police went through their missing persons files and didn't come across any report that matched the woman's description."

"Did you try later? Perhaps the parents waited a few years before becoming sufficiently concerned to file one."

"I'm here now, and I mean to find his relatives before I leave. So if you can't help me, I'll ask elsewhere."

"Madame, I am sorry I can't be of more help. You can try the Haida Nation council. They'll have a better idea about the children who left Haida Gwaii twenty years ago. Now if—"

The sound of the front door slamming cut off the rest of his sentence. We all ducked back into the reception area in time to see Sherry stomping into the detachment as best she could in her spiked heels.

She pointed a finger at the Mountie. "Have you arrested them yet? They killed Bo-Bo."

THIRTY-THREE

Behind Sherry sauntered in Ernest Paul as if he hadn't a care in the world. *About time you showed up*, I thought. I felt Cloë stiffen beside me. When the carver nodded in our direction, Cloë turned her head away, while I, feeling one of us should be polite, smiled back.

"Tell him, Ern. Give him the guys' names," Sherry said.

Sergeant Galarneau held up his hands. "Please, madame, I don't know what this is about. Who has been killed?"

"My Bo-Bo, Frank."

"Are you referring to François Champagne?"

"Who else?"

He glanced in our direction before turning to Sherry. "Please, come into my office."

It was obvious the sergeant didn't want us listening in, but I was too intrigued to let this go, so I crowded into the narrow room with them. Cloë, probably more out of a desire not to share the same room with the carver than out of politeness, remained in the reception area.

"Now, madame, please tell me your name."

For a moment Sherry seemed taken aback. "Yeah, right. I guess I wasn't talking to you at the hospital, eh?

I'm Sherry Monaghan."

"And what is your relationship to Monsieur Champagne."

"I'm his girlfriend … *er* … I guess I have to say *was*, don't I?" For a moment she seemed flustered, but then her resolve returned. "I was there when it happened. But I told the other cop all this."

"I imagine you mean Constable Murray. Since you are here, I would like to hear directly from you what transpired." Indicating one of the wooden chairs, he said, "Please have a seat." Then he noticed me. "I'm sorry, madame, I will have to ask you to leave."

As I crept out of the room, I heard him ask, "And Ernest, what's your involvement?"

"He knows who killed Frank," Sherry cut in. "It was those awful men at the restaurant."

"What men?" the cop asked.

"The bastards who spat on Frank."

"Look, Sherry," Ernest said, "I have no idea whether they killed Frank or not. I just told you I know them."

"But they have to be the ones. They hated Bo-Bo."

"Okay, both of you please sit down and let's start from the—"

The door clicked closed.

"Do you think those men in the restaurant really could've done it?" Cloë asked me. She'd been listening in after all.

"I imagine they're as good candidates as any. They sure didn't hide their hatred of François," I replied.

"Nah, they couldn't've done it." Both of us jumped at the sound of the voice behind us. I whirled around. It was Jimmy, the owner of the restaurant. "Sure, Vinny's got a temper, but, hell, he's got an alibi that can't be beat. He spent the night in the clink to dry out after smashing his truck into a pole."

"Which one was he?" I asked.

"The big guy. The skinny guy with the crazy beard's Siggy. But hey, he couldn't've done it either. He's all bluster. Doesn't have a mean bone in him."

"How can you be so sure? He didn't hesitate to spit on François," I said.

"I know the guy. I worked beside him for close on fifteen years. Same way I know Vinny."

"That's right, you said were a logger too."

"Yup, for twenty-three years. It's what brought me to the islands. Good money in it too, until the tree huggers started causing problems. Once the Haida started their protests, I knew our days were numbered. That's when me and my partner decided to open up a restaurant. Bruce was camp cook, and a mighty good one at that."

"He is, if last night's meal is anything to go by."

Jimmy beamed. "Best chef on the island."

"Tell me about these two guys. Why did they hate François so much?"

"Like I told you, they hated him, like a lot of people around here, because of the scab loggers he brought in."

"But did this affect them personally?"

"Now that you mention it, I think Siggy might'a been fired by the company that guy headed up. I don't think Vinny ever worked for them. He was just pissed off with the scab loggers." Jimmy tried to brush the few strands of his comb-over back into place and failed. "Jeez, what a way to go. To think, the dead guy was in my restaurant last night, enjoying Bruce's cedar-plank salmon. I sure hope he didn't see it coming."

"I've heard of people killing someone for less reason than being fired."

"I suppose. Siggy was outta work for a long time after."

"Sounds like a possible motive to me."

"I suppose, but I'm not sure how hard Siggy was lookin'. He seemed to spend a lotta time in that hideaway of his. Besides, no way he could'a killed that guy this morning. Like Vinny he's got an alibi too. He wasn't anywhere near here. He'd just come in to quaff a few beers before heading south."

"But the ropes could've been cut right after they saw François."

"No way. Vinny smashed his truck not more than a hundred metres from my door."

"What about Siggy?"

"No way I'm gonna believe he could'a done something like that."

"I guess it's up to the police to find out. I expect Ernest is telling the staff sergeant about the two of them right now."

"Ern knows Siggy pretty good. He's good at finding the big cedar Ern likes to use for his totem poles."

At that point, the door to the staff sergeant's office burst open and out walked Sherry with a smug smile plastered across her face, followed by Ernest, whose face, as per usual, was unreadable. His jacket was partially open. I noticed a thin black cord hanging from his neck with something greenish attached.

"Jeez, Ern," Jimmy said. "You don't think Siggy or Vinny could'a done it, do you?"

"No idea. But I did see Siggy this morning coming out of George's cabin where he usually stays when he's in town."

191

"Jeez."

"See, didn't I tell you they did it," Sherry piped up, giving the carver a stab in the ribs with her elbow.

Ernest winced. "Come on, Sherry, let me get you back to the hotel."

As I watched them leave, I wondered if the cops knew Ernest had told François to stand next to the pole and what they would read into it, if anything. Getting the police to focus their attention on someone else was one way of deflecting suspicion from oneself.

"Mesdames, you have something to tell me?"

"Sarge, before you get caught up, can I give you something?" Jimmy said. "The constable asked me to drop them off."

"What is it?"

"Last night's receipts." He brought out a thick envelope from inside his jacket. "I don't know why he wanted me to bring them. Maybe he thinks they have something to do with the case."

"Thanks, Jimmy. I'll give you a receipt." He scribbled on a piece of paper and passed it to the restaurant owner.

"Now, mesdames, could you please come into my office."

I was about to mention Ernest when Cloë, who had been watching the two through the front door, cried out, "Arrest him."

"What do you mean?"

"He killed my son."

"Why do you say that?"

"He's wearing my son's pendant, the one he was wearing when he died."

THIRTY-FOUR

The Fateful Voyage

His fingers were itching to cut into the wood, to feel the adze slice through the red cedar like a knife through the buttery flesh of a fat Coho, to carve the first curve of the story. But it had to wait. He had to be patient. One quick slice without thinking and the carving would be wrecked.

Some carvers could carry an image of the complete carving in their heads. They didn't need to draw it first along the length of the pole. He wasn't that skillful. He had to sketch the entire story to make sure the different figures flowed one into another with balance and harmony, the Haida way.

Besides, he hadn't figured out how to depict certain parts of the story, like this next bit. He'd wanted to ignore it, pretend it never happened, but he couldn't. It was too important. It was the beginning of the end.

Nanaay had told him the clan's troubles began when members of the Blue Shell Ravens came to Llnagaay in their big cedar canoes to attend a potlatch. They had just returned from a sea voyage of many days far to the south, to the mainland across from the Big Island. They were bragging about the strange yellow metal they'd seen. They said it glowed in the night and that the Iron Men considered it so valuable they would kill for it. They spoke of paddling to the mouth of a big river, to where many Iron Men were preparing to walk far into the mountains to find this glowing metal.

When Chief Blue Shell held a tiny pebble of the yellow metal up to the sun, everyone gasped at the sight of its brightness. After the Blue Shell Ravens left, Old Chief told the Greenstones that they would make the journey to this big river far to the south to get some of this yellow metal. They piled their massive dugout canoes high with otter skins to be used in trade. Old Chief knew the Iron Men valued these pelts almost as much as they valued the yellow metal.

Throughout the night, the carver tossed and turned trying to come up with a traditional Haida figure to depict this fateful voyage. Frustrated, he threw off his sleeping bag and walked in the waning moonlight along the beach beside the lapping waves, until the grey light of dawn spread across the sky. He was hoping the rhythms of nature would open his mind, but they didn't.

If Scav had been at his house in the neighbouring bay, he would've paddled over in the kayak. Scav was always full of good ideas. But Scav wasn't there. He'd gone north to Queen Charlotte a couple of days ago and was still there. He'd probably stuck around for the pole raising.

Even though there was no way he could witness the raising, he was sure curious to know how this false chief would behave. Would the Geek act with the dignity befitting Old Chief's title or would he grovel and squirm like the little man he was, the way his ancestor had grovelled and squirmed.

After he drank his morning tea and ate some of Scav's dried salmon, an idea for the design finally came to him. It was more like the log telling him, which was as it should be. He was running his hand over the wood below Old Chief's eagle when he sensed a sea otter with a ball of gold clenched between its paws. He'd been thinking of a killer whale, known for its ability to travel great distances. But it didn't fit with the story. A killer whale was supposed to be a symbol of good, but no good came from this journey.

The otter worked, even if it wasn't a traditional Haida crest. Old Chief and his men had taken their canoes filled with the rare pelts and had succeeded in trading them for gold. At least that was what Nanaay said. The otter spent most of its life in the sea, although it didn't travel great distances, not like a killer whale. But he figured it didn't matter. The pole had spoken. Besides, the sea otter was a symbol for family and loyalty. That was what this trip was about— loyalty to the family and to the clan.

Sliding his fingers over the smooth wood, he sketched out the ebb and flow of the otter in his mind. Flowing lines for the haunches and front paws, in which he placed the orb of gold in much the same way that a real sea otter holds an abalone shell he is trying to open. Mind you, he'd only seen this in pictures. Otters hadn't swum in these seas for over a hundred years, not since the Iron Men had killed them off for their pelts. Once the otter was carved, he would paint the orb a brilliant yellow, so there was no mistaking what it was supposed to be.

He took up his black marker and began sketching. He drew the otter's eyes as two ovoids, the Haida way for making animal eyes. He gave him a long tongue that stuck far out of his mouth. He wasn't sure what it meant, but he liked the effect and would paint it a bright red. Under one arm, he drew the outline of a bottle. He knew it wasn't a traditional Haida form, the same way that the picket fence in front of the otter's haunches wasn't traditional. But he needed these to tell the story. The picket fence would symbolize the Iron Man's river camp, where Old Chief's troubles began. He took the idea from one of the ancient poles still standing at a nearby village. People thought the picket fence that ringed the bottom of this pole stood for a chief's visit to Fort Victoria.

The bottle would symbolize the booze that led to his clan's shame. Nanaay said that when Old Chief landed with his men in their mighty canoes on the beach near the miner's camp, he made them stay in the boats to guard the pelts, while he went in search of gold. They stayed, so the story goes, until someone gave them a bottle of booze. After their first drink, they wanted more. And we still do, he snorted to himself.

When Old Chief returned, several of the clansmen were missing along with some of the pelts. Old Chief managed to round up all but two of his men. When they didn't return by the time the trading was finished, he left the men behind. Things were getting ugly in the camp and he didn't want anyone stealing their gold.

Despite how much he'd bugged Nanaay, she wouldn't tell him how much gold Old Chief brought back to Llnagaay nor what he did with it. She would only say that it was a clan secret but that if his destiny came to be, he would find out. But she died before he was ten. As for his destiny, Hah! That was a laugh. A failed fisherman. A drunken carver. Not exactly what she'd had in mind.

The night she first told him of the gold he went to bed dreaming about it and had dreamt about it many times since.

When he asked other clan members about the gold, he received mostly blank stares. One or two thought that it might have something to do with Old Chief's death. No one talked about it, because no one wanted to talk about the clan's shame.

He was outlining the last tooth in the otter's mouth when he heard a shout coming from the water. Although it sounded like Scav, he wasn't sure. Just in case it wasn't, he threw the green tarp over the pole and blended further into the trees. It couldn't be the cops. No way. The only one who knew he was here was Scav, and Scav wouldn't tell them. Scav hated cops almost as much as he did.

He worked his way toward the lagoon's beach, being careful to remain hidden behind the massive tree trunks. But when he heard the roar of a boat engine, he walked out onto the beach grinning. He'd know that sound anywhere. Sure enough, there stood the familiar figure in his bad-ass boat, long hair streaming out in the wind like it was a flag, his arm raised, his fist clenched in victory.

THIRTY-FIVE

The police sergeant raced out the front door and managed to flag down Ernest before he drove out of the parking lot.

"Have you caught the bastard?" Sherry yelled through the open window of the Range Rover.

"Ernest, something's come up. I would appreciate if you could come back into the detachment."

Sergeant Galarneau stopped a discrete distance away from the SUV. Although he appeared outwardly relaxed, I sensed him tense up as if preparing for the unexpected.

Sherry screwed up her face. "What do you want from Ern?"

The carver's face, no longer expressionless, appeared more confused than wary. Still, he hesitated before getting out of his vehicle.

"Ernest, this won't take long," the cop insisted. "I just have a few questions I want to ask you."

"About what?"

"I'll tell you inside. Now please get out of your vehicle." His hand rested on his hip, close to his holster.

Ernest glanced at Sherry and shrugged. He climbed out and stood next to the SUV.

"I want you to remove your hands from your pockets, then turn around and place them on the roof of your truck."

Ernest hesitated.

"Now!"

The carver shrugged, removed his hands, and held them up as if to say, "See, empty."

The cop grabbed Ernest by the arm, whisked him around and slammed his body against the side of the SUV. Cloë sucked in her breath.

"Hey, whaddya doing?" Sherry shouted. "Ern ain't done nothing. He wasn't even at the pole raising."

Ernest started to protest, but the sergeant yelled at him to keep quiet while he patted him down.

Finding no weapons, he said, "Okay, let's go into the station."

"Are you arresting me, sergeant?" Ernest asked.

"I just want to ask you a few questions. Now get moving."

"You can ask them out here."

"Ernest, I don't want to have to arrest you for obstruction, but I will if you won't come voluntarily into the police station."

"Look, I had nothing to do with Frank's death. I wasn't even there. In fact, I have an alibi."

"This has nothing to do with Monsieur Champagne."

"This is police harassment, that's what it is!" By now the carver's face was twisted in anger. "I'm going to press charges, Sergeant."

"Murderer!" Cloë shouted. "You killed my son, and I can prove it."

"Fuck."

"Are you going to go into the station willingly or do I have to arrest you?"

The carver held up his empty hands. "Okay, okay." The two of them started walking toward Cloë and me. We moved out of the way to let them pass, then followed them inside. Sherry climbed out of the Range Rover in her bare feet and pattered into the station behind us.

She nudged me. "Hey, did he really kill this lady's kid?"

"I've no idea, but Cloë seems to think so."

The sergeant led the carver toward a closed door. We followed. "I am sorry, mesdames, but you will have to stay here."

"But you need me to identify my son's medallion," my sister-in-law said.

He nodded in the direction of the chairs where we'd sat earlier, "Please sit over there, madame, and I will bring it to you."

He shut the door behind them with a resounding click.

"Jeez, I'm sorry," Sherry said to Cloë. "I didn't know your boy was killed. I guess we're kinda in the same boat, eh?"

"Hardly." Cloë stared straight ahead.

"Yah, well I guess you're right. It's not as if Bo-Bo and I were related. But he was the love of my life and I'm sure gonna miss him."

"As will his wife."

With these words Cloë succeeded in stopping the conversation.

Sherry shuffled in the chair on one side of me, while Eric's sister remained stonily still on the other side. I heard a few sniffles and realized the former mistress was crying. I patted her gently on her knee.

"I loved him. I really did."

"I know you did."

We sat in silence, while Sherry wiped her eyes.

"Wonder what he's doing to Ern," Sherry said. "Sure hope he ain't hurting him. Ern's not a bad guy."

"He's a bastard!" Cloë hissed.

At that moment the door to the office opened and the staff sergeant walked out dangling a Ziploc bag. He placed it on the counter. "Could you please come over here, Madame Zakharov, and see if you recognize this."

Sherry and I crowded in behind Cloë. Inside the bag lay a flat piece of jade with a thin braided cord strung through a small hole at the top. It wasn't large, about the size of a tablespoon, and very thin, like stones used for skipping. Apart from what appeared to be the faint outline of a Haida carving etched into its surface, the jade was as smooth as glass, as if from years of handling. The black cord, however, appeared new.

Cloë reached for the bag, but was stopped by the cop.

"Please, madame. Do not touch it. It could be evidence in your son's case. Tell me if this belonged to your son."

"It's his. See the silk cord is new. The old leather one broke about a month ago."

"Was he wearing it the night he was killed?"

"Yes, he was. At least I think so, because I didn't find it in his belongings."

"So you don't know for certain if he was wearing it or not."

"Of course he was. He always wore it, even when he showered. It was very precious to him. It once belonged to his birth mother."

"When was the last time you saw your son wearing it?"

"The morning before he was killed."

"Are you sure, madame?"

Her hands gripped the edge of the counter so hard her knuckles turned white.

"Of course. Why don't you believe me?"

"Because Ernest says that he found it on the floor of his carving shed a couple of days before the murder."

"He's lying. He took it off my son's body after he killed him."

"Ernest also says he has an alibi for the time of your son's death that has been confirmed by the Vancouver police. I believe that alibi is you, Madame Monahan."

"Wait a minute. You talking about that Indian kid that was killed in Ern's shed?"

"That's right, madame."

"Jeez, I didn't know that was your kid." She ran her eyes over Cloë's blond features as if trying to reconcile it with Allistair's darkness.

"He was adopted. His birth mother was Haida. But I've been his mother since he was a baby."

"Jeez, I'm real sorry. I wish I could help you find his killer. But it ain't Ern. He was having dinner with Frank and me."

"But the police told me that my son was killed between 11:00 p.m. and 2:00 a.m."

"Yeah, well, ah, Ern and I went off to a couple of clubs after. You know…. Besides, Frank had to go home to that wife of his and I wanted to party."

So much for true love.

I thought Cloë was going to spit on her. Instead, without another word, she turned and stormed out of the police station.

After a hasty apology to Sergeant Galarneau, I turned to run after her.

But the sergeant stopped me. "This won't be needed as evidence. Could you please give it to Madame Zakharov." He dropped the baggie containing Allistair's jade pendant into my hand.

As a parting shot, I said, "You might want to ask Sherry the name of the man who told her boyfriend to stand under the pole. Could be you can't rule out Ernest as a murderer completely."

Ernest glared at me, while Sherry stood back and scrutinized the carver carefully.

THIRTY-SIX

"Wait up," I shouted as I raced up the hill after Cloë. With my lungs burning and my heart pounding, I managed to catch up to her at the entrance to the Eagle's Nest parking lot.

"Sergeant Galarneau wanted me to give this to you." Gulping down great lungfuls of air, I held up the medallion.

She snatched it and clasped it to her breast. "My dear, sweet son." She kissed it. "I miss you so." With tears seeping from her closed eyes, she clenched it tightly. Then her anger returned. "That man knew it belonged to Allistair. Why didn't he return it to me?"

"Are you sure he knew?"

"He knew. He made a big deal about it one day when I was picking up Allistair."

"Maybe he forgot."

"Hardly. It was only a couple of months ago. He was examining it when I arrived and made some comment about it being very old. He told Allistair to take good care of it. Allistair asked him if he knew where it came from, but I don't remember him answering."

"Maybe someone at the Skidegate Band Office would know. Look, Eric's here. He can take us."

We backed out of the way as the blue Honda Civic turned into the parking lot and stopped.

Eric hopped out. "Out for a walk, ladies?"

"We were down at the police station," I said. "I thought you weren't coming back here before the pole raising."

"The men I hoped to talked to were busy. I came back to get my buckskin and then I'm off. Are you sure you two don't want to come? It looks like the rain might hold off for a while."

He glanced up at the clouds that were no longer one solid grey mass. I even spied a line of emerging blue above the mountain ridge to the west.

"Sorry," I answered, while Cloë simply shook her head. "How are your hands? Did you have any problem driving?"

He held up the bandaged palms and grinned. "They worked like a charm, but I'm glad the car's an automatic. Moving a stick back and forth would've been a touch painful."

"Cloë and I want to go to the Band Office to see if they know anything about the bracelet. Do you have it with you?"

He pulled it out of his jacket pocket and passed it to his sister. "I was going to ask around this afternoon. If the band office can't help, we can do it tonight at the potlatch."

Cloë kissed the cold silver and wrapped it around her wrist, probably for the same reason that prompted her to loop the pendant around her neck: to be close to her son.

"Since we only have one car, do you mind if I drop you off at the pole raising and come back later to get you?"

I glanced at his wet hair. His jeans didn't look too dry either. "You look a tad damp. You should dry off. You don't want to spend the rest of the afternoon outside in this cold wind with a wet head."

He squinched up his face. "Yes, Mummy." Then he sneezed.

"See, didn't I tell you."

He chuckled and sneezed again before blowing his nose loudly. But I felt this was more an act than a necessity. Still, he could be coming down with a cold. Serve him right for not putting his hood up.

"Cloë, you might want to change into some dry shoes."

A short while later, Cloë, wearing a pair of light hiking boots, and I were walking up the dirt path to the front door of a squat, white vinyl–sided building that looked more like a bungalow than an office. A bell tinkled when we opened the door, but it took several minutes before a gum-smacking teenager, her head bristling with red dyed spikes, bounced out of a back room. Her boobs jiggled with her energy, while her black T-shirt barely covered the quivering flesh overflowing the waistband of her jeans.

"Hi. Whaddya want?"

Cloë explained about the bracelet and pendant.

The girl hollered, "Cath, can you come out here! You maybe can figure out what these guys want. Somethin' about jewellery, eh? You know more about this stuff than I do."

An equally chunky but older woman, her abundant flesh more tightly cinched into jeans and a red sweatshirt sparkling with purple sequins, walked out of the same room. Her long black tresses flowed over her shoulders.

"What can I do for you, ladies?" The woman smiled. "Here on a holiday?"

"Sort of," I muttered while Cloë took off the bracelet and laid it on the counter. She removed the pendant from around her neck and placed it beside the bracelet.

"I'm wondering if you know who these pieces might have belonged to," she said.

The woman picked up the bracelet and ran her fingers over its carving and examined it carefully while the young woman picked up the pendant. "Awesome." She held it up the light. "Hey, it glows."

She was right. The jade had taken on an eerie green sheen.

"Where'd ya get this?" the older woman asked.

"From my son." Cloë went on to explain his history.

"So you saying his mother came from here?"

"I think so, but I don't know for certain. I only know that she was Haida."

"You don't know if she was eagle or raven?"

Before Cloë could answer, the woman answered the question herself. "She's gotta be eagle clan. Look at those eagles. You're saying it was hers."

"As was the pendant. They were found on her body."

The woman continued studying the bracelet. "It's Haida all right. I recognize the style." She ran her fingers over the inside. "See here, there are some markings. But they're too faint to read."

"Do they mean anything?" Cloë asked.

"It'll be the carver's mark. Nowadays they etch in their initials or name. But in the old days, they'd use their personal crest."

She rubbed her hands over the bracelet. "This is old. Don't think I've ever seen one this old. Used to make them out of melted down silver coins."

"Is there any way you can identify who it might have belonged to?"

"I don't know enough about these crests. One of the elders might know."

"We should ask Louise," I said to Cloë.

"If you're talking Louise O'Brien, she would know," the woman said. "She knows a lot about the old stuff. But wait a minute, here comes Flo. She might be able to help you."

A small, hunched over woman with grey hair, still clad in her red and black ceremonial button blanket, was struggling to open the door. I hastened to help her.

"Pole raising finished?" the woman asked as the elder stepped into the room.

The woman seemed a bit out of breath, so I slid a chair toward her. But she brushed it aside. "I'm okay. What's that you say, Cathy?"

"I asked if they finally got the pole raised," Cathy repeated in a louder voice.

The old woman nodded. "They did. It didn't take long with that fancy equipment. Should'a used it from the start. That poor, poor man. I'm so sorry for his family."

"Yes, a real tragedy," I said. "We were there this morning when it happened. In fact, he was staying at our lodge."

She turned to look at me. "What's that you say?"

I started to repeat it, but then thought it didn't matter, so instead just shouted, "A real tragedy."

She nodded. "I don't know what this is going to do to the *Hlgaa K' inhlgahl Xaaydaga*. It is a very bad beginning.

The shame continues …"

While she rambled on I noticed Cathy making sign motions to try to stop her talking. Finally the old woman noticed. She glanced at us, then back to Cathy, and nodded. "You're right. Best keep this to ourselves."

Her eyes alit on the bracelet. She reached up and grabbed it. "Where'd this come from?"

Cathy pointed to us.

"How d'you get it?"

Cloë tried to explain, but the elder misunderstood most of it. Cathy took over and finished by shouting. "They want to know if you know which clan it belongs to."

The elder peered into Cloë's face as if trying to see beyond her pale features. "Son Haida, eh?"

"Yes, his birth mother died when he was born."

"What was her name?"

"Mary was her first name. Do you recognize this bracelet?"

The old woman seemed to have no difficulties hearing Cloë now.

She closed her eyes as she continued to hold the bracelet. When she opened them, her gaze fell on the medallion. She reached for that. "What's this?" She turned back to Cloë. "This belonged to your son, too?"

"Yes, it also came from his birth mother."

Clasping both objects in her hands, she thrust them toward Cloë. "You take them and go back to where you come from. We don't want them here." Turning her back to us, she said to the teenager, "Carrie, take me home now. I'm tired."

"I'm sorry," I said, "if these items are causing you pain, but it is important that we let Allistair's Haida family know what happened to him and to his mother."

She whipped her head around. "They don't care. Now go."

I started to say more, but Eric's sister grabbed me by the arm and pulled me to the door. We stepped into a sudden downpour. The edge of blue had been only a teaser. The rain had returned with a vengeance.

"Why did you shut me up?" I asked once we were safely inside the car. The rain pounded against the windows and the car roof. "I think she knows who they belonged to."

"She's not going to tell us. No matter how much you pester her. Did you catch the faces of the other two women?"

"No."

"The minute that old woman started talking, their smiles disappeared and their faces clouded over. I've seen those same closed expressions before, on the carvers' faces whenever I came by Ernest's shed looking for Allistair. They hated me. They didn't want anything to do with me. These women don't want anything to do with us either."

I knew what she meant. During a couple of tumultuous times on Eric's reserve I had encountered the same stony faces from his people, people who a short time before had been my friends. In those moments, I knew that I had become the enemy. I never liked it. It made me feel ugly. But I knew that it had nothing to do with me, rather it had to do with who I was, a white woman, a member of the race who had changed their way of life forever.

I started up the car. "We'd better get Eric before he gets drenched again."

THIRTY-SEVEN

The Coward

He let out a war whoop when his brother told him. Served the jerk right. The matriarchs would never make him chief now, no matter how much money the geek had.

Too bad the kid was dead. But who would've thought he even existed? He sure hadn't thought his cousin had it in her. Yet she produced this boy, and a fine one at that. He would've made a good carver, too. He wondered where his cousin was now. Probably dead.

That's what happens when we turn our back on our clan. We become adrift, like a piece of timber floating in the sea. Then some big wave throws us onto a foreign shore, where, without the lifeblood of our roots, we slowly wither and die.

It sure happened to him. He was so upset by the loss of his boat he had to leave the islands. He went to Vancouver, where he got sucked into the booze and drugs. Half out of his mind, he wondered the streets of the Downtown Eastside looking for what, he didn't know. He never found it. It was the carving that found him. It brought him back to life, back to his roots, back to Haida Gwaii.

Bro wasn't so lucky. Although he never left the land of our people, he left us in his mind. He was trying too damn hard to be like a white man, and it wasn't working. It never would.

But enough of these crazy thoughts. He had to get back to the story. Time was running out. He wanted to make sure it was laid out on the pole from the beginning to its tragic end. So if he couldn't complete the carving, someone else could.

Bro had brought a bottle with him. But he needed to work, so he told him to take it over to Scav's and to wait there. It was great seeing his brother. It'd been a long time. But for now he needed to be alone. And he sure didn't need the booze. It would only mess with his head. But he'd be good and ready for a drink when he finished drawing this next part of the story.

Like Old Chief, he didn't have to think hard to come up with a crest for this guy. It had to be a raven to show the guy's clan. But he wouldn't make it a proud raven with its chest thrust out as if it owned the world. No way.

He took up his marker and drew the bird small, half the size of Old Chief's eagle, and hunched over like the coward Chief Blue Shell was. He outlined a short, blunt beak with a lopsided twist at the end. Though it wouldn't make the figure symmetrical like totem pole figures were supposed to be, he didn't care. Chief Blue Shell was a yellow-bellied bastard who didn't deserve the honour of harmony and balance.

Sure, clans fought. That was the Haida way. But they didn't sneak up on each other in the dead of night. No, they announced their arrival by banging their paddles on the sides of their canoes and shouting war cries before swooping down onto the village beach of their rivals.

But Chief Blue Shell and his men had snuck up Otter Inlet on the other side of the headland and had landed just as dusk was closing in. They were guided by the traitor along one of the secret trails known only to the Greenstones, a trail that took them up and over the mountain and down to the back end of the village, to where Old Chief's regalia was hidden in the only place where no Haida would dare go — the mortuary house. Though the Blue Shells were as terrified as the Greenstones were of the spirits guarding the dead, they had two men with them who weren't, two Iron Men who didn't think twice about entering the house filled with the rotting bones of the clan's dead and scattering them about in their search for the riches the drunken clansmen had bragged about when they waited by the big river for the gold.

He drew the raven's eyes sly and shifty and gave him a long skinny tongue, like a snake's. To remind everyone of the coward's terrible deed, he depicted the raven's talons clutching a bone with two bulbous ends. So there was no mistaking the identity of this raven, he outlined the Blue Shell clan crests, a frog and a sea lion, onto both of its wings. He wasn't going to let the Blue Shell Ravens pretend their long-ago chief was anything other than what he was: a coward who betrayed the Haida people when he helped the Iron Men.

THIRTY-EIGHT

"I can't accept these gifts, Eric. They make me feel very uncomfortable." I fingered the pair of intricately beaded earrings the new chief's mother had placed moments ago in my hands. She was handing a similar pair to a woman farther along our table.

"Just your protestant inhibitions taking over." He grinned. "Relax and enjoy them. It's the Haida way." He held up a woodcut print of an eagle, hummingbird, dogfish, and beaver intertwined and flowing one into the other. "Quite something, isn't it?"

I had one too. In fact, everyone at our table had been given the same print, as had the people sitting at the surrounding tables. "I think the figures are the crests of the Greenstone Eagles. They look similar to the ones carved into the totem pole."

"You're right." Becky held up hers. "And everyone gets one."

Caught up in official duties, Louise sat at a table several tables from ours, next to the head table where the new chief and Matriarch were seated.

"But there have to be over five hundred people here. That's a lot of prints."

"A lot of gifts, period." Eric pointed to a blue iPod nano and a small woven cedar basket lying next to his print. "And a lot of money invested in them. I can see why Harry didn't want to cancel the potlatch."

Becky was struggling to insert a dangly earring similar to mine, but without success.

"Here, let me help you." The silver wires slipped in easily. The red and silver beads shimmered as she shook her head, laughing. "They look very chic. They match your sweater perfectly."

Thinking my copper and black pair would compliment my new black dress nicely, I laid them on top of some fluffy teal blue towels, another potlatch gift.

"Eric, I can see you being given all these gifts because they probably consider you a V.I.P. And Becky, because she's a member of the community. But me? I'm just a mere wife. I don't deserve any of this. Besides, I ended up not witnessing the pole raising. I thought that was the purpose of these gifts."

Eric leaned over and kissed me on the cheek. "You're not a mere wife to me, nor are you a mere wife to the Haida. Remember, women rule here."

Becky raised a clenched fist into the air. "Yes!"

It was nice to see her enjoying the evening with little hint of the sadness that seemed to lurk in her eyes whenever I saw her.

"I suppose. But I still can't help feeling embarrassed by all this generosity. And I'm terrified we'll have to hold a potlatch to repay them."

"Not unless I decide to become a Haida chief," he said, chuckling. "Do you fancy wearing one of those button

215

blankets? I think you would look rather fetching. And you certainly have the shy retiring personality of a matriarch."

I punched him in the arm. "A totem pole is just the accent we need at Three Deer Point. It'll fit right in with the pine trees."

"Please, enjoy these gifts without feeling guilty," Becky said. "It's our tradition."

From the moment we arrived in the overcrowded community hall it had been a whirlwind of sights, sounds, and smells, starting with the ceremonial drum entrance of the Haida chiefs wearing elaborate headdresses and ornate blankets. The room burst into thunderous applause when the new Chief Greenstone entered accompanied by his mother, the new Matriarch.

This was followed by a brief ceremony, which looked a bit like a coronation as the Matriarch placed a curious-looking headdress on her son's head. Around the back and sides of this headdress dangled long white ermine tails topped by a ring of upright feathers, giving the headdress a crown-like appearance. The front piece appeared to be made of wood with a carving of an eagle sporting a menacing hooked beak. This eagle was edged on either side by a line of tiny objects that sparkled green under the brilliant lights of the hall.

"Are those emeralds?" I jokingly asked Becky.

"Wouldn't that be nice?" She laughed. "I imagine they are pieces of cut glass meant to represent the green stones of the clan."

"Is the clan really named after a green stone?"

"So our storytellers have told us. No one knows where the stone came from or even if it existed. You see, these islands don't have any rocks or minerals that are green, like jade or tourmaline."

"Or emeralds?"

"I wish." She laughed again. "According to our stories, a long-ago chief of the Greenstone Eagles brought some curious green stones home after a sea voyage to a distant land. He liked their pretty sparkle and placed them in his headdress and other items of his regalia. Traditionally we use abalone shell."

"So they could've been emeralds?"

"I suppose, but more likely they were just pieces of green glass like those in Harry's headdress. Harry commissioned an artist from Old Masset to make it for him."

"What happened to the regalia of that long-ago chief?"

"The story goes that the Matriarch at that time hid it in a secret location known only to her. The knowledge of this location was supposedly lost when the Matriarch died from smallpox. It happened long ago when the clan still lived at its hereditary village of Llnagaay."

"Would Louise know if it ever existed?"

"She might. But if it's still around, Harry would be wearing it. He is Chief Greenstone, whether she likes it or not. Besides, regalia that old wouldn't survive this long. Feathers, fur, and wood don't age well unless they're kept in optimum conditions, and my people never worried about that. With such a plentiful supply of materials, things could easily be replaced."

"Except for green stones."

Her brown eyes twinkled. "If they were made of glass, replacement is easy, as you can see with Harry's headdress."

I rather liked the idea of emeralds. It appealed to my sense of romance. I would continue to think of the ancient green stones as emeralds lost in a secret location where the Greenstones used to live.

"There've been stories of men nosing around Llnagaay searching for treasure, so some people thought they were more than just glass," she continued.

"Did anyone ever find them?"

"Not that I know of. But if someone did, they wouldn't exactly broadcast it."

I thought of the piece of green stone I'd seen only a few hours ago, and was about to ask Becky about Allistair's pendant when someone tapped a microphone to say Chief Greenstone was about to speak, ending further conversation.

Harry started off by welcoming everyone to the potlatch. Next he pledged his allegiance to his clan as their chief and to the Haida Nation. He finished with one minute of silence in the memory of François Champagne. At a nearby table, I saw Sherry wipe away tears with one hand while the other clung to Ernest, who was sitting beside her. It would appear that the carver wasn't high on her suspect list.

Although Eric had already shown Allistair's bracelet to a number of people, no one had yet identified it. While most commented on its age and the high quality of workmanship, a couple of the older women and an old man reacted much like Flo had. Their expressions went blank and they insisted that we keep it out of sight. One of the women went so far as to say the bracelet was cursed. But they refused to tell us who it had once belonged to. Cursed or not, we needed to know. I was holding out for Louise, but we couldn't show her the bracelet until the end of the potlatch.

Thunderous drumming accompanied by boisterous clapping and shouting announced the arrival of the dancers. A swirl of sea, avian, and forest creatures sporting flying capes and brilliantly coloured masks with jutting beaks and snouts and threatening eyes cavorted into the hall. After several raucous dance sets, the dancers were joined by others, including Eric dragging a reluctant me. Within minutes the two of us were hopping and gyrating with the best of them and I found myself enjoying the hoopla. Someone even plunked a cedar hat onto my head.

The delicious aromas wafting from the mounds of food arriving into the hall sent us back to our table. There we remained for the rest of the evening, feasting on the bounty of the Haida Gwaii seas. I particularly liked the Haida delicacy of strips of dried salmon and kelp covered in herring roe and dipped in warm oolichan oil.

Feeling very replete, I sank back into my chair to savour the last of evening. But the sound of scraping chairs soon filled the hall, as people headed to the exits laden with gifts.

"It looks like the potlatch is over," I said to Eric. "Maybe we'd better grab Louise before she leaves, to see if she can identify the bracelet."

After piling our gifts into a bag Becky had given us, we started over to Louise's table.

But before we reached her, loud shouting broke out behind us.

I turned around and saw Sherry. She was yelling, "Arrest that guy!"

She was pointing directly at the skinny man with the braided beard who had spat on François, the man whose name I now knew was Siggy.

219

THIRTY-NINE

"Eric, we should do something."

More and more heads were turning to look at the shrieking Sherry, who was half-hidden by the craning necks in front of us.

"He killed my Bo-Bo!"

Siggy, the man she was screaming at, tugged thoughtfully at the tail of his braided beard. He didn't appear the least bit upset by her accusation. He said something to the hysterical woman before turning on his heels and striding away. Her yelling went up several decibels. I figured it was nothing complimentary.

"Do you think he did it?" Eric asked, pushing his way through the crowd. I clung to his arm to avoid being swallowed up.

"I've no idea. But if he were guilty, you'd think he wouldn't show his face where he's probably known by most of the people in this room. Excuse me." I jostled with a man who'd just stepped in my way. "Besides, she accused him in front of the police. So if he really is a suspect, surely they'd have him behind bars."

"Someone grab him! Pleaaase!" Sherry hollered.

Although I could no longer see her, I could hear her heels clattering along the floor.

"Christ," Eric muttered at the same time as I heard something land on the floor with a thud.

"I've got him," a gruff male voice shouted.

Eric bent down. The people in front of me parted to reveal a disheveled Sherry sprawled out on the floor, her short leather skirt pushed up to reveal her nether regions, barely covered by a thong.

"Are you okay?" Eric asked reaching down to help her up.

"I'm fine. Just get that man," she shot back, not bothering to pull her skirt down. I watched her give Eric one of those challenging looks that dared him to ogle her.

I hastily intervened. "I'll help her, you go after Siggy." The first thing I did was tug her skirt down. Then with the aid of another woman, we helped her to her feet.

"Ouch!" she shrieked as she hopped on one foot. "Goddamn it, I've twisted my ankle."

Someone passed her a chair. She collapsed into it with a groan and started rubbing her sore ankle. "Did they get the bastard? He killed my Bo-Bo."

The crowd moved back to reveal Eric walking back to us. Although he strode with determination, I noticed a faint twinkle in his grey eyes, almost as if he were trying to keep himself from laughing. Next to him ambled Siggy. The two men were about the same height, but Siggy was much slimmer, almost too thin. His jeans and flannel shirt hung loosely from his slightly stooped frame, while his belt was cinched in as far as it could go. His weathered face was creased in a broad, gap-filled grin. With his straggly long hair and curious beard, he looked more like an aging hippy than a former logger.

On the other side of Siggy strode the RCMP officer from the detachment, a tad shorter than the other two, but his girth considerably wider. I barely recognized Staff Sergeant Galarneau in his potlatch attire: pressed jeans, crisp button-down shirt partially hidden by a vest resplendent with Haida creatures. A traditional headband edged in fur ringed his short-cropped hair. He, too, looked as if he was sharing in the joke.

I started to ask them what was so funny, but was stopped by Sherry. "Where're the handcuffs? Isn't that what you do with prisoners?" she rasped.

Before Galarneau could answer, another voice interjected. "Is this the man that ruined my pole raising?"

Harry strode over with the confidence of a new chief. Although he no longer wore his headdress, he still appeared very regal in his button blanket. His mother had remained standing in front of the head table, arms crossed over the shelf of her bosom, her lips firmed in a smug grin. Behind me I heard restless stirrings and whispered exchanges.

"Please, everyone, calm down." Sergeant Galarneau held up his hands.

Harry walked up to the suspect. "You're Siegfried de Jong, aren't you?" He stood back and surveyed the glibly smiling hippy. "I don't get it. What do you have against me that you would want to ruin my pole raising?"

Siggy ran his eyes up and down his accuser. He curled his lip in derision and answered with a grunt, neither confirming nor denying the accusation.

"Please," Sergeant Galarneau said, "I'm sure you both have good cause to accuse Siggy of cutting the ropes, but he didn't do it. He has an alibi, which I have verified. There's no way he could've cut the ropes that killed Monsieur Champagne."

"That is correct, *mijn vrouw*." He bowed at Sherry while completely ignoring Harry. "I had drunk too much beer and spent the night passed out at the house of my friend. I could not have cut this rope." He tugged at the thin braid of his beard, which was strung with three wooden beads — a red one, a yellow, and a blue. "I may have hated your husband, but I did not want him dead. Please accept my condolences." He gave her another bow. If he'd had a hat on his head, I swear he would've doffed it in troubadour fashion.

"You're lying. I bet your friend is covering for you."

"Think about it, *mijn vrouw*. If I had wanted to kill your husband, I would have chosen a method more direct like a gun. Hoping for a totem pole to fall on an intended victim does seem a little too much like Russian roulette. I prefer more certain methods."

"He is right, madame," the policeman offered. "It is more likely that Monsieur Champagne's death is a result of a tragic accident."

"But you said someone cut those ropes."

"Yes, our evidence suggests this is the case."

"So if this guy didn't do it, who did?"

"Someone who wanted to embarrass me," Harry interjected. "And we all know who that is."

Sherry turned to the policeman "So if you know who it is, why haven't you got the guy?"

"Harry, are you referring to Johnnie Smith?" the policeman asked.

"Yup, my useless cousin. You saw what he did this morning."

The cop nodded. "Do you have any evidence that he cut the ropes?"

"Ask Denny. He saw him lurking around the carving shed yesterday, near where they were storing the ropes. He could've done it then."

"He didn't do it," said a new voice. I turned to see Louise approaching. "My nephew would never harm anyone."

Harry and Sergeant Galarneau exchanged glances before the policeman said, "*Bonsoir, madame*. You are looking very nice in your regalia. This must be a very proud moment for you. Finally you have a Chief Greenstone."

"Thank you, Jean-Louis. It is a wonderful moment for my clan. But I tell you, Johnnie didn't do this. He would never do anything that could hurt someone."

"That may be so, madame. But you can't deny that he was pretty hostile to Harry this morning."

"Yes, I know. He should never have done that. And I apologize for him." She paused. "You're the policeman. Do what you think is right."

He nodded grimly. "Harry, a word with you."

The two men disappeared through the crowd, their heads slanted toward each other in conversation. Siggy, on the other hand, after bowing once again at Sherry, strode away whistling in the opposite direction.

FORTY

"I like Siggy's beard decorations," I said to Louise. "Except the colours clash with his orange shirt." The ring of her laughter belied the exhaustion in her face. But she brushed aside the chair I offered with a dismissive wave.

"A lot of curious people wash up on our shores. We have our share of hippies, draft dodgers, escape-to-nature types, all wanting to get as far from their own world as possible. Most came in the late 1960s and '70s and set themselves up as homesteaders, though not many of them live out in the bush today. It's pretty tough living off the land ... unless you're Haida. Mind you, not many of us doing that either. We love our modern conveniences too much." Her laughter rang out again.

"Where's Siggy from?"

"I think he's Dutch. He's been on these islands a long time. We don't see him much in Skidegate. He pretty much sticks to himself on that property he's got way down on the south end of Moresby Island. I've never been there myself, but my nephew says it's a strange place, an old abandoned whaling station. It's not far from Llnagaay."

Eric yawned. "Man, I'm tired. It's been a long day. I think I'll sit down. Why don't you join me, Louise?"

This time she didn't hesitate to collapse into a chair. Trust Eric to come up with a way to overcome her pride. Exhausted myself, I slumped into the chair beside her.

"Do you visit your ancestral village much?" he asked.

"I haven't been there in years. When the kids were young, I and my family and my sister's used to visit it once a year to remind our kids of their roots. We tried to do what we could to keep the few remaining poles from falling over, but it was a losing battle. Eventually we let the moss, wind, and rain return them to Mother Earth. I imagine there isn't much left of the village today." She sighed.

"In its day Llnagaay was one of the most important villages in Haida Gwaii. I've seen photos taken from around the time of Old Chief. There must have been more than twenty-five longhouses with a good thirty or more poles of all varieties. I think Old Chief had at least five in front of his longhouse, which, of course, was the largest." She grinned. "Our chiefs always had to have the biggest and most of anything. We're a competitive lot, we Haida."

"No different from other peoples I know." Eric chuckled. "It looks as if the potlatch has wound down. Can we drive you home?"

Apart from twenty or so people cleaning up, the hall was empty. Many of the tables and chairs were already stacked against a far wall.

"Thanks, Eric, but Becky promised to take me. Here she comes now."

We watched the long-legged young woman approach, her satiny hair swinging to the rhythm of her confident stride, her new earrings dancing. She held a basket overflowing with potlatch gifts.

"You ready, Auntie?" she asked. "Wonderful potlatch, wasn't it? Especially when you consider how badly things started out. I think Harry behaved very respectfully, don't you? He'll make a good Chief Greenstone."

"I'm sure he will, child. Still, until we find out who cut those ropes, we will always have that stain on our clan."

Louise started to get up.

"Wait, we almost forgot," I said, suddenly remembering. "We have a bracelet we're hoping you might be able to identify."

"That's right." Eric withdrew the gleaming silver bracelet from his jacket pocket and held it out to Louise.

Becky sucked in her breath. "That's Allistair's. I recognize the eagle and salmon design. In fact, Auntie, now that I—"

"Where did you get this?" Louise cut in. She appeared shaken, her face stark with shock. I could see her aching to touch the bracelet, but something was preventing her.

"It belonged to my boyfriend." The young woman didn't hesitate to pick it up. She ran her fingers over the cold metal and kissed it. "This is the bracelet we had the fight over. If only I had accepted it … he wouldn't have gone to the carving shed and …" Her voice faded, while her tears covered the bracelet's eagle.

Louise's lower lip trembled. "Please, tell me where you got this."

"Are you sure you're feeling okay?" I was worried by her sudden frailty.

"Don't worry about me. Just tell me where it came from."

"Like Becky said, it belonged to Allistair, my sister's adopted son," Eric answered. "It once belonged to his birth mother. You recognize it, don't you?"

"Yes." Her voice was barely above a whisper. "It was mine."

"Did Allistair's birth mother steal it?" he asked.

"May I touch it?"

Becky gently placed the bracelet into the elderly woman's hands. This time she didn't hesitate to run her trembling fingers over the gleaming silver. As Becky had done, she brought it to her lips and kissed it.

"The mother may have been my daughter."

"You had a daughter?" Amazement washed over Becky's face. "What happened to her?"

"She left her homeland a long time ago, before you were born, child. She was a year younger than you are now and the youngest of my three children. She was my little angel."

"But you've never talked about her. I've never seen a photo of her anywhere in your house."

Louise remained silent, her eyes glistening with tears. She continued to stroke the bracelet.

"Lizzie was my dear sweet little girl. After two sons, I was thrilled to finally have a daughter who could follow me as Matriarch. When she was young she absorbed all things Haida. She was a model child. But when she hit her teenage years everything changed. She spurned me and her Haida roots. She took up with a bad crowd and started drinking. I think she might have even tried drugs. There was nothing her father or I could do. Any attempts we made to help her only seem to make her behaviour worse. One day she was here; the next she was gone. We never saw her again." She stopped and closed her eyes as if grappling with long-suppressed emotions.

"She disappeared at about the same time as a sailboat that had been docked for a couple of weeks at Queen Charlotte. We discovered that she had been spending her nights with the owner and his two friends. When the police eventually located the boat on Vancouver Island, the owner vowed that my daughter had gone willingly with them and left the boat when they reached the island. The police were never able to prove otherwise.

"Thinking that she would probably go to a city, my husband made several trips to Victoria and Vancouver, but never found her. A couple of years later, our marriage died. He blamed me and wouldn't let me forget it. I've never forgiven myself either. If only I hadn't been so hard on her." She shook her head. "I was a bad mother."

"Please, Auntie, don't say that. You've been like a mother to me, a wonderful mother." She bent over and kissed her on the cheek.

"Don't blame yourself, Louise. These things happen," Eric added, glancing in my direction.

"They sure do," I agreed. "My mother and I didn't get along either, but I realize now that neither of us was to blame. We just have conflicting personalities. I imagine that was probably the case with you and your daughter."

Conflicting personalities was putting it mildly. We'd been like oil and vinegar. Mother never stopped haranguing me and I never stopped shouting back at her. In fact, my ultimate solution had been to run away, though she wasn't the only reason for my leaving

Toronto. Still, even though I stayed away from her for a good five years, she knew I was alive and well and living at Three Deer Point. She'd hammered the good daughter too far into me. I'd dutifully kept in touch with pro forma phone calls.

"I guess your daughter was wearing the bracelet when she left," I said.

Louise nodded. "The bracelet disappeared at the same time she did. I figured she'd taken it to sell for drugs. Though I'd always wondered why she didn't take my wallet at the same time."

"If it's any comfort, she didn't sell it. She was wearing it …" I paused, hesitating to tell her. But surely she suspected. "When she died."

She sighed. "Although I hoped and prayed life had turned out well for Lizzie, deep down inside I knew as only a mother can know. When she didn't contact us or anyone else in our community, I suspected she was dead, either killed by those men on the boat or later from too much drinking or a drug overdose." She kissed the bracelet again, then placed it carefully around her wrist and patted it as if saying "welcome home."

"Please, can you tell me what you know about her?"

Eric told her what little we knew of her tragic death. Although he left out the part about her being a prostitute, Louise filled that in for herself. "There is only one way a young native woman with no high school diploma and an addiction can keep herself in alcohol and drugs, and that's on her back." She shuddered. "My poor angel. But she left the gift of life. Please tell me about my grandson."

"You should hear it from my sister, who loved him as if he were her own," Eric said. "It's getting late, Louise, and you look tired. I can bring Cloë over to your place first thing tomorrow morning."

"Yes, it's been a very difficult and long day. But I need to know something else. Another family valuable disappeared with my daughter. A pendant made from a green stone. Do you know if my daughter had it with her when she died?"

FORTY-ONE

There was no changing the elderly matriarch's mind. Though she was almost keeling over from exhaustion and needed Eric's sturdy arm to guide her to our rental car, she was determined to visit Cloë right away.

"Why is this pendant so important that it can't wait until morning?" I asked, once we had loaded ourselves into the Honda. It was closing in on midnight and we were all struggling to keep our eyes open.

"Does it have any carving on it?" she asked, ignoring my question.

The road was wet from a recent rainfall, but the sky was clearing, with stars glinting intermittently through the scudding clouds. A gale-force wind buffeted the car as we rounded a bend. In the side-view mirror, I watched the headlights of Becky's father's truck waver behind us as it caught the same gust.

"Yes, but it's quite faint."

"Are there any markings on the back?"

"I didn't look. Do you know what the greenstone is? Is it jade?"

"I suppose it could be. I never thought about it. We've

always called it *hlgaa k' inhlgahl*, meaning 'greenstone.'"

"Is your clan named after this greenstone?"

"No. The name is much older."

"Why is the pendant so important?" I asked again.

"The greenstone has been in my family a very long time. It goes back to the time of Old Chief and has been passed down from Matriarch to Matriarch. The bracelet is more recent. My grandmother's father made it for her mother out of silver coins. Curiously, he carved the old Greenstone Eagle crests into it: the eagle, salmon, beaver, and frog. The man who became Chief Greenstone after Old Chief changed the clan crests to the ones you saw on the new totem pole."

"Why did he change them?"

"As much as Old Chief was admired in his day, he suffered a terrible shame before he died. His nephew who took over didn't want to be reminded of this shame."

"Is that why several elders who saw the bracelet today refused to have anything to do with it?"

"Unfortunately we Haida have long memories. Events of long ago, particularly shameful ones, aren't easily forgotten … or forgiven."

Cloë's bedroom window was dark as we drove up to the main lodge.

"Eric, it looks like Cloë's asleep. She was pretty tired. Do we really want to wake her up?"

"Please do," Louise replied. "It won't take long. I just want to know the greenstone is safe."

It had been a good twenty years or more since she'd seen the pendant, surely she could wait another day. Her persistence begged the question, if it was so important, why hadn't she moved heaven and earth to find it along with her daughter?

"I'll nip inside and get it from her, while you two stay here, okay?" I suggested.

"You'll need this." Eric passed me the front door key.

I signalled for Becky to park behind us and wait with Eric and Louise.

Feeling more lead-footed than fleet of foot, I tramped up the stairs to the front door. The wind had managed to push most of the clouds from the sky, revealing a tableau crowded with a trillion dots of light. Far below, the running lights of a boat chugged through the channel toward the docks. Even in the lee of the building, the wind still managed to whip my hair into a frizzy frenzy.

When I placed the key in the lock, the door creaked open. Figuring the last person had forgotten to shut it tightly, I crept inside and gave the door an extra push to ensure it remained closed. I could hear a television in one of the rooms on the same floor; otherwise, the place was as any hotel would be after midnight, deathly still.

A brass lamp at the far end of the sitting room provided enough light for me to see my way to the stairs leading up to Cloë's floor. Two of the three doors on the second-floor landing were firmly closed and there was loud snoring coming from one of the rooms. But the door to Cloë's room was partially open, which made no sense. Surely she would keep it locked.

"Cloë, you awake?" I whispered, pushing the door open farther.

Was she even here?

Maybe she couldn't sleep and had gone for a walk or was waiting for us in our cottage? But surely she would've locked the door … unless she'd been too upset to care.

Worried, I gingerly pressed the door open wider and the landing light poured into the dark room. "Cloë, it's me, Meg," I whispered.

Cloë was here. I could make out her shape under the thickness of the white duvet, her long hair sprawled over the pillow. So why was the door open? Had someone been in her room? I glanced around nervously, but nothing appeared disturbed, nor were there any shapes that didn't belong.

"Cloë, wake up. I have something important to tell you."

I tiptoed to the bed, expecting her to wake up at any moment. But other than the steady rise and fall of her breathing, she remained motionless. I hesitated touching her, in case I scared her.

I ran my eyes over the surface of the night table and chest of drawers, hoping to see the medallion but failing to spot it in the dim light. My fingers touched her earrings and a couple of rings and felt the buttery softness of her leather purse, but they didn't feel the coldness of the stone. Last time I'd seen her, she was wearing the pendant. Maybe she wanted to continue to feel the memory of her son close to her skin. I would have to wake her.

I touched the shoulder peeking out from under the duvet. "Cloë, wake up."

No response.

I shook her gently.

Still no response.

I noticed a dark splotch on the white pillowcase next to her head and reached out a hand to touch it. It felt sticky.

When I held my fingers up to the landing light, I saw blood.

I shook Cloë more vigorously. "Come on, wake up!"

I grabbed the phone on her night table and dialed 911.

With the promise that the police and ambulance would be here within minutes, I ran back outside to Eric.

"Something terrible has happened to your sister. You'd better come inside."

Before he had a chance to ask me what was wrong, I was racing back up to her room with him clambering up the stairs behind me.

"Slow down, Meg, and tell me what's going on."

"I don't know whether she's been shot or what, but look at all the blood."

He snapped the light on beside the bed and leaned over his sister. He held his hand to her forehead and felt the pulse at the side of her neck. "She's alive. Thank God. Cloë, can you hear me?"

He gingerly turned her head one way, then the other. "I don't think she's been shot." He patted his fingers gently over her scalp and stopped near the top of her head. "I feel the wound here."

Blood clung to his fingertips.

The rising sound of sirens cut the stillness of the night.

Cloë groaned. Her eyes fluttered open.

"Are you okay?" Eric asked.

"God, my head hurts." She reached up to the spot Eric had found. "What happened?" She struggled to get up.

"Leave her alone. The girl needs time to collect her wits." Louise, her breathing heavy, pushed her way around us and gently settled Eric's sister back down on the bed. "Does it hurt anywhere else, child?"

Directly behind her, Becky shrugged as if to say "I tried to stop her."

"No, just my head. What time is it? It's still night, isn't it? What's everyone doing here?" She tried to sit up again, but Louise, sitting on the bed beside her, kept a hand firmly on her shoulder, forcing her to remain down.

The sirens drew close and stopped.

"It's best you stay lying down. That nasty bump on your head might make you dizzy," Louise said.

"I remember," Cloë said. "It's coming back. I woke up and someone was in my room. He, I think it was a he, was rummaging through my things on the night table. I could see a pinpoint of light shining on my rings. I must've made a noise because he turned the light on me. Then everything went black. Are the rings still there? One of them is my diamond engagement ring."

"Yes, they are," Eric said. "So you didn't recognize him?"

"It was too dark. I just remember a black shape leaning over the table."

"I know what he hit you with." I pointed my toe at a slender black object about twenty-five centimetres long lying on the carpet.

"It looks like an argillite totem pole," Louise said. "That could give you a nasty bump."

She started to reach down to pick it up, when a voice from the landing yelled, "Don't touch that!"

In walked Staff Sergeant Galarneau, and behind him two paramedics.

"Good evening, *messieur-dames*. Please move away from the victim and let these paramedics do their job. And don't touch anything, okay?"

As one of the paramedics leaned over Cloë, she suddenly brought her hand to her neck. "It's gone," she cried out. "My son's pendant is gone!"

FORTY-TWO

Time Is Running Out

He felt goddamn awful. He should've never drunk that bottle last night. Cheap booze'd do it every time. Made you feel like crap. But he could never convince Bro to spend the extra bucks for some good stuff. Still, it was as much his fault as his brother's. He knew it was rotgut stuff and yet he downed almost a full bottle on his own.

He sure didn't feel like doing any drawing today. No way. His hand shook too much and the hammers pounding away in his head made thinking hurt. While the booze had dulled the pain last night, it was in full flare this morning.

Hell, Bro was still passed out on the ground where he'd fallen at whatever hour of the morning they finally finished the two bottles. Even the downpour hadn't woken him up, although he looked pretty well dried out now, except for his arm lying in a pool of water.

He poured what was left in the cold teapot into his mug, swished yesterday's tea around his mouth and spat it out. Tasted like hell; but at least it got rid of the booze taste. He should make a new pot, but no way he felt like going through the effort of lighting the stove. He swirled more tea around his mouth and spewed it out onto the ants crowding around the last splotch of tea. Weren't fussy eaters, were they?

He must've slept in a bad position. His back hurt like hell. No way he could spend the day bent over the log, drawing. But time was running out. He had to get this story finished before they came for him. From the way Bro talked last night, it could be any day.

Some big-time Vancouver cop had arrived in Queen Charlotte and was now working with the RCMP. They'd tracked him to Haida Gwaii. They just didn't have a name yet. But he figured it wouldn't take long for them to put two and two together and come up with his. So he had to finish the drawing. Then he had to find someone to carve it, because one thing was for sure, he wasn't going to get to do it himself. He knew just the carver. He figured when the guy recognized the story in the drawing, he'd do his damndest to carve it into the kind of pole the storytellers would talk about for years.

But he couldn't do any drawing until he had a couple more hours of sleep. By then his hand wouldn't be shaking so much, the crick in his back should be gone, and the pounding in his head stopped. As for the pain, it wasn't leaving anytime soon, but he was learning to live with it.

His mind also needed to be alert, for it was going to be a challenge to come up with the right figures for this next part of the story.

FORTY-THREE

By the time we were finished with the police and were waiting for the doctor to finish examining Cloë, the faint light of dawn was creeping through the hospital windows.

Louise and Becky hadn't come to the hospital. Visibly upset by the pendant's theft, the matriarch had said little other than a few muttered words in Haida. Something about the shame continuing, Becky whispered. When I tried to question the elderly woman, she brushed me aside and insisted that Becky take her home immediately.

She wouldn't even talk to the police about it. She dismissed their questioning by insisting the stolen pendant couldn't be the greenstone that had once belonged to her clan. Though how she would know this without having seen it, I had no idea.

Despite her denial, I was convinced it was her family pendant and she didn't want the police knowing. I decided to go see her once we were sure Cloë was going to be okay. I would take Eric with me and let him charm the answer out of her. If it was her family heirloom, she might know who would have wanted it so badly that they hadn't hesitated to knock Cloë out in order to steal it. It certainly wasn't stolen for its monetary worth; otherwise the far more valuable rings would've been taken. Nope, it was stolen for another reason, and Louise knew what that reason was.

After a thorough examination, Eric's sister was declared well enough to return to the hotel. The doctor believed she had a mild concussion, but would suffer no ill effects other than some nausea and a bad headache. However, if these symptoms persisted or the headache grew worse, she was to return immediately.

Eric carefully loaded his sister into the backseat and we drove slowly back to the Eagle's Nest, into the red streaks of the sun rising over the mountains.

It was only when we reached the lodge that I remembered: "Shit, we've missed our flight! It leaves in an hour. There's no way we can catch it now."

"Yeah, I know. I thought of it as we were leaving the hospital." Eric smiled wryly. "But we can't leave my sister here on her own. I'll let the guy know I can't make the interview."

"He'll just postpone it, won't he?"

"I doubt it. CBC was wanting to tie it in with some special they're doing the next day on Aboriginal housing."

"Oh, Eric, I'm so sorry. It would've given your campaign for Grand Chief a big boost."

"Yeah, well, you can't win them all." He sighed.

I leaned over and hugged him as best as I could with a steering wheel in the way.

I heard Cloë stir behind us. She'd fallen asleep the minute we'd tucked her into the backseat.

"Cloë, you awake? We're here," I said. "How are you feeling?"

"Not good. My head feels like crap."

"Hopefully after a good sleep, you'll feel better," Eric said. "We'll get you up to your room and Meg'll stay with you as a precaution, okay?"

Together, the two of us half-carried, half-supported Cloë up the two flights of stairs to her room, where we gently laid her down on her bed, but not before replacing the bloody pillow with a clean one. After kissing Eric goodbye, I laid down beside her. I swear I was asleep before I felt the softness of the pillow under my head.

I awoke to a tap on the door and tiptoed over to find Eric on the other side. His eyes filled with sleep, he was trying to suppress a yawn.

He gave me a gentle kiss and said, "It's after two in the afternoon. I figured I'd better check on you guys to make sure you're still alive."

"You barely look alive yourself. Did you sleep?"

"Like the dead, but I tell you, Meg, I'm getting too old for these all-nighters. Long gone are the days when I'd party all night and head off to hockey practice without a wink of sleep."

"What about the interview?"

"They're going to look for someone else, but the producer said they'd keep me in mind for next time."

"I'm sorry, but I don't know what else you could've done. What about flights?"

"I've changed them to Wednesday. I figure we should give Cloë a couple of days to make sure she's going to be okay." He nodded in her direction. "How's she doing?"

"As far as I know she slept soundly, but maybe I'd better wake her up, as the doctor suggested, to make sure she is just sleeping."

"I'm awake," came a weak voice from the bed. "God, I feel awful. My head won't stop pounding."

I tensed. "Is your headache worse?"

She gingerly patted the bandage where it covered the wound. Her once perfect hair was a snarl of tangles and kinks under the layers of gauze.

"No … I don't think so." She struggled to get up, but only made it half way before dropping back onto the pillow. "I'm dizzy too."

"Do you feel nauseated?"

"No … not really."

"Do you want to go back to emergency in case there's any swelling?"

"It's not that bad. I'll be okay if I stay in bed."

"Are you hungry?" Eric asked. "I was just going to ask Meg if she wanted to get something to eat. We could bring something back for you."

Food. Good. I was starved.

"I'm not that hungry, but a bit of soup might be good." She pulled the duvet up to her chin, closed her eyes, and within seconds her breathing had taken on the regular rhythm of sleep.

A couple of hours later, Eric and I returned, both of us feeling considerably rejuvenated after a sumptuous meal of Jimmy's special fish and chips made from fresh haddock. Eric carried a paper bag containing the chef's special homemade chicken noodle soup and a beef and tomato sandwich — not the fresh salmon and dill sandwich the chef had wanted to make until I mentioned my sister-in-law's aversion to fish.

Cloë was propped against a pile of pillows, reading. She had regained some colour in her cheeks.

"Good, you're awake." I took the bag from Eric and placed it on the dresser. "You must be feeling better."

"I am. The headache's not quite so bad and the dizziness has gone. I hope you brought something good. I'm famished."

I removed the lid of the soup container and passed it to her, along with a metal spoon, which Jimmy had given us with the proviso that we return it. He'd also given us a china bowl to serve it in, but I decided the Styrofoam container was easier. "It's still pretty hot, so be careful."

She'd made an attempt at untangling her hair, but with the gauze covering much of her head, it was nearly impossible. Nonetheless, the hair surrounding her face appeared less unruly.

"This tastes wonderful." She smiled.

"Maybe we should've brought you more food," Eric said.

"This will be fine. Thanks for bringing it." Without another word she finished the soup and demolished the sandwich.

This was the first time I'd seen her eat so quickly and so completely. Normally she left food on her plate. "Nothing wrong with your appetite."

"Nope, I'm feeling a lot better. " With a sigh, she leaned back into the pillows. "While you were at the potlatch last night, one of the RCMP officers dropped by. They've finally identified Allistair's killer."

"That's good news," Eric said. "Have they arrested him?"

"Not yet, but he said shortly."

"Is it the man that stole the totem pole?"

"He didn't say, but I assume so."

"Did he give you a name?"

"No, the cop just said that the man was Haida, but that he hadn't spent much time on the islands in recent years."

"But he's here now?" I asked.

"Yes."

"Do they know where he is?"

"Not yet, but they're narrowing down the places where he could be hiding."

"Given the hundreds of uninhabited islands, I think it would be worse than trying to find the proverbial needle in a haystack," Eric said.

"Constable Murray seemed pretty confident."

"I hate to dash your hopes, Sis, but I imagine if the guy is used to living off the land, he could hide out for years."

"Maybe I'll rent a helicopter and go looking for him."

"A helicopter isn't exactly quiet." I wasn't sure how serious she was, but thought it best to dampen her enthusiasm. "The guy would run for cover the second he heard it coming."

Eric nodded in agreement. "I think it best we leave it to the cops to find him. By the way, did the cop interviewing you last night give you any idea who they think broke into your room?"

"He didn't say. Though he did say he thought I was targeted since the medallion was the only item stolen. I can't for the life of me imagine why anyone would want to steal a worthless piece of jade."

"Maybe Ernest didn't like giving it back to you," I said. "Apart from us and the police, he and Sherry were the only ones who knew you had it."

"He didn't look too happy when he had to hand it over either, did he? But why would he want it back? Allistair meant nothing to him. He was just a student he used for free labour."

"I agree it's very strange. I also think Louise knows something."

"Louise? What would she know?"

Right, we hadn't had a chance to tell her.

"Sis," Eric said. "We have some terrific news for you. We've found Allistair's birth family. It turns out Louise is his grandmother. She recognized the bracelet as a family heirloom."

At first Cloë was flustered, not quite able to absorb the sudden news. "Is this true? Really?" Then her eyes lit up as a smile spread across her face. "How wonderful! I really like her. So Allistair's mother was her daughter?"

Eric recounted the sad story, and when he was finished I added, "She'd love to talk to you about Allistair. But let's wait until tomorrow, when you're feeling better."

"No, I want to go now." She threw back the covers and climbed out of bed, but when she stood up, she wobbled.

"I don't think this is a good idea," Eric said. "Spend the rest of the day in bed and we'll go tomorrow."

"I'm going now, and if you won't take me, I'll get a cab." She started to pull clothes from the drawers. "Leave, I want to get dressed."

"Okay, we'll take you," I said.

FORTY-FOUR

Louise's house was not what I expected. I assumed that since she'd been the Greenstone Matriarch for so many years, she'd have a house befitting her highborn status. Failing the big house, I thought she would at least have a totem pole or a painted wooden plaque proclaiming her rank and her clan.

Not so.

Louise lived in a discrete bungalow like any one of the millions of rectangular bungalows that crowd Canadian suburbs. Hers sported pale green siding, which I thought appropriate, with navy trim and a black roof. The only objects decorating her yard were a couple of gaily painted cement gnomes and a frog.

While the drawn drapes suggested she wasn't home, her Corolla in the driveway said otherwise. The other vehicles parked behind her car told us she had visitors. I recognized Becky's father's silver pickup, but the third vehicle, a black BMW X3, was unfamiliar.

"I wonder if this is a good time, Eric."

"Why not?"

"Remember, Louise erased her daughter from her life.

She might not want to talk about her in front of other people. Although Becky knows, we don't know about the other visitor."

"Maybe we should come back later," Eric said.

"No, I want to talk with her now." Cloë opened the back door and stepped out onto the dirt road, dragging the bag containing her son's heavy urn with her. Hefting it up with both hands, she pressed it against her breast. She staggered either from the weight or from dizziness before steadying herself against the car.

"Are you sure you're alright?" I asked.

"I'm fine." She pushed herself away from the car. Her navy and gold Hermès scarf didn't quite hide the bandage covering her forehead.

"Why don't you leave the urn in the car? If Louise wants to see it I can come back for it," I suggested, worried the sight of her grandson's urn might upset the elderly woman.

Cloë hugged the bag closer. "No, I need him with me."

"Let me carry it for you," Eric said.

"No." Without another word she walked to the front door. Her step seemed surer, stronger. Maybe she would be okay.

When Louise answered our knock, her unusually cool manner suggested that our visit was indeed inconvenient. Though when her eyes fell on Cloë they creased with joy as her smile broadened. However, within seconds the shutter snapped back into place. "I'm not sure if—"

Cloë, in her eagerness, cut in. "I had no idea you were Allistair's grandmother. I couldn't have picked a better one for him." She thrust the velvet bag into Louise's hands.

Caught unawares, Louise struggled to hold on to the heavy bag. Before she dropped it, I grabbed it.

Becky's smiling face appeared over Louise's shoulder. "Hi guys, come on in. We're just having some tea."

"But Becky, I don't think—" Louise said.

Too excited to notice her aunt's reluctance, the young woman stepped around her and opened the door wider to allow us to enter. "I think it's fabulous that Auntie is Allistair's nanaay. No wonder I fell in love with him." She gave the Louise a quick hug.

I was about to suggest coming back later, when a female voice from around the corner said, "Allistair? Who's that?"

"He was my boyfriend," Becky answered. She led her boyfriend's mother down the short hall. Unable to stop them, the three of us reluctantly followed them into the living room. The new Matriarch sat resplendently on the sofa, her red-and-white-checked skirt fanned out over the pale green cushions.

"I thought Becky said something about you being his nanaay, Louise." Rose said.

"If that means grandmother, she is." Cloë beamed.

"What's this to do with you?" With a sneer, the woman ran her eyes over my sister-in-law's fair features and the blond hair peeking out from under her scarf.

"I'm Allistair's mother ... or at least his adopted mother. His real mother was Louise's daughter."

"Please, I'd rather not—" Louise tried to intercede.

"Sis, let's save this visit for another time." Eric tried one last time to save the situation by grabbing his sister's arm but she shook it off and walked farther into the room.

An exuberant Becky didn't help matters. "Auntie is my boyfriend's nanaay and I didn't know it."

Rose frowned. "Your boyfriend? Where? In Vancouver?"

250

"We met at school." The young woman gave Cloë a sideways glance as if uncertain of her reaction. "He used to come on the tours I'd give at the museum. One thing led to another, and well, you know …" She stopped, realizing she'd probably gone too far.

Biting her lower lip, she continued to watch her dead boyfriend's mother, who seemed more interested in a reprint of an Emily Carr painting hanging on the wall than looking at her son's girlfriend. I couldn't understand Cloë's indifference until I remembered that she'd been against his relationship with this young Haida woman.

I was searching for something to say to break the uneasy silence when Cloë reached for the young woman's hand and said, "He loved you very much."

"Imagine that," Rose muttered. "A raven and an eagle." She lumbered to her feet. "I must be going, Louise. I only stopped in for a chat. Let me know when you find those papers, okay?"

She trundled past Louise toward the hall. Louise didn't move. I assumed she was finding it difficult to deal with this awkward situation, until I noticed the glint in her eyes. If looks could kill….

Rose stopped. "When do I get to meet this young man?"

For a moment, silence reigned. Finally, Louise spoke up. "He's dead."

"What a pity." She disappeared into the hall.

The click of the front door closing broke the tension.

"That awful woman!" Becky exclaimed. "Auntie, you can't let her be Matriarch."

"I have no choice, child. We must follow our traditions." Motioning to the sofa where Rose had been sitting, she said, "Please, my grandson's mother, sit down beside me and tell me about your son."

As we sipped tea and ate homemade date squares, Eric, Becky, and I watched and listened to the two women as they talked, one hungering for every word about a grandson she would never know and the other reliving her memories of a beloved son.

As the sun sank lower, I watched it mark a path across the grey broadloom. The living room was crammed with furniture, knickknacks, and prints of Haida and West Coast art. The sun lit up a collection of family photos crowded onto a bookcase. Most were pictures of what I assumed were the families of Louise's sons: three boys in one family and two girls and a boy in the other. They spanned the passages of youth from birth and baptism to graduation, and in one case marriage. In several I thought I could see a family likeness to Allistair, if my memory of his photo served me correctly. There were also shots of Becky at various points in her life.

It was Eric who noticed one particular photo that was partially hidden by a chair.

He walked over and picked it up. He held it up to Louise. "Is this your daughter?"

Louise nodded.

"She's beautiful, Auntie." gushed Becky.

And she was. She looked to be in her mid teens. Her long black hair spread over the brilliant red of her button blanket. She had the same engaging smile as Allistair and her eyes were the same bright amber colour. She even had the same slight droop of her right eye. I tried to see in those eyes any hint of her life to come, but nothing was revealed. She appeared to be a happy young woman filled with the promising dreams of youth. I wondered what so shattered that dream that within a few short years she was giving birth to a son as she lay dying on a cold hospital bed.

"Yes, that's my little angel."

"Is this her graduation photo?" Becky asked. "You gave me a button blanket like that for my own high school graduation, except it had ravens on it instead of eagles."

"Sadly, she lost interest in school before she could graduate. I gave her the blanket when she was still interested in learning our Haida ways. Curiously, just before she disappeared, she gave it to a girlfriend whose parents couldn't afford to give her one."

"She sounds as if she had a kind heart," Becky said. "I'm glad you've put her photo back where it belongs, with the rest of your family."

"Yes, it was time." She paused before turning to Cloë. "Please tell me everything you know about my daughter … and her death."

FORTY-FIVE

Uncertain how much to divulge, Cloë looked to her brother for direction, but Louise answered for him.

"Please, you don't need to protect me. My daughter left these islands an alcoholic and likely a drug addict. I doubt she turned her life around in Vancouver. So please tell me the truth."

Cloë took a deep breath. "I'm afraid I can't tell you much. I only know that she died shortly after giving birth to Allistair."

"From an overdose?"

"No, she was stabbed."

"My poor Lizzie." Louise's shoulders slumped. "Did the police ever catch the person who did it?" She stopped. "Why do I bother to ask? Of course they didn't. They probably didn't lift a finger, figuring either a john or her pimp killed her."

"I think they did some investigating because I remember one officer mentioning that the circumstances surrounding her death were a bit unusual. But I'm sorry, I can't tell you more. I'm afraid I didn't pursue it. I'm so sorry."

"There's no need to blame yourself. You didn't know her."

"I didn't even know her last name. Mary was the only name I was given."

"Elizabeth was the name she was baptized with. Her Haida name was Maada. Mary was my mother's name."

"You can see why I had no way of finding you, although I did try. I felt that if there were any grandparents they should know about the child."

I was taken aback by Cloë's bald-faced lies. But perhaps this was her way of admitting that she'd been wrong in not giving Louise a chance to enjoy her grandson while he was alive.

"You've made the effort to find me now. That's all that counts," Louise said, as if sensing the truth. She reached for Cloë's hand and squeezed it tightly.

"I had to … for Allistair's sake." She paused. "There is a bright side to your daughter's sad story. I think she was trying to turn her life around. According to her friend, she was looking forward to the baby and didn't want to bring it up it on the streets. With the help of her boyfriend, the father of the child, she'd stopped drinking and was in a program to help with her drug addiction. She'd started collecting welfare and was supposed to be in line for social housing."

"Does this mean she wasn't turning tricks when she died?"

"The friend never said. Maybe that's what the policeman meant by unusual circumstances."

"So why in the hell didn't they try to find her killer?"

Unable to give a fitting answer, Cloë closed her eyes and placed her hand on her bandaged forehead as if in pain.

"Are you okay, child?" Louise asked. "You should be in bed."

"I wanted to tell you about your grandson. I felt it couldn't wait." Her voice sounded weak and she appeared paler than when we arrived. This was as hard on her as it was on Louise.

Eric stood up. "I think we should take you home, Sis."

"No, I'm fine. The headache isn't as bad as it was."

"Nothing beats a cup of tea for making you feel better," Louise said. "Becky will make another pot. Do you mind, dear?"

"Happy to." The young woman strode out of the living room with the empty teapot.

"What about this boyfriend?" I asked. "Did the police ever identify him?"

"They never mentioned him. But her friend told me he took off after the couple had a big fight, a month or so before your daughter died. She never saw the man again. She assumed he'd gotten cold feet about the baby."

"Did she know his name?"

"Just a strange nickname that sounded like 'Guyga.' I've no idea what it means. This friend thought he was also Haida."

"It could be from the Haida word for carver *Gya ḵ'id ll Gaay Ga*. We Haida do love to use nicknames."

"There can't be that many carvers," Eric said. "Any chance you might know who he is?"

"I suppose I could ask around, but I don't think I want to. If this man were from here he would've known she was my daughter. He would've contacted me if he had wanted to and he never has. It's best to keep things as they are."

"I see your point. But speaking from a man's perspective, he might have been reluctant to approach you given your exalted position. You know you can be a bit intimidating." Eric chuckled. "I've even had to summon my own courage in some of our heated Grand Council discussions."

Louise laughed. "That's never stopped you from disagreeing with me."

"Because underneath I know you're as soft as eagle down."

"You charmer you. Meg, if you hadn't nabbed this man first, I would've gone after him myself."

"Yeah, but I saw him first, so hands off. Still, I could do with some cash…. How much are you willing to pay for him?"

"I have a few spare loonies."

We chortled together while Eric frowned.

Becky returned and poured steaming tea into all our cups.

"Joking aside," Louise said to Cloë, "did this friend know which clan he belonged to?"

"If she did she never mentioned it, and I didn't know enough to ask. Does it matter which clan the man belonged to?"

"Not really, not now. Just wishful thinking on my part. If he was a Raven, he would have been the right partner for my daughter."

"That would mean that your daughter cared enough about her Haida heritage to choose the proper mate, wouldn't it?" I said, trying to follow Louise's train of thought.

"It does, but it also would've meant that my grandson had the perfect parentage to become Chief Greenstone."

Becky clapped her hands. "Of course. He was a direct descendent of Old Chief's Matriarch. Awesome. Imagine that, my Allie a chief." Then her joy vanished as she remembered.

"A double tragedy for you, Louise," Eric said. "The naming of the new Chief Greenstone has not been an easy time for you, has it?"

"That's life, eh?" She sighed. "Besides, we Greenstone Eagles have survived much worse. Harry'll be okay. He won't be a great chief, but I don't think he'll be a terrible one either. Believe me, we've had some pretty bad ones throughout our history. Unfortunately he'll probably be spending more time in Vancouver than here with his clan. He has to pay off that potlatch somehow."

"Does that mean that his mother, as the Greenstone Matriarch, will be looking after clan affairs?" I asked.

She gave me a long, hard stare before answering. "I don't know what she will do. Traditionally the Matriarch advises the clan in the chief's absence. She doesn't take charge."

"Rose is going to be a disaster," Becky cut in. "I bet she does more than advise. She'll try to run it and make sure her family gets everything."

"Now child, Rose has her good side. She can be kind and generous."

"Yeah, to those who suck up to her."

Louise turned her attention to the coffee table and the green velvet bag. "Tell me, what is this very heavy object that you've brought me?"

"That's your grandson," Cloë replied.

Louise didn't blink, but took it in stride. Becky, on the other hand, gasped and tentatively reached out as if she meant to touch it, but she couldn't quite bring herself to do it.

"I imagine you mean his ashes. They're in an urn?" the grandmother said.

"Actually, a bentwood box. I wanted to honour his heritage."

Louise smiled.

"I had his ashes divided between a traditional urn and the bentwood box. I brought the box so that part of him could be buried with his ancestors."

"My dear, how thoughtful. I know just the place."

"I hope it's beautiful and wild, the kind of place Allistair loved."

"It is a very beautiful place and very wild. It is where all Greenstone Chiefs have been buried. At Llnagaay or *Hlgaa K'inhalgahl Llnagaay*, the full name of our ancestral village."

The sudden ringing of the phone stopped the conversation.

Apart from a few clipped *yes*'s and one or two *when*s, it was impossible to know what the call was about; however, the deepening furrow in the elder's brow suggested it wasn't good news.

After she replaced the receiver, she continued to stare at it for a few moments before turning her attention back to us.

"Tomorrow we go to Llnagaay."

FORTY-SIX

The One in the Sea

He swore he'd only been asleep a few minutes when Scav woke him up bursting with his news. But with the sun no longer lighting up the stones on the beach, he could tell it was well into the late afternoon. So he'd ended up sleeping longer than a couple of hours, but it hadn't helped. His head still throbbed, though not as much as this morning. And his hands still shook. But he couldn't wait until tomorrow to draw the next figure. If Scav's news was anything to go by, he had to get it done today.

According to Scav, the cops had finally identified the thief of the boy's pole and their prime murder suspect. The name they had come up with was his. Scav heard it from a couple of off-duty cops at Jimmy's last night. They even asked Scav if he'd seen his carving buddy lately, but of course Scav lied like the expert he was.

They said they'd got his name from his tugboat buddy. Some friend, eh? But maybe Joe wasn't a complete traitor, because the cops had drilled him after a witness reported seeing a log being loaded onto his tug in Richmond. Scav figured Joe hadn't told them the whole truth. The cops told Scav that he and the log had been dropped off at the north end of Graham Island. They also told him that the Masset cops were searching the area around Rose Spit.

He and his bro had laughed till their sides almost split when they heard this. Rose Spit was at the opposite end of Haida Gwaii, a good three hundred kilometres or more from where they were devouring Scav's ham sandwiches in Llnagaay.

Why the cops believed he'd be hiding out in the north, god only knows. He wasn't a northern Haida. Showed you what little they knew about the community they were supposed to be policing. But he figured it was only a matter of time before someone let slip that his clan was southern and that he'd most likely be hiding out on one of the many islands in the south. Eventually they would clue in about his ancestral village and come looking. Now if it were just the cops he was worried about, he'd probably have enough time to finish the drawing and start carving the pole. But it wasn't.

He was more worried about the new chief. It looked like the geek would be coming sooner than expected. At the potlatch Scav had overheard him telling that bloody mother of his that the new boat had finally arrived. With a ready means of getting here, it was a matter of days if not hours before the Geek came to pay homage to his ancestors. Homage. Yeah, right.

So he'd better get down to work. Thank Salaana he still had plenty of daylight left. He flexed the fingers of his drawing hand. They felt better. He took another big gulp of cold tea to help clear his mind. He was glad his brother had gone with Scav. He didn't need the distraction, for this next part in the story was going to be difficult.

He'd been giving a lot of thought to how best depict the crux of the story: the treasure. Since he had no idea what this treasure was, only hints of gold and glittery green stones from his nanaay, he had been at a loss about which crest to use until he had a sudden brainwave. It must've come to him while he was passed out, for when Scav shook him awake, there it was, fully formed in his mind: The One in the Sea.

In the old days, his people had highly prized the sea turtle's green, bumpy shell. When a chief potlatched, he used to dress up as The One in the Sea. Haida longhouses were said to resemble the curved and ridged outline of the shell and the chiefs' coppers were said to resemble the shape of the plates of a sea turtle's head.

While he'd seen lots of bentwood boxes with The One in the Sea crest, he'd never seen one carved into a totem pole. Maybe there was some kind of taboo about putting them on poles, but he neither knew nor cared. After all, he was probably breaking a lot of Haida rules with this pole. So he'd just have to use his imagination and see what he could come up with, though drawing the formline to represent the shell was going to be tricky.

He took another swig of the cold tea, wishing he had a bottle to add zip to it. But he'd made Scav take back the new bottle of rye he'd brought. He needed a clear head to talk to the log, to feel what it was trying to tell him.

He brushed away the needles from the overhead branches and ran his hands lightly over the pole, starting with the top of Old Chief's eagle head and on down to Blue Shell Chief's raven feet. His fingers tingled with Old Chief's pride, buzzed with the daring of the sea voyage and throbbed at Blue Shell chief's treachery. When he reached the point where the lines would flow into The One in the Sea, they itched with greed.

The marker flew over the wood as the treasure took shape. He drew ovoids within ovoids for the eyes. He gave the mouth a pointed beak, not as large as an eagle or raven beak, but a beak nonetheless. This he topped with two nostrils, which he would paint black. On either side of the large head, he drew smaller ovoids for the flippers. Resting on top of the head was the shell, a series of seven ovoids. He would paint The One in the Sea green. He thought it only fitting. But he would paint the flippers a bright yellow for the gold.

In his childhood dreams, he'd imagined the treasure to be a bentwood box filled with Old Chief's gold. He'd tried to guess where Old Chief's Matriarch had hidden the treasure. Maybe it lay within the tangled roots of an ancient tree or buried under a mound of thick moss or deep within a crevice in the granite cliffs that hung over the village.

For many years, whenever he visited, either with his family or alone, he searched for likely places, but always came up empty. Finally, he decided that if it had been in a place he could easily find then the treasure was likely long gone. And if it wasn't, it was in a place so secret that a map would be needed to locate it. Since he didn't have the map, he stopped looking.

FORTY-SEVEN

The idea of Allistair's ashes being sprinkled on the land of his ancestors rather appealed to my romantic sense of symmetry. The only problem was the journey to the southern end of Haida Gwaii would require three days — one day longer than we had. While Louise was saying we needed two full days of travel with a full day in between for the ceremony, Becky thought we could shorten it to two if we held the ceremony first thing in the morning and left immediately after. This would allow us to make our outbound flight the following morning. Louise, however, was adamant that she would need the entire day. She brushed Eric off with a mumbling answer about tradition when he queried her about a simple burial ceremony requiring an entire day. The phone call was beginning to make me wonder if there was another reason for this sudden trip.

While I had no pressing need to get back to Three Deer Point, Eric felt he couldn't afford any more time away from GCFN business. So we proposed that I go on the trip to keep his sister company.

But no matter how much Eric cajoled, pleaded, and flat out refused, there was no dissuading Louise, and for that matter Cloë. Both were convinced that he, as Allistair's closest male relative, even if only through adoption, needed to be there to help ease the boy's passing into the Haida spiritual world. In the end he agreed and set about charming the airline into changing our flights yet again without charging a big penalty.

Unfortunately, Murphy's Law reigned. Various conferences and sporting events conspired to fill the different combinations of connecting flights so that in the end we would be travelling separately. Although we'd leave Haida Gwaii together four days from now, I had to layover an extra day in Vancouver, which I ended up pushing into three at Cloë's request. She wasn't quite ready to face her future without Allistair.

None of this served to put Eric in a good mood, particularly when Cloë rushed up to him after he agreed to go to Llnagaay and clung to him, gushing, "Oh Eric, thank you, thank you. You are my rock. I couldn't do this without you."

This prompted him to say, "I'm only doing this for the boy." He removed her arms from around his neck, which surprised me as much as it did her.

From the sympathetic way he'd been treating her so far on this trip, I thought he was beginning to put their past history behind him. Not so. It came out as one big rant when I raised the subject once we were finally alone.

"She's too damn spoiled. Always the little princess wanting her own way and not prepared to think of others. Always trying to get others to do things for her. She never faces up to her responsibilities ..." And so on and so forth.

When I suggested that she was in a fragile state and needed our understanding more than our hostility, he brushed me aside with "She sure didn't show me any understanding when she tried to cut me out of Mom's will." So I left it.

The next three days were going to be very interesting. Either he would decide to accept her, warts and all, and make her a part of our family, or he would severe the connection once and for all.

His continuous tossing and turning during the night told me that come morning his spirits wouldn't be any better. When it did arrive and he could barely growl "Morning," I knew it was a day for being the dutiful wife and keeping my opinions to myself.

Running out of shaving cream didn't help. Though I offered to go out and buy some he, in true pigheaded male fashion, insisted he could scrape his skin without it. And scrape he did. When I saw the tissue-covered cuts on his chin, I was sorely tempted to shout "Told you so," but bit my tongue instead and offered to make us a nice pot of English Breakfast tea.

Heading down the hall to the kitchen, I almost collided with Sherry coming out of her room. She was dragging a large black suitcase with one hand and with the other juggling a clothes bag and her leather purse in the shape of an exceedingly large flower, complete with petals. Her fingers slipped and the purse landed on the floor with a thud.

"Are you leaving?" I asked, retrieving the purse.

"Yah." She grabbed the purse, slung it over her shoulder, along with the clothes bag, and headed down the hall in front of me.

"Once again, I'm so sorry about François."

"Thanks." She continued walking. "But it never should'a happened."

"No, it shouldn't have. It was just a dreadful accident."

She stopped and turned around. "So some people say, but I know the guy wanted Frank dead."

"Do the police have a line on who did it?"

"They're not saying, but Ern says he's got a pretty good idea."

"Who?"

"Some guy by the name of Johnnie. He's suppose to be a cousin of the new chief and I guess was all jealous because he wanted to be the big honcho."

Poor Louise. Someone else who thinks her nephew guilty.

"Did you tell the police?"

"Ern doesn't want to. He wants to talk to him first."

"Are you sure this is a good idea? If this guy did cut the ropes, he could be dangerous."

"Ern says he knows how to handle him. They go way back."

"I assume Ernest knows where to find him."

"Yeah. We're taking Ern's boat to get there."

"What does Ernest plan to do? Talk him into turning himself in?"

"I guess. Ern's taking his rifle. If he won't use it, I will."

"Aren't you worried you could get yourselves or Johnnie killed?"

"I'm a good shot. I've been hunting since I was a kid."

Amazing what could be disguised by a beehive hairdo, skin-tight pants, and spiked heels. Except today she was wearing running shoes and cargo pants, although they were considerably tighter than mine. And her hair had

267

been collapsed into a more functional ponytail. This time she wasn't going to let man-luring fashion slow her down.

A car horn sounded from outside.

"That's Ern. Gotta go."

"Be careful," I said to the closing door.

Eric was more sanguine when I told him about their plans. "If this Johnnie can be so easily found by Ernest, the police will eventually find him. Since the two men know each other, I'd say we let Ernest handle this without bringing in the police, not at this stage. Bringing them in could complicate things. The Haida might have traditional ways for dealing with situations like this."

"Whatever you say," I said, although I didn't entirely agree. A rifle and someone as hot-headed as Sherry didn't always lead to a peaceful solution.

I passed Eric a freshly poured cup of tea along with a shortbread cookie to help raise his spirits.

After taking a long sip and a bite of the cookie, he chuckled. "Sorry for growling at you. I guess I'm still trying to sort out my relationship with my sister."

"I know."

"These three days in close proximity with each other are going to be very interesting."

"I know."

He laughed. "You have it all figured out, eh?"

"No, I don't. But I'm hoping you can come to accept her. She's really struggling. With the end of her marriage and the death of her son, she needs a shoulder to lean on, and that's something neither your brother nor your father can provide."

"You're right. I'll try not to be so judgmental."

"Thanks." I gave him a lingering kiss.

He glanced in the dresser mirror and ran his fingers lightly over the cuts. "I guess I wrecked my chin, didn't I?"

I laughed.

He tried removing one of the bits of tissue but the cut started bleeding again. I tore off another a piece and dabbed it on the cut. When it stopped bleeding, I said, "Why don't you make breakfast while I pack, okay? And please, leave those cuts on your chin alone."

"Yes, Mummy." He chuckled and gave me a slap on the behind before heading to the kitchen, while I gritted my teeth. I wasn't anyone's Mummy.

We, together with Cloë, had been sitting packed and waiting in the living room at the cottage for a good hour before Louise and Becky finally arrived. Cloë seemed better this morning. She'd gone straight to bed after our visit with Louise, and apart from waking up to eat the dinner Eric had brought back from Jimmy's, she'd slept through. None of us, though, felt like talking, so we waited in silence, flipping through magazines or staring out the window at the rain.

"Sorry we're late," Becky said, bounding into the cottage. Louise had apparently stayed in the car. "We were all set to leave when the cops showed up."

"Not bad news, I hope?"

"I'm not sure. The police were asking questions about her nephews, Johnnie and Colin."

"Is it related to François's death?" I asked.

"The cops didn't say. Jeez, I sure hope it wasn't them who cut the ropes. That would be so hard on Auntie. She

269

loves them like they were her own sons. But Col couldn't have done it. He lives in Vancouver."

"What kinds of questions were they asking?"

"Mostly they wanted to know if she had seen either man recently, and if she knew where they were."

"And?" I pressed.

"She kept saying she hadn't seen Col in a long time and that as far as she knew he was in Vancouver. As for Johnnie, she last saw him on Saturday along with everyone else when he made that horrible scene at the pole raising."

"Does she know where he is now?"

"She just said if he wasn't at home, she had no idea where he could be. You know, I sensed she knew more than she was saying, but I don't think the police picked up on it."

"Is there a place south of here where he could be?"

She stopped and gave me a querying glance. "Yeah, maybe. Why?"

"No reason. Just wondering." For the moment I didn't want to mention Sherry's plans in case it turned out to be nothing.

We collected our bags and headed to the door. Before we stepped outside, Becky said, "Look, guys, I'd appreciate it if you didn't let on I told you about this business with the police. Auntie might not want you to know."

FORTY-EIGHT

I was very glad the rain had stopped by the time we reached Moresby Island on the ferry — the same one we'd taken over three days earlier. With my rain jacket nearing the end of its water-shedding life, I hadn't been looking forward to spending a day out in a deluge. Unfortunately, low dark clouds still hid the mountaintops and a mist had closed in, blotting out the distant shore of Graham Island. I figured it was only a matter of an hour or two before the rain returned.

But I was pleasantly surprised when we emerged from under the forest canopy an hour later. After bumping, grinding, and zigzagging our way over a treacherous logging road that wound its way up and down through the dense bush, we were greeted by an expanse of blue sky, sparkling water, and rising green mountains. In the distance, snow-covered summits shimmered in the sun. Only a handful of fluffy whites remained.

Amazingly, our rental car survived, although I wouldn't want to be around when the agency checked its undercarriage. Despite Eric's best manoeuvring, the bottom scraped roughly along the road's surface numerous times when the tire-swallowing potholes couldn't be avoided. Even Becky's father's truck, with its much higher suspension, had its problems.

We drove along the shoreline of an estuary that at the moment was more tidal flat than water, before turning into a parking lot for boats. Next to a wooden shed stood six boat trailers, each topped with an oversized grey Zodiac with a rigid hull.

Becky stopped the truck beside the shed and hopped out. "We're renting one of these boats from an adventure company that I work for in the summer. I figured it would be safer and more comfortable to use one of these than to try to cram the five of us plus our gear into my dad's boat."

She unlocked the shed door. "By the way we'll be camping out for two nights. I hope that's okay."

While Eric and I enthusiastically greeted this opportunity to sleep in the great outdoors, his sister didn't bother to hide her annoyance. "Doesn't this place have an inn?"

"Just the wind, the sea, and the trees," Louise said. "You'll be okay. Becky will find us a nice soft carpet of moss to sleep on. Close your eyes and you'll think you're sinking into a bed of feathers."

Grimacing, Cloë muttered, "For Allistair."

Besides, being packed with lifejackets, ropes, gas cans, and other boating paraphernalia, the shed also had racks crammed with rubber wet weather gear. Thank goodness.

By the time Eric and I struggled into dark green rubber overalls, doffed mid-calf dark green rubber jackets, clamped ourselves into bulky lifejackets, and stuck our feet first into two pairs of heavy wool socks and then into roomy rubber boots, we looked like two very fat penguins. Becky, on the other hand, looked very svelte in her form-fitting chest-high waders and yellow Gore-Tex jacket. Though Eric's sister was not the least bit amused at having to wear such unflattering and unfashionable attire, I thought she handled it gamely with barely a disdainful twitch of her lips. Initially she hesitated to take the pair of overalls Eric handed her, but with another muttered "for Allistair" she gritted her teeth and put them on.

While Becky was helping her auntie with her gear, she said, "Did you know Harry has a new boat?"

"Good. A boat means he's planning on spending time here," was Louise's response.

"I thought he was going to live in the house where the pole was raised," I said.

"That's his mother's place, although he owns it," Louise replied. "I suppose they'll call it the Greenstone longhouse. But I don't imagine he's going to move in on a full-time basis. Since he won't make any money being clan chief and he has that big loan to pay off, I expect he's going to continue spending most of his time in Vancouver, where his job is."

"He spent a bundle on the boat, too," Becky added. "I hear it's a forty-eight-foot Sea Ray, bigger than Ernest Paul's Sunseeker."

"He certainly didn't buy that on the island, did he?" Louise said, struggling to get the overall straps over her shoulders. I grabbed the one hanging down her back and handed it to her.

"They say he bought it in Vancouver and hired someone to bring it here," Becky continued. "It arrived a couple of days ago."

"More money. I hope he's got it," Louise said.

"You said he's made a lot of money in the computer business. Maybe he owns one of those web startups the big computer companies pay millions for," I suggested, removing my lifejacket and undoing the jacket. I was beginning to feel very warm encased in all this rubber.

"I doubt it. He's not that smart." Louise laughed. "Though to believe Rose, you'd think he was the next … ah … what's the man's name?" She eyed each of us for the answer. "You know, the man who owns one of the biggest computer companies in the world. He lives not far from my son in Seattle."

"Bill Gates," we replied in unison.

"That's the guy. At bingo a few weeks ago, Rose was bragging about the millions Harry was going to make. *Harrumph.* He doesn't have it in him." She tried on the jacket Becky handed her and was quickly lost from view. "A little big. You got a smaller one?"

"Oh Auntie, don't be so hard on Harry. He's a nice guy." Becky riffled through the rack. Finding a smaller size, she handed it to Louise. "This should fit."

"Louise, I have what is probably a stupid question," I said. "I'm having difficulty understanding why Harry would want to spend all this money to become chief, if he's not going to get any money from it and won't be living here."

"Simple. Prestige and status." While this jacket wasn't quite so roomy, it still reached almost to her ankles and the sleeves swallowed her hands.

"I'm sorry, Auntie, that's the smallest size here."

"It'll be fine, child. I figure if I fall out of the boat, I'll float like a fat blubbery seal." Her laughter filled the dark shed.

"Louise, if you don't mind my saying so, the prestige and status is only within your small community. Being Chief Greenstone won't mean much in Vancouver." I ignored the darts Eric's eyes were shooting in my direction. He thought I was being insensitive.

"You're right, Meg." I shot a triumphant glance at him. "It's one of the reasons why my sons chose not to pursue it. Neither of them thought the debt was worth it."

"I would've given Allistair the money to become chief," Cloë said, more to herself than to the rest of us. "He would've made a good one."

Louise patted her gently. "I'm sure he would've."

"So why did Harry want to be chief?" I asked.

"His mother put him up to it. She'll be the one to benefit with her higher status as Matriarch. Mind you, not much comes with that other than people pestering you at all hours of the day to help them solve their problems." She removed the jacket and placed it on the bench with her lifejacket.

"But, Auntie, you love helping people, and you're so good at it."

She shrugged. "I doubt that'll change. Rose is about as approachable as a snake. Come on child, we're wasting time. Let's get the boat into the water. It's closing in on noon and we have a ways to go. I want to get there before suppertime."

Along with the others, I threw my gear into the back of the truck. With Eric directing, Becky then backed the vehicle into one of the boat trailers. After Eric attached the hitch, Louise climbed into the cab beside her. The rest of us followed behind on foot. We arrived at a point of land that appeared more man-made than natural with its almost vertical sides and long, rectangular shape jutting far out into the water.

Taking over as driver, Eric backed the trailer down a steep stony slope into the water until the boat floated.

With the advantage of her hip waders, Becky ventured out into the deeper water and pulled the boat up onto the stones. With help from Louise, Eric and I passed the gear to Becky, who stowed it away in two long wooden lockers built side-by-side lengthwise into the centre of the boat. Though Cloë made no effort to help, we wouldn't have let her anyways. But when it came time to pass over the urn, she grabbed it from Eric and raised the heavy bag into Becky's reaching hands almost as if it were a ritual.

Included with the gear were two large gas cans. Becky attached one of these to the high-powered outboard motor and tested it. It started on the second try.

While she parked the truck, the four of us struggled back into our gear. Once fully dressed, we waddled like a parade of penguins down to the water.

Getting into the boat over its high, rounded side was challenging. Despite a leg up from Eric, I landed like a beached whale on the bottom. Cloë climbed in with considerably more finesse. Louise, with the help of Eric, Becky, and I, arrived inside the boat as gently as we could manage. Eric, after pushing us farther out into the water, sprang into the Zodiac as if he were born to it.

Becky lowered a row of four seats over each of the storage lockers. Straddling the seat like a horse, each of us wedged into a spot bounded front and back by a metal railing. Becky started the motor. This time it took three tries.

"Not to worry," she said. "Although the motor was overhauled recently, it hasn't been used much since last fall. It'll be working fine after a good run."

It roared to life and over the sparkling blue we flew.

FORTY-NINE

We needed the wet weather gear not only for the frigid waves splashing over the bow, but also for the cold wind pummeling us. To get a good view, Eric and I had sat in the seats closest to the bow. We were paying for it now. On the other hand, Louise and Cloë were avoiding the worst of it by sitting in the more protected seats near the stern, just in front of Becky, who was at the helm. Eric's sister had her hood pulled down over her face to keep the water out but Louise seemed to be relishing the wind ripping through her curls.

Becky deftly steered us across an expansive body of water. Surrounded by an undulating ridge of forest-covered mountains, it looked like a lake, but I imagined somewhere ahead of us would be an outlet to the sea.

I ducked my head as another wave crashed over the bow and felt coldness course over my hood and down my back. I laughed at Eric, who'd taken it fully in the face. But he didn't seem to care. Beaming, he looked like he was having the time of his life. He loved speed. Why else would he own a Harley?

This was my kind of fun too: being in the great out-doors, surrounded by the majestic splendour that only nature can provide. Although I respected the gravity of the situation, I'm afraid I was viewing this trip more an adventure than a funeral.

We passed the rotting remnants of an abandoned pier rising high above the water. Bits of greenery and small trees sprouted atop the platform, while the low tide revealed barnacles clinging to the log pilings.

"It belongs to an old logging camp, dating back to the 1930s," Becky shouted. "The camp used to be over there." She pointed to the shore directly behind the pier, which appeared as densely forested as the rest of the shoreline.

She veered the boat toward a kelp bed, where several small brown heads poked up through the glistening leaves. Though their eyes watched as we passed, they didn't seem alarmed by our presence.

"Seals," she shouted. "I'll show you some starfish."

She turned the boat in the direction of a rock outcropping that rose out of the sea a couple of hundred metres away.

"We don't have time," Louise yelled. "We need to get to Llnagaay."

"No problem. We'll get another chance later." Becky pointed the boat's bow at the open expanse of water.

"Why aren't you taking the shortcut?" Louise demanded. She pointed to the right, to a distant mountainous shore that looked impenetrable but must have a passageway through it. Becky slowed the engine so she could be heard.

"It's low tide, Auntie. We can't get through, not unless you want to drag the boat."

"What's my old lady's mind coming to that I would forget the tides?" She shook her head in frustration. "What are we doing about lunch?"

My stomach was growling, and I was glad she'd asked that question.

"I thought we could have it at Blue Shell Village. It'll give us enough time to ensure the tide is high enough in Burnaby Narrows to allow us to get through. I want to avoid as much open water as I can. It's going to be rough out there with this wind."

"Good." The elderly woman settled back into her seat.

Becky revved the engine. For a second it coughed, but then it caught and off we zoomed again, heading to what I could now see was a break in the mountainous shore, where open water must lie.

Cloë remained hidden in the folds of her rubber gear, her hands stuffed into the sleeves. When the wind finally blew the hood off my head, I kept it off. I enjoyed the feeling of it ripping through my hair, as did Eric. He was letting his mane ripple behind him like a flag.

A flock of black and white sea birds burst from the water in front of us. They flew just far enough to get out of our way before returning to float once again on the undulating water.

Until now the surrounding mountains had been a healthy deep forest green with the occasional patch of lighter green where I assumed logging had taken place. But looming off to the right of us was a mountain where the forest looked as if it had been eaten away by an angry brown cancer. It stretched from the water's edge to the summit and covered the entire mountainside. Although it was tinged with the faint greenish hue of new growth, it was riddled with the deep fissures of erosion.

Eric shouted, "Becky, it looks as if someone didn't care much about sustainability when they clear-cut that mountain."

"Nope, they sure didn't. That's the island where the guy who was killed stole our forest."

"No wonder people hated him," I said. *But was it enough to kill him?*

"Yup, he and his scab loggers did a lot of damage," Becky said. "Even with the high levels of rainfall, it'll be many years before trees will take hold and hundreds more before they become the mighty giants that covered these mountains when our ancestors lived here."

We were leaving the calmness of the bay and heading out into a vast empty sea that stretched all the way to the B.C. mainland more than a hundred kilometres away. A large wave splashed over the bow. I didn't duck in time and got drenched. Eric, equally soaked, laughed. "Yahoo!" he shouted as we plowed through another wave. Though he vowed his hands didn't hurt, I caught him wincing when he grabbed the railing. Ahead the water looked to be in a boil; behind us it was almost mirror calm. I gulped as a particularly large wave hovered above us, then broke over the bow in a cascade of white as the boat climbed up its height and slid down the other side. I was a fair-weather boater who preferred gentle waves. Angry seas like these made me nervous.

Eric, knowing my fear, motioned for me to take the empty seat behind him. Holding on to his arm for support, I managed to change seats without falling, despite the bucking of the boat.

"You'll be okay now," Eric shouted. "Just hang on to me."

I gripped his shoulders with probably a little more force than he intended. I glanced back at Cloë and Louise to see how they were faring. Eric's sister had completely withdrawn into her coat. With her head bent down under her hood, she seemed to be praying. I worried over the effect this pounding could be having on her injured head. Unfortunately, the only solution was to turn back, and I doubted she would agree to that.

On the other hand, the smile stretching across Louise's face said she was enjoying this as much as Eric. So was Becky. I put it down to the Haida seafaring blood flowing through their veins. As the boat climbed up another wave and crashed through to the other side, I prayed Becky was as good at seafaring as her ancestors.

I noticed with alarm that the shore was falling farther and farther behind us, while the waves seemed to me to tower higher and higher above us. Eric would probably call them your standard ocean waves. I became quite scared as the boat became almost vertical, then slipped back before righting itself and surfing down the other side of the wave. To make matters more unnerving, there wasn't a hint of land, not even a tiny island or a boat in the raging, empty sea in front of us. *Where in the world was Becky taking us?*

After what seemed like an eternity, Becky steered the boat back toward the shore. The waves now ran behind us. Rather than climbing them, we were lifted almost gently and then settled back down into a trough. I relaxed … a bit. We were angling along the coastline at a distance I realized was far enough away for the boat not to get caught up in the backwash of the waves crashing against the shore, a most unfriendly shore I might add. The precipitous mountainside plunged into the sea, leaving a tangle of rocks strewn along the waterline. The trees were so closely packed, the incline so steep, that I doubted anyone or anything other than squirrels could travel through it. Not a shore on which to run into trouble.

At last we rounded a rocky point and moved into the calmer waters of a lagoon. Ahead lay a steep, grey-stone beach edged with massive lengths of driftwood. A cottage built in the Haida style was nestled at the top of a grassy knoll.

"Blue Shell Village," said Louise. "One of our ancient villages. It was the home of the Blue Shell Ravens.

Becky stopped the Zodiac just short of the beach. She jumped out into the shallow water and held the bow while the rest of us, with Eric's help, struggled to maintain our dignity as we lumbered over the side and into the water. After removing a box containing our lunch, Becky tied the boat to a solid length of driftwood and let it float out into deeper water.

"We can eat our lunch here, and then do a bit of exploring."

"Becky, we can't spare the time. We must get to Llnagaay," Louise insisted.

"I know, Auntie, but it's still another three hours before the tide will be high enough for Burnaby Narrows to be passable." Becky checked her watch. "It's about a two-hour distance from here. I figure we have a good forty-five minutes, so I thought our friends would appreciate seeing an ancient village."

"But child, they will be seeing Llnagaay."

"I know, but there isn't much left to see. At least this village still has some standing poles."

"Whatever you say," Louise said, not bothering to hide the resignation in her voice. Clearly she wasn't happy with the delay.

"Is there a pressing need for you to be there?" I asked, remembering the earlier phone call.

For a moment she seemed startled by the question, but then she smiled. "Just call it an old woman's impatience. It's been many years since I've visited my ancestral home. I'm anxious to see it."

FIFTY

It Exists

Since making the decision to tell the story of shame, he'd been racking his brains to come up with a crest for the worst villain in the story, the bastard who'd dared to betray his own clan by leading the rival Blue Shell chief and the Iron Men to where Old Chief's treasure was hidden. Problem was, he didn't know who the traitor was. He just knew it was a member of the clan. Nanaay had refused to tell him the name, no matter how much he'd bugged her. He figured it was one of those secrets the Matriarchs passed down from generation to generation. Auntie would know, but she wouldn't tell either. Too bad he couldn't use a real-life model. He knew just the person. The owner of the silver trinket he'd found beside the kid's body.

He was running his hands over the log to see if it would speak to him when his brother's boat landed on the beach with a screech of scraping stones. Bro wanted him to come to Scav's place for a booze-up. He was sorely tempted, but time had almost run out. He could feel in his bones that they'd be coming soon. Bro got pretty upset when he turned him down, so he figured Bro wanted to talk. He made tea and the two of them sat on a piece of driftwood in the sun.

But Bro didn't say anything; just sat staring out to sea with his face looking as if it were going to crack. He figured it had to do with the pole raising, but when he brought it up, his brother told him it was better he didn't know.

Finally, just as the sun was about to sink behind the ridge, his brother started talking, but it wasn't what he was expecting.

"Two Finger, has the Geek ever asked you about the Greenstone treasure?"

"Only once. But since I know nothing, I had nothing to tell him."

"He wouldn't leave me alone," Bro said. "I guess he thought I should know something, since the Chief Greenstone name was by rights mine."

Two Finger eyed his brother thoughtfully. "What do you know?"

"Hell, if I knew where it was, do you think I'd be sitting here hanging out in Scav's shack. Nope, I'd be raising my own pole and declaring myself Chief Greenstone."

"Auntie told you something, didn't she?"

His brother wiped the sweat off his brow with the back of his hand, though it was too cold for sweating, and threw some stones into the water before answering. "Yeah, she did. Not much, but enough to tell me the treasure's for real."

"Did she say what it was?"

"Nope, just that if I ever became Chief Greenstone, I'd find out."

"Did she say where it's hidden?"

"Nope. Just said it's where the Matriarch hid it after the shame," Bro said.

"So it's gotta be around here somewheres, eh?"

"I guess. But, hell, I've searched this place all over and haven't found a thing other than some old bones and a kid's rattle."

"Yeah, me too," Two Finger sheepishly admitted. "Do you think Auntie's gonna tell Fat Momma?"

"Tradition says she has to. But once that damn woman finds out, it won't stay hidden for long. She'll be showing it off to everyone."

"Or selling it. I thought you were bad with money, but I've seen money go through her fingers like it was *oolichan* oil."

"I remember Auntie saying its location was marked on a special talisman."

"Did she say what it was?" Two Finger asked.

"Nope. But she said it had gotten lost. But she wasn't worried. She figured Salaana would return it, when it was needed."

FIFTY-ONE

Out of the wind, the heavy rubber gear was hot. I struggled out of it, as did the others, and left it draped over a massive timber that looked as if it had drifted onto the beach when the Haida called this shore home. The five of us sat in a line along the log watching the tide creep ever closer us as we ate our lunch. From the calmness of the bay, the open water didn't appear so angry. But noticing the number of white caps, I could tell it was going to be another white-knuckle ride when we headed back out.

"Becky, is there ever any boat traffic out there?" I asked.

"Barges and Alaskan cruise liners make up most of the traffic on Hecate Strait, but they travel closer to the mainland, too far away to be seen from here. There isn't much local traffic with only four people living down here. It's mostly tourist traffic from a handful of outdoor adventure companies, like the one I work for, and the odd sailboat that dares to venture this far from the mainland. But it's early in the season, so I doubt we'll see any other boats. In the summer, kayakers come here too, but they stick to the internal waterways. The only time a kayak travels along this shore is when the open sea is a dead calm."

"Calm? I didn't think that was possible."

"It happens, but only when the wind drops." Her eyes twinkled. "I guess that's the way you'd like it, eh? Like a mill pond."

I laughed. "My favourite kind of water."

"Once we're beyond this stretch of coast, we'll be back into calmer waters. Can you hang on until then?"

"I'll just hang on to my husband."

His attention elsewhere, Eric started at the word *husband*. "What? You talking about me?"

Becky and I broke into giggles.

He frowned, which only made us giggle more. Choosing to ignore us, he glanced at his watch and said, "We don't have much time. Why don't we go explore that village."

Becky stood up. "Auntie, you coming?"

"No, child, I'll only slow you down. But don't take long." Louise was well settled on the log and was using another as a back support. "I'll sit here and enjoy the peace. I always find an ancient village so in harmony with Mother Earth. All the tensions of past lives, the clan rivalries, and the sickness have long since been calmed. Whenever I walk on the ground our ancestors walked on, I like to think their spirits are watching over us."

She was right. There did seem to be an otherworldly calmness as the four of us headed up a narrow path through wavering grass toward the cottage. Two small deer, their black-tipped ears and soft brown coats barely discernible in the high grass, served to emphasize the peace. One raised his head to watch our progress, then returned to his feast, unfazed by our intrusion.

We passed the cottage. Although it had weathered to the silvery sheen of old cedar, the relative newness of the wood suggested it had been built long after the village was abandoned. On the porch stood a waist-high carving of a bird that could be a raven.

"Does someone live here?" I asked.

"Only in the summer. This is the watchman's house. Each month, from June until September, two people from our community live here and watch over the site to make sure no one damages it. It gives them the chance to get away from all the modern conveniences and immerse themselves in Haida ways. We call them watchmen, after the watchmen that sit on top of totem poles."

"Not completely electricity-free," I said, pointing to a solar panel strung up on a tree next to the cottage.

Becky laughed. "You know how it is. You've got to keep your iPod charged."

Her warm brown eyes sparkled. Her shimmering black hair rippled in the breeze. She really was quite a pretty young woman. I hoped she didn't linger too long on the memory of Allistair before moving on to another young man. I'd noticed several giving her an approving eye at the potlatch.

We reached the top of a rise and were beginning our descent along a grassy pathway lined with white shells when I heard what sounded like a motor. Though I could see the grey stones of a beach at the bottom of the slope, a line of trees blocked the view of the water.

Eric walked down and moved some branches aside. "It's a dinghy with two people in it. They're headed to a cabin cruiser moored farther out."

"I doubt they're tourists, so they're probably from the islands," Becky said.

When we joined Eric on the beach, I saw a long, sleek yacht about fifty metres out. The Zodiac was stopping next to a ladder hooked over the transom. Two people, cloaked in rain jackets with the hoods up, climbed up onto the boat. Cloë, who'd been straggling behind, came up beside me. "Where'd they come from?"

"Judging by the tightness of the pants on the smaller one, I suspect it's Sherry, with Ernest."

"What in the world would they be doing here?"

"She's got some crazy idea about going after the guy who killed François. Apparently Ernest thinks it's Johnnie, too, and says he knows where to find him."

The dense forest behind us suddenly seemed more threatening. "It's not here, is it?"

Eric waved his arms and called out to them. Either they didn't hear him or they chose to ignore him, for the yacht's engine started up. Within minutes the boat was moving away.

"Where would he stay?" Becky asked. "There's nothing here but ruins."

"There is the empty cottage."

"Yeah, right. I forgot." Both of us glanced at the roof of the cottage rising above the grass at the top of the hill.

"Wait a minute," I said, "Johnnie can't be here, or Ernest wouldn't be leaving."

"Yeah, right. Ern was probably showing her his ancestral village."

"Is it possible Johnnie could be hiding out somewhere around here?"

"I suppose. If you wanted to disappear, this part of Haida Gwaii would be the place to do it. But like I said, I don't see Johnnie cutting those ropes. Look, we'd better go see the poles. Auntie's going to be hopping mad if we aren't back soon."

She walked over to where Eric was standing, arms crossed, pondering two cantilevered silvery-grey poles that seemed to be defying gravity in their desire to remain upright. One pole, with its surface smoothed by a hundred or more years of wind and rain, revealed little of its past glory, while the other still bore the faint lines of carving.

"What do you think the carving is?" I tucked my hand into Eric's.

"He has quite the commanding eye, doesn't he?"

"Yes, he does look like he's trying to put the fear of god in us. From the size of the downward pointing beak, he could be a raven."

"You're right," Becky said. "The pole probably belonged to the village chief, who was a raven."

"Does that mean Ernest is a raven?" I asked.

"He's a Blue Shell Raven. He and Harry McMillan are cousins. His mother and Harry's father are siblings." She paused. "You know, Meg, I think I know where Ernest could be going to look for Johnnie."

"Is it far?"

"It's where we're going — Llnagaay."

At that moment, a head of white hair emerged above the grass near the cottage. "Oh dear, there's Auntie. We'd better get going."

Becky took off, with Eric and me in pursuit. Then I realized Cloë wasn't with us.

"Stop. Where's Cloë?"

"Damn that woman," Eric muttered under his breath, then shouted, "Cloë, where are you?"

He started walking back along the path. All that remained of her presence was the indentation where she'd knelt in the grass to examine a half-rotten pole lying on the ground.

Eric called out again.

The area was fairly open with only a scattering of upright poles and a few scraggly trees to block the view. Although the grass was high, she would need to be lying flat on the ground for us not to see her.

"She's not here."

Becky ran up. "What's happened?"

"My sister's wandered off. Any idea where she could've gone?"

"Shit, I hope she hasn't fallen into one of the house pits. One of them is pretty deep." She ran to the far side of the clearing and stopped beside a moss-covered mound that looked to have once been a massive length of timber. On the other side of the mound was a wide, deep rectangular hole, also covered in a thick carpet of green moss. Thankfully, it was empty.

"What is it?" I asked. "It looks dangerous."

"It's the interior of a chief's longhouse. The main floor was dug deep into the ground and surrounded by one or two layers of wooden platforms, where family members and slaves lived. The bottom floor was used for cooking and for ceremonial gatherings such as potlatches."

At that moment a faint sound of singing drifted from the direction of the beach.

"What the …" Eric exclaimed. He started to walk toward the sound and Becky and I followed. As we slipped through the trees and onto the beach, Eric was already bent over his sister, who was sitting cross-legged on the pebbles above the tide line. She was clutching something to her breast.

"What're you doing?" Eric demanded. "We have to go."

Ignoring him, she continued to rock side-to-side, singing a tune that reminded me of the lullaby my nanny used to sing. She was clearly in distress.

"Are you all right?" I asked.

My question only made her rock harder.

"What are you holding?" I tried to get a glimpse of it, but could only make out that it was a reddish colour.

"It looks like a carving," Eric answered.

"It's my son's. Isn't it beautiful?" Cloë held it up. "I have one just like it. When Eric reached for it, she brought it back to her breast.

"It is beautifully carved," I said. "Do you mind if I take a look?"

She placed it gently in my outstretched hand.

It was identical to the whale sculpture we'd seen at her home. With its back arched, its long thin dorsal fin pointed threateningly upward, as if it had just leapt out of the water in pursuit of prey. Jagged teeth lined its gaping mouth, giving it a menacing look.

"Allie's initials should be on the bottom." She turned the whale upside down and pointed to the letters *AZ* carved into the wood. "He only carved two of them, so where did this one come from? I found it on the beach propped against that tree." Cloë pointed to a flat boulder wedged against the base of a tree. There were several bluish white shells scattered on its surface and a folded piece of textured paper. I walked over and picked up paper. On the front was a Haida design of an eagle and a raven and on the inside were words written in what I assumed was Haida. I passed it to Becky.

"Sorry, I can't read Haida. Auntie knows some, so she might be able to translate. But I don't know whether we should take it. I think the carving and the shells were left as a sort of memorial. This might be a message to Salaana."

"We should respect the wishes of the person who left it," Eric said.

Becky nodded and placed the paper back amongst the shells. Eric propped the orca against the tree, partially covering the note to prevent it from blowing away.

"Do you think Ernest left it?" I asked.

"That's my guess," Eric said.

"But why?" I asked.

"This *is* his clan village," Becky said. "But where did he get the carving? Besides, why would Ern want to pay homage to Allie, especially here in a place that has nothing to do with him?"

"Because he feels guilty," Cloë spat out.

FIFTY-TWO

We were heading away from the serenity of the beach and back out into the rough open water when, without warning, the boat's outboard motor coughed and sputtered. I tensed. It caught and continued going. But after just a few minutes it stopped altogether with an unnerving puff of smoke.

"Stupid motor," Becky muttered as she scrambled to restart it.

The starter whined, but the engine didn't catch.

As the waves tossed us about like driftwood, Cloë and I clung to the railing. While our faces mirrored each other's fear, Louise's was twisted in annoyance. "Can't you get the stupid thing going," she said.

"There might be air in the gas line. Let me see what I can do," Eric offered.

He lurched toward the stern, bumping into us as he squeezed his way past. Struggling to keep his balance, he fumbled with his bandaged hands until he managed to undo the gas line. He sucked on the line carefully and spat the tiny amount of gas that found its way into his mouth over the side of the boat. Becky reattached the line to the motor and tried the starter again.

I held my breath.

Once, twice … and on the third try, the motor roared to life. A cheer went up and we were soon ploughing smoothly through the waves, which wasn't too soon for me as I'd begun to feel the first twinges of seasickness.

"Thanks," Becky called out to Eric. Louise smiled her thanks.

Eric gave them the victory sign and settled in to enjoy the ride.

"How're your hands?" I yelled into his ear.

He turned around. "They'll survive. You okay?"

"I'm fine, but will be a lot better once we get into calmer waters."

"That's my girl. Always up for a bit of adventure, eh?" His eyes twinkled, his dimples erupted.

"Yeah, right."

"If it's any consolation, we'll soon be out of this chop. Look where we're headed."

I was too busy hanging on to him to notice that we had veered away from the open sea and were now heading toward the far more civilized-looking water of a large bay surrounded by forest-covered peaks. Within minutes the boat's bucking diminished to a gentle undulation and I was able to relax. Though I wasn't sure about Cloë. She was still gripping the railing as if her life depended on it.

I also noticed a Cheshire Cat grin on her face, which was soon explained when I saw the tip of the orca carving sticking out of her pocket. I wondered what Ernest's reaction would be, but then realized that he would likely never find out. But if his offering had been homage to his gods, *they* would know. How would they react to the missing gift? With anger or understanding?

After the scene on the beach I was beginning to wonder if this trip was going to be too much for her. She seemed to be clinging more and more to her son's ashes. Would she be able to let them go?

I found it curious that Allistair's teacher had brought his pupil's carving all the way from Vancouver and left it as an offering on the beach of his ancestral village. Was it out of guilt, as Cloë suggested, or was there another more personal reason? Perhaps he truly mourned the untimely loss of a star pupil and this was his way of showing it. It could also be his way of returning this lost Haida boy to his roots. I was sorry Cloë had removed the carving. I liked the idea of the tiny killer whale being reclaimed by the sea.

For the next hour we wound our way down what seemed like a fjord, but turned out to be a channel separating Moresby Island from several smaller islands. The water was calm but achingly cold, as I was reminded when inadvertently splashed. Apart from one or two soaring eagles, it was an empty land. Given the steepness of the slopes and the denseness of the forest, I doubt there was much traffic of even the four-legged kind.

The channel came to an end and once again we journeyed out into a large protected waterway dotted with islands. As we motored along, I kept an eye out for Ernest's boat, but didn't see it. The Zodiac's engine would occasionally hiccup. Each time I held my breath and waited for it to die, but thankfully it didn't.

The tree-lined heights closed in again and Becky slowed us to a crawl. Peering intently into the water, she carefully manoeuvred the boat around a rock outcropping and down the middle of a narrow channel.

"This is Burnaby Narrows," she said. "The tide is high enough for us to go through now."

The waterway seemed no wider than a canal, but judging by the tide line it would broaden substantially as the sea level rose.

"The water is so clear you can see right to the bottom. I'll slow down so you can see some of the fabulous sea life that we share our homeland with."

"As long as it doesn't slow us down too much," Louise said.

"This won't take long, Auntie. When we're through, I'll go extra fast, okay?"

"Good." Unsmiling, Louise crossed her arms and prepared herself for the wait. After a minute or two, she seemed to have second thoughts, for she smiled. "Please, my friends, you must excuse the impatience of an old lady. Becky is right. This is the perfect place to view them."

Becky steered closer to the rocky shore. Eric and I hung over the side of the Zodiac. It was like looking into a giant aquarium — nature's aquarium, or more aptly, Mother Earth's. A myriad of purple, brown, and green sea anemone waved in the current. Among them lay a tangle of red, orange, and purple starfish. Drifting beside us pulsed numerous brilliant yellow jellyfish and one or two smaller orange ones. Eric pointed to a shifting school of tiny silvery fish that Becky identified as salmon fry.

We were so intent on watching the gallery below the water that we almost missed the happening on shore.

"Oh, dear," Cloë whispered. Her plaintive voice barely registered with me as I bent over the side of the boat, but Eric, more attuned to her moods, looked up.

"What did you say, Cloë?"

"I see something moving over there." She pointed to the opposite shore. "I think it's a bear."

We all turned to look. A massive black bear it was and a well-fed one at that, if his thick, glossy black coat was anything to go by. He was strolling along the boulder-strewn shore flipping rocks. He'd sniff the wet undersides and then move on.

"He's looking for crabs," Becky explained.

We watched as the bear clamped its mouth onto a large orange crab. The hard-shelled body slowly disappeared inside its mouth, the legs left wriggling outside. They quickly vanished, though, and I winced at the thought of all that shell going through the bear's digestive tract. *Better him than me*, I thought.

"*Taan,*" Louise said. "It's the Haida word for bear. In difficult times *taan* has brought great strength to my clan." She sighed. "Perhaps it will now." She said this in a voice that was barely louder than a whisper.

Uncertain if I'd heard her correctly, I glanced back. She looked troubled. Perhaps worry was the driving force behind her need to get to her village quickly, not just an old woman's impatience.

But what was causing this worry? As far as I knew, our trip was nothing but a simple visit to an abandoned village to sprinkle her grandson's ashes. Though I did find it curious that the trip's timing was suggested immediately after yesterday's phone call. She'd seemed unduly troubled when

Becky mentioned seeing the carver and his boat at Blue Shell Village. But when the young woman had brought up the possibility of Johnnie being at Llnagaay, the Matriarch had quickly dismissed it as being a ridiculous idea.

"Becky, we need to get going," Louise said.

"Sure, Auntie." Becky revved up the motor. Once more it hiccupped and sputtered and almost died. She swore, but managed to catch it in time. Soon the engine roared back to life and we were slicing our way through the narrows at perhaps a faster speed than was prudent.

Eric shouted back to Becky, "I don't like the sound of that motor. When we get there, I'll take a good look at it, okay?"

She nodded in agreement.

We soon left the channel and entered another large bay.

"Sorry, Meg," Becky said. "I'm afraid we'll hit more rough water when we head back out into Hecate Strait. There's no interior route to the village."

"Thanks for the warning."

Soon the waves were crashing over the bow and I was clinging to Eric for dear life again. But Becky piloted the boat like an expert and I kept telling myself that an adventure tour group wouldn't use such a boat unless they had complete confidence in its abilities to keep clients safe and dry.

Once again, the motor coughed and died.

"Shit," Becky cried out. "What's wrong with this stupid thing?"

I muttered, "Oh no, not out here." I gripped Eric harder.

The starter motor whined and whined and whined, but I didn't hear the heartening roar of the engine igniting.

Eric gave me a reassuring pat before standing and lumbering back to the stern, where he tried to clear the gas line again, this time without success. Believing it must be a problem with the gas tank, Becky switched to the spare tank, but the engine remained dead.

"I'm afraid we'll have to paddle to shore." She passed Eric one of the wooden oars. "You take the right and I'll do the left."

The shore seemed miles away from us, with nothing but giant tumbling waves in between.

FIFTY-THREE

After watching Eric trying to pretend that his hands weren't hurting, I grabbed his paddle and picked up the stroke. It proved impossible to keep the boat on course, so Eric steered as best he could with the dead motor. With my attention riveted on the paddling, I forgot about my fears, despite noticing that we weren't heading to the immediate shore, but to a point a few kilometres away.

It was hard work, so it didn't take long for me to run out of energy. Eric convinced Cloë to take over. Although she only lasted a short while, it was enough for me to recharge. So we continued, with Cloë spelling me off whenever I ran out of oomph. Becky, on the other hand, seemed to be running on high octane and kept going and going like the Energizer Bunny.

By the time we rounded the point into the calmer waters of a bay, I was exhausted, but I did manage a weak cheer at the sight of a beach a short paddle away. Once my feet were on solid ground, I collapsed on the hard stones. Becky, who wasn't so invincible after all, joined me, as did Cloë. The three of us lay stretched out, breathing in great gulps of air, until the incoming tide forced us to move.

"Becky, I'll take a look at the motor," Eric said. "We often have problems with the damn things at the fishing camp I run. Usually a few jiggles and a couple of whacks get them going." He chuckled. "And in case it doesn't, do you have an emergency tool kit?"

"I'll get it," she said.

"I think all of us could do with some warming up," Eric suggested. "Meg, see if you can rustle up some nice hot tea."

While Eric worked on the motor, Becky and I carried the heavy food pack, the water container, and the Coleman stove above the tide line to a clearing in the forest that crowded the edge of the beach.

This was my first up-close look at Haida Gwaii's famed rainforests and I was overwhelmed. Since old growth white pine grow on Three Deer Point, I was used to the size of tree Mother Earth can produce when left to her own devices, but never in my wanderings in the forests of Eastern Canada had I encountered such monsters. With diameters in excess of five to seven metres, the heights of these red cedars were in back arching territory reaching seventy or eighty metres. According to Becky, these were babies, only a few hundred years old. The six- or seven-hundred-year-old grandmothers were twice the size, but were only found in the inaccessible reaches of the archipelago where loggers had never tread.

Thick green moss carpeted the ground and anything that lay on it. Rocks, deadfall, and protruding tree roots took on amorphous otherworldly shapes. I even spied a forgotten hiking boot partially consumed by the moss. Though the wind must be buffeting the canopy, at ground level the moss muffled sound to a deadened silence.

The clearing where we set up our kitchen was relatively flat and large enough should we end up having to camp here. Settling herself on a rock, Louise took control of the stove, saying she'd cooked on stoves like this since long before any of us were born. In short order, she had the kettle heating up on the hissing flame.

"I think we could all do with some hot soup. We packed some, didn't we, Becky?" Louise asked.

While Becky passed her a couple of packages of dried chicken noodle soup and a pot, I searched for the tea bags and mugs. When I started to place a tea bag in each of the mugs I was summarily chastised by Louise. "Sorry, dear, I'm fussy about my tea. You will find a tea pot in the pack."

Sure enough, I discovered a large eight-cup Brown Betty carefully wrapped in tea towels and buried amongst the softer items. Given the amount of crazing in the royal blue glaze, the crack along the spout, and the black-stained interior, I'd say Louise had been using this teapot since before we were born. And it did make an excellent cup of tea. Well, almost. I prefer real milk to canned concentrate. But stranded in the back of beyond, I could hardly be choosy.

I waded out into the water to pass Eric a mug of hot tea and another mug of steaming soup. "How goes it?"

"Not good." The cover was off the motor and various parts lay strewn on the floorboards. He held up a tiny piece of metal. "This should've been replaced during the overhaul, but it wasn't. I've been trying to jury rig something, but I'm not having any luck."

"Not what we want to hear." I looked out over the vast empty bay. The distant mountainous shore appeared equally empty. I realized with a shiver the sun had gone. Dense rain-gorged clouds were moving in fast. "We're kind of far from help, aren't we?"

"Check if Becky brought a satellite phone. I also think you'd better start hauling the tents and the rest of our gear onto shore. I have a feeling we'll be camping here tonight."

As luck would have it, Becky hadn't brought a satellite phone. Louise hadn't wanted to pay the additional rental fee, figuring there was little that could go wrong. *Yeah, right.* She went on to say that in the old days her people got along very well without such luxuries. I almost shot back about her not thinking twice about using the luxury of the Zodiac and its motorized power, but held my tongue. If we had used a Haida canoe, we wouldn't be in this fix.

While I was returning to the Zodiac for my third load, I saw a white boat emerge from around the point that we had rounded. It was on a heading that would take it across the bay toward the next point of land. Unfortunately, it was a fair distance away.

I ran back onto the beach, jumped up and down and waved my arms and hollered. Louise and Becky joined me. Becky even waved her yellow jacket, but the boat continued chugging across the bay without so much as a shift in our direction.

"I think that's Ernest," I said. "It looks like the cabin cruiser we saw at his village."

"Yup, it looks like his Sunsucker," Becky answered.

"Where do you think he's going?"

"It's hard to tell. My ancestral village, SGang Gwaay, is in that direction, and so is Llnagaay."

"I bet he's going to Llnagaay," I said.

"Yup, after Johnnie, if he's there." She glanced at Louise, but the elder's only response was to purse her lips.

"How far away is it? Could we walk?"

"Totally impossible. Look at the terrain. Would you want to walk through that stuff?"

Nope. It was the same impenetrable shoreline we'd been passing since starting our journey: near vertical slopes plunging into the sea, trees so tightly packed a mouse would have difficulties getting through.

"I suppose in the old days there might've been a trail from here to Llnagaay, but no way it's still there," Becky said. "We've got no choice. We have to stay here until someone finds us."

"Yikes. Unless Ernest comes back this way that might never happen."

"My Dad'll come. He said if we weren't back in three days, he'd come looking."

Thank goodness for concerned fathers, I thought. "How will this affect your plans, Louise? You wanted to get to your village tonight." I watched the first drops of rain land on the water near Eric.

Louise sighed, turned her eyes to the lonely grey sea, and shrugged. "There is nothing more I can do. What will be, will be."

FIFTY-FOUR

Old Chief's Shame

By the time rain started seeping through the trees and splashing onto the pole, he was connecting the last line of the traitor's crest to the boy's eagle. It was only fitting that the link between the two should be the knife that killed the kid. It had taken awhile, but eventually the cedar had told him what the figure should be for the betraying clansman who almost destroyed the Greenstone Eagles. He wouldn't know if it was right until Auntie saw it. If he'd got it wrong, she would frown. But if he had it right, she would smile in her matriarchal way.

Even the shame of Old Chief he had to figure out on his own. No one knew, and if they did they weren't telling. But someone once mentioned a sailing ship; another said something about otter pelts. Then he remembered a story about another great Haida chief who'd been shamed by the Iron Men. He figured something like that must've happened to Old Chief.

He figured when Old Chief learned his treasure was stolen, he loaded up his canoes with clansmen and paddled out to the Iron Men's ship still moored in the bay. They would've invited him on board, just him on his own. They probably laughed as he struggled up the unfamiliar rope ladder and made snide remarks about the primitiveness of his chief's regalia, for it was certain that Old Chief would've been fully robed in his fancy goat's wool blanket and ermine-tail headdress. He might've even carried a copper or two to emphasize his highborn status.

He would've gone in peace, knowing their few rifles and spears couldn't win against cannon power. He probably was prepared to negotiate in true Haida fashion for the return of the treasure. Old Chief would've offered them something the Iron Men would consider of equal value, like canoe loads of otter pelts. But it didn't work.

Instead the bastards laughed at him. Not only did they keep the treasure, but they helped themselves to the pelts. To add to the shame, they stripped him of his regalia, forcing him to return to his men naked. Old Chief never recovered. Within a couple of years he was dead.

But the treasure was eventually returned, for why else would people continue to believe it was hidden near Llnagaay? He wouldn't be surprised if Old Chief's Matriarch had had a hand in its return.

Hearing the rain strengthen out on the water, he covered the pole with plastic sheeting. He felt good. He'd finished the story in time. Though he may not get to carve it, he knew it would get carved.

He watched his brother's grey boat skim across the water toward him. He limped down to the water. The pain was bad today.

Bro raised his fist in triumph. "The boat's come. It's show time."

FIFTY-FIVE

"Hey, anyone there?" a man's voice called out.

I was burrowing myself into a hole of thick, velvety moss, trying to find a missing gizmo.

"Louise, this you?"

Louise?! Where did Louise come from? I was alone. No wait. That's not true. Eric was here ... somewhere. I snuggled further down into the comforting moss.

"Hello, who's there?" called out another voice.

No, wait. That's Eric.

"Come on Meg, wake up. Someone's here."

I struggled to climb out of my dream although I didn't want to. I realized the soothing warmth was Eric and nestled deeper. We'd joined our two sleeping bags together to make for a warmer and more interesting night, although it had been a challenge with the three women sleeping almost on top of us in the other tent. The rain that had sent us scurrying into our tents was still beating down on the fly.

"My name is Siegfried," the stranger said. "I am seeking Louise O'Brien. Is she with you?"

"Yes, yes, Siggy. I'm here," came Louise's sleepy voice from next door.

"Eric," I whispered. "That's the guy from the restaurant."

"Un-hun."

"The one Sherry accused. Maybe Ernest is going after this guy and not Johnnie."

"The cops cleared him, remember?"

"Maybe, but alibis can always be broken. Do you think we can trust him?" I whispered.

"How did you know where to find me, Siggy?" Louise called out.

"When you didn't show up, I worried you might have run into trouble, so I came looking," the man answered.

Eric started putting on his clothes. "I think if Louise can trust him, we can too."

"How are things at Llnagaay?" Louise asked.

"Starting to heat up."

"I guess we'd better get going."

FIFTY-SIX

The Wait

He and his brother made their way to the inlet where Scav said the boat was moored. To keep their presence a secret, they left Bro's boat tied up in a cove not far from the inlet's entrance. They scrambled along the steep, rocky shore in the pouring rain until they could just make out the white shape of a cabin cruiser in the growing twilight. Thank Salaana, the tide was going out, making for easier walking, otherwise Bro would've had to do it on his own. Not a good idea, even if he was carrying his rifle. The situation would likely need both of their guns.

It was pretty dark by the time they reached a spot where they could see straight down the inlet to where the lights from inside the boat rippled across the water.

"There's only one boat," Bro said. "You sure the other's coming?"

"I'm sure." Just the way he was sure the end of this inlet was where the Iron Men's rowboat had tied up more than a century and a half ago. "It'll be here soon."

"You sure there'll just be the two boats?"

"I'm sure. They won't want anyone else in on this." The same way the Coward had kept the number of his men down to one, as had the Chief Iron Man.

"I guess we'd better make ourselves at home."

His brother scrambled over the rocks to where a tangle of overhanging spruce branches offered a degree of protection from the wet. He propped his back against the trunk and pulled out a flask from his jacket pocket.

"Bro, we don't need that."

"Best way I know to stay warm in this shit."

"We need to stay sober. We don't know what's going to happen."

"Yeah, but like you said, the action ain't likely to start till morning. We can sleep it off by then."

"Yeah, and wake up with the mother of all hangovers. That'd make us real alert, eh?"

"Okay, okay. Have it your way." He started to put it back in his pocket.

"I'll take it." Two Finger held out his hand, the one which had given him the nickname — though technically it was a finger and a thumb. The other fingers he'd lost in a fishing accident.

Bro jutted out his jaw in refusal, but after trying to ignore his brother's sneering stare, gave in and handed him the flask. Two Finger slipped it into his back pocket.

"Who do you think is here first?"

"I can't see the Geek getting here none too quick. He may have a fancy new boat, but I'm not sure he knows how to run it." He clenched his teeth as a jolt of pain ran right through him. He wondered how much worse it was going to get.

"What a laugh if he sunk it, eh?"

"Yup. It'd sure solve everything." But then they would never know.

"What're we gonna do when it gets here? Attack them?"

"Nope. We need to see if they find it. We need proof."

"So we gonna follow them and watch them dig it up?"

"Nope. No point in traipsing along a trail that hasn't been used since our people left. Let them get all scraped up. They've got to come back to their boats to get out of here, so we'll be sitting inside waiting for them."

"You sure Auntie is coming?"

"Yup. I told Scav to call her. She knows what's going to happen. She's going to do whatever it takes to stop them. The clan's her life. She won't let these guys destroy it."

He heard the sound of the boat before he saw it cutting through the water toward them. Although he didn't think they could see him in the dark and the rain, he ducked under the foliage to stand beside his brother.

"Sure hope they didn't see our boat," his brother said. "We should'a hid it better."

"They won't see it in this weather. Besides, they weren't looking for it. They think they're all alone on the edge of the world."

He could make out the blur of two faces in the light of the cockpit as the boat slipped by. He smiled in the blackness at nothing in particular other than his own sense of destiny. A hundred and fifty-five years later the story was playing out again with the same players, well, not quite, their descendents. He was going to make damn sure it had a different ending. This time the Matriarch would stop them.

FIFTY-SEVEN

The five of us scrambled into Siggy's Red Rocket, as he called his red Zodiac, and headed in the direction Ernest's boat had taken. The short journey ended in a small bay beside a rather unusual habitation. Although it appeared to be a normal two-storey house, closer examination revealed that it had been built one room at a time in lean-to and stacking fashion from an odd assortment of building materials. Siggy later bragged that he'd spent almost nothing on its construction. For the most part he'd scavenged logs and other items from nearby beaches and the Queen Charlotte garbage dump. He even bragged that some friends called him Scav, short for Scavenger.

In the interests of speed we left most of our gear behind. The only items we brought were clothes and sleeping bags and, of course, Allistair's urn, although in the turmoil of leaving it was almost forgotten. Although Becky didn't want to leave the boat and the gear unattended, Siggy assured her that they would be fine. He also promised to fix the motor, but only after it was over.

The only hint Louise gave that the purpose of our trip was other than to scatter her grandson's ashes was when she said to Siggy, "I hope I'm not too late. I can't let it happen again."

What the "it" was, neither was saying, despite Eric's offer of help. Louise merely made some cryptic comment about events in the past affecting events in the present. She finished by telling us to get some sleep, that tomorrow was going to be a long day.

Next morning we awoke to clear skies and a delicious breakfast Siggy had prepared on his woodstove. It included eggs collected moments before from a chicken coop and pancakes made from freshly ground millet flour using a grinder propelled by a stationary bike. With the only power source being some small solar panels, which ran the lights and his computer, Siggy had become very ingenious in providing himself with modern-day comforts.

As far as I could tell his was the only house on this shallow south-facing bay. The shore across the channel appeared as wild and devoid of human presence as every other shore we'd passed on our way to this southern tip of Moresby Island.

I thought Three Deer Point was isolated, with only one other habitation on Echo Lake, but we did have electricity and easy road access to stores and friends. Though surrounded by endless forests and lakes, I didn't feel as if Eric and I lived on the edge of the world.

Siggy, on the other hand, lived on the edge of the world with nothing but hundreds if not thousands of kilometres of empty ocean beyond the few islands that protected him from the ravages of the sea. The closest stores and people were back the way we'd come, a good five-hour boat trip away.

I was amazed to discover that he'd been living here for more than thirty years. No wonder he was a bit strange, with his carefully braided foot-long beard, which today sported purple and pink beads, and his single pirate-like gold hoop earring. All he needed was a black eye-patch to complete the impression.

"Where are they?" Louise asked, not bothering to identify who "they" were.

But Siggy knew. "The two of them went to Otter Inlet last night. I didn't see their boat when I last checked the lagoon, so I assume they're still there."

"What about the others? Have they arrived?"

"A boat came by late yesterday afternoon and headed toward Otter Inlet. Then, after dark, another passed by heading in the same direction."

"Just the two boats?"

"*Ja*. How many are you expecting?" Siggy asked.

"Two sounds about right. They're going to want to keep this to as few people as possible."

"They haven't passed back this way, so I assume they're still in the inlet, unless they took the other coast."

"They'll be moored in the inlet. They won't leave until they get what they came for."

I was dying to ask what was going on and whether one of the boats was Ernest's. I could tell from the Eric's arched brow he wanted to know too. But the intense resolve on Louise's face told us that she wasn't about to satisfy our curiosity.

"How long do you think it will take?" Siggy asked.

"I've no idea. It depends on how well they can read the map. Did Col tell you what this was about?"

"He just said it had to do with saving the clan's honour and something to do with correcting past wrongs."

I waited, but she deflected Siggy's ignorance with "It's a long story and I don't have time to go into it now, but when this is over I will tell you the story of our shame." She included all of us in her gaze.

"Col also said it had something to do with stopping a killer. What's that all about?"

"So it's true. I wasn't sure."

"Who got killed?" Siggy asked.

She sighed. "My grandson, the man who should've been Chief Greenstone."

"Gotverdomme," Siggy swore at the same time as Cloë cried out, "What? Allistair's murderer is here?"

Until now she'd been playing with her food and paying little attention to Louise and Siggy. Occasionally she'd smile sweetly to herself and caress the bag containing her son's ashes.

"Where is he?" She stood up. "I need a gun."

She glanced frantically around the crowded room. Her eyes passed over the book-filled shelves, the jumble of dirty dishes on the counter, the assortment of clothes hanging from a line of wall hooks, until they rested on a rifle propped next to the back door. But Eric, anticipating her move, blocked the gun just as she was about to grab it.

"Cloë, get a hold of yourself. You can't settle it this way. Let the due process of law be the judge," he said.

"Hah! You believe that shit. He'll get off on a technicality. They always do. Give me the gun."

As she reached behind his back, Siggy grabbed the rifle and removed the cartridges.

"Child, I feel your pain," Louise said. "I've lost him, too. But killing the person who put an end to his short life won't heal your pain or mine. We must let destiny take its course. What will be, will be. Come, sit beside me."

Cloë continued to glower at Eric and Siggy, then, with a deep sigh, she sat beside Louise on a sofa. But before she did, she retrieved the urn and placed it between the two of them.

FIFTY-EIGHT

We waited as the morning sun gradually lit up the red geraniums on the sill of Siggy's bay window. After the unsettling conversation between Louise and Siggy, Eric and I had been expecting something to happen. But the elder remained sitting beside Cloé. Occasionally she would pat her grandson's urn as she sipped her Darjeeling tea. Not once did she choose to break her silence.

Meanwhile, Becky and I busied ourselves by doing the dishes with hot water scooped from a large battered pot simmering on the woodstove.

Cloé hummed softly to herself. I was worried about her. After she had tried to grab the rifle, she'd returned to this almost trance-like state, seemingly oblivious to what was happening around her. I wasn't sure whether it was a result of her overwhelming grief or her concussion. She no longer wore the bandage. In a fit of fury yesterday, she had ripped it off when it slipped down over her eyes. After checking the wound, Eric felt it was healing nicely and no longer needed the bandage. She hadn't complained about dizziness or headaches in well over a day. So I was hoping it was only her grief that was affecting her. That we could deal with. A worsening brain injury we couldn't, not this far away from medical help.

Eric tried distracting her by suggesting a walk, but she ignored him. After several more rebuffed entreaties and a "best leave her alone" from Louise, he turned his attention to the strange apparatuses strewn around Siggy's house.

An initial query about a web-like piece of wire attached to the ceiling brought Siggy running to proudly declare it was an aerial for his shortwave radio, which he immediately turned on to some Japanese station to show how effectively it worked. He then set out to explain all the other gizmos he'd invented to make life easier on the edge of the world.

After a couple of hours, Louise finally stood up and declared that it was time to go. She walked across the room to where her pack lay propped against the rest. After putting on a heavy wool sweater, she pulled out her red and black button blanket and draped it around her shoulders, snapping the clasp into place. Next she rummaged around in the pack until her ceremonial cedar bark hat appeared in her hands. She shook it vigorously to get rid of the creases. Placing it over her short, curly white hair, she tied it securely under her chin with a thin strap of braided cedar bark. A leather pouch came next. This she placed in the pocket of her jeans.

Taking this as a sign that we were about to leave for Llnagaay for the scattering of the ashes, I put on an extra sweater and my Gore-Tex jacket. I was hoping I wouldn't need the cumbersome wet weather gear. For the moment the sky was cloudless. Hopefully if rain were coming we'd be back inside the dryness of Siggy's house by the time it arrived.

I insisted Eric wear an extra sweater too. Though he showed no signs yet of a cold after his soaking, I wanted to make sure he didn't get one.

Cloë remained seated, her eyes focused on her son's urn, which now rested in her lap.

"You better put on some warmer clothes," I said. "We're going."

Louise looked up. "Oh dear, I'm sorry. I should've told you. We're not going to Llnagaay right away. There's something I have to do first and I need to do it on my own, although I want Eric and Siggy to come with me. I will need them as witnesses."

"Happy to," Eric said. "What will we be witnessing?"

"I'd rather not say."

"I want to respect your ways, Louise, but I would feel much better if my wife came with me. I don't feel comfortable leaving her here on her own."

"She will be quite safe here, as will Becky and your sister."

"You're going to this Otter Inlet, aren't you?" I said. "You want to confront your grandson's killer. Is it Ernest?"

As if I hadn't said a word, she continued, "If we don't return within a few hours I want you to call the RCMP on Siggy's satellite phone."

"Why not bring them in now?" I asked.

"Because there are things I must do that don't concern the police."

"I don't want my husband going."

"I know it's asking a lot of you, but I need him. Besides, he won't come to harm. This only concerns me and my family."

"It's okay, Meg. I'll be careful."

"But Eric, I almost lost you once. I don't want to lose you again."

He wrapped his arms around me. "My *Miskowàbigonens*, don't worry. I won't do anything silly. Besides, I've only used up two of my nine lives. I still have seven more." He grinned.

Louise walked over to Cloë. "Child, do you mind giving me your son, my grandson."

"Why?" The distraught mother clung to the velvet bag. "I want to scatter his ashes, too."

"I promise you we will do this later, together, but first I need him. He has one last duty to perform."

Cloë continued to clutch the heavy bag to her breast. Louise waited.

Finally Cloë spoke. "I don't understand why you need my son, but he *is* Haida. He must follow your ways." She brushed her lips against the soft velvet before handing it to Louise.

Siggy, decked out in a black and red lumberman's shirt with a black watch cap pulled down over his unruly hair, tossed Eric a rifle from a cupboard. "I'm assuming you know how to use this."

Eric nodded grimly. I didn't like this at all.

Siggy helped himself to the other rifle in the cupboard, but left the one Cloë had gone after propped beside the door.

"Auntie, be safe." Becky gave her a long hug.

"You take care of yourself too, child." She patted the young woman gently before turning to leave.

While Cloë remained inside the house, Becky and I escorted the three of them down to the water and watched silently as the Red Rocket, with Louise sitting proudly in the bow gripping her hat, sped across the bay and disappeared into the channel beyond.

We returned to the house with the instructions to call the RCMP if they didn't return by 4:00 p.m., six hours from now.

I chose to ignore those instructions. I called the number Siggy had given us to let them know that the killer of Allistair Zakharov could be found on Otter Inlet at the south end of Moresby Island. I didn't care if Louise got angry with me. My husband's life and hers and Siggy's were more important to me than letting her keep her secrets.

I asked them to hurry.

FIFTY-NINE

While I anxiously watched the clock, waiting for the police to arrive, Becky tried to hide her own nervousness by flipping through a book. She was in complete agreement with my decision to call the police. If I hadn't, she would have.

The house was quiet, almost too quiet, but for the ticking of the clock and the rustling of the pages. None of us was interested in talking. Surprisingly, Cloë had roused herself a short while ago and gone outside. She'd said nothing since passing her son's ashes over to Louise, so I had no idea what she was feeling or whether she appreciated the danger her brother might be in. And I hadn't asked. I was too worried about Eric.

"You know, in the old days the matriarchs were often the ruling force in our communities," Becky said, putting the book down. "When the men screwed up, the women took over." She laughed and then grew serious. "I think that's what Louise is doing. But I'm worried. Whatever this is about, it might be more than she can handle."

"She has Eric with her. If any man can handle a difficult situation, he can. I suspect Siggy would be a good man to have around too. Still, I'm worried. When someone has killed, they won't hesitate to do it again." I shuddered and said a silent prayer for Eric. "Do you think the murderer could be Ernest, even if he has an alibi?"

"I don't know him that well. But apart from shouting at Allie whenever he screwed up, Ern always treated him with respect. Besides, what reason would he have for killing him?"

"That's the problem. There doesn't seem to be any motive. What about Louise's nephews? Could either of them have done it?"

"God, I sure hope not. But, you know, I was surprised to hear Siggy say that Col was here."

"You said he lived in Vancouver."

"Yeah, that's right …" She began pacing back and forth in front of me. "He used to be a fisherman until the industry went under. He's a carver now."

"Do you think it could've been Col who stole Allistair's totem pole and brought it here?" I asked.

"That would make him a suspect too, wouldn't it?" She shook her head. "For Auntie's sake, I sure hope not. It would destroy her."

"Let's not forget Johnnie's a suspect in the rope cutting."

"I know."

"I hope the police come soon."

"I don't understand. They're both great guys. Sure they've got their problems, like a lot of people. But I don't see either of them being capable of doing such terrible things. Two Finger, that's what we call Col, because he has only two fingers on one hand, he saved Dad's life. It was when they were working on the fishing boats. Dad got tangled up in a net and fell overboard. Two Finger jumped in and saved him."

She suddenly stopped at a window. "Hey, someone's out there in a kayak. Where'd they come from?"

I ran to join her. A yellow and white kayak was about halfway across the bay, headed in the direction the Red Rocket had gone. I felt a sudden chill when I realized the person paddling had blond hair and was wearing a bright blue jacket. "Where's Cloë?"

We raced outside, screaming her name. I ran one way around the house, while Becky ran the other. But the only answer to our repeated calls was the waves lapping against the rocks and the cry of gulls from across the water.

"I'll check back in the house in case she came inside when we weren't looking," I offered as a last hope.

But I knew deep down that she was the one paddling as fast as she could toward her son's killer. To confirm my suspicions, the first thing I did when I went back in the house was check to see if the rifle was still leaning against the wall. It was gone. And scattered on the floor was a box of cartridges.

"The rifle's gone!" I shouted, running back outside in time to see Becky emerge from some crumbling brickworks.

"That's got to be Cloë in the kayak," she said. "I've looked all over."

The kayak was moving at a fair clip and had almost reached the channel. I was surprised at Cloë's paddling skill, given her decidedly urban bent.

"We have to go after her. Does Siggy have another boat?" I asked.

"I don't know, but I'm not sure we should go. Auntie was pretty insistent that we stay here."

"Cloë could cause a real mess, especially with that gun. We have to stop her."

I ran to where I remembered seeing a couple of overturned kayaks lying on the shore. There was an empty space where one of them had been. When I turned over the other, I groaned at the sight of several gaping holes in the deck and a smashed bow. "Is there anywhere else Siggy might keep a boat?"

"Maybe in the cove beyond the old whaling station." She pointed in the direction of the decaying brickworks.

I ran past her and onto a path that wended its way through crumbling brick buildings, rusting iron vats, and other debris. It opened onto the shore of a rock-lined cove. Moored in the middle of the cove was an aluminum fishing boat, very much like my own putt-putt, complete with an outboard motor. Although there were a few dents in the hull, it appeared seaworthy. Jammed into the rocks next to me was an overturned lightweight plastic kayak with a paddle underneath.

"Becky, there's a boat," I shouted. "I'm going to take it." I hefted up the kayak and began carrying it down to the water. "Are you coming?"

I dropped the kayak onto the water, squeezed myself into it, and paddled out to the boat. I gingerly transferred from one boat to the other and fixed the kayak's rope to a cleat. Crossing my fingers that this motor wasn't going to be temperamental, I pulled the starter. Miraculously, it caught.

I shouted Becky's name again, hoping she could hear me. Although I didn't want to go on my own, I didn't have time to coax her. As I was untying the mooring line and securing the kayak to the buoy I heard a noise on the shore and looked up to see her standing on the rocks wearing a life jacket. In one hand she carried another life jacket and in the other a gas can.

"I think we'll need these," she said.

After paddling the boat close enough for her to climb in, we took off after Cloë. The putt-putt motor might not be a racing machine, but it would be faster than her paddling. Although she'd already disappeared around the point, I was hoping we would catch up to her before she reached the others. Thankfully, the water conditions were with us, not quite flat calm, but not choppy enough to slow us down either. When we moved into the channel, the wind picked up along with the waves. Fortunately they were going in our direction.

"I don't see Cloë. Do you?"

"No, but the entrance to Otter Inlet is another kilometre or so ahead. She's probably already reached it," Becky yelled from her seat in the bow.

"It's a bit rough for a kayak. Do you think she could've dumped?"

"We'd see the yellow bottom of the kayak. She looked like she knew what she was doing, so I think she made it to the inlet."

We skirted along the inhospitable shore and passed an opening to a lagoon with a sizeable beach. In the trees beyond, I could make out something orange.

"Keep further out," she shouted. "There are some rocks up ahead."

I saw their jagged tops in time and dipped around them.

We chugged along for another fifteen or so minutes, then Becky said, "The entrance to the inlet is just beyond that dead tree."

I reduced our speed. "I'll go slow. No telling what might greet us when we round the corner."

We skirted the carcass of a once-mighty Sitka spruce and inched along the shore until it fell away to reveal the calm waters of a deep narrow inlet surrounded by steep mountain slopes. At the far end, a kilometre or two away, I could make out the white hulls of two large boats. Siggy's Red Rocket floated closer to shore beside another boat, grey in colour. Halfway between us churned Cloë's yellow and white kayak.

The scene appeared deceptively calm. I couldn't make out anyone on the boats or on the shore. More importantly, I didn't see Eric's bright red jacket.

Where was everyone?

SIXTY

Revving the engine, I yelled, "We've got to get to Cloë before she reaches the boats."

We churned through the water toward the blond head. She glanced back at us and I could sense her horror as she realized she was being chased. She paddled harder. For a second she seemed to move away from us, until I opened up the throttle completely.

"Come on, old girl," I muttered under my breath. "Don't conk out on me now." My own aging outboard sputtered at the mere hint of going full speed. But this one seemed to thrive on it. Thank god.

Despite Cloë's frantic paddling, we were gaining on her. But she was closing in on the first moored boat, a sleek, expensive-looking seagoing yacht whose pristine newness made me hazard a guess on the ownership. I waited for someone to emerge.

Eric's sister slowed down and scanned the boat carefully as she drifted past. When no one appeared, she picked up her speed and paddled to the next high-class yacht. This one I did recognize.

"Becky," I shouted, "that's Ernest's boat, isn't it?"

"Yup. My cousin made those curtains in the main cabin."

"Sure has done well for himself, hasn't he?"

We were nudging the kayak's stern by the time Cloë reached the boat.

"Leave me alone," Cloë shouted. She dropped her paddle onto the kayak deck, lifted out the rifle from between her legs, and pointed it at us. "I'll shoot, if you come near me."

I put the engine into neutral. "Please, Cloë, come with us. It's not safe here. You could get killed."

"I don't care. I'm going after my son's killer. Do you know which boat is his?"

"Killing him won't solve anything."

"With Allistair dead my life is over anyways. I wasn't always there for my son. This time I will be. I'm going to make damn sure this man pays for what he has done to me."

"Look, Cloë, the police will soon be here. Let them deal with him."

"Hah! You honestly think our judicial system will give him what he deserves. Like hell. Even if they manage to convict him, he'll be walking free in five years or less while my poor Allistair is gone forever. Now back off or I'll shoot." As if to emphasize the point, she fired the rifle into the air, sending a flock of gulls soaring. She aimed the rifle back at us.

What to do? I figured with one very forceful thrust, I could overturn the kayak and Cloë into the water along with the rifle, rendering it useless. But could I do it before she shot us?

Before I could make up my mind, a shout came from shore. "Cloë, put the rifle down."

Eric stood astride a boulder at the water's edge. In his hand he held a rifle. He motioned for me to move away from her and out of the line of fire.

"If you don't, I'll shoot you," he yelled above the sound of the boat's motor.

"You wouldn't kill me, Eric. I'm your sister."

"And Meg's my wife, and she means more to me than life itself. If you harm her, you're dead. Now throw the gun into the water."

Oh Eric, my love. Watch out she doesn't shoot you instead.

I moved the boat farther away and watched her chin rise in resistance and her shoulders brace for action. The rest of us remained frozen, not daring to move.

"My brother doesn't love me either," Cloë muttered.

Oh shit. Here goes. I started to shout, "Watch out, Eric!" when I heard the splash. It took a few seconds for the sound to register. When it did, I felt limp with relief. She had thrown the rifle into the water.

Then the tears came. "Oh Eric, I'm so sorry. I don't know what came over me. I'm just so angry at everyone and everything for what they did to Allistair."

"I know. I feel your pain. Can you get to shore?"

She began paddling toward her brother.

"Meg, you and Becky go back to Siggy's. I'll keep Cloë with me."

"No, Eric, I'm staying with you."

At this point a man emerged from the trees and strode onto the beach. He wore a traditional Haida vest over his jean jacket and a woven band around his head, much like the ceremonial clothing the men had worn at the potlatch. "Auntie says they stay."

He raised a hand to his face to brush something away. I stiffened. It wasn't a complete hand. I glanced at Becky to judge her reaction. But she was waving a greeting at Two Finger as if she'd forgotten our earlier conversation.

Fortunately, when Becky and I were talking about the possibly of this man being Allistair's killer, Cloë was frantically paddling away from us. Though it probably didn't matter; she was going to suspect any strange man she met on these shores.

With his rifle relaxed at his side, Eric seemed at ease with the man, suggesting that he didn't believe him guilty of murder. But Eric wasn't with us either when the possibility was raised. Yet Louise had said that the reason for this visit was to stop a killer. So if it wasn't the man talking to Eric, who was it?

I didn't give my husband a chance to convince Two Finger we weren't needed. I drove the boat up onto the pebbles and jumped out.

"Hi," I said, "I'm Meg Harris, Eric's wife." I held out my hand and felt a firm handshake. I searched for guilt in his gaunt, almost skeletal face, but saw only worry and something else, maybe resignation.

He gave Becky a bear hug. "It's been a long time, kiddo. You sure ain't the little pipsqueak who used to steal jelly beans from my pockets." His eyes twinkled with admiration as he eyed her slim yet curvaceous figure. "Sorry to hear about your boyfriend."

While they talked, I turned to Eric. "What's going on? Where's Louise and Siggy? Are they okay?"

"They're fine. In fact, Louise seems to have everything firmly under control."

"Where are Ernest and Sherry?"

"With Louise."

"Does the other boat belong to —"

Two Finger interrupted. "We should go. Auntie's expecting us." He headed up a path leading away from the beach, Becky not far behind.

Eric and I started to follow, but I noticed we were missing the last member of our group, again. "Where's your sister?"

The kayak lay abandoned on the pebbles, along with the paddle. But Cloë was nowhere in sight.

"Christ, where's she got to now?" Eric said.

"Maybe she went on ahead."

"Who knows? Given her current frame of mind, she could be anywhere. I'd better look for her. You go on ahead."

"No, I'll look with you."

After many futile minutes of calling out her name and searching the bush around the beach, we decided she must have snuck past us and gone up the trail after the others.

"Thank god, she doesn't have the rifle anymore," Eric said as we started up the path.

SIXTY-ONE

We tramped along a barely discernible trail, more like an indentation in the all-pervasive moss, through the dense rainforest. The trail wended its way up, in and around giants whose enormous moss-covered roots crisscrossed the forest floor. I stumbled over them several times. If not for Eric's steady hand, I would have fallen. Because the going was so tricky, it was difficult to keep an eye out for Cloë. Every once and a while Eric or I would stop, hoping to catch sight of her, but finally realized that in the thick forest she could be walking only metres away and we would never know.

Sound was once again muffled into silence by the relentless moss. Like the calm before a storm the stillness had a menacing feel to it, no doubt augmented by the eerie half-light we were walking through. Although Becky and Two Finger had a fair lead on us, because of the man's slow, almost halting gait, we were closing in on them. Apart from the four of us, the forest seemed devoid of life. Not a squirrel twitched or a bird fluttered. I wondered where Louise, Siggy, and the others were.

The path grew steeper, the trees smaller— if you could call a metre-thick tree smaller. At one point I thought I heard singing, but when I didn't hear it again I blamed it on an overactive imagination. We caught up to Becky and Two Finger and slowed our pace to match theirs. The funereal speed didn't bother me. I wasn't entirely convinced I wanted to get to wherever Two Finger was taking us.

The trees abruptly stopped and a rock face appeared out of the gloom. Almost vertical, with no obvious footholds, the granite wall looked to be at least ten metres high. It disappeared into the shadows in either direction, with no apparent way around it.

Two Finger stopped and took a few minutes to catch his breath. He seemed unusually thin, so much so that I wondered if he was ill.

"Do you know where we're going?" I asked Eric.

He shook his head. "I've only seen the beach, where Louise told me to stay. She's good at giving orders." He grinned. "She wanted me to stop people from going inland."

"It's new to me, too," Becky said.

"Follow me." An unsmiling Two Finger pointed to the right and started shuffling along the uneven ground next to the cliff face.

Judging by the footprints in the odd patch of bare earth, Louise and Siggy and maybe the others had scrambled along here recently. Given Louise's stiffness, it wouldn't have been easy for her. But I had a feeling that her iron will would overcome any pain.

I was concentrating so hard on my footing that I failed to notice Siggy until Two Finger said, "Hey, Scav, any action?"

The Dutchman was sitting on a boulder next to where part of the cliff had crumbled. On his lap rested his rifle.

He stood up as Two Finger approached. "I haven't seen anybody since Auntie and your brother headed up." He nodded in our direction. "I see you have company. Auntie said if they came, they were to go too."

He motioned to a cleft in the wall. About a metre and a half wide, it sliced through the granite to the sky above. Two Finger disappeared into it, as did Becky.

I turned to Eric. "What should we do about your sister?"

"I'm sure she's around here somewhere." He looked back the way we'd come. "She's in rough shape, isn't she?"

"I'm afraid she might be having a nervous breakdown."

"She's always been kind of flighty, but I've never seen her this bad. I shouldn't have let my anger get the better of me. I should've stayed in touch."

"Don't blame yourself. These things happen. I don't think there is much either of us can do for her at the moment other than to be there for her while she works her way through her grief."

"I know, but hell, she could get us killed in the process. I should've recognized how fragile she was and insisted she stay in Queen Charlotte."

"But we thought this was going to be a simple scattering of Allistair's ashes. I was hoping it would help."

"I did too. Instead, it's become something far riskier. I sure as hell wish I knew what it *was* about." Balancing the rifle in his hand, he turned to Siggy. "What's waiting for us on the other side of this passage? Should I have my gun ready?"

"You won't be in any danger. If I know Auntie, she will have the situation under control. The rifle is only a precaution."

"And what is the situation?"

Ignoring Eric's question, he said, "You better get going."

"Eric, I'll wait here in case Cloë comes, okay?" I said. "You go."

Siggy shook his head. "You can't stay behind. She wants all of you with her. If the woman comes this way, I'll send her on. And don't make any noise. This is a sacred place."

I entered the defile with the comforting sound of Eric's footsteps close behind. My nostrils twitched at the dank smell of decay emanating from the darkness. Although light seeped down from above, it was not enough to light up the floor. To help guide me, I kept one hand on the cold, damp wall. I was glad I did when my foot smashed into an unseen rock jutting up from the floor.

"Careful," Eric whispered placing a bracing hand on my back.

I could just make out Becky's yellow jacket several metres ahead of me. She appeared to be moving at a higher elevation. Then I felt the gradient rise, until it became fairly steep. The walls grew lower and it got brighter until I could see Becky and Two Finger clearly as they climbed up through the pass. Soon they were in full sunlight as they disappeared over the lip. I stepped into the brilliance with Eric right behind me.

Although I was momentarily blinded, I kept walking until I felt Eric's restraining hand on my arm. "Stop," he said.

I'd been walking toward the edge of a cliff.

"Wow!"

Before us stretched the magic of Haida Gwaii; at our feet the undulating forest canopy, and beyond that lay shimmering blue inlets and bays and the rich green of the neighbouring islands. Beyond the islands stretched the endless cerulean expanse of the Pacific Ocean. We were truly at the edge of the world. On either side of our granite perch the mountains continued to rise. We seemed to be in a high valley.

"Fabulous, isn't it?" Eric said. "But we've got to go. The other two went through the trees over there."

Once again we found ourselves back in the gloom of a dense forest, but these fir trees were neither as tall nor as thick as the giants below. After meandering a short distance, the trail ended at a clearing at another cliff face, this one not as high as the last, but with several yawning gaps in its jagged, lichen-covered surface.

Four people were sitting cross-legged on the moss in a semi-circle facing the wall. One was Louise, resplendent in her ceremonial blanket and cedar hat and looking none the worse for her difficult trip up here. Another was the man I'd seen accosting the new chief at the pole raising, the man Louise said was her nephew Johnnie. He resembled Two Finger in height and facial features, but carried considerably more weight on his tall frame. Like his brother, he wore a ceremonial vest and headband.

As I'd done with his brother, I tried to read guilt in his deeply bronzed face. After all, he was the man being accused of cutting the ropes that killed François. But once again I saw only sombre resignation.

A rifle rested on the man's legs. Its muzzle was pointed in the direction of the other two people, whose identities came as no surprise: Ernest Paul and Sherry. Neither appeared pleased. Fighting mad was more the expression on Sherry's face, while Ernest firmed his lips in defeat.

On the ground directly in front of Louise sat a bent-wood box with Haida figures painted in red and black on the sides. How sad, I thought, that the only time Allistair was truly Haida was in death. What a difficult decision it must've been for Cloë to finally admit that her son belonged as much to the Haida world as to her own.

Without saying a word, Louise motioned for Eric, Becky, and me to join the circle beside her. Raising her eyebrows, she mouthed, "Cloë?" Although she seemed unperturbed by Eric's response, I thought I heard her mutter, "What will be, will be."

Two Finger, his rifle firmly gripped in his good hand, took up a position closer to the rock face.

When I sat down I realized we were facing what appeared to be an entrance to a cave, and Two Finger seemed to be guarding it.

Louise continued to sit in silence. Johnnie, his body stiff with tension, flicked his eyes back and forth from the carver to his brother to the cave. Sherry also glanced nervously at the yawning hole, while Ernest ignored it.

Someone was inside. Friend or foe? Probably foe. Why else the guns.

Everyone stiffened as a sudden noise came from the cave. It sounded like something scraping along the ground.

A woman's voice that seemed familiar said, "Jeez, this had better be worth it."

Suddenly the filthy back end of a man appeared in the opening. He backed his way out of the hole dragging a wooden box. It, too, was covered with dirt. Pushing the other end of the box was a woman, also crawling on hands and knees and equally dirty. The man, his back still to us, lumbered to his feet and with a forceful tug pulled the box free of the cave. He bent down to help the woman up. Her face was hidden by her long hair. Given her size, I thought for a moment she'd become wedged in the hole, but the man was able to pull her free, and with a "Never again," she lay splayed out, panting, face down on the soft moss.

Louise coughed.

The man wheeled around and gasped.

The woman raised her head. She narrowed her eyes and directed them straight at Louise. She hissed, "It's ours. You're not going to stop us."

SIXTY-TWO

I wasn't surprised, and judging by the expression on Eric's face, neither was he, to see the new Chief Greenstone and his mother emerging from the cave. The fancy new yacht had been the tip-off. But the shock mirrored on Becky's face told me she hadn't suspected.

"What are they doing here?" she asked.

"Yes, tell us." A smile verging on smugness crept over Louise's face.

"I don't have to tell you anything. You're not the Matriarch anymore," Rose retorted. "Now get out of my way."

Gripping the box like a battering ram, she pushed her bulk forward, her son close behind. Before she had gone two steps, Johnnie blocked her way. Even though his rifle remained pointed away from her, the message was clear. His brother, his rifle likewise crossed against his chest, pulled up behind Harry, squeezing the two of them into a vice grip.

"Why don't the two of you sit down," Louise said. "I'd like us to discuss this like reasonable Haida."

The former Greenstone Matriarch sat like a Buddha, calm and serene. From the slight upward twitch of her lips, I thought she might even be enjoying this.

Harry remained standing, as did his mother. When his gaze fell on Ernest and Sherry, he started, as if noticing them for the first time. Ernest shrugged. With the bravado gushing out of him, Harry sank cross-legged to the ground. His mother, on the other hand, continued to stand, her chin jutting out in challenge, the box crushing her bosom.

"Awaay, sit down. It's over," Harry said. "Look who else is here."

"They took us by surprise," Ernest said.

Rose whirled around to face him. "That woman's got no rights. We're still going through with it."

Sherry bit her bottom lip. "You sure? She said she'd have me arrested."

"Rose, take a seat and show us what's inside that marvellous box," Louise said.

It was indeed a marvellous box, as fine an example of a bentwood box as any we'd seen at the museum. The wood wore the rich mellow sheen of old cedar. Although the colours of the painted Haida creatures were faded, the carving on the lid didn't appear to have been blunted by time. Unfortunately the creeping darkness of rot marred one of the bottom corners. This box was very old.

When Rose leaned over to place the box on the ground, a necklace dangled from her neck.

"Hey, that's Allie's," Becky cried out. "I'd know that jade necklace anywhere."

Rose grabbed the pendant and slipped it under the neck of her sweatshirt. But not before I also saw the familiar green stone.

"You stole it!" I hissed. "You broke into my sister-in-law's room, knocked her unconscious, and stole it."

For a moment, Rose seemed at a loss for words. Then she turned to her son and was about to say something when he spoke up. "I did it. But I didn't mean to hurt your sister. It was an accident."

"I don't think Cloë would agree. What's so valuable about the necklace that you had to steal it?" I asked.

"Yes, tell us," Louise said.

"Why should I?" Rose shot back. "You're the one who knows all about it." With a groan she eased herself to the ground.

"But your son stole it. He must've had a good reason."

Harry looked at his mother and started to speak, but she cut in. "What can I say? He loves his mother. I saw the white woman wearing it. Admired it. And Harry, wanting to please his mother, borrowed it."

"Borrowed? Yeah, right," I retorted. "But more importantly, when could you have seen Cloë wearing it? The only time she had it was when you were caught up in the pole raising and potlatch, and she didn't go to either."

"Okay, okay, I told Harry," Ernest said. Rose glared at him.

"Why? What would it mean to him?"

"Yes, do tell us," Louise said.

"You know perfectly well," Rose answered.

"I want to hear it from you."

Rose clamped her mouth shut and jutted her chin out in a show of refusal. She jammed the box against her thigh and kept her hand firmly on it.

"Come on, Awaay. It's over. Tell her what she wants to hear. If not, I will," Harry said with a sudden display of independence.

"It's a map," his mother said through gritted teeth.

"Why don't you take it off and show us."

Rose wrenched the pendant from around her neck. In the process it became entangled in her long hair. When she finally freed it, she threw it at Louise. It landed out of reach, so Johnnie retrieved it. He looked it over thoughtfully before passing it to his aunt.

Louise gently brushed off the dirt. "It's been a long time since I've held this. A family heirloom you Europeans might call it. My nanaay many generations back made it. We don't have a term for 'great' in Haida, but she would be a great-grandmother several times over." She glanced over at Rose. "I guess she was your nanaay too."

"Damn right," Rose spat out. "I have as much right to it as you."

"No, you don't. And you know why."

The two women locked eyes for what seemed interminable minutes. Rose was the first to look away.

Louise continued. "This long-ago nanaay was the sister of Old Chief and the Matriarch of the Greenstones. Before she died she gave this pendant to her daughter, who became the next Matriarch and so it has been passed down through these many years, from Matriarch to Matriarch." She caressed the greenstone, then clenched it tightly in her fist. "But only the Matriarchs know its secret. So Rose, how do you know? I've never told anyone, not even my own daughter."

"Yeah, well someone in your la-di-da family squealed," Rose spat out. "My nanaay knew about it. She told me."

"She must've learned it from her mother, our common ancestor, the Greenstone Matriarch at the time. But

she would've known she couldn't tell anyone about it."
Louise paused. "But, of course, your nanaay was a drunk,
wasn't she? Like most of your kin. So she must've been
drunk when she told you."

"At least my daughter wasn't a thief. The minute I saw
the greenstone around Lizzie's neck, I knew what it was."

"But she ran away before you could get your hands on
it, didn't she?"

Rose's answer was to clench her lips tightly.

"Your nanaay also told you the secret to reading the
stone, didn't she?" Louise held the stone in her palm,
carved side up. She traced a finger along the intricate lines.

Rose remained silent.

"She did. Because you found the box … or 'treasure' as
you probably call it."

At the mention of the word *treasure*, Sherry started.
For a second I thought she was going to rush forward and
seize the box, but Ernest held her down firmly.

"So let's open this box and see what it contains. But
first, I should tell our witnesses the story of this so-called
'treasure.'" She shifted her position so that she had Eric,
Becky, and me in her view.

"I told you about Old Chief, didn't I?"

"You said he was a famous Greenstone chief in the late
1800s," I replied. Becky nodded in agreement.

"That's right. He was our last great chief. Our storytellers say that he used to go on great sea voyages to distant lands and bring back goods he traded otter pelts for.
Most of these goods he gave away in potlatches. During
his time as chief he held eight potlatches, which is a very
high number and emphasizes his importance. But some

of these goods he kept, particularly those that glittered."

"Like gold," Two Finger said. Although he was supposed to be guarding Rose and her son, his attention had also turned to the box. He couldn't keep his eyes off it. "That's what Nanaay told me."

"That's right. He brought gold back to Llnagaay. Our stories say he also brought back some strange green glittering stones. Some think they might have been emeralds."

"Is that what's in the box?" Two Finger asked.

"I don't know. My mother told me that it is Old Chief's regalia. That's all." She paused. "There's a curious story about this regalia. It was stolen once, a long time ago. And now it's being stolen again."

"I'm not stealing it," Rose shot back. "I am taking what is rightfully mine … I mean my son's. It belongs to him as Chief Greenstone."

"The most curious thing …" Louise ran her eyes around the circle, stopping at each individual as if ensuring she had our undivided attention. "The most curious thing is that the people who are stealing the regalia today are descendents of the people who stole it from Old Chief more than a hundred and fifty-five years ago."

SIXTY-THREE

Rose and Harry remained silent.

"That's right, isn't it, Harry?" Louise said. "Your father was a descendent of the Blue Shell Raven chief who helped the Iron Men steal the regalia."

"What the …?" Ernest muttered.

"You and Harry are cousins, aren't you, Ern? I guess your mother never told you about this blot in your clan history. And here you are stealing the regalia again." The Matriarch sighed.

Two Finger slapped his leg and hooted. Johnnie joined him.

"It's true what they say about history repeating itself," Louise continued. "But Ern, at least you aren't a descendant of the real traitor." She paused. "Unlike your aunt."

Her gaze shifted to Rose. "Not only does your son have the blood of one traitor in his veins, but Harry also has the blood of the other through your line. Your mother was a descendent of the Greenstone traitor, the person who betrayed the clan by revealing the secret hiding place to the Iron Men."

"You're lying!"

"You know I'm not. Your grandfather was the grand-son of the traitor. When your grandmother had a child by him, the clan shunned her. As the oldest daughter, she should've become Matriarch when her brother became Chief Greenstone. She tried, but no one would accept her, so my grandmother, her younger sister, became Matriarch."

"It's all lies. Stories your family made up to keep my grandmother from becoming what was rightfully hers. But now I'm Matriarch and things are where they should be."

"Not for long."

"You no longer have any say in clan affairs. Harry does, and he made me Matriarch."

"The clan has the ultimate say and we'll see what happens after I tell them how your ancestor brought shame to the Greenstones."

"It'll be your word against mine."

"Ah, but I have proof."

"You're lying."

"I'll show you when we open this." Louise tapped the ancient bentwood box with her knuckle. "After the regalia were stolen, Old Chief's Matriarch found an item belonging to the traitor on the floor of the burial house where the regalia had been hidden and where the traitor had no right to be. To ensure we never forgot who brought shame to the Greenstones, she placed it with the regalia inside this box." She tapped it again, this time harder. It gave off a dull thud that told us the box contained something.

"There's another reason why you can't be Matriarch." She brought Allistair's bentwood box onto her lap. "Do you know what's inside this, Rose?"

Rose gave a dismissive shrug and started fiddling with her gold bracelet.

"It's considerably newer than the box you dragged out of the cave. It comes from Vancouver. Does Vancouver mean anything to you, Rose?"

Rose stopped fiddling.

"You went there recently to visit Harry, didn't you?"

Eric and Becky tensed, as did I.

"So...? I go to Vancouver often like a lot of people on Haida Gwaii. You were there not long ago yourself."

"On this last trip you left something behind."

Louise reached inside her blanket to a pocket in her sweater and pulled out an object that glimmered in the light. This she dangled over Allistair's ashes. It was a silver earring in the shape of a salmon.

"Look familiar?"

Rose reached for her ear, then, as if realizing what she was doing, dropped her hand back down into her lap. "It could belong to anyone. It's a common enough design."

Her son's eyes were fixed on the earring.

"It's very old. The silver looks to be made from silver coins. Not many of these left from the old days. You like to brag about the silver salmon earring that's been in your family for a very long time. Funny, I haven't seen you wearing it since you came back from Vancouver."

"So what? I lost it."

"You're probably wondering how it came into my possession. Two Finger found it." She looked at her nephew, who nodded grimly.

While Rose tried to act as if she didn't care, a nervous twitch in her right eye suggested otherwise.

"By the way, this is my grandson." Louise caressed the smooth, painted top of the box.

Rose's eyes locked onto it. Harry's eyes locked onto his mother.

She watched the two closely for a few seconds before continuing, "I didn't know I had a grandson until Eric and Meg showed me a bracelet that was passed down to him from his mother, my daughter." She pulled up her sleeve to reveal the familiar band of etched silver looped around her wrist.

Ernest started at the sight of the bracelet. "Are you saying you're Allistair's grandmother?"

"I am."

"Fuck, I should've known." He ran a hand through his thick salt and pepper hair. "She said her name was Mary, but I knew it was a lie."

"You knew her in Vancouver?" It was Louise's turn to be surprised.

"Yup, even loved her in my drunken haze."

"Could you be Allistair's father?"

"Yup. When the kid walked into my studio I recognized the bracelet right away. Mary wore it all the time. When I saw that greenstone pendant, I knew for sure. I could see he was searching for his roots, so I took him on as a carving apprentice." He sighed. "I never told him I was his father."

What would Cloe's reaction be when she discovered that the man she hated, the man she accused of being responsible for her son's death, was his real father? I glanced at the forest behind us, wondering if she was hiding close by, listening.

Louise remained silent while the trees began moaning with the rising wind almost as if they were sympathizing with the tragedy unfolding beneath them.

Harry, obviously startled by this news, leaned forward as if hanging on every word. His mother, on the other hand, leaned back in indifference as if it was of little importance. The nervous twitch in her right eye increased.

At last, Louise roused herself and said in a subdued voice, "Now we come to my grandson's, your son's untimely death."

At this point, Rose struggled to raise herself from the ground. "We've heard enough," she rasped. "I'm sorry to learn of your grandson, Louise … if he really was your grandson. But it has nothing to do with us. Come on, Harry, grab the box and let's be on our way."

She lumbered toward the path that led to the gap in the wall. Although Harry stood up, he didn't follow his mother. Sherry had no qualms. She scooped up the ancient box and sprinted after the woman, which made me wonder about the real reason for her presence. I was beginning to think it had nothing to do with finding her lover's killer.

Ernest didn't stir from his seat on the ground. When Rose stood up, both Johnnie and Two Finger jumped to their feet, firmly gripping their rifles. But they didn't go after the two women. They waited, as if seeking direction from their aunt.

"Rose," Louise called out. "Don't you want to know where Two Finger found your earring?"

"Nope." Rose continued walking.

"It was found where it shouldn't have been, just like the trinket your ancestor left behind. Once again, history repeats itself."

Louise nodded in Two Finger's direction. He pointed his rifle at the retreating women, but fired into the forest canopy above their heads.

Sherry screamed and dropped the box. "Okay, okay, don't shoot me. It's yours."

Rose kept on walking and was soon lost from view amongst the trees.

"Rose, you won't get away with it," Louise shouted. "I know you killed the boy. Two Finger saw you."

Another blast from a rifle was followed by a howl. But neither Johnnie nor Two Finger had fired a shot.

"You killed my son. You deserve to die!" shrieked Cloë.

SIXTY-FOUR

Eric and I ran. We found Rose sprawled on the ground against a tree, moaning and clutching her ankle, her face screwed up with pain. Cloë stood over her, aiming the rifle at her head. Although my sister-in-law's hands shook, there was no doubting the determination on her face.

"You don't have the nerve," Rose sneered. "I dare you to kill me."

"Cloë, think carefully about this, please," I said, terrified she'd pull the trigger again and actually kill the woman.

Eric slipped silently through the trees and came up behind her. He kept his rifle pointed at her. The look of outrage and shock on his face told me he wouldn't hesitate to shoot his sister if she dared fire again.

I couldn't let that happen.

"The police will be here soon. Please put the gun down," I pleaded.

She continued to aim the rifle at Rose.

"You won't achieve anything by killing her, other than putting yourself in jail for the rest of your life."

"Dear God," muttered Louise, as she limped up beside me, supported by Becky. "I didn't mean for this to happen."

"Please, Cloë, give me the gun," Eric said. "This isn't you, not the sister I love. Where's my big sister, who once stopped her brother from shooting a rabbit because she couldn't bear to see it hurt." He lowered his rifle and held out his hand. He stepped closer. "Where's the sister who took a lost little boy into her heart and made him part of her family? Where's the mother who opened her heart to an orphan baby and made him her own. Cloë, please, put down the gun and take my hand."

The anger had left him. Thank god.

Although the tears began to flow, the gun still pointed unwavering at the injured woman. "Please tell me why you killed my son."

"Simple, he was in our way. Harry needed to become chief. When I first saw the boy at Ern's studio a few months ago and recognized the pendant around his neck, I knew it would only be a matter of time before Ern clued into who he really was."

"But Allistair was just a boy, with a boy's dreams. Becoming chief would not have been one of them even if he had known it was possible," his mother said.

"Maybe not, but once that woman knew," Rose glared at Louise. "She would've done everything in her power to make him chief."

"But being chief is nothing but status," I said. "That's hardly a reason to kill someone."

"You're wrong. Being chief gave us access to the treasure. Ernest knew someone who was prepared to pay us more than a half a million dollars for it."

François Champagne! That was his real reason for coming to these islands.

"But you don't even know what it is," Louise said.

"Sure I do. My nanaay talked of a headdress made of gold and emeralds, a one-of-a-kind Haida treasure."

"Wait a minute," I cried out. "Where's Sherry?" One minute she was standing behind Rose. Now she was gone … and with her the bentwood box.

"She's taken the treasure!"

"Go after her, Johnnie," Louise ordered.

Her nephew started after the fleeing woman, just as she disappeared amongst the trees. He, too, quickly vanished. We listened to the pounding of their running until the forest swallowed the sound.

"I'll go after them," Eric said, poised to take off.

"No, he'll catch her."

At that moment, loud cursing broke out, followed by an abrupt silence.

A short while later, Johnnie returned, grinning broadly with the box gripped in front of him. Behind him walked Siggy, rubbing the back of his head with one hand and pulling the squirming woman with the other.

Eric quietly removed the rifle from his sister's hands and held her weeping in his arms.

"I'll take my rifle back," Siggy said, picking it up off the ground. "*Gotverdomme*, she surprised me. I didn't hear her until she hit me on the head. Next thing I'm waking up on the ground with my rifle gone and a bump the size of an apple." He rubbed the back of his head.

"You've got a hard head, Scav. You'll survive." Two Finger grinned and slapped his friend on the back.

"I guess we should see what the fuss is about, eh?" Louise bent over the box. "Gold and emeralds, you say,

Rose?" She tried lifting the lid, but it held fast. Johnnie reached down and tried, but without success either.

"The wood is swollen from too many years in that cave." Two Finger ran the fingers of his good hand over the carved lid. "Beautiful workmanship, eh? Look at how the cedar was steamed and bent to make a perfectly square box. And look at the pegging." He pointed to a barely visible line of wooden pegs along the corner where the two ends of the single piece of wood were joined. "You don't see that done much these days. Most artists use glue. It'd sure be a shame to destroy it. Maybe Scav has something back at his place that could ease the lid off."

"Okay, let's take it there." Louise turned to Rose. "I don't see any blood, so I assume you're okay."

"I've broken my goddamn ankle, that's what. That stupid woman tried to kill me."

"A pity she missed. Harry, help your mother up. Johnnie, you help him."

The two men tried to haul the heavy woman to her feet. Defiant, she refused to budge. Louise leaned over and whispered into her ear. Glaring back at her cousin, Rose struggled to pull herself upright. With the help of the two men she eventually made it, but cried out in pain when she placed her injured leg on the ground.

"A little pain won't kill you, Rose," Louise said.

Rose again glared at her cousin, then threw her arms around the shoulders of the two men standing on either side of her. The threesome crept along the path toward the split in the rock.

Louise consigned the ancient box to Eric. Becky helped her aunt, who seemed to be favouring her hip. I

357

placed my arm around my sister-in-law and guided her after the others. As for Sherry, she could stay here for all I cared. But I thought I heard her footsteps joined by the slow shuffle of Two Finger coming behind me.

We arrived at the gap without further mishap. Steep and narrow, it would be impossible for the two men to continue supporting Rose on either side. In fact, there was barely enough room for her on her own. But she had made it up the defile, so she should be able to make it back down. Eric came up with the idea of creating a sling for her out of Louise's button blanket.

"I can always have another one made," Louise said, passing it over to Eric.

After giving Two Finger the box, Eric, with Harry's help, wrapped the blanket around Rose. With her son ahead of her, Rose shuffled down, her hands on his shoulders for support. Eric followed, keeping the sling tight as best he could with his sore hands to keep her from falling forward.

Two Finger carried the treasure through the gap, careful not to let the fragile wood scrape against the rock. His brother helped Becky guide his aunt. I'd almost forgotten about Ernest until I heard his footsteps behind me and turned around to see him carrying his son's ashes. The rest of us had become so caught up in Rose and the treasure that we'd completely forgotten about Allistair.

My heart caught at the despair reflected in his face. I imagine he was blaming himself for his son's death. If he hadn't introduced François to Harry and his mother, Allistair would be alive today. So Cloë had been right after all.

Although Cloë's tears had stopped, she hadn't spoken a word since threatening to kill Rose. She walked in front of me like an automaton, but shook my hand off when I tried to comfort her. Thankfully, she was stable on her feet and didn't need support as she made her way down the uneven terrain.

As I drew closer to the growing light at the end of the gap, I heard loud voices. I assumed Rose was causing trouble, until I emerged to see several uniformed police with their guns drawn ranged out in front of us. Two were approaching Two Finger, one with handcuffs ready to snap around his wrists.

Louise was shouting at them not to touch him.

With the ancient bentwood box clutched against his chest, the gaunt man swung erratically around as if looking for an escape route.

Sergeant Galarneau shouted, "Colin Smith, I arrest you for the murder of Allistair Zahkarov."

"Please, he didn't do it," Louise pleaded.

Ignoring her, the sergeant yelled, "Put that box down immediately."

"But I didn't do it," Two Finger said, still gripping the treasure.

"We have evidence that says otherwise. Drop that box."

Two Finger appeared confused, as if uncertain what to do. The other cop came up behind him and grabbed his arm, pulling it away from the box. Two Finger tried desperately to hang onto it with his damaged hand, but was yanked back roughly. The fragile box landed on the ground and began bouncing down the incline. It caught on a rock, flipped over, and continued tumbling until it slammed into a tree. The ancient wood shattered.

A collective gasp resounded.

As one, we peered down the hill, anxious to see the treasure. But it was impossible to see anything other than splintered wood.

"Becky, do you mind going down and bringing it up to us," Louise said.

"Madame, no one moves until we have this man fully apprehended," the sergeant said.

The other cop slammed Two Finger's chest against a tree, wrenched his arms behind his back, and clipped on a pair of handcuffs.

"Stop," Louise shouted. "Colin didn't kill my grandson. She did." Her finger pointed at Rose, who was being helped down the hill by one of the other cops. Amazingly, the woman seemed to be walking with only a slight limp now.

I read nothing but confusion on the staff sergeant's face. Nonetheless, he ordered the other cop to stop.

Meanwhile, Becky picked her way down the slope to the smashed box. She carefully moved the splinters out of the way, then reached down and lifted up what looked to be a Haida headdress similar to the one Harry had worn at the potlatch. It glittered. She scooped something else from the ground and tucked it away in her pocket. Holding the headdress securely with both hands, with the front piece facing her, she climbed back up to where all of us were waiting. Eager anticipation was reflected in everyone's eyes. Finally we would get to see this treasure that had been hidden for more than a century, the treasure that had caused the death of an innocent young man and ignited the greed of others.

From the back it didn't look like much, pieces of dried-out fur pelts hanging from a circular frame.

Rising above the pelts were spikes of varying length that reminded me of extra long porcupine quills, but which I learned later were sea lion whiskers. Becky kept the front piece from view as she passed the headdress to Louise.

She examined it closely. "Ah," was all she said before turning it around to show the rest of us.

For a moment there was stunned silence as each of us took in the square piece of cedar with the carved hooked beak of an eagle, as befitted the headdress of a chief of the eagle clan.

"Hey, where's the gold and emeralds?" Sherry shouted, voicing the question that was foremost in the rest of our minds. "I want François's thirty-thousand down payment back," she shouted at Rose, who was being firmly held by two cops.

Yes, indeed, where were they? The eagle carving was surrounded by something that glittered, which at first did look like gold and emeralds. But the tiny hole in the centre of each of the tiny circles betrayed them. They were sequins, gold and green sequins. I almost let out a laugh, but caught myself in time. One broke loose and fluttered to the ground, followed by another and another.

I picked one up. It was definitely a sequin, something that might have been prized by a culture that had never seen such glittering objects.

"You betrayed us!" Rose shouted, trying to break away from the cops. "You matriarchs lied and pretended it was valuable."

"Look to your own ancestors. Seems to me betrayal runs in your genes, not mine."

"But Auntie," Two Finger said. I could see that he was almost as upset as Sherry and Rose were. "What about the old stories of Old Chief bringing back gold and sparkling green stones? Aren't they true?"

She shrugged. "I guess we'll never know, unless another bentwood box is hidden deep within these forests." I thought her smile had a slight secretive twist to it.

"I also found this inside the box." Becky held out her hand. Resting on the palm was an earring. Although badly tarnished, the gleam of silver shone through. It was in the shape of a salmon.

Louise held up the earring Rose had left beside Allistair's body. The two earrings matched.

SIXTY-FIVE

We were a sombre group of people squeezed around Siggy's long, narrow dining table, which looked more like a door that had floated onto a nearby beach, if the faint Japanese characters at one end were anything to go by. We were finishing the dinner Siggy and Eric had prepared. Although Siggy had insisted he didn't need help, Eric, unable to sit still, dove in anyway.

It was a delicious meal of rockfish caught earlier by Siggy and vegetables fresh from his greenhouse garden. But it was a meal mostly ignored. None of us had much of an appetite. It was also a meal eaten in silence. We were all trying to come to terms in our own way with the traumatic events of the afternoon.

Cloë sat between Eric and me. Thankfully, she'd come out of her zombie-like trance and was responding to the world around her. She no longer felt the need to keep her son's ashes within reach. She'd let Ernest bring them to Siggy's house in his own boat. Throughout dinner she cast only an occasional glance at the bentwood box resting on a nearby table. I felt this was her way of saying goodbye to her son.

Rose had been so busy trying to convince the cops she wasn't guilty of murder that she forgot to tell them about her own attempted killing, and none of us were going to mention it. It was an event best forgotten. Maybe someday it would be resurrected in a Haida story.

Eric had used Siggy's satellite phone to call and delay his flight to Ottawa. He had decided his sister needed him more than the Grand Council. The two of us were going to stay with her until we felt she was strong enough to continue on her own.

Louise sat with the same serenity she had displayed throughout the ordeal. Nonetheless, she couldn't hide the tremor in her hands or the exhaustion in her face. So far she'd made no comment about the day's events or the impact it would have on her clan. But she had insisted that both Harry and Ernest come to Siggy's house. She now sat between the two men, so perhaps the healing was beginning. Tomorrow at dawn we were going to Llnagaay to put her grandson to rest; another step in the healing process.

The ancient headdress was propped against Allistair's box, where Becky had placed it, along with his orca carving. The fabled glitter had mostly disappeared. During our walk down to the beach, many of the sequins had dropped off, leaving a sparkling trail in their wake. Perhaps some distant day, a venturesome soul will follow the flashes of gold and green up to the clearing and the cave. Maybe the stories recounting today's events would draw them. Or maybe it would be the lure of Old Chief's treasure, for I suspected the full secret had yet to be revealed.

Neither Two Finger, Johnnie, nor Sherry was with us. While we stood on the beach watching Rose being half-pulled, half-pushed into the police seaplane, Sherry managed to cajole them into taking her with them as well. Even though the sale of the ancient headdress would've caused great pain to the Greenstone Eagles, it wasn't a criminal offence, so Sherry Anne was free to go. Hotly declaring that she wasn't going to spend "one more fucking second in this fucking hole," she'd jumped into the police boat without so much as a backward glance, let alone a goodbye.

After Ernest declared that the totem pole had been a gift, the police couldn't charge Two Finger with its theft. So Louise's nephew took off in the grey fibreglass boat moored next to Siggy's. Louise told us that he was returning to Llnagaay to complete a project. We would get a chance to see it tomorrow when we visited the village.

As for his brother, Johnnie, the man suspected of killing François, he had disappeared. In the melee of apprehending Rose and discovering the true treasure, he'd slipped away. We forgot about him until we were all standing on the beach with the police waiting to leave. I'd noticed first Two Finger glance around as if looking for someone, then Louise, and finally Becky. I counted heads and, realizing one was missing, whispered to Eric.

He whispered back, "Let the Haida deal with him. I'm sure they have their traditional ways for punishing a person who has not only killed a man but in doing so has brought shame to the clan."

So we kept mum, as did Harry and Ernest. I doubted Cloë even noticed he was missing. And Sherry was far too busy extricating herself.

Most of us were still toying with Eric's apple crumble when Louise put her fork down beside her empty plate and, turning to Ernest, said, "Please, tell me about my daughter."

The carver shrugged. "There's not much to say. Mary … I guess I should call her Lizzie … was a high point in my otherwise dismal life. I didn't know how much she meant to me until I lost her."

"Cloë said she was living on the streets."

"We both were. We were just a couple of drunken Indians trying to make sense of the world and not succeeding. That was before I found carving and turned my life around. At that point I was only interested in the next drink."

"If you loved her so much, why weren't you at the hospital when she died?" Cloë asked.

"I was in the clink. I'd been caught shoplifting. Funny enough, it was some maternity clothes for Lizzie. I only found out after I got out four months later that she was dead and the baby adopted."

"Did you try to find the baby?" Louise asked.

"What was the point? I had no way of taking care of him."

"Did you even think to look for us, her parents?"

"What good would it've done? I felt the kid would have a better chance with the rich people who adopted him. Besides, I figured Lizzie's parents were probably a couple of drunks too. There had to be a good reason for her running away."

Louise sighed and ran her fingers over the silver bracelet. "Yes, they were difficult times … and painful. I don't like to think of it now. But that's when my husband's drinking was at its worst. Drink brought the violence out in him. It was hard on Lizzie, but at the time I could only think of myself. After she ran away, it took me a few years to accept he was probably the cause. That's when I divorced him. Still, I am very sad I never knew my grandson, or held him in my arms, or laughed and played with him, or had a chance to teach him our Haida ways."

"I'm real sorry, too, that I only got to know him at the end," Ernest said. "I could see his step-parents had done a good job of bringing him up. He was a good kid. The kind of kid any man would be proud to have as a son." Ernest acknowledged Cloë with a smile. She reached across the table for his hand and squeezed it.

He finished by saying, "Allistair would've made a good Chief Greenstone."

Harry spoke next. "Auntie, I don't feel right holding the name any longer, but I'm not sure how I resign. I figure you as the Matriarch should know."

"It's an unusual situation and I'm afraid I don't know myself," Louise said. "I will ask the other matriarchs. In the meantime, I think it best you leave Haida Gwaii. After you pay off all your bills, I think you should look to providing financial help to those in our clan who need it the most. Perhaps in time you will earn the right to reclaim the name Chief Greenstone."

Harry, nodding in agreement, crossed his arms. "That won't be a problem. If I need to, I'll put the company up for sale."

"Good. But first thing tomorrow morning, I want you to get in your fancy boat and go directly to Queen Charlotte, where you will surrender yourself to the police. You assaulted this poor woman and stole the pendant."

"It doesn't hurt so much now." Cloë touched the back of her head.

"I'm very sorry. I never meant to hurt you," Harry said.

"That's okay. I won't press charges. I imagine your mother pushed you into it. But tell me, what happened to the pendant?"

Louise reached inside her sweater and brought out the greenstone. "If you don't mind, I'd like to keep it, but please take the bracelet."

She slipped the silver band off her wrist and passed it to Cloë, who brought it to her lips and kissed it. "My son." She wrapped it around her wrist and caressed it several times before removing it. She held the bracelet out to her son's girlfriend. "Please, I want you to have it. I know he loved you dearly."

Becky hesitated. "No, I can't."

I imagined thoughts of that fateful evening when she turned it down were foremost in her mind.

"Please." Cloë pushed it closer to the young woman. "I know I didn't always treat you fairly. I'm very sorry. When you're back in Vancouver, I want you to visit me. I'd like us to get to know each other better."

Her eyes brimming with tears, her fingers trembling, Becky reached for the bracelet and gently slipped it onto her wrist. "I'd like that," she said barely above a whisper.

Louise clapped her hands. "Perfect. You ladies are going to have more than Allistair to talk about."

Confusion spread across Cloë's face, while Becky blushed.

"Come on, Becky, if you don't tell her I will," Louise said.

"I'm pregnant," was the young woman's simple reply.

SIXTY-SIX

Harmony Restored

Though the pain wasn't so bad today, he knew it was only going to get worse. The doc said there were drugs he could take. But he figured he could live with it for now. Besides, a good bottle of rye went a long way to dulling everything. Six months, the doc said, before the cancer killed him. That was four months ago. Whether he took the drugs or not, it didn't matter. What mattered was he was here where he belonged, in the land of the ancestors. When the time came, if the Queen Charlotte hospital didn't have the right drugs, he would do without. There was no way he was going back to Vancouver to die.

After lying awake most of the night, he'd finally fallen asleep, only to have his brother wake him up. He'd seen his brother sneak off without the police noticing, so he'd been half expecting him to come to Llnagaay. Still, when Bro crawled into his tent, it had scared the hell out of him. It'd taken several nips of rye to settle his nerves.

The first thing Bro said was, "I killed that guy. I never meant for anyone to get hurt when I cut those ropes. I only wanted to shame Harry."

"I know," Two Finger answered. "But it doesn't matter. What matters is someone died because of you."

"What am I suppose to do? There's no way I can go to jail. I won't last six months."

Two Finger nodded. He knew how his brother felt. During his time in the asphalt jungle of Vancouver he'd lived with this dull ache in his soul. It only disappeared when he sighted the mist-shrouded islands of his people's land and inhaled the rich, cleansing air. He'd flung his arms wide to embrace the forest-covered peaks and the bountiful seas and felt the sense of freedom flowing into his soul. Bro was right. He'd wither and die in jail.

He felt really sorry for his brother. But not only had he killed someone, he'd also brought shame to the entire clan. So he had to be punished. Tradition dictated it.

Though he hated to do it, he had no choice. Auntie had told him what to do if his brother came. Now that he was here, Two Finger was forced to pass sentence on his closest kin. But Bro saved him from having to say the damning words. Instead he passed sentence on himself.

"I've done a terrible thing," Bro said. "I will accept the traditional Haida punishment of banishment. I only came to say goodbye. I'm sorry I can't be with you in your final days. You've been a good brother. I'll miss you."

The two brothers embraced.

Two Finger could feel wetness on his face as he watched his brother vanish into the forest's darkness as the first of the sun's rays reached Llnagaay. He didn't want to think about what was in store for his brother. He knew word of his banishment would spread throughout the Haida Nation before the day ended. If his brother dared seek help, he wouldn't get it. But he figured Bro had something else in mind. He hoped it would be quick.

Though the day was still early and he hadn't slept more than an hour, he couldn't go back to bed. He had one last job to do. Auntie had said they would be coming after breakfast. He needed to have it finished by the time they arrived.

Now that he knew the identity of the long-ago traitor, he could finish drawing the crest. He thought it fitting that it was an ancestor of Fat Momma. That long-ago woman likely betrayed the clan for the stupidest of reasons: a man. Funny that he'd already drawn a salmon for the traitor's crest. But maybe the cedar had known. When he'd set out to draw the crest, an image of a salmon had jumped into his mind as his fingers touched the spot where it would go. The salmon also worked for the other traitor, Fat Momma, so the two would become one in the totem of shame. To complete the drawing he would add a tiny salmon on either side of the fish's head to remind people of the pair of earrings, and how they had revealed the betrayal.

He would regret until he died that he arrived too late to save the boy. He got there just after the stabbing. He watched Fat Momma search the boy for the pendant and then kick his body in frustration when she didn't find it. Although he should've called the police, he knew this killing was a Greenstone affair and had to be dealt with by the Matriarch before the police were called in. And so it had played out.

He never suspected the treasure was the motive. He was bowled over when the gold and emeralds on Old Chief's headdress turned out to be duds. But, hey, the old stories couldn't be all lies. There had to be some truth in the gold and the emeralds. He figured they still remained hidden in the hills behind the village. And he was damn sure Auntie knew where they were.

It was good Ern turned out to be the boy's father. He figured the man wouldn't hesitate to carve the pole for his son. He wished he would be around for the pole raising, but it would be nip and tuck if he survived the two months it would take to complete the carving. He knew just the spot, on the rise of a grassy knoll overlooking the lagoon. He'd tell Auntie.

Speaking of Auntie, there she was, just entering the lagoon perched in the bow of Scav's Red Rocket. Her white curls flickered under her cedar hat while her button blanket flapped in the breeze. Becky sat behind her, along with the folks from away, the Algonquin bigwig and his red-haired wife. It looked like Ern had made a new friend for he seemed to be cozying up to the crazy blond lady who was supposed to be the boy's mother. He could just make out the small bentwood box resting on the seat between them. He didn't see Harry, but maybe Auntie had already sent him on his way. Scav, looking suitably serious with black beads in his beard, was steering the boat to the beach.

Two Finger grabbed the pouch of eagle down Auntie had given him and the other things needed for the ceremony and shuffled down to the water's edge to greet them.

The healing had begun.

ACKNOWLEDGEMENTS

Part of the fun of sending Meg to another wild part of Canada is that I get to go too. While Vancouver isn't exactly wild, I had an intriguing time exploring Granville Island and the south shore of False Creek and came up with some fabulous story ideas, many of which found their way into *Silver Totem of Shame*. But the highlight of my West Coast adventure was Haida Gwaii. I fell in love with these magical forest-covered mountain islands on the edge of Canada. I enjoyed getting to know the Haida and their culture better, especially "the woman rule" part.

A number of people helped me reflect Haida culture and life on Haida Gwaii as accurately as the story would permit. I'd like to thank: the staff at Gwaii Haanas National Park Reserve, National Marine Conservation Area Reserve, and the Haida Heritage Site; the elders with the Skidegate Haida Immersion Program (S.H.I.P.); totem pole carvers Clarence Mills, Tim Boyko, and Huuyaah; Leona Clow; Jay Bellis; Albert Hans; watchman, Jordon, Shirley, Sean and Aileen; Carolyn of Caro-on-the-islands blog; Heron, Vivian, and Laura with Moresby Explorers; Susan Cohen; and Götz Hanish. I also want to extend a big thank you to three special people who helped open the door even further into Haida ways. You know who you are.

I gleaned valuable information from various Internet sites by and about Haida and found several books invaluable, including *Raven's Cry* by Christie Harris and *Solitary Raven* by Bill Reid.

I also want to thank my readers Vicki Delany and Barbara Fradkin and my editors Sylvia McConnell and Allison Hirst. Bringing a book to publication is never a solitary affair.

And last, but far from least, Jim, who enjoyed Haida Gwaii as much as I did. I couldn't continue on this writing adventure without your enduring support. Thank you.

More Meg Harris Mysteries by R.J. Harlick

A Green Place for Dying
978-1926607245
$17.99

*Meg Harris confronts police
indifference as aboriginal
women go missing ...*

Meg Harris returns to her home in the West Quebec wilderness after a trip. Upon her arrival she discovers that a friend's daughter has been missing from the Migiskan Reserve for more than two months. Meg vows to help find the missing girl and starts by confronting the police on their indifference to the disappearance. During her investigation, she discovers that more than one woman has gone missing. Fearing the worst, Meg delves deeper and confronts an underside of life she would rather not know existed. Can she save the girl and others with little help and in the face of grave danger?

The fifth installment in the acclaimed Meg Harris series.

Arctic Blue Death
978-1894917872
$16.95

*The sparsely populated
Arctic is no stranger
to murder ...*

The fourth in the Meg Harris series follows Meg's adventures into the Canadian Arctic as she searches for the truth about the disappearance of her father when she was a child. Many years ago, her father's plane had gone missing in the Arctic and he was never seen again. What happened on that fateful flight?

Thirty-six years later, her mother receives some strange Inuit drawings that suggest he might have survived. Intent on discovering the answers, no matter how painful, Meg travels to Iqaluit to find the artist and is sucked into the world of Inuit art forgery. *Arctic Blue Death* is not only a journey into Meg's past and the events that helped shape the person she is today, but it's also a journey into the land of the Inuit and the culture that has sustained them for thousands of years.

Finalist for the Arthur Ellis Award for best crime novel.

Available at your favourite bookseller

🏛 **DUNDURN**

Visit us at
Dundurn.com | @dundurnpress
Facebook.com/dundurnpress | Pinterest.com/dundurnpress